NOT YET LOST

NOT YET LOST

a novel

JANIS M. FALK

SHE WRITES PRESS

Copyright © 2025 Janis M. Falk

Detroit Moan
Words and Music by Victoria Spivey
Copyright © 1936 SUGAR HILL MUSIC PUBLISHING LTD.
All Rights Administered by SONGS OF UNIVERSAL, INC.
All Rights Reserved Used by Permission
Reprinted by Permission of Hal Leonard LLC

All rights reserved. No part of this publication may be reproduced, stored in a retrieval system, or transmitted in any form or by any means, electronic, mechanical, photocopying, recording, or otherwise, except for brief quotations in reviews, educational works, or other uses permitted by copyright law.

Published in 2025 by

She Writes Press, an imprint of The Stable Book Group

32 Court Street, Suite 2109
Brooklyn, NY 11201
https://shewritespress.com

Library of Congress Control Number: 2025909431
ISBN: 978-1-64742-960-7
eISBN: 978-1-64742-961-4

Interior Designer: Katherine Lloyd, The DESK

Printed in the United States

This is a work of fiction. Names, characters, places, and incidents are either products of the author's imagination or are used fictitiously. Any resemblance to actual persons, living or dead, is purely coincidental.

No part of this publication may be used to train generative artificial intelligence (AI) models. The publisher and author reserve all rights related to the use of this content in machine learning.

All company and product names mentioned in this book may be trademarks or registered trademarks of their respective owners. They are used for identification purposes only and do not imply endorsement or affiliation.generative artificial intelligence (AI) technologies to generate text is expressly prohibited. The author reserves all rights to license uses of this work for generative AI training and development of machine learning language models.

To all the scrappers who work hard to improve their lives, and to my mother, Celia, who gave me a work ethic.

POLISH WORDS AND PHRASES

aniołeczek	Angel.
Basia	Diminutive form of Barbara. A main character. Pronounced bă-schă.
Boże	Oh, God! Used as an interjection throughout. Pronounced bō-schă.
Boże błogosław	God bless.
Boże kochanie	Dear God.
braciszek	Brother.
chodz tu	Come here.
Damski	Ladies.
Dobry wieczór	Good evening.
dupek	Asshole.
dziecko	Child.
Dzień dobry	Good morning.
Kurwa	Curse word, the F–word.
malutka jeden	Little one, term of endearment.
Na zdrowie	Cheers.
No nie	Oh, no!
pierzyna	Down quilt.
Powodzenia	Good luck.
przekaski	Refreshments.
Rozumiesz	You understand.
staruszka	Old women.
Towarzysze	Comrades.

CHAPTER 1

Tuesday morning, January 26, 1937

Ricocheting off the bottom cupboard, the breakfast sausage skidded across the linoleum floor, bounced off the kitchen table leg, and came to rest adjacent to her husband's polished work boot. Holding the empty tongs in her hand, Florence watched Alex arch an eyebrow as he peered at her over the top of the newspaper. Florence retrieved the saucepan she knocked off the stove with a hurried elbow; the lid still danced on its back on the floor.

"*O Boże, Boże*, oh God, I'm sorry!" She retrieved another kielbasa from the ice box and placed it in the pot. She rinsed the rogue sausage and laid it next to the sink. People didn't waste meat nowadays, so she'd take it to work for her lunch. Florence retreated from Alex's disapproving eye to their bedroom to get ready for work. Her abysmal cooking skills, once a shared amusement, now divided them as a bone of contention.

She rummaged through her dresser drawers in search of a sweater. Her shabby cotton dress, stained deep umber by the tobacco leaf dust at the cigar factory, presented no match for chilling January winds. She pulled two sweaters from the drawer, weighed them in her hands, chose the heavier one, changed her mind, and took them both. Florence threw her thick brunette hair, straight as boiled noodles, on top of her head any which way, her fingers fumbling with the hairpins.

She still needed to wake the boys before meeting Basia to walk to work. With Lucien fifteen, just, and Frank ten, she respected their privacy more than when they were little boys. She knocked on their bedroom door before opening it a few inches. "Time to get up! Don't dawdle. Get to school on time!" Returning to the kitchen, she served Alex his sausage. He remained silent, engrossed in the newspaper. When they'd first arrived in Detroit in the 1920s, Alex encouraged her to pursue her art, even endorsed her working in a gallery. The market crash changed all of that, and more, much more.

After washing the dishes, Florence stepped out the back door, pausing to kiss her fingers and touch the scarred cheek of the painted Black Madonna hanging in the hallway. Though an inexpensive reproduction, she revered it. The original, said to have been painted by St. Luke, hung in the Jasna Gorna monastery in Częstochowa.

Brutish wind funneled through the alley between Florence's house and the Sikorskis'. Basia and Romek lived straight behind her, their house a mirror image. She blew into her cupped hands, and even though she wore gloves, the damp chill nipped through them. Basia should be out any minute now. The friends walked together every morning to Detroit's White Eagle cigar factory. She stomped her feet, but her knees hadn't yet worked out their morning kinks and they ached. Sooty plumes from smokestacks lost themselves in gunmetal gray cloud cover. If she were painting, which blue would she add to achieve that specific pewter color? Exhaust from the smokestacks would require red or orange undertones for the heat. These days she only painted in her mind. Who had time? A sharp metallic sound, followed by a cat screech, reverberated from the end of the alley. A stray must have knocked over a trash can. Fat chance it'll find any food in it. Florence pulled her scarf tighter around her head and over her mouth. Just as she considered approaching to knock on her friend's door, an earsplitting shriek jolted her around.

"*Pomóż mi!* Help me! *Proszę!* Please, *pomóż mi!*"

Basia! Florence pushed open the gate to her friend's yard and raced inside. Basia hunched over a man's body sprawled face down, limbs akimbo, over the three wooden steps of the stoop. Florence pulled up short, her hand to her mouth. "*O, Boże!*

"Henryk!" Basia shook the man by his shoulders. "Wake up! Wake up!"

Florence skirted around to the other side of the stoop. She kneeled.

"Help me turn him over." Florence pulled the left shoulder toward her while Basia pushed Henryk's chest from the other side. Once Henryk was on his back, he slid down the stoop, twisting at odd angles. Basia continued to shake Henryk, searching for life Florence knew wasn't there.

"He's gone, Basia. Gone," she whispered, her hand on Basia's shoulder. Her friend stood. Steamy breath burst from their lips. They looked down. Ice crystals were embedded into his blue and red mottled cheeks. Thank goodness his eyes were closed. Florence didn't know if she could bear looking at them.

"Go inside. Call for ambulance. See if you can get message to Romek. Tell him to come home," Basia ordered.

Florence complied, returning moments later. "The operator at the plant said she'd get a message to Romek." She descended the steps and sat on the lowest one next to her friend.

"Ambulance?"

"They won't come. I called the fire department. Should we call the police?" Florence hesitated to suggest it. Not all policemen were friends of the community.

Basia held her head in her hands and sobbed. Florence wrapped her arms around her and rocked. She stared at Henryk's long, skinny legs clad in worn canvas pants. They lay limp yet frozen in place, like the rest of Henryk's body. Her eyes wandered to his head, which he must have hit when he fell. Crusty rust-colored clumps snarled his light brown hair. No hat. She thought she knew what icy blue looked like. She'd never seen the preternatural shade permeating his lips. His ears tipped reddish purple. Lifeless. His left arm had been reaching forward when he'd fallen on the steps, the door handle just beyond reach, so close to warmth, so near to living. His right arm hung over the side of the stoop. On a hunch, Florence released Basia from her embrace and ventured to the side of the steps. She retrieved a brown pint bottle from the snowy ground cover. Without a word, she deposited the empty bottle in the trash can in the alley. She spotted her bag, which she'd dropped at the sound of Basia's shriek, and retrieved it. Her gaze rested on the windows in her own house. Had her boys heard the shriek?

"How long do you think he'd been there?" Florence queried.

"I don't know. I was coming to you. I opened door and—Romek leaves in front. He wouldn't see."

"What should we do? Should we take him inside?" she asked.

Romek lumbered around the corner of the house. "Basia! You're safe." He enveloped his wife in a bear hug. "At the factory, they said emergency at home. I didn't know . . ."

Basia turned him toward his cousin's body.

"Dear God in heaven!" Romek kneeled beside Henryk's body. He tried to grasp Henryk's hand, but it wouldn't bend. He checked for a pulse. None. Just to be sure, he placed his ear close to Henryk's mouth, then bowed his head in prayer, finishing with the sign of the cross. "Let's go inside."

"Should we bring him in?" Again, the thought of leaving Henryk in the cold disturbed Florence.

"No. Best we call the police." Romek, in his gentle manner, directed the women toward the door. Florence was grateful for permission to flee the elements. In the enclosed porch, on the way to the kitchen, she noticed a crocheted blanket thrown over the back of a chair. She almost nabbed it to cover Henryk, paused, hesitant to sacrifice her friend's coverlet, then snatched it and returned to cover Henryk's body. In no time she could crochet a new one for Basia. In the kitchen she returned the still-warm coffee percolator to the burner. Romek telephoned the police from the front hall. Florence joined her friend at the table with two cups of reheated coffee.

"Months now. We tried to help," Basia spoke. Florence remained silent. She let her friend speak of the many things she already knew. Henryk came to America alone, like many men. He planned to send for his family when he'd saved enough for their passage. Last year an accident at the factory crushed his left forearm, robbing it of full use. "He'd drink. Constant pain." Basia stared into her cup. "We never said, but Wally told us one time he caught Henryk drinking Ginger Jake in alley. You know, some bad people add poison to that. Sell it cheap. It makes your muscles go all wobbly. Especially the legs."

Florence remembered Henryk's limping gait. Basia'd told her how his legs would seize up and she'd bring him hot compresses. She didn't know that was the reason. Was that why he'd fallen on the steps?

"After that, Wally let him drink for free. He got lower and lower. Felt he was failure. *Rozumiesz?*"

Florence nodded. She understood. Henryk wasn't the first man to fall victim to the broken promise, the one that seduced those in the maelstrom of Eastern Europe.

"The police will be here shortly. They'll notify the coroner." Romek returned from the front hall. Florence rose to pour a cup of coffee for Romek. He waved it away. "I'll go back to work. *Proszę*, call Father Maletski." Romek kissed Basia on the top of her head.

"I'll call Father," Florence offered. Romek nodded at her and left, never having taken off his jacket. She completed her task and assured Basia the priest would visit in the evening to plan a service. The women sat in silence until the knock on the door.

Florence directed the police to the backyard, then she and Basia donned their coats again and went outside. The officers elicited the relevant information. Yes, it was Basia's husband who called, yes, he'd gone back to work, yes, Henryk was a boarder, yes, distant relative from Poland. Florence used her coat sleeves as a muff since she'd left her gloves inside. She stood in the shadows, shivering, while Basia answered questions. Soon the coroner arrived with two assistants. The men laid out a canvas stretcher and a sheet. The women watched them execute, with practiced maneuvers, the grim task of straightening Henryk's remains the best they could to roll him onto the stretcher. She noticed Henryk's bare ankles. Surely Romek would have lent him socks.

"Do you know this man?" the coroner queried.

"Know him? Do I know him?" Basia's voice became shrill. "He's our cousin. He lives here."

"There's been a lot of thefts, burglaries goin' on lately. Street bums. Just the other—"

"There's been no crime here. We've discussed everything," the police officer intervened.

"He is *not* street bum," Basia stated. Florence put a hand on her arm in gentle restraint. The officials dispatched their duties, undoubtedly eager to retreat from the cold.

The women resumed their places at the kitchen table. Florence listened to the sounds from the street, imagining the actions. The slam of the back doors of the hearse, men's voices, first one, then a second, closing of a passenger door, an engine sparking then fading away to nothingness. She rose to fill the coffee cups and found the pot empty.

"Should I make—" Basia shook her head no. Florence sat again. After a moment of watching her friend stare into her empty cup, she rose and began to wash the Sikorskis' breakfast plates. She couldn't cook, but her mother had taught her to clean. Working her way through the dishes, she proceeded to the countertop, wiped down the cupboard handles, and had begun to scrape small debris from around the stovetop burners when Basia spoke.

"No crime committed here! *Psia krew!* Just the crime of being poor!"

Florence didn't respond. She wiped down the backsplash.

"Should we go to work? Nothing to be done here," said Basia.

"No, I suppose not. Are you sure you feel up to going?" Florence scrutinized her friend's face.

"Yes! Yes, I am." Basia stood. "To honor Henryk. He wanted job. That's all he wanted. We should go work ours. Pitiful as they are."

She had a point. Florence doffed Basia's apron that she'd thrown on when she'd begun cleaning. For the third time that morning, she bundled up.

"What do you think Resnick will say? Us showing up so late," Florence asked.

"I dare that *dupek* to say anything to me!"

Leaden clouds hung low over the alley. Florence searched above. The sun had risen. She was grateful the wind had abated, though chilling eddies encircled her ankles.

If anything good had come from these dark days, it was Basia's friendship. They were so different, yet extraordinarily compatible. Florence's family, a combination of Polish and French Canadian, relocated from the rural plains to Montreal. As farmers, they knew food and opened a grocery store. They became city folk and, hoping to launch Florence into Montreal society, sent her to an elite girls' school. Basia emigrated to the States a dozen years ago from rural eastern Poland. She'd had little book learning but was whip-smart in the ways of life. Florence admired her.

"Basia?" she asked. "I was wondering. I don't mean to imply anything—"

"Out with it! What do you want to know?"

"I noticed Henryk had no socks. Surely Romek would've lent him socks?"

"Yes. He lent him socks. First one pair. Then two. After three, Romek found out Henryk sold them. So we stopped."

"*O, Boże!*"

"He didn't have hat, gloves, belt, undershirt." Basia continued to recount how Henryk had made money in the summer. Florence knew but let her friend talk. Fishing in the Detroit River, foraging berries and mushrooms, and washing windows had sustained him, though barely, in nicer weather. "Once winter set in, nothing. Here we are. Another day, huh? In just another week." They arrived at the White Eagle cigar factory on Grandy near Warren.

Numerous square windows, opaque with tobacco resin, lined the five-story red brick building. They entered through the side door, the employees' entrance. In the hallway lined with rusty, cubbyhole-sized lockers, Florence leaned an outstretched arm against the grimy wall for balance while taking off her old boots. Basia proceeded to the lunchroom, where the walls were studded with wooden pegs for coats. Florence joined her and removed the layers between her cotton dress and the moth-eaten wool overcoat. Florence chewed her already chapped lip.

"Good morning? Or is it *afternoon* already?" Resnick greeted them. Florence cringed at his mock obsequiousness, though she tried to mirror Basia in both stride and demeanor. Heads held high, backs straight, they situated themselves at their worktables and went about their business. Florence approached the bin of wrapping leaves. Another woman joined her.

"Careful. He's been fuming all morning," whispered the woman in Polish.

Resnick was hovering over Basia's worktable when Florence dropped off a stack of leaves to her friend.

"Did you ladies go out to breakfast? Or maybe you decided to shop downtown?" The supervisor looked around their desks in an exaggerated fashion. "No shopping bags?"

Florence prayed for God to give her friend self-control, today of all days.

"Don't worry. We'll make our quota. We always do," Basia replied. Her friend was in no mood today to abide Resnick's bullying, not with what had happened.

"Mr. Resnick, please come with me to the bins. I think I saw some mold there. I'm worried about the leaves." Florence led Resnick to the bins.

After examining the leaves and finding no problem, Resnick yelled through the megaphone. "Time to get goin'. No slackin' off. Been hearing complaints about wrappers comin' loose. Make sure you use enough gum. And when you strip those leaves, make sure you get close to the stem. I went through the discards last night and look how much I salvaged." Resnick held up a bowl of shredded leaves.

"Like hell he did! Bet he scooped them off top of hopper five minutes ago. *Dupek!*" Basia whispered over her shoulder. Florence laughed.

"You dames got a joke you want to tell us? What're you laughing at?"

"I was just coughing, Mr. Resnick," Florence deadpanned while waving the air in front of her mouth. "Inhaled tobacco dust. That's all. Sorry to interrupt, Mr. Resnick." She retrieved her Chaveta knife from her bag. Workers supplied their own specialty knife for cutting cigars, at their own expense.

Resnick continued his lecture, strutting among the worktables. When he came upon one of the younger women, Resnick bent way over her shoulder as he shoved a bowl of shredded leaves under her nose. "Do you see these? Do you? They're perfectly fine leaves. Not waste! Now use them." He emptied the bowl onto the young woman's worktable. He picked on the younger ones, closer to his own age. Florence felt grateful to be older.

For the next two hours, the women stripped, crushed, bound, and wrapped the leaves over and over again. Finally, Resnick announced the lunch break. The women crammed into the same small rooms housing their coats. They formed pods of three to five to eat lunch on their laps. Some turned boxes upside down for a table. Florence produced a small bottle of vodka from the pocket of her sweat-stained dress. Each woman drizzled a few drops in her palm to wash her hands before eating.

"I don't know which is worse, having the windows shut and breathing tobacco dust or opening them and freezing," Anna, a neighbor and coworker, said.

"Romek and I joke about whose lungs will give out first, his from foundry or mine from this place. Romek's going to try for job in salt mines at edge of town. His brother, in Poland, works in salt mines under Krakow. He says it's like spa." Florence couldn't believe Basia could converse after the events of the morning. She could barely speak.

"The mines are dangerous. My grandfather, he died in the collapse back in the 1890s digging the first mines here in Detroit. I never knew him. Ma talks about it. He loaded dynamite into holes in the salt and he was crushed when the whole thing collapsed," a younger girl said.

"*O, Boże, Boże.* Jesus, that's terrible," muttered several of the women.

"Basia, tell us about this meeting coming up tomorrow night," one of the women implored, lowering her voice to a whisper, "What's Romek going to talk about?"

"Yes, tell us! Is there going to be a protest?" piped in another wide-eyed young woman.

"We talked last night, and he said—" Basia began to reply when Florence interrupted.

"Ladies, ladies!" Florence clapped her hands to get attention. She gestured toward the doorway, worried Resnick might hear. "Talk about something else."

"I have a new job," one of Florence's other neighbors chimed in. "The bakery needs extra help. We need the money. It's just for a while, until Lent. I go for a few hours before I come here. I help make the *paczki.*"

"Those filled doughnuts! Makes me miss Krosno. My folks have a bakery there. Easter season's the best. I started rolling dough at six years old," commented another.

"Maybe that's why you're so good at rolling cigars. You're wrapping those half coronas and perfectos after only two years! Took me four with my fat fingers. If I didn't work so fast, Resnick would still have me making filler." Florence examined her hands, knuckles bulging like an aneurysm ready to burst, and she wasn't yet forty years old.

"I don't know how my Romek can still smoke these things. He lights one up, and I shoo him out of house. I tell him it's bad enough I smell tobacco all day. My home's going to stay clean and smell fresh." Basia lowered her voice. "But still, I bring him one each week. Old cheapskate will never miss it." Basia wiped horseradish from her lips.

"I bring one to Stephan, too, once in a while," said Anushka, Florence's godchild. At just sixteen she was one of the younger workers. "I get so scared though. Filing out last Friday, I caught Resnick staring at my chest. I just knew he knew I had a cigar there. I told Stephan it was his last one for a while. I don't want that creep looking at me like that."

"Not having a cigar there won't stop him from staring at your chest," another younger woman said, letting out a caustic laugh.

"You be careful, Anushka," Florence admonished, cleaning up lunch things. "Concentrate on your work. Don't talk so much you don't get your work done. You don't want to stay late and be here alone with Resnick."

"Back to your tables! Fifteen minutes is over. C'mon. No dawdling." Resnick herded the women out of the cramped lunchroom, and he brushed Anushka's behind as she passed through the doorway.

"What do you think you're doing!"

Anushka's head snapped around.

Florence gripped Anushka's arm, guiding her away. "Think of Stephan! What would your hardworking young man think if you lost your job before the wedding?" Florence admonished.

"He'd be glad I stood up to that pig."

Florence stood in front of Basia in the line for the bathroom. She fingered the pocket of her work dress, finding security in the small bottle of vodka she'd used at lunch for hand washing. She hoped the bathroom wouldn't be broken again. Only two toilets and one sink for so many women, all of which the women cleaned themselves. The women did the best they could with their own cleaning supplies. The owner wouldn't provide any. Tobacco leaves remain pliable in high humidity, so management ordered all windows to remain closed. Hundreds of women working in a veritable humidor. Mold and mildew ravaged the bathrooms, but management dismissed complaints.

"Is Alex coming to meeting tomorrow?" Basia leaned over Florence's shoulder and spoke close to her ear.

"I don't know. He said none of this should concern me."

"What does Alex think about taking action?"

"Hard to know." Florence deflected the question. Alex was dead set against labor organizing, but she didn't want people to think he wasn't supportive. "You know him. Cold as a Siberian sturgeon."

Basia laughed, then it was Florence's turn for the bathroom.

The afternoon dragged on as usual, though the friends worked diligently. Florence and Basia typically rolled the cigars at a good clip in the morning and then maintained a more tolerable pace in the afternoon. Pay was based on piecework—how many cigars were produced. Neither had to stay late or rush before quitting time to meet the quotas. Today they missed the first few hours, so they would need to hustle throughout the afternoon. Better to keep busy, though, to keep the dark thoughts at bay.

At the end of the day Florence wrapped herself in layers again for the journey home. Same as the morning, darkness enveloped the streets. She'd survived another day. If she hurried, she might be able to reach Kowalski's shop and pick up some sliced *szynka* by the time Alex came home from the tavern. Dinner would have to be quick so she could get to the hall, Dom Polski, to clean and set up chairs for tomorrow's meeting. Fingers crossed her sons hadn't caused too much aggravation in the neighborhood. Maybe with a miracle they'd started their homework. Then she might squeeze in washing clothes, at least a few, before making ham sandwiches and leaving for Dom Polski. The meeting had been the talk of the neighborhood. Florence hoped Resnick hadn't caught wind of it from the lunchtime conversation. She suspected he knew more than he let on. She, too, had wanted to know more about Romek's plans and intended to question Basia on their walk home. She'd have to wait. Resnick made Basia redo about one-quarter of her work, and it kept her late. Florence offered to help, but Basia refused. She asked her to give Romek some dinner and tell him she'd be home late. The chill in the wind swirled around Florence. Frost seemed to form between the layers of her clothes, which moments before had been damp with perspiration.

Basia worked efficiently at her worktable. She didn't mind so much working late. The room was quieter, the atmosphere more relaxed. She minded redoing cigars she'd already made. Instead, she'd just make new ones and she'd be paid more when her piecework was counted. Resnick wouldn't notice the difference. Both knew nothing was wrong with the ones he'd told her to remake. At home Romek would be preparing for the meeting. He'd have notes and papers all over the kitchen table. He'd be talking and mumbling to himself. She smiled. Her husband still embodied the hope and fervor he'd held when she'd fallen in love with him. They'd met on the *Hamburg* during their passage over. He had stood out among the crowd. He was generous and kind amid the most egregious conditions below deck in steerage. A natural leader, he'd quelled petty squabbles, kept the calm, and buoyed spirits. Without his leadership many more would have perished in the crossing of the Atlantic.

"Excuse me, Mrs. Sikorski." Basia looked up to see young, blonde Alicja, just a child, smiling at her.

"Ah, Alicja. Do you need something, *malutka jeden?*" Such clear blue eyes!

"Would you teach me how to roll these cigars faster? You're so quick! I don't like being here late so often."

"I don't blame you, dear. Sit next to me. I go slow. You watch." Basia worked her magic over and over.

"You see how I do that? You try."

For the next while, Basia and Alicja worked together, slender young fingers mimicking the seasoned and experienced. Alicja had worked in the curing area downstairs until recently. Mostly she was assigned to wrapping filler, but now and then Resnick let her roll the low-end cigars. She was an eager learner. She had ambition. Basia knew Alicja had responsibilities at home.

"I want to earn more money when I get better at rolling these."

"Takes time, my dear, and practice."

They worked side by side now, Basia with more fragile high-end leaves and Alicja with cheaper scraps.

"Mine looks like a snake swallowed a rat." Alicja held hers up, offering a wry smile. Basia laughed and showed her how to prevent leaves from clumping, how to roll a uniform cylinder.

"Is there a comedy show going on here?" Resnick approached with his usual swagger.

"Yes, working late so much is joke. We laugh all time. Ha, ha."

Alicja gasped at Basia's remark.

"It's no joke for me either. I don't like to stay here," Resnick said.

"Then go home!" Basia knew Resnick tolerated her cheekiness more after hours than during the day. He didn't like being embarrassed in front of the entire workroom.

Resnick counted the finished cigars on her table. "Looks like you made up for your shoddy work today. You may go, Mrs. Sikorski."

"Come on Alicja. We go home now." Basia shepherded the young woman out of the factory, leaving Resnick to lock up. She knew Alicja was only fourteen but had said she was sixteen to get hired.

"You would've made a wonderful teacher or mother, Mrs. Sikorski. Didn't you want children?" So innocent this girl.

"Children are gift from God, dear. Now you scoot along home." Basia knew the girl should be safe now they were in their neighborhood. Basia had been pregnant once, shortly after she and Romek arrived in America. They'd been renting a room from an older woman who had allowed them to live in her basement. While the landlady preferred renting to single women, she agreed after Romek pointed out the house repairs he could do for her without pay. One afternoon, while Romek was out, Basia confided in her landlady, her only friend. Basia had raised her younger siblings in Poland and knew the work. Romek didn't have a steady job yet, and no one would hire a pregnant woman. Like a couple of fish washed up on shore, they were gasping for breath. No reason to bring a baby into the world. Not at that time.

The landlady empathized in her reserved manner. For a few minutes, they danced around the topic of addressing Basia's predicament. It took a moment for Basia to catch on, though she'd heard of farm wives who ended pregnancies in Poland. The brusque landlady, as streetwise as she was practical, knew people and offered to escort

Basia to an appointment. She agreed, at least to talk. But Romek must never know. Her decision, the only overt lie she'd ever told Romek, remained buried deep in her heart. Her other secret, the reason she left Poland, was a lie of omission. As the years passed, and they found their footing in this new world, they'd hoped and prayed for children, she and Romek, but it was not to be. She remained in contact with the landlady and became part of the underground network helping other desperate women. Another secret not even shared with her closest friend Florence.

She quickened her pace, wondering how things were going at the community hall. She would stop there for a minute before going home.

CHAPTER 2

Wednesday, January 27, 1937

Alex winced at the shriek of the whistle signaling the lunch break. Lunch seemed to come later and later these days. Management also thought the workers didn't notice the conveyor belt accelerating ever so slowly over the weeks. He was certain production increased by five to seven percent since the beginning of the year. He silenced his pneumatic tools and rivet guns, tidying them on the wooden bench at his station.

"Hey, Falkowski, we're goin' to speed over to the luncheonette. Need somethin' hot today?"

"Thanks. I brought lunch," Alex responded. "I'm going to work in the lab."

"Keep it up, Alex. I believe in you. You're goin' to invent the next automobile."

"When you do, just remember your pals here and hire us on," another coworker chided.

With a ham sandwich in waxed paper tucked into his hand, Alex headed to the machine shop where employees could work with tools and scrap metal. Management hoped an employee would invent something or have an idea they could steal. Alex spent as much time there as he could, even after hours. He had an idea, but he'd be damned if he'd share it with the company. As Alex worked on his project, his sandwich, half eaten, sat on the workbench, all but forgotten.

Fred, the supervisor, stuck his head around the door frame. "Hey, Falkowski! Knew I'd find you here."

"I've got a few more minutes. Lunchtime isn't over yet."

"I'm not here to bust your chops." Fred perched on a stool not far from Alex. Over the years Fred had been friendly with him. Fred at least respected him.

"It's the boss. Moore." Fred gestured toward the ceiling with his thumbs. "He's ready for you. Time to get your picture painted by that artist Rivera."

"I've been meaning to ask you. Why did Moore pick me? I was surprised when you told me about it."

"You want my opinion? You're one of the few 'round here doesn't look half dead. But I think it's because you speak English pretty good."

"Tell me about Diego Rivera. Why's he here at a Dodge plant when Edsel Ford hired him? Nobody understands what this is about." Alex sorted the myriad parts in front of him back into their proper bins.

"Edsel's the head of that art museum downtown. He's paying for it, but it's really the museum directing it. Rivera's painting the walls at the museum. He's supposed to document all the industries here in town. Out of my league, all this art stuff."

"Seems an odd choice, Rivera. Rumor has it he's a communist from Mexico." Alex tested the waters.

"Yeah, I heard that too. Ford's all in tight now with Mexico. He's building a factory there. Some say he's trying to appease workers, avert a strike. Maybe avoid another showdown like what happened near the Rouge plant. Ya know, throwing a bone to the rank and file."

"I see." Alex finished sweeping off the top of the workbench. "Scraps for the dogs," Alex muttered under his breath.

The shrill whistle signaled the end of the lunch break.

"Let me wash up." Alex excused himself to the washroom. He retrieved a small celluloid comb from his rear pocket. With a practiced flick of the wrist, he flipped the wide swath of still-golden hair back off his face, then he liberated a few strands to hang over his forehead.

"If you're all purdied-up there, we better get upstairs." Fred popped a piece of chewing gum in his mouth and started smacking and cracking with salivary pleasure.

Trailing up the stairs behind Fred, Alex surreptitiously flicked grease and dirt from under his fingernails. He ran his hand over his smooth cheeks, glad he'd taken extra time shaving this morning.

"Here we are." Fred opened the door with gold leaf lettering on the panel's frosted glass.

Diego Rivera appraised the factory worker entering the office-turned-art studio. Tall, slender, good posture.

"This here's Alex Falkowski," the gum-cracking supervisor said. "He's the chump you asked for, right?" Fred slapped Alex on the back a couple of times. One corner of Rivera's mouth turned up. He'd seen the disdainful sidelong look the worker shot at the annoying supervisor. He coughed to mask a chuckle. Yes, he and this Falkowski would get along just fine.

"Yes. You may go now." The artist dismissed Fred.

Fred didn't budge. "But I—"

"Go on," Rivera prodded. Fred huffed as he left the office. Alex suppressed a chuckle.

Rivera faced Alex and extended his hand. "I'm Diego Rivera. My pleasure to meet you, Mr. Falkowski," the artist said in Spanish-accented English. His brown curls danced as he bowed his head while shaking hands. Alex returned a respectful nod.

"Please sit down." Rivera motioned to a chair pressed up against the wall adjacent to an exterior window. He observed his subject's graceful movements as he navigated the narrow aisle around three easels, a center table full of paint jars, and office furniture relegated to the room's perimeter. Rivera analyzed the shadows cast across Alex's Slavic cheekbones and aquiline nose. Alex's eyes followed his every movement as he arranged charcoal, pencils, pastels, and paints. "I like to talk with my models while I sketch them. Do you like working here?"

"It's all right," Alex responded, his voice neutral as pabulum.

This one's a little wary—it may take time to get him warmed up. "I see. How long've you worked here?" The charcoal in Rivera's hand flitted like a hummingbird.

"Nine years."

"You must make good money then?"

"Ha! Nobody here makes good money working in the factory. Our wages were cut a few years ago. And we work more than twice as hard. Half the people were laid off."

"I see." He tried to draw out the essence of Alex and posit it onto the easel. He smudged the wisp of bitterness into the paper with his charcoal.

"You know how it is," Alex continued. "I heard you're sympathetic to workers. Someone said you were at the workers' march on Ford's Rouge plant."

Perhaps his subject was becoming, if not warm, at least tepid. "I *sketched* the march from the bridge. I didn't participate in the march. Were you there in the fray?"

"On the sidelines." More pabulum. Rivera's hand paused. His subject's expression slid away like the moon behind the clouds.

"You're not active in the workers' movement then? Perhaps like some of your colleagues?" Rivera pointed toward the window, which offered a panoramic view of the factory floor.

"Once the Dearborn police started with the tear gas, I took my wife and we fled. I don't join in with the activists. No good to come of it," Alex stated as though it were a fact.

"No? The workers' demands seemed quite reasonable."

"Of course they're reasonable!"

Success. Rivera elicited a reaction.

Alex presented the list of simple demands: shorter workdays—eight hours instead of twelve, breaks, heating fuel for the Ford-built homes, medical care. The artist picked up speed as Alex became more animated, more emotive. He spoke of companies cutting costs to survive right after the market crashed in '29, and now that people were buying cars again, companies were enjoying profits on the workers' backs. Alex emphasized the logic of companies supporting their employees so they would produce their best work.

"Logic! It's elusive, my friend," Rivera egged him on as he moved to the second easel. He began working in pastels without missing a beat. Out loud, Alex debated with himself whether the support of the people should be provided through the government or through companies. He made a compelling case for each approach.

"You are a communist then, no?" asked Rivera.

"No!" balked Alex. "The Communist Party has ruined everything! America's running scared of communism. The government thinks any small attempt by workers to get even the most basic of rights is driven by communists. That gives carte blanche to companies to take advantage, abuse immigrant labor!" Rivera smudged the pastels, blending reds and blues on the ecru background, capturing the colors of indignation.

"You're not a communist, yet you see the evil of greed. You support the workers' movement, yet you don't participate? You don't think tools of labor agitation effective?"

"Maybe, maybe not. At that march on the Rouge plant, five people were killed, fifty injured. Some were arrested right out of their hospital beds. That's a high price for a maybe."

"Perhaps so." With a yellow pastel crayon Rivera executed long, strong strokes to capture Alex's thick, straight hair. His round face and colorful hues ensured his face would be a focal point in the mural.

"There's nothing to be done." Alex sighed, dropping his chin. "My neighbor tried to stand up for a coworker at a Ford factory, and the Service Men—you heard of them? Ford's own police, like the Cheka, the Bolshevik's terrorists, took him down. He was fired. Beat up."

The Cheka. Now Rivera recognized the blended accent. Eastern European, perhaps Russian, top-dressed with French. "I had a lady friend once, actually a wife, when I lived in Paris. Angelina Beloff. She's an artist from Saint Petersburg. She left Russia before the Bolsheviks and their Cheka, but I know of them. Have you lived elsewhere? Maybe Paris?"

"I'm Polish, from Tsarist Russia."

Rivera paused his pastel. His subject's facial expression had fossilized again. "*Je vois.* Aristocrats spoke French in Russia." This man posed such an enigma. Peasant or aristocrat?

"Yes, and so did those who served them and the Cossacks who protected them."

"A politician, I see." Rivera perused his supplies, searching for a color. "Cover all your bases in case I have an opinion, no?"

"And do you?" The quizzical look broke Alex's stony visage.

"I'm a man of many opinions, Mr. Falkowski, which is why I can be so prolific in my art."

"Why did you select me?"

"I paint every man. The hero of working people. Workers like to see their own nobility in a handsome man, no?"

"I see." Alex's pride radiated.

"You seemed to like being photographed when I walked the factory floor. And you're a bit spruced up compared to the others." Rivera smiled. His eyes remained on the canvas. The artist selected a blue-hued rose to capture the color developing on his model's cheeks. Alex remained quiet, embarrassed at being called out.

"What I'm doing here is sketching several versions of your face. I'm not sure yet where exactly I'll use it. I'm still designing the various walls of the murals."

"How did you come to work for Ford? Your reputation for being sympathetic to workers seems like it wouldn't endear you to Henry Ford, or his son Edsel for that matter."

"I see you've done your homework, Mr. Falkowski. Edsel is on the Board of Directors of the Detroit Institute of Arts, so I work for him in that capacity. Please turn to the right. Thank you." Rivera moved toward the third easel. "You see, I'm no longer involved with any political parties. Maybe, like you, I remain outside. They like to hear themselves talk, so much so that nobody listens." He could see Alex agreed with him, nodding his head. "Me? My art is my weapon. If you don't talk to the people who need to hear, what good is it?"

"Makes sense." Alex fell silent again.

"Lift your chin. Please put on those glasses you removed before taking a seat."

Alex retrieved the spectacles from his shirt pocket.

"You see, Mr. Falkowski, if my art is to speak to all people, they must see themselves. Today's American aristocrats, 'captains of industry' I believe they're called here, might just recognize themselves in a face like yours."

Alex straightened his shoulders and lifted his chin.

The door from the hallway burst open, propelling Fred into the room. "Hour's over." Fred pointed to his watch. "Falkowski needs to get back on the line. All right with you, Mr. Rivera? You said an hour or so."

"Yes, *or so*." Rivera placed his pastel crayon onto the easel's ledge. He approached Alex, now standing, and extended his hand. "Thank you, Mr. Falkowski, for sharing your time, your thoughts, and your likeness." Rivera dipped his head in a small bow. "I may need you again, if that would be acceptable?"

"Yes, of course. *Au revoir.*"

"*Au revoir.*"

Fred's head switched back and forth between the two men. "You speak French?"

Alex and Rivera exchanged small smiles.

Fred steered Alex in front of him, through the hallway, toward the top of the staircase. Rivera winced at the sound of gum cracking. He went to close the door. Before he did, he saw a man in a suit pop out of a doorway.

"How'd it go, Fred?"

"Good, good. Falkowski here's a champ!"

The man raised his eyebrows. "Good to hear."

Alex, unacknowledged, moved past the man in the suit. Fred looked back over his right shoulder, nodded, and winked at the man in the suit who receded from the hallway.

"Hey, Falkowski, whaddya say we meet up at the gun club Saturday? It's a swell place, and I can get you outfitted with equipment if you want."

Always the observer, Rivera paused while shutting the door. Alex stopped and turned to face Fred, who almost ran right into him.

"The invitation is quite unexpected," mused Alex.

"Well, you know. One good turn deserves another. You really helped me out with the boss. Not many guys on the floor could speak like that to an artist. In French even! Look at you. I don't get what all the hubbub's about, but I was told to treat Rivera like royalty. Not many of those shop rats coulda pulled it off like you."

Alex sighed. Shop rats indeed.

CHAPTER 3

Wednesday, January 27, 1937

A morass of men exited the factory. Their galoshes plowed through slush, the men too tired to lift their feet. A huddle formed at the train crossing, one of the four track lines in a square that encapsulated Poletown. The screeching sound of steel wheels abrading steel tracks muffled the noise of men shuffling their feet to stay warm. Bleary-eyed, the men watched the train cars feed raw materials to the ever-voracious factory loading docks. Alex covered his ears with his gloved hands and pondered whether the conveyor speed would be just a tiny bit faster tomorrow. A strong hand gripped his shoulder.

"Going to Wally's? I'll walk with you."

"*Dobry wieczór*, good evening, Joe," Alex greeted Florence's brother. "How're things in the electrician's shop?"

"Same old, same old. At least there's job security. They need us to keep the conveyor going."

A train car full of taconite ore, raw material for making steel, ambled by, the last of many hoppers. The throng of men crossed the tracks, thinning out into different directions. Joe and Alex headed toward Wally's, their neighborhood tavern and so much more. Now twilight, the temperature dropped. Moisture, atop the creosote-soaked wooden blocks paving the street, froze. The men almost skated to their destination. Wally's Bar, known for its affable owner, could easily be overlooked. A bland wooden-frame structure with no glass storefront identified itself with a humble painted sign above a single door. A few windows, narrow and high up, had been painted black during Prohibition, which had ended a few years prior. A small round window, head height in the entrance door, afforded the only view in or out. The window reminded Alex of the monocles European gentry and the literate class wore before the Great War. Afterward, they'd become a symbol of aggression by the Weimar Republic.

The men entered the tavern. Amber light bathed the blue-gray pallor of the patrons, offering a tinge of warmth. Wally stopped polishing the mahogany bar top to pull a couple of Altes draughts and pour a couple of shots. Wally placed shots of vodka and the mugs in front of the two men as they settled onto the bar stools.

"What gives?" Joe quietly queried Wally while his eyes scanned the line of men hunched over the bar.

"Henryk. The guys've been talkin' about him dying. Look, even bought him a drink."

Joe and Alex glanced to the other end of the bar, where a full shot was perched in front of an empty bar stool, a shrine to the lost. Wally stepped away to help his wife, Helen, who bustled through the swinging kitchen door with a large pot of Bigos stew. Fresh cabbage, sauerkraut, mushrooms, and a little pork mixed together exuded steam, sure to warm empty bellies. Single men who boarded in rooming houses often took meals at the tavern. Wally and Helen tried to keep a lid on the costs as a service to the community.

Alex, feeling he'd had a good day by meeting Rivera and being invited to the gun club, waved Wally back over.

"Give a round to the men. My tab."

"You sure, Alex? There's a lot of guys here."

"Yes. I can't stand this gloom. It's depressing." Besides, Florence always said he should engage more with the community.

"Joe, I've been thinking about something," Alex turned to his brother-in-law. "Times aren't great, but they're not as bad as a few years ago. Automobile sales have been improving. If you lay off workers, produce more with a faster line, *and* cut wages, shouldn't there be extra money? Something's not adding up."

"Are you going to the meeting tonight? I heard Romek's going to talk about that." Joe knew he could speak freely at Wally's.

"Yes. I'm curious what he has to say. Although I don't put much stock in some of these labor actions."

"Hey, everybody! Quiet down. Nowak's coming on the radio. I want to hear the latest." Wally listened to the radio much of the day. He could always talk to the guys about current events. Stanley Nowak was a labor leader who organized his countrymen across several industries. He reported on unionizing activities at different Michigan factories.

"He's gutsy. He doesn't mind being front and center. One of these days he'll end up shot in the back like Johnnie Bielak," a man at the bar said.

"That's the guy who tried to organize the Hudson automobile plant." An old-timer listening in brought a young rookie next to him up to speed.

"Hey, Alex," a man at the opposite end of the bar called.

Alex looked up, and the man, with a full shot glass in his hand, nodded his gratitude. A few other men saluted Alex with their drinks as well.

"Showing off, Falkowski? What, did Fred give you a raise?" Chet, one of the younger men, said, slurring his words.

Alex started to comment, but Joe put a hand on his arm. "Ignore him. He's all piss and vinegar."

Chet persisted. "I saw you goin' up to the boss's office with Fred. Are they promoting you?"

The men at the bar snickered sourly, sarcasm infusing their muttering. Promote Polacks? Not likely. Management thought all Eastern Europeans were Bolsheviks or revolutionary sympathizers. They knew little about Eastern Europe and understood even less. Corporations feared communists infiltrating their organizations. Alex tried several times to advance in the company, only to be shunned. Chet had pulled a scab off Alex's wound. Alex started to rise from the barstool, but Joe's strong hand pushed him back in place.

"Let him be. Just a jealous hothead."

"You might be better served spending your evenings at English school rather than sitting here," Alex, religious in studying English in the community language schools, admonished Chet. "Instead, you sound like an ignorant hunky." Once again Alex rose, blocking Joe's hand with his forearm. He retrieved his fedora from the hook under the bar and made for the door. Chet sprang from his stool and tackled Alex from behind. Alex fell forward, stumbling, knocking over a coat rack and a newspaper stand. He remained upright with the help of a table. Newspapers scattered across the speckled linoleum floor, yesterday's events soaking up melted mucky slush from the workmen's boots.

"You're not jus' goin' walk outta here after insulting me."

"I didn't insult you! I told the truth." Alex secured his scarf and retrieved his hat from the floor.

Chet cocked his fist down at his waist, released, and landed a powerful uppercut beneath Alex's chin. Alex's head snapped back into the small round window in the exterior door. Glass shattered. Wally, now in the middle of the fray, pulled Chet's arms around behind his back. Using his grizzly-bear frame, Wally pushed Chet out the door.

"Don't come back 'til you learn to behave!" He turned to Alex. "Sorry. You know Chet can't hold his booze. Should've been keeping an eye on him."

"Not your fault, Wally. I'll fix that window tomorrow."

"Are you going to the meeting tonight?" Joe, now at Alex's side, asked Wally.

"Want to but can't leave Helen here alone. All these guys are wound so tight these days. They just snap."

Helen appeared with a bar towel wrapped around a large chip of ice and handed it to Alex.

"For your jaw."

NOT YET LOST

Alex lay prone on the floral couch in the front room, his head in Florence's lap. She held an ice pack to his head and a towel with ice chips on his chin. His long legs hung over the scrolled arms, almost touching the lion-paw sabots.

"At least you didn't lose any teeth," Florence conceded when Alex recounted the events at Wally's. She'd checked that first when Alex came home with blood on his chin.

"It's a good thing I'd prepared dinner early tonight because of the meeting, or you would've interrupted my cooking coming home like this," she chided, trying to tease out a smile. He obliged, barely able. "Nick stopped by earlier looking for you."

"Nick Starovitch?" Alex sat up and looked at his wife. Her extended hands held the ice packs like an offering, her fair skin red and ruddy from the cold.

"Yes. He is such a dear man. So kind."

"I wonder what he's been up to. I haven't seen him in a long time."

"He didn't say. I invited him in, but he said he had to run. I told him you were likely at Wally's, so I thought you might've seen him there."

"No, he wasn't there."

"No matter. You should call him. Invite him to Sunday dinner. I'm going to clean up before the meeting. You rest."

Alex stretched back across the couch, resting his head on a pillow Florence had embroidered. He had known Nick in the old country. Nick was a real Cossack, born in the Caucasus along the Dnieper River, unlike Alex, who had joined the military group under peculiar circumstances. Alex had left Eastern Europe on his own and never looked back. One evening a few years back he was out on Hastings Street in the entertainment district. He made his way from one club to the next, sampling different jazz music. The bartender at the last club he visited seemed familiar, the short stocky build, straight black hair slicked back, and a round Slavic face accented with a sharp slant to the eyes. When Nick asked him for his order with the familiar intonation, their eyes met in recognition. They stayed in touch for a while, but Alex distanced himself when he thought Nick too entwined with that notorious criminal mob, the Purple Gang, during Prohibition.

"Time to go." Florence stood in the doorway. Alex took his time hoisting himself from the couch and retrieving his outerwear. Florence waited, holding a large heavy sheet cake, before the couple departed for the evening's meeting.

CHAPTER 4

Wednesday evening, January 27, 1937

Groups of twos and threes climbed the concrete steps to enter Dom Polski, a red brick building that served as the center of Polish life. An eagle embossed in concrete kept a watchful eye over the entrance. White concrete also trimmed the rows of arched windows, contrasting with the red brick and encompassing the Polish national colors. After dinner, the community drew together for the evening's activities. Women busied themselves on the first floor, arranging tables and chairs and decorating for an upcoming baby shower. Men gathered in the daylight basement, though daylight was long gone. Many men puffed cigars, talking politics and shaking their heads in bewilderment. Others gesticulated with their stogies, sounding off, bellowing their ideas.

"Glad you're here." Florence caught up to Mrs. Koseba, who was descending the stairs. "I understand my boys stole potatoes from your root cellar again."

"No matter. I have extra. I let them take a few, then shooed them away as if I hadn't seen. If we run out, my husband will bring some home from our grocery store."

"You're too kind. You and I, we're so lucky. Lucien and Frank eat enough at home, believe me. But those other boys? I just don't know. I tell my boys to leave that food for the others. They don't need it."

"They're just trying to fit in. Be one of the gang. You're the lucky one. Those boys of yours, both darling as can be, but Lucien—if I could have children—I would want him."

"Yes, he's all charm. Comes naturally, just like his father."

"But he's got your heart." Mrs. Koseba patted her on the arm. Florence blushed at the compliment. Indeed, Florence found joy in her boys. She was also fortunate Alex had insisted they save money during the bountiful 1920s. They had set aside most of her earnings from the gallery and the occasional art sale. Alex hadn't put it all in the stock market, and those funds had cushioned them in recent years. No arguing he was a smart man.

"We need some fresh air in here," a woman piped up, opening the windows facing the street. "We breathe tobacco dust all day long. Don't need it in here."

Florence went to the basement windows on the other side of the room and threw open the bottom of the double-hungs. Startled, she found her sons, Lucien and Frank, and their friends, Jerry and Bogie, crouched between the bushes and the brick wall.

"What're you doing here? You're supposed to be at home."

"Mama, we heard the meeting is important. We want to know what's going on." Lucien's voice, now usually low, cracked just a bit.

"You shouldn't worry about these adult matters."

"But, Mama, we're almost men now. We're old enough."

"*Tak*, yes, you and Jerry probably are. Now take these younger ones home and keep an eye on them! Hurry up. You don't want your father to see you out." She looked over her shoulder and saw Alex occupied, preparing mugs with a finger or so of vodka for the men. "Now shoo!"

Florence joined the women laying the buffet table with desserts. Others brewed a semblance of coffee. Joan, who worked at *Głos Ludowy, The People's Voice*, unpacked her old Corona typewriter from a carrying case. Joan served de facto as the community scribe. She prepared to take notes. Florence knew Basia had alerted her that tonight's meeting could be newsworthy.

NOT YET LOST

"*Badź chicho! Badź chicho!* Quiet please! We're ready to begin." Romek stood behind the podium on the elevated platform. His burly body dwarfed the diminutive wooden podium salvaged from St. Florian's church storage room. His hand, massive from years of foundry work, raised a glass of water to his mouth. He sipped, licked his lips, took a slow, deep breath, and began. He projected his voice without benefit of a microphone.

"*Dobry wieczor, przyjaciele!* Good evening, friends! I hope you're all as well as can be expected in these dark days we live in. We need to talk about what's happening in our community, not just our neighborhood here, no, but the Polish community, our community of workers. All over Detroit, workers lost their jobs. When trouble started in 1929, the companies, they asked us to work for less money. We understood. We said *tak, tak*—yes, yes—we'll help you out. We thought it would be just for a short time. Then they'd pay us again. No, that hasn't happened." Romek panned the audience. Florence looked around, too, and saw heads nodding in agreement.

"Then, the companies, they wanted more." Romek's voice was getting louder. "They make the lines go faster and faster. Just a little bit at a time." He made a tiny space between his thumb and index finger. "They think we don't notice. We don't say anything. We understand. We're agreeable. Happy to have a job, those of us who still do. Now they produce more with fewer workers. They say it's the economy. But no, no, that's not it. All it does is save them more money. They got greedy. Our coworkers, toiling hard to keep up, get hurt, maimed, and can't work anymore."

"That's right! Look at me." Andrew held up his arm, truncated at his elbow, the stump wrapped in make-do cloth bandages. A factory machine severed his arm. Florence recalled the day it had happened. She remembered, too, the day Henryk's arm was crushed. Maybe this man will fare better.

"The companies, do they pay this man who can't work anymore?" Romek pointed to the man who kept his maimed appendage raised. "No! Companies don't pay him. No one pays him. What's he supposed to do? What're *we* supposed to do?" Romek pounded his fist on the podium. Florence jumped. He paced side to side across the front of the room, running his hand through thick sandy-brown hair. The audience remained quiet, letting him gather his thoughts.

"We endure. That's what Poles do," he spoke through clenched teeth, a charging dog tied to a fence. "Now the companies, they see we can work ten, twelve hours a day, day after day, six days a week. We pride ourselves in our ability to work. Send a little money home. Don't take time off. Don't be late. They dock our pay if we're late." Romek wiped sweat from his forehead with his sleeve. He sipped some water.

"Today, first time in fifteen years, I was late." People in the audience strained to hear him. "I had to write a letter. I wrote to Henryk's wife, Danuta, in Poland. I had to tell her Henryk was gone. Dead! Tell her she would never see him again. Tell her she'd already kissed him her last goodbye. Their children, especially the one born soon after he came to America, wouldn't know their papa. They didn't have a papa anymore."

The crowd quieted. People looked at their shoes. Florence and other women dabbed their eyes with handkerchiefs. She could hear the wind whistling around the bushes and in through the window she had opened.

"Henryk was a distant cousin, sure. More importantly, he was my friend. We came from the same village in Poland. We worked together, worshipped together, shared our dreams, shared our sorrows—and we drank together." He paused, and one corner of his mouth turned up ever so slightly. Nervous laughter spread through the audience, glad to turn their faces away from stark reality. Romek retrieved an extra chair from the side of the room and swung it into place next to the podium. Florence faced the empty chair.

"This here is Henryk's chair. This is where Henryk is *supposed* to be, alongside each and every one of us. But he can't be. He's no longer with us. Why? Because I failed him. We failed him. Our brother. Together, you and I, our Polish community, *we* failed Henryk."

Romek didn't bother to wipe away the tears coursing through the dark stubble on his cheeks and chin. "We didn't see, behind his stoic face, the toll this world took on him. No job, no money, no respect!"

An auto worker stood up. "We didn't fail Henryk. We tried to help! We gave him what we could, didn't we?" He looked to the crowd for agreement. Heads nodded, looking back and forth, seeking affirmation.

"That's right! What could we do? We can't even feed ourselves!"

Florence could see both sides were right, Romek and the others. She didn't know what to think. People in the crowd chimed in.

"It's not us. It's those *dupeks* who run the factories. Criminals. Just because we don't speak English they think we're stupid. They make their money breaking our backs."

"Just like in Russia. Work the Poles hard, they'll do it. Harvest their food. Pay for their palaces."

"We came here for better. Look what happens?"

Romek allowed the crowd's indignation to roil. He allowed the heat to ratchet itself up. Florence examined Alex's face while Romek fanned the crowd like the flames in the foundry. The men stood up, taking turns berating those in power, those who held their precarious future in their hands. Alex said nothing.

"What you say is true. But still, we failed Henryk. We failed Henryk by not standing up! By allowing companies to abuse us. Use us up and throw us out! Just waste to be added to the slag pile. The companies, they made us hungry, they made us tired. Poor. But now they're *killing* us! Driving us to despair." Romek's face flushed red with fury, his navy blue eyes half crazed with ire. The attack dog escaped its leash. Florence worried he could have a stroke.

"Prussians rolled over Poland from the West, Russians from the East. Turks and Tatars couldn't kill us! The Cossacks couldn't kill us! And we're not going to let these companies kill us! Because we're better than that! We're Polish, we *survive!*" Romek's colossal fist pounded the podium, pitching his water glass to the floor, shattering it into shards. He waved away the woman who aimed to clean it up.

"We need to take action. For ourselves, our children, our friends who lost their jobs. And for Henryk. We're going to fight back!"

"That's right!" Murmurs of agreement floated above the crowd.

"The jobs we lost—we want them back!"

"We just want to work. They need us."

"How 'bout a shorter day? They work us like mules. Then more people can work."

"Safer conditions!" Andrew hollered, waving his damaged arm.

Florence spoke up. "I just want a clean bathroom!" The women nodded their heads. Romek laughed.

"All of it, my friends, all of it! We're going to demand it all. We're not going to let them drive us to despair, kill us inch by inch while they get fat. Let's do it for Henryk!"

"For Henryk!" Basia jumped up, her fist in the air. She motioned for the crowd to stand.

"For Henryk! For Henryk!" Basia led the cheer. Florence watched Basia beam at her husband in the front of the room. He smiled back. She scanned the room for Alex. He was refilling mugs.

"Anyone interested in making a plan, meet me here tomorrow night. In the meantime, let's start with slowdowns. It's worked elsewhere. Pretend to be busy, but don't do anything. It'll make them *crazy*. But you won't get in trouble."

Alex returned to his seat next to his wife with a half full mug. Florence noted his bloodshot eyes.

Joan, now standing up behind her typewriter, began to sing.

> Stand up! Ye wretched ones who labor,
> Stand up! Ye galley-slaves of want.
> Man's reason thunders from its crater,
> 'Tis th' eruption naught can daunt.
> Of the past let us cleanse the tables,
> Mass enslaved, fling back the call,
> Old Earth is changing her foundations,
> We have been nothing, now be all.

NOT YET LOST

> 'Tis the last call to battle!
> Close the ranks, each in place,
> The staunch old International
> Shall be the Human race.

"'Internationale,'" Alex whispered to himself, though Florence heard. Originating in France but sung the world over, "Internationale" had become a rallying cry for laborers, socialists, and communists.

With the song wrapped up and plans in the works, the group dispersed. While others gathered their coats, Joan stood by the door with a bowl, collecting donations for Henryk's family. Florence contributed a few coins, others passed by, hands in their pockets, averting their eyes, avoiding the shame of having nothing to give. On the walk home Florence held Alex's arm as he swayed to and fro. He had refilled his own mug often, two fingers to the others' one.

"Don't they understand? It won't help. It's suicide."

"Help Henryk?" Florence tried to understand Alex's slurred words.

"No, not Henryk. Their demands. They'll lose. Just like Rouge. Just like Narva." Alex ranted in a mix of French, Polish, and Russian. Florence didn't understand a word. She didn't need to, as she was all too familiar with this situation. Alex only spoke of life in the old country, Imperial Russia, when he drank too much.

"I know that song. 'Internationale.' Marchers in the mud, horses," Alex babbled.

Entering through the side door, she watched Alex slip in the puddles surrounding the boys' boots. She took a rag and wiped up the icy slush. She helped Alex undress, and he slipped into bed. On her way out of their bedroom to check on the boys, she heard Alex, still vitriolic.

"'Internationale.' I know it. The coda. Coda. Always the same."

She knew he'd sleep it off. The boys must have been tired. They had fallen asleep in their day clothes. Florence returned to her room to undress. Alex's raspy snore caught her attention. His lungs had never been good. Whenever she tried to apply a poultice or garlic rub, he became angry and stubborn. A difficult man, but he still took her breath away, especially while sleeping. In slumber his face forgot the hardships of his life.

In her flannel nightgown she propped the pillows against the headboard, then slipped under the covers. She laid hairpins on her nightstand as she pulled them out, one by one. Using the silver brush Alex had given her years ago, she brushed her long hair. Maman always brushed her hair 100 strokes before bed. Old habits die hard. Under her breath she counted.

Nineteen, twenty . . .

She rested her hands on the covers. Noticing the contrast between her tortured fingers and decorative filagree on the brush, she grimaced. Alex had given her the toilette set soon after their engagement. He'd beamed when she opened the *cadeau* wrapped in silver paper with gold ribbon. The classic monogram was a particular point of pride. She traced the curves of the large fancy F in the center. F for Falkowski, her new last name. How far they had come from those heady days of youthful romance. She missed her mother, though she hadn't always. People didn't travel these days.

Twenty-one, twenty-two . . .

They'd been the talk of the town in her Montreal neighborhood, she and Alex. Her girlfriends from her exclusive school envied her. Alex, swanky and handsome, intrigued them all with his murky background and formal, deferential manners. In school, they'd read *Anna Karenina*. Alex was her Vronsky. Silly schoolgirls, they imagined themselves swept up in dramatic, high-society intrigue.

Thirty-one, thirty-two . . .

Alex was sophisticated, though perhaps only the age difference made him seem so, ten years her senior. Papa respected his work ethic. Maman couldn't find fault exactly but cautioned her. She would say, "Alex has a dark soul. *Gris ou noir*." How could she take her mother seriously? Maman was all heart, but she read tea leaves and threw salt over her left shoulder. After they married, Florence wondered if Maman had been right. Now she knew with certainty. Nightmares disrupted their slumber, often after Alex imbibed. She glanced at him now, hoping he'd sleep through and not wake in fear.

Fifty-three, fifty-four . . .

She pulled a stray hairpin from the back of her head. Her brush lay in her lap and she fidgeted with the hairpin. Never had she understood the entire story. Alex talked nonsensically about St. Petersburg, Narva, the stampede, screaming. Workers in Imperial Russia had risen up against the tsar time and time again. She set the hairpin on the nightstand and resumed brushing. All she knew was that whatever had happened, it turned him into a lone wolf. He was rabid in his opposition to labor unions. Whenever he read an article about workers organizing or heard the radio news, he'd launch into a tirade.

Seventy-five, seventy-six . . .

The uprising had been in 1905 when she was still a child. She'd probably heard about it in school, but she found history boring. The past was the past. She liked to create, make something new. Studio art had been her life, and Alex loved that about her. He appreciated beauty. They'd always shared a love of the possible. What could they make their future be? An artist and an engineer?

Ninety-seven, ninety-eight, ninety-nine, one hundred!

A few gray strands highlighted her chestnut brown tresses. Soon she'd be making up hair dye from walnut shells like her *maman*. Hair color seemed an insignificant problem compared to the talk at the meeting. Whatever future she and Alex had envisioned, the life they have now certainly isn't it. She turned off the light. Alex murmured, his breathing rapid. Her rustling around must have disturbed him. She stroked his cheek with the back of her hand and smoothed his hair off his forehead. He rolled toward her and flung his arm over her waist. His grip tightened, and his fingers dug into her back.

"Shhh now. Everything is fine." They lay facing each other. He was still asleep. She hummed a lullaby Maman had sung to her. He relaxed his grip. Now she could sleep.

CHAPTER 5

Thursday, January 28, 1937

In contrast to the spirited evening at Dom Polski, Florence and the others cut, rolled, and stacked cigars in machine-like monotony. At breakfast, Alex had been grumpy and morose. Besides the hangover, his tortured dreams often agitated him for days. How was he faring at work? Men at the factory didn't understand him. She crossed her fingers that he wouldn't snap at someone and get into another fight.

"Flo," Basia said over her shoulder from her worktable, "you're humming."

"Am I? I didn't notice."

"The song from last night at Dom Polski. You know, 'Internationale,'" Basia whispered the song's title, rolling her eyes toward Resnick, whose head was shielded by a scrim of newspaper.

"Aaahh. I was thinking about what to cook for Henryk's wake." She chose not to disclose her concerns about Alex.

"I have idea. Start humming again. Louder. I'll join in after I pass word." Basia went to the cart and lifted a pile of leaves to replenish the supply at her table. As she walked by each table she whispered in Polish, "Listen and hum along, pass the word." She smiled pleasantly at Resnick when he looked up to watch her movements.

Soon, table by table, pleasant humming supplanted chatter, sounds rose from the rolling tables, mixing in the air with the tobacco dust. Basia, back in her seat, thrummed along with verve.

"I don't know that tune," Resnick said, looking directly at Basia. "It's lively."

She just smiled and nodded her head.

"Is that a Catholic song? Church melody?"

"Something like that. Originally French," Basia replied, switching to English.

"Basia! I hope you know what you're doing!" Florence muttered in Polish under her breath, yet she, too, continued humming.

Resnick, parked in his chair, crossed his right leg over left and spread out the newspaper, the *Detroit Free Press*. Resnick's chair sat not far from Florence's workstation. She could read the headlines. Labor actions in Detroit, Chicago, New York. She saw a small article. Strike in Flint, in the middle of the state.

Boże kochanie, dear Jesus. What's the world coming to? People should be happy they had a job. So many didn't. Like Henryk. Besides, if they didn't work, they didn't get paid. Soon, maybe soon, the world would settle on an even keel. Perhaps their reduced wages would return to normal.

Basia started to giggle and turned over her shoulder to catch Florence's attention. "Look! Look at him!" Basia jerked her head toward Resnick. She made an up-and-down motion with her hand. Florence glanced over, and sure enough, Resnick's foot at the end of his crossed leg bounced in rhythm to the revolutionary tune. Florence's eyebrows popped up, and she used the back of her wrist to cover her snicker. Basia dropped her head to her forearm on the table in an effort to control her mirth, tears running into the rolled-up cuff of her work blouse. Like a couple of schoolgirls, every time they looked at each other giggles spouted forth with abandon. Once she composed herself, Basia ratcheted up the volume and intensity of her humming in a way Florence didn't think possible. The women smirked as Resnick's foot moved in tempo.

"We shouldn't make fun," Florence said, guilt washing over her. Basia shrugged. Florence knew Resnick hated his job and resented his uncle, but he was beholden. Schwarz, who owned the factory, had accepted the young man into his home when Resnick's parents banished him from Germany. He was young and alone. Sometimes Resnick would chat with her. She likely reminded him of his mother, though the age difference wasn't sufficient. Girls in the factory called her Mother Flo; they said she was everyone's mama. Once in a while, Resnick shared his troubles with her. His loneliness, bottled up tight, leaked out, even gushed forth, on occasion. Yesterday he'd shown her an advertisement for a Dodge D2 convertible coupe. He'd been all agog pointing out the wide whitewall tires and suicide doors. He'd said, "With a swell car like that, surely I'll be able to get a date." Then he caught himself, blushed, closed the paper, and slinked away. Just looking at his sloping shoulders and defeated gait brought tears to her eyes.

The woman to Florence's right started singing some words from the chorus, shyly. Florence heard her and met her eyes, incredulous. Basia said, "If you're going to sing, then sing!" Basia belted out the next lines of the song. The other women in the room stopped their humming, aghast. All eyes were on Basia. She sat straight up. Her rich, low voice flowed over her lower lip, compelling others to follow. Florence, too, began singing the words, pianissimo, testing the waters. By twos and threes, the others joined. Soon the voices reached the rafters, enveloping the room with strident harmony.

Resnick dropped the newspaper onto his lap. His eyes panned the workshop.

Boom! The steel door that had been propped open slammed shut. Mr. Schwarz announced himself. His white, starched shirt collar jutted above a double-breasted gray wool suit coat. He glowered across the workstations, blinking aggressively, commanding his eyes to adjust to the hazy light. Silence covered the room, a wet blanket doused flames.

"Good morning, Mr. Schwarz." Resnick never addressed the man by "uncle" at work. "Hope the noise didn't annoy you. One of the gals propped open the door for some fresh air."

Schwarz strode over to Resnick, now standing and resting the newspaper against the leg of his gray corduroy work pants. Schwarz snatched the *Free Press*, threw it on the floor, and spit on it.

"What is the meaning of this, you lazy fool!"

Resnick shrugged.

"You sit and read a rag while these dames sing revolutionary songs? Are you out of your mind?"

"Uh, I didn't know, sir. They sing in Polish, sir. I thought it was a church song. I don't know what they're saying."

"Not sure *you* know much of anything, you tin-eared twit!" Schwarz smacked Resnick's cheek almost as hard as the steel door had slammed. Florence winced.

"Everybody knows that tune is the 'Internationale.' It doesn't matter what language. It means insolence, insurrection! Revolution! It's *your* job to put the kibosh on it," Schwarz continued.

"Yes, sir. I will, sir. I surely will!" Resnick nodded his head, eyes lowered, his hand holding his left cheek. Schwarz stormed from the room. The steel door slammed closed once again.

Florence's shaking hands broke the cigar she was rolling. All the while the other women continued working in silence, heads down, eyes averted. She hoped the lunch break would come soon.

Resnick's voice crackled through the megaphone. "No more singing. It's not allowed!"

Without looking up, Basia started humming. Florence feared her friend's moxie would cause even more trouble.

"And no more humming! I'm adjusting quotas. Every day this week we'll produce ten percent more. Starting today. It's already midday, so you'll have to work fast. The lunch break will be ten minutes only. That's all."

Groans and curses created an undercurrent in the room. Muted comments slipped out from bowed heads. Fingers grudgingly rolled leaves faster. Finished cigars slapped down on growing piles. Time for lunch.

Florence followed Basia, with the square set of her shoulders, into the lunchroom. Hesitating for a moment, Florence looked at Resnick's face as he stood with arms folded across his chest at the doorway. His front teeth gripped his lower lip. His hazel eyes, a cistern of tears, refused to meet hers. Basia and Florence sat to the side, away from the others, and far from the doorway where Resnick loitered, swaying back and forth on his feet.

"Basia, you need to be careful! This could turn bad."

"I know, but I'm tired. Why not do something? What can he do to couple of overripe cabbages like us?"

"He's just a kid in over his head, thinks he has to be a tough guy. He told me once his uncle took him in unwillingly. Doesn't even pay him much. Tells him he's working for room and board." Florence laid out her hard-boiled eggs and a piece of rye bread on her lap.

"He's got it easy. Besides us old ones, he's surrounded by young girls who don't cause trouble. He doesn't have to deal with auto workers. Those men make bulls look feeble."

"Still, his uncle didn't need to dress him down in front of us. Now there's a bull."

Miller, the owner's flunky and right-hand man, charged through the door to the work area. Florence couldn't see him from the lunchroom, but she didn't need to. She heard him.

"Resnick! What're you doing? Why aren't those broads back to work? It's a lunch break, not a drawn-out banquet!"

"No, sir. Definitely not, sir. In fact, I cut their lunch break. Only ten minutes. Increased quota too. Ten percent more. We can increase prod—"

"Do what you need to do, Resnick," Miller interrupted. "I need a handpicked box of perfectos. Only the best. Get it now and bring it up to the offices. Make sure all the exterior wrappers are perfect." Miller's purposeful footsteps faded away. Missive delivered.

Florence looked up when Resnick entered the lunchroom. His hazel eyes, harboring injury just a few minutes ago, radiated loathing. Florence grabbed her friend's arm.

"Back to work now. Picnic's over. We're staying here tonight until we not just meet but exceed quota."

Eight minutes had passed.

NOT YET LOST

All afternoon, the women rolled tobacco leaves in the somber workroom. Most still wanted to leave on time to reach the food markets before they closed. No one wanted to spend the early evening hours with Resnick. They had taken to leaving in at least couplets, if not larger groups.

Resnick sauntered up and down the aisles, a hawk circling for prey. His hands, behind his back, cradled a Chaveta knife. Sidling up behind a young woman, Resnick reached over her shoulder and stabbed a cigar from the top of her pile with the point of his Chaveta. He shoved the cigar in her face. She recoiled. Florence flinched.

"Do you think *this* is a perfectly wrapped cigar?"

Dumbstruck, the young woman was mute.

"Do you?" Resnick shoved the cigar so close to her face that her eyes crossed.

"Yes, it's as I always make them. Sir."

"Then you can't make them worth a damn! In fact, they all look like turds. Resnick sliced through the pile of finished cigars with his knife. They scattered like shot. Florence gasped.

"Do them over," commanded Resnick.

Two women working nearby started to retrieve the cigars. "Stop! She'll do it." Resnick pulled the shabby metal stool out from under the young woman. She kneeled to retrieve the cigars from under the worktable. Resnick slapped her on the rump. Her head, jerking up in surprise, slammed into the underside of the worktable. The young woman's tears puddled in the piles of dry tobacco dust. Resnick chuckled.

Florence whispered a prayer with her head lowered. She made the sign of the cross, uncertain who was most in need of the prayer.

"What's he doing? I've never seen him act this bad. What is *wrong* with him?" she implored.

Basia turned to answer. No words came, but her eyes could have burned down the factory with their fire.

Resnick continued striding with an affected casualness. "Just because you make more doesn't mean you get sloppy." Resnick approached Alicja. Once again, the Chaveta knife gored a cigar, like a toothpick spearing an olive. This time Resnick waved the cigar with his right hand under his own nose. He inhaled the bouquet as if searching for tertiary flavors in a fine wine, as if he'd know. All the while his left hand stroked Alicja's fine blonde hair. Resnick's protracted evaluation of the cigar, slower than the most exacting sommelier's, coincided with his fingers' exploration of Alicja's neck, cheek, and décolleté. Basia hurled herself from her stool, shoving Resnick off his feet.

"How *dare* you take liberties with Alicja! Who do you think you are?" Basia stood erect, one hand on her hip and her own Chaveta tight in her fist.

Resnick, recovered from the shove, faced off with Basia. Staring at each other, Chavetas poised, arms cocked, eyes locked, a twisted tango about to start. Just as Florence approached to pull Basia back to her corner, the steel door slammed. Miller appeared.

"Got my perfectos? I thought you'd have 'em up in the office by now."

"Yeah, I got sidetracked. Mrs. Sikorski here was just about to gather 'em up."

Basia found a new wooden box, the White Eagle insignia burned into the lid. She held each perfecto up to eye level, making an opera of examining each wrapper. She laid each cigar in the box with mock precision. Florence caught her breath as she gripped the edge of the table, bracing for an explosion. Beads of sweat emerged on Resnick's temples. The veins in Miller's neck rose, red ropes around his neck. Just as Miller's snarling lips opened to speak, Basia snapped the box lid shut. With two hands and mock obsequiousness, she offered the box to Miller. She almost curtsied.

Florence exhaled. *"O Boże!"*

CHAPTER 6

Saturday morning, February 6, 1937

Immediately after Alex left for the gun club, Florence retrieved her coat and scarf from the hooks in the small vestibule leading to the back door. Maybe in the spring Alex would build a porch around the back stoop like the Sikorskis did. She stepped through the maze of men's shoes on the landing between the door and the basement stairs. When did the boys' feet get so big? She paused for just a moment when she noticed the cardboard in one of Lucien's shoes. She picked it up and turned it over, confirming what she already knew. A hole. He needed another pair. Fitting her wool bucket hat snugly on her head, she approached the alley to meet Basia.

"*Dzień dobry!* You're here already." Florence usually arrived before her friend.

"Today an exciting day, no? Not like going to work." The women walked toward Michigan Avenue. Florence smiled at the spring in her friend's step.

"*Tak*, it should be interesting, yes." She still was in disbelief she'd agreed to go with Basia to the Westside Polish neighborhood. Basia had arranged for them to meet a group of women who worked at General Motors' Ternstedt factory. She'd heard ten, maybe twelve, thousand people worked there, mostly women. Automobile parts such as door handles, locks, trim pieces, all small parts, were dipped in chrome. They'd heard reports of conditions there. Rumors had spread that Ternstedt workers were planning action, maybe even organizing. Basia pounced on the hearsay with bulldog tenacity and focused on little else until she'd orchestrated this meeting.

"I think we learn from them. And them from us. They know more about Flint." Basia referred to the sit-down strike at General Motors' plant in the mid-state city. "They have same problems. Not enough pay. Too much work. It's bad. It's so big. Many people from down south. They blame people who come here from other countries for working!"

Florence didn't interject much. Basia was just thinking out loud. They joined the group waiting for a streetcar on Michigan Avenue. The cream-colored streetcar approached from the southeast. The line started near Tiger Stadium and angled northwest, one of the spokes of Detroit's wagon wheel layout. They stepped up, paid, and settled into their seats. By tacit agreement, they did not discuss the purpose of their journey in public.

"Where's Alex today?" Basia sat primly, holding her clutch purse on her knees.

"His boss invited him to go shooting at a gun club. A surprise for sure. I'm glad for him. He needs a little fun. Romek?"

"Working."

"The boys are going to a boxing match. Lucien, he likes to watch this boxer. Joe Louis, I think his name is."

"Boxing is so popular now."

Each retreated into her own thoughts as the streetcar inhaled and exhaled its passengers, block after block. In the 1920s, when Florence and Alex first arrived in Michigan, she marveled at the opulence and style of Detroit's Michigan Avenue. Hesitant to leave Montreal, she found a welcome surprise in the sophisticated culture and commerce of their new hometown. The industrial bedrock of Detroit generated innovation and wealth at an unprecedented rate. A main artery of the city's hub, Michigan Avenue housed the crème de la crème of hotels, shops, medical offices, furniture stores, custom dress shops, fur emporiums. She enjoyed spying the new advertisements painted on the sides of the brick buildings, unable to imagine painting such large areas. The art deco architecture for which the city was famous shouted modernity and the forward-thinking spirit of the city. The 1929 stock market crash prematurely snipped off the bloom of the twenties. She hoped the precipitous deadheading would result in more blooms, and soon.

Now, gazing through the streetcar's dirt-mottled window, she noticed paint peeling from advertising murals. Garish signs announcing goods at discounted prices hung under tattered striped awnings. People used to line up for movies and shows, for new product introductions, and to dine in fine restaurants. Just past the next street she saw a queue stretching down the sidewalk and wrapping around a corner. She craned her neck for a better view. A soup kitchen. Darkness eclipsed this city that once shone providentially on so many. Thick sadness oozed through her veins.

"Next stop is ours." Basia put on her gloves and collected her clutch, all business. Florence wrenched her gaze from the window and followed Basia to a place near the exit door. Panning the riders, she realized the view inside the car offered no more hope than outside. Regardless of shoddy clothes and scrawny bodies, it was the faces. Despair branded on most, scored deep. Florence knew she must rise above this angst or surely she would drown.

"I'm ready. Yes, I *am* ready!" Why had Basia looked at her so quizzically? The streetcar doors opened. They walked a few blocks on Junction Street past Kopernick Street to arrive at the Westside Dom Polski. Each Polish neighborhood had built their own. A small committee of gracious women welcomed them.

Basia turned the conversation after the pleasantries. "We're very interested to hear about events at Ternstedt." The three women spoke spiritedly of their factory, sharing their knowledge of manufacturing. They spoke of the die-casting process, the alloys. Florence recollected Alex's conversations with his coworkers, all technical and engineering terms. Such pride this cohort had in their knowledge and skill. She and Basia were experts at their jobs, but finely rolled handmade cigars didn't carry the panache of the alluring automobile industry.

The Ternstedt women liked their work, except they wanted to be paid fairly and treated with respect. Also, they weren't impervious to safety concerns. Smoke generated from the process permeated the factory. Wet rags over their eyes, used only at the break, provided some relief. Die-cast parts need to be chromed, and their job was to clean the dies, treat them with acid, handle the chrome, electroplate, buff, and polish.

Florence perused the wall hangings of so many scenes of pastoral Poland. Farms, lakes, mountains, forest creatures. She noticed the clock. Still enough time before she had to be home. Basia was enjoying herself, drawing comparisons to their own work situation. Florence was just as glad to remain quiet. She lugged the heft of her melancholy with her after all.

"This is good time to know you and your factory. We need to learn about organizing and strikes. How to make plans?" Basia directed them toward their mission.

"We thought you might, so we invited a special guest to join us," one of the Westside women said, glancing at the clock. "She should be here any time now."

"Ah, who is this special guest?"

"Mary Zuk."

"The communist?" Florence uttered. She covered her mouth with her hand.

"My hero!" Basia said at the very same time.

"And what if she is?" the second Westside woman challenged her. Florence looked to Basia, whose searing brown eyes warned her to remain silent. She heard the front door close.

"*Dzień dobry! To ja!* Mary." The diminutive woman whisked into the room, dropped her coat and hat on an empty chair in the corner, and joined the group, assuming the head of the table. She tamed a few strands of dark brown hair escaping from the bun low on her neck, her dimpled smile genuine.

"I've only a short time, but this is important. Especially after the firings last month at General Cigar." All agreed. The Westside women wasted no time serving Mary coffee and cake and refilling Basia's and Florence's cups.

Mary worked at Dodge Main some months ago. With the explosion of activity and labor unrest, she quit to work full time organizing and supporting work stoppages. When Mary Zuk quit Dodge Main, Alex told Florence, "Good riddance." He didn't want communists near him or his place of employment. Florence sat back and listened.

In spite of herself, Florence warmed up to Mary. The woman included her in the conversation through eye contact and warm smiles, though Florence said little. Impressive. Basia pelted questions at Mary, who answered them all with patience and enthusiasm.

"I work with Stanley Nowak. He's so busy now with the situation in Flint." Mary referred to the massive sit-down strike at the General Motors Fisher Body plants. Nowak led the charge of organizing workers from Eastern Europe. A Pole from Chicago, he carried sway through his Polish language radio show.

"This is our time for Ternstedt." Mary explained that organizing the Ternstedt plant while the United Auto Workers, or UAW, was on a streak would be good. She was enrolling Polish women from the plant and advising them on work slowdowns.

"The AFL has a cigar workers' union. Have you approached them?" Mary queried, referring to the American Federation of Labor.

"I've been making inquiries, but they're not interested in helping us. Our wages are so low, even the unions don't want us." Basia elicited a chuckle with that comment.

"That might be helpful," asserted Mary. Responding to Basia's questioning eyebrows, she explained how useful the element of surprise could be by catching management off guard. In Flint, management expected a strike at a different factory from the one in which the sit-down occurred. Workers had the advantage of time and preparation.

"You see, if the existing cigar workers' union doesn't want you, the owners won't anticipate any action. They'll be shocked."

"Like ambush." Basia nodded, absorbing Mary's every word.

"Yes, like an ambush." Mary and Basia nodded at each other, their brown eyes locked. Florence looked from one to the other. These two are kindred all right, cut from the same cloth.

"Now let me explain. You ladies from Ternstedt too. Here's what we do." Mary laid the framework for a successful labor action. No question, her organizing skills were second to none. She listed committees required for food, cooking, watching children at home. Reserves of women would be needed to switch in and out every few days so workers could take a break and go home and bathe. They would need money, and this was the hardest part when they weren't part of a union yet.

"I need to go now. Think about all I said, and we can talk more. To be realistic, until Flint and Ternstedt are settled, it may take time."

The women shepherded Mary out and cleared the table. Basia and Florence thanked the Ternstedt women for their hospitality and the introduction to Mary Zuk. They departed for the streetcar.

"She's quite a woman." Basia walked, scarf untied and coat open.

"She is. But, *psia krew*, she's a communist!"

"You don't know that!"

"There are rumors. We should ask Joan." Florence alluded to their friend who wrote for *Głos Ludowy*, the left-leaning Polish newspaper.

"I don't care if she is. Maybe what it takes to get something done. When she started boycott of butchers, we got lower meat price."

True. Florence couldn't argue. Two years ago, Mary Zuk instigated a boycott of butchers and meat packers in Detroit. Newspapers reported five thousand people followed her tiny frame to a rally in a park. She organized picket lines, even garnering support from women outside of the Polish community who shopped in Hamtramck. Everyone had to eat, regardless of race or ethnicity. Of course Florence didn't participate. Alex forbade her. Basia walked in a picket line but was otherwise uninvolved. In a matter of weeks, turbulent and sometimes violent, the boycott proved successful.

NOT YET LOST

On the streetcar Florence crossed her tired ankles. Her head hurt and she felt flushed. Maybe too much coffee. Or the walk from Dom Polski. Basia had walked like a racehorse. The scene around her was the same as in the morning—different people with the same dejected demeanor. A bone-thin young mother, scarf tied under her chin, held her little boy's hand. He sucked on a cloth with the other hand. Maybe his mother had put a hint of syrup on it. Their deep-set, hollow eyes matched each other's, mother and son. Women, including the young mother, held handbags. What was in them? A comb, a handkerchief. Most bought too few items to warrant a list for the markets. Handbags lay flat, deflated, a mirror of the world. A few men passed around a newspaper, checking for the numbers they'd gambled on the previous day. Their faces crestfallen—but not surprised—at confirmation they didn't win a payout.

A communist. Did they really need a communist to help them? People were already suspicious of Eastern Europeans. If Alex found out? *O, Boże!* What about the boys? She didn't want them branded. The opening and closing of the streetcar doors grated. She slid her tongue between her teeth to avoid grinding. Maybe Mary Zuk wasn't a communist? She was called one during the boycott. People accused others of all sorts of things these days. The world had gone mad. She used her gloves, paired up in her hand, to fan her face. Bulging blue veins formed bumps on the back of her hands. She was angry. But why? With whom? The street signs indicated only a few more blocks. She needed to get off this streetcar and nudged Basia to move toward the exit.

Falling wet, sloppy snowflakes refreshed her face, and she felt she could breathe again. They moved toward the alley that would take them home.

"A lot to think about, yes?" Basia said.

"Yes. The things you get me into."

"Those women are smart. They're taking control. Not sitting back."

"Do you think what they said was true? About the mice in the factory having strange growths all over them? It sounds grotesque."

"They've no reason to make up stories. I think it's true. Those women? They'll die of cancer just like rodents. The shiny car parts they make? Last forever."

CHAPTER 7

Saturday morning, February 6, 1937

Alex paced in front of the Eppinger's Sporting Goods store in Cadillac Square. His hands, rattling coins in his trouser pockets, itched to wrap around a trigger again. Fred had invited him to meet at the club and should arrive soon. The unexpected invitation from his supervisor remained an enigma. Maybe there was nothing more to it than gratitude for modeling for Diego Rivera, as Fred had said. In the meantime, he enjoyed watching the patrons come and go, recognizing more than the occasional political or sports celebrity. Surprising that this club occupied such tony real estate. But then again, maybe only the well-to-do could afford to join. The *clang clang* of the streetcar approaching caused him to stop pacing and lean nonchalantly against the exterior wall. Fred jumped down from the second door of the cream-colored streetcar, waited for the Saturday morning cars to clear, then crossed to greet Alex.

"Morning, Alex." Fred Lynch extended his hand.

"Good morning," Alex replied, accepting the proffered hand.

"Ready for a bit of target practice?" Fred held the door for Alex, clapping him on the back as he passed through.

"I sure am. I may be a bit rusty. Living in the city here, I don't get out hunting or shooting often."

"I'm sure you'll be in fine form in no time. Let me get you set up here with some ammo. Club gets it for free from the War Department."

"Is that so?"

"Yeah, it's their way of training the next army. Once we're set, we'll go up to the ranges." Fred greeted or nodded to several men as they walked through the hallway to the elevator. "Mornin'. Fourth floor please," Fred addressed the elevator operator perched on his stool.

"Yes, sir." The operator scanned Alex up and down, proprietarily assessing an obvious newcomer. Other than Fred's incessant gum cracking, the men rode in silence. When the elevator operator retracted the bronze gate and opened the glass door, the staccato noise of bullets firing and acrid smoke enveloped them. Alex's pulse quickened. The attendant behind the counter provided paper targets and directed them to adjacent shooting lanes. They fired away.

Alex kept an old long rifle at home along with his handgun. When he first emigrated to Canada from Poland, he acquired the rifle in Montreal. In his early days there he thought for a short time that he might return to the farming life of his boyhood, but easy access to wilderness areas and abundant wildlife proved hunting to be more profitable. The great influx of immigrants demanded food, and he sold a variety of meat to taverns, inns, and grocery stores. Florence's parents owned a grocery store, which is how they met. He favored selling to them because Florence's father would accept the meat minimally field dressed. His years in St. Petersburg with the Cossacks destroyed any affection, of which there wasn't much, for agrarian ways.

Alex's old long rifle was an antique compared to this new Winchester bolt action Fred lent him. He admired the metal components inlaid into the wood stock, and he appreciated the front and rear iron sights. Clumsily at first, Alex manipulated the bolt lever to eject spent cartridges, but after practicing twice, the sequence flowed. After an hour, the stores of ammunition were depleted and they stopped. He was glad to be finished shooting. His head still ached from cracking the window at Wally's. Fred pulled the clothesline-style wire, retrieving their paper targets. They rifled through them, analyzing their shots.

"Hey, Falkowski, you're a regular marksman. Look at that!" The men reviewed the pattern of holes circling tight to the bullseye.

"Guess it's like putting the left foot in front of the right. Comes back to you." Alex nodded, quite satisfied with himself.

"That's great. Really great. Aces, just aces, as they say!" Fred slapped his thigh with enthusiasm.

"Not so bad yourself there, Mr. Lynch." Alex remembered his manners and with whom he stood.

"Fred. Call me Fred. Come here often enough, I should be a good shot. Great way to spend a day, ain't it? Just spotted a couple of the guys over there I need to get with."

"Thanks again for inviting me. I'll see you at the plant on Monday."

"Sure will. Next time we'll shoot revolvers. Club's got some Smith & Wessons."

"I would like that. Thank you."

"Abyssinia!"

"Pardon me?"

"Aah-be-see-in-ya. Abyssinia."

"Right. Good afternoon." Alex shook his head and returned to the elevator. The elevator cab slipped into view through the wired glass doors. He stepped aside to allow the passengers to exit and was surprised to see his old friend among them.

"Hello, Nick, I didn't know you came here. You never mentioned!" Alex greeted his friend as he stepped over the threshold.

"Well, you know I keep it quiet." Nick shifted his gun bag back and forth, hand to hand. "Didn't know you were a member. New?"

"No, I'm not a member. First time. Lynch brought me as his guest."

"I see. It's a swell club. Belyaev owns it. Third generation. Remember that place in Petersburg?" Nick put his hand up to the side of his mouth and whispered, "Best thing is he's a White Russian. Like us."

"Yes, I can see why you would like that." Alex sighed. His friend still carried a torch for their beloved homeland, the strip of land overlapped by eastern Poland, western Russia, and Ukraine, where many ethnic groups converged. Nick hoped to return there one day. Alex did not. He mourned the culture, the arts, the intellectual discourse. Twenty years now since the Bolshevik revolution decimated the spirit of his homeland. The ghosts haunted him. He wasn't a tsarist. No, he understood all too well the wreckage in the wake of serfdom. He wished Nick would stop assuming they were alike. He'd given up on politics a long time ago.

"Why don't we meet up at Wally's tonight after dinner. Did you keep your targets? We'll see who's the better shot."

Alex had, in fact, shoved the targets into his coat pocket. Wadded paper sheets rested on top of his own handgun nestled down deep. Not knowing what to expect, Alex had packed his Smith & Wesson .38 Special, snub-nosed and compact. He often carried it because of the recent groundswell of crime.

"We'll make some bets beforehand. How about 7:30 tonight?" Alex suggested.

"I'm game. Just don't make the stakes too high. You're a damn good shot as I recall." Nick went on his way.

Alex decided to walk home. The streets weren't crowded. These days, few people window-shopped for things they couldn't afford to buy. He preferred the chilly wind over rubbing elbows with people on the streetcar. Surveying the despair of humanity made him uncomfortable, akin to witnessing a gruesome accident from which one averts the eyes yet is compelled to look back. He evaded that anguish since he left Russia.

His galoshes leaked from a small tear near the sole. They protected his leather shoes, though the persistent rattling of two broken buckles drove him mad. At winter's end he would take them to the shoemaker for repair. The sleeves of his long navy blue wool coat looked like a mouse had nibbled the cuffs. Alex pulled up his gloves as far as possible to cover them. The gloves were new. At the

NOT YET LOST

next intersection, Alex stopped for a streetcar, passengers loading and unloading. On the corner, tucked up in the lee of a building, a downtrodden man wore a cardboard sandwich board, strings over his shoulders connecting the signage. "I speak three languages, I have two children, I want one job." The man walked a few steps in one direction, then the other, traversing the building's corner. Alex looked away, then back. He approached the man, removed a glove, and dug deep into the pocket of his trousers. He pulled out a copper Lincoln penny and pressed it into the man's palm. Their eyes met for just a moment. Alex nodded and turned away, relieved the streetcar had moved on and he could cross the street. Alex, too, spoke several languages: Polish, Russian, French, and English, not that fluency meant much in today's job market. Today, if you hailed from Eastern Europe, you needed to work with your hands and have endurance. That's all the bosses wanted. He considered Fred Lynch. The supervisor's slang and idioms were colorful at best and often amusing. Alex avoided slang. Such language often reflected nuances or associations with undesirable groups. He didn't risk possible missteps. Monday may prove interesting. Fred might put upon him to do extra work or up the ante on the "dues" Alex paid him for use of the workshop. He didn't know what the price for today's adventure at the gun club would be, but there would be a price. Of that he could be certain.

A pack of boys exploded from a doorway on Alex's right, nearly knocking into him. They ran to beat the devil, their feet slipping and sliding in the slush as they turned into an alley. He knew two of those boys. His own. Lucien and Frank. Mr. Kowalski exited the shop right after them, yelling and cursing.

"Thieves! You delinquents, you. I'm sending the police. I know where you live." Hearing Mr. Kowalski's threats and immediately understanding the situation, Alex hung back on the sidewalk. Kowalski turned to enter his delicatessen and stopped short, sticking his landing like an award-winning gymnast.

"Falkowski! What're you doin' here? Your boys—did you see them?" Kowalski jerked his thumb back over his shoulder. "Did you put them up to this? I'm shocked! You of all people."

"Woah, just a minute. Don't you dare accuse me of stealing. Or sending my boys to steal." Alex's lapis lazuli eyes iced over. A few people on the sidewalk stopped to watch.

"Let's go inside and I will cover my family's debt." Alex opened the door for Kowalski and gestured for the man to enter, bowing slightly at the waist. After addressing his boys' transgressions and buying some fragrant honey cakes to make nice, Alex exited the shop. Old man Kowalski smiled and waved through the window as Alex resumed his walk home. From the end of his street, he saw Florence scraping slush off the wooden porch steps. Their porch faced south and slush on the steps thawed with the sun and froze again at night. He admired her resilience. She'd been schooled in high-minded academia—philosophy, the arts—yet she could roll up her sleeves and work like a farm wife. Her parents had seen to that. Fortuitous, since no one foresaw the end of Detroit's halcyon days.

"How did it go?" Florence wiped her forehead with the back of her forearm.

"Good. It was a lot of fun." He kissed her and presented the white baker's box.

"What's this? What occasion?" Florence leaned the shovel against the porch railing.

"You work so hard. You deserve a treat."

She untied the string and opened the box. "Honey cakes! Thank you." She loved the golden honey-soaked sponge cake crowned with a red maraschino cherry.

"Now where are the boys?"

CHAPTER 8

Saturday evening, February 6, 1937

Alex left Florence to clean up after dinner. Once again donning his worn navy blue coat and galoshes, he descended the shoveled front porch steps and turned left on Denton. He anticipated with relish both the ice-cold Polish vodka Wally kept on hand and the ever-greater boasts he and Nick would swap about their shooting prowess. Alex patted his pocket. Yes, the folded targets were still there, but he had removed his revolver for safekeeping. He'd ask Nick about membership in the shooting club. Maybe he would join.

Aooga! Aooga! Alex turned his head to see a Ford coupe pull over to the curb. Nick hung out the window of the front passenger seat.

"Hey, Alex, c'mon. We got a change of plans. Get in back." He gestured to the back seat of the car.

Alex peered from the sidewalk into the car and tried to identify the driver. The driver faced out his own window, and in the dark, Alex didn't recognize him, though something in his bearing, or maybe just the red hair, was familiar. Alex shrugged and hopped into the back seat of the black car.

"Evening, Alex," Nick said, twisting over the front seat to look at him. The craggy skin of Nick's round face resembled a full moon, which this evening was absent from the night sky.

"Good evening, Nick. What's going on?"

"Let me introduce you to Mike Crane. Mike, my good friend Alex."

"Nice to meet you." The red-haired driver met his eyes in the rearview mirror.

"Mr. Crane, I'm pleased to meet you. How do you two know each other?"

"We just met. Mike here's a member over at the shooting range," Nick explained.

"Yes, that's why you look familiar. I saw you there this morning, Mr. Crane. I was waiting out front for a friend." Alex wondered if he should have referred to Fred Lynch as a "friend." Crane hadn't seen him with Fred, so it probably didn't matter.

"Mike, please, call me Mike. We're just friends here."

"Thanks, Mike." Alex rubbed the seat's black leather. It had been a long time since he'd felt something so fine. The rich smell of new leather pierced the overlay of cigarette smoke wafting back from the front seat. He gave way to the embrace of the seat back and looked out the window.

"Where're we off to?"

"A group of guys're getting together for a little late-night barbecue out in the woods. It's a good group. I think you'll like them," Nick responded, stretching his arm out along the top of the bench seat.

"All right." It was a little strange, the time of night, the place. A barbecue? What else did he have to do? Florence would be busy darning socks or some other sewing chore. Lucien would be out with his friends. Frank would listen to the hockey game or a detective show on the radio. Maybe it was high time for a little diversion. He hadn't even been to Hastings Street in a long time.

"Here you go." Nick handed a flask over his shoulder. Alex took a welcome swig. Warm and smooth, the bourbon caressed his esophagus and pooled delightfully in his stomach. He pulled a second mouthful, pausing this time, allowing his tongue to bathe in the amber liquid.

"Good stuff you got in here." Alex held the flask up to the window and admired the textured silver in the light from the streetlamps. He brought it closer to his eyes and lifted his glasses. A date was inscribed just below an Old English style capital "D."

"Hmm, 1935. The Tigers won the series. Hey, you're not a player, are you?"

"Found it in a pawn shop." Crane reached his long arm back and confiscated the flask from him.

Odd, this Mike Crane driving a nice car and using a flask from a pawn shop.

"Nick, I brought my spent targets. Did you? I thought we'd compare. See who's the best shot."

"I already know, Alex. You've always been better than me. Say, you didn't bring your gun too, did ya?"

"No. I thought we were going to Wally's. You know he doesn't like guns in the bar." He noticed the two men up front exchange a quick glance. "Why? Should I have? Is there going to be shooting at this barbecue, get-together, whatever it is we're going to?" Again, the men exchanged side-glances.

"No, Alex, hopefully not. This group's just a bunch of gentlemen sharing a little Southern hospitality," Mike answered. Alex noticed the almost feigned drawl of "Southern hospitality." He was leaning forward, head almost in the front seat. Mike kept his eyes on the road and Nick looked out of his passenger window, offering him only his left shoulder. He settled himself in the back seat, though his mind was anything but.

The men up front fell silent. Initially surprised by the change in plans and the perturbing ambience, Alex failed to notice how far up Michigan Avenue they'd driven. Up ahead was the overpass from which Henry Ford's private security force and the Dearborn police sprayed fire hoses, tear gas, and bullets into a crowd of unemployed workers not long ago. Scores of destitute, bankrupt, and hungry former Ford Rouge plant employees had been looking for help when there was nowhere else to go. Before swooping below the overpass, he saw the sign, displaying in fancy script, WELCOME TO DEARBORN. Alex clenched and unclenched his hands on his thighs. Perhaps this hadn't been such a good idea after all. He had plenty of experience being where he wasn't wanted.

Crane nosed the car through a labyrinth of parking lot aisles, gravel rustling beneath the tires. At last he parked at the edge of the woods lining the River Rouge. The three men, in single file, Mike in the lead, Alex in the middle, tromped over the rough, uneven path without benefit of a light. The mud, now frozen in the evening's cold, formed hard ridges from what must have been slush earlier in the day. A melody of logs popping in a fire overlaid the subdued sound of the river, its flow tamped down by ice patches. Woodsmoke wafted up Alex's nostrils and his stomach rumbled in anticipation. He'd eaten an adequate dinner, but American barbecue never failed to entice. He hoped for baby back ribs, almost tasting the tang of the sauce. They said "Southern hospitality," right? Trudging one behind the other limited conversation. Alex navigated his steps with caution, each step a tripping hazard.

"Sure am looking forward to swapping stories with the guys," Mike bellowed, his voice overly loud for their compact group of three. "How 'bout you?"

"Sure, sure. It's always a good time. I like bringing new people too," Nick's voice boomed in his ear.

They entered a clearing. Flames danced alluringly in a ring of stones, seizing Alex's attention. Orange and gold shifting light illuminated pointed shapes circling the tract, seemingly a grove of small fir trees. He couldn't quite make it out. Oddly, the pointed cones moved around, even in the windless night. Light from the flames blinded him and smoke from damp wood caused his eyes to water. He rubbed his eyes.

"Good evening, gentlemen," a raspy male voice emanated from below a set of free-floating eyes. Alex squinted to bring the image into focus. A tall figure cloaked in a black robe with a black pointed hood stepped forward from the circle. He held a flashlight at his chin, shining red, beaming upward. Alex recoiled.

Click, click, click. In quick succession, several other flashlight beams, also crimson, illuminated multiple sets of eyes. Viscerally, he recalled the moment in his youth when he was surrounded by wolves in the dense primeval forest on the Polish–Russian border. In the evening blackness, he had climbed a tree. No such option here.

"Nick, what's going on here?" He allowed no affect in his voice.

"No names are spoken here," boomed the voice from the one who seemed in charge. The voice punctuated his command with a sharp snap of a copper-studded leather whip.

"Then let me rephrase, what the hell is going on here?" Alex demanded. He pulled himself up to his full height.

"I brought you here to join the Bullet Club. It's a group I thought you'd be interested in," Nick stammered. Alex looked around. Some of the cloaked figures sported bicorne hats perched crookedly on their pointed hoods, a white skull and crossbones appliquéd poorly on the front of the Napoleon-style headpieces. He repressed a chuckle. Was this a joke?

"Let me explain," the leader took over. "We're a group of American patriots who don't like what we see going on around us. We're a political organization. We don't like Roosevelt. We don't like trade unions, and we don't like socialism, communism, or any other isms." The pointed hoods flanking the speaker bobbed up and down in agreement. "America was running fine, just fine. Before all you hunkies arrived."

Alex bristled at the term hunkies, a slur applied universally to Eastern European immigrants who worked in factories. "What does that have to do with me?" he spit his words.

"You're going to help us with our plans." The leader paced while fingering his whip's copper studs like worry beads. "But before we share our plans, we need to ensure your loyalty. Shall we administer the initiation, fellas?" The group converged, tightening the circle around him. Alex smelled the blood lust. He wished the .38 was still buried below his spent targets. Alex put his hands up, palms forward as if to slow the advance of the masked predators. "Now wait one minute—" He took a few steps backward. *Thwack!* Pain behind his knees. He lost his balance. His arms flailed. He lurched forward to recover. His hands broke his fall and his forehead broke the frozen crust of snow. For a moment he fixated on the toes of highly polished black boots a few inches from his face. He breathed in and out once, twice. Buy time.

"He's one of them knee-bending Catholics, ain't he? We don't like Catholics neither," a new voice from behind gleefully declared. Alex envisioned a drooling Doberman.

Alex pulled himself up onto his knees, straightened his glasses, and retrieved his hat.

"What then, pray tell, do you want with me?" Alex pulled a handkerchief from his pocket and wiped the snow from his face.

"Your friend here vouched for you. Said you're not a believer. It's just your wife," the leader said. Alex looked around for Nick and Mike, but they'd been subsumed into the group of black-hooded men.

"Besides, we saw you shoot. We need a marksman like you. And we hear you're anti-union," another hood spoke up.

Who are these people? They must've been at the gun club. He supported workers' rights movements but was realistic enough to know communists manipulated the workers for their own political advantage. He'd seen it all before with the Bolsheviks. Those who were powerless, once tasting a morsel of power, became ruthless.

"Let's get on with it then. Who brought him here?" The leader looked around until someone stepped forward. "You! Hold the gun." The leader waved over the cloaked man and handed him a gun.

"Forgive me," barely audible, Nick implored in Russian, holding the gun to Alex's head. The fire's light reflected in Nick's dark eyes.

"What's wrong with you? What're you doing?" Alex spewed in Russian.

"Enough! None of that here. We speak English!" the leader commanded as he wrenched the gun from Nick's hand and handed it to another cloaked figure. "I'll deal with you later," the leader promised Nick.

"You'd better listen up." It was the Catholic-hating Doberman's voice. "You fish eater. Make one move and you'll get it in the head." Was this man a bad radio actor? Or just a club stooge?

"To join our fine brotherhood, you will repeat this oath as I say it," the leader said. "Afterward, you will live by this oath and execute the commands of the Legion. Now raise your right hand." What choice did he have with the gun poised at his temple? He wished Nick was still holding the gun. The man handled the gun with pleasure as he danced foot to foot, almost giddy with the possibility of using it.

The leader spoke the oath of the Black Legion one line at a time. Alex repeated line by line, word for word.

"I pledge and consecrate my heart, my brain, my body, and my limbs, and swear by all powers under heaven and hell, to devote my life to the obedience of my superiors and that no danger or peril shall deter me from executing their orders. That I will exert every possible means in my power for the extermination of the anarchists, the Roman hierarchy and their abettors, socialists, communists . . . I swear that I will die fighting."

Once Alex completed the oath, the leader relieved the giddy man of the gun. Alex exhaled. Though he was offered a hand up, he refused, standing of his own volition. He brushed snow off his knees. In the moment of silence he thought he heard the ear-thwacking sound of someone cracking chewing gum.

"What's next?" His eyes now accustomed to the dark, Alex could see the white patches depicting a skull and crossbones insignia, also shoddily sewn, on the chest of the black robes over the heart. For a fleeting second, he expected—he hoped—someone would announce it was all a gag. The men would laugh, remove their hoods, shake hands all around, and get on with the barbecue. No one did.

"Now that you're one of us, we'll assign you tasks. Before we do, though, it is customary to give new members time to let the words of our oath sink in. The final step of initiation is the presentation of these two bullets. Most of us keep them in our pockets. You show them to signal your allegiance if need be. More importantly, keep them as a reminder of your oath. If you fail to uphold your responsibilities to the Legion, there will be a bullet for your head and one for your heart," the leader warned. "You won't see them coming."

One of the bicorne-adorned robes stepped forward. "Now you see, we don't think the government's doin' enough to protect the old red, white, and blue. The country's goin' downhill. All of us men used to have jobs. Detroit was the place to be. Now bread lines stretch 'round the blocks. Lines at the soup kitchens. We think America should be for Americans."

"Yeah!" the giddy gun holder spoke up. "Just 'cause you don't like your own dirty rotten countries don't mean you can come here and take our jobs." Alex doubted this halfwit understood a scant shred about the rise of fascism and communism in Europe.

"What do you want me to do?" Alex asked the bicorne-adorned man.

"A man like you? Many ways you can make yourself useful. We need a spy at Dodge Main. See, we run a business, provide a service to companies. Help them defend themselves. Purge labor agitators from their payroll. Anarchists. Socialists, communists. All plotting to overthrow the government of the US of A."

"You expect me to provide you names? Then these so-called agitators get fired."

"Something like that. In some factories the union makes it more difficult. We find ways. Dodge Main ain't got a union yet," the bicorne hat intoned.

A man with a pointy hood, devoid of a bicorne, spoke up. "I could use you to disrupt labor meetings. Also on the gun squad. I hear you're a pretty good shot."

Alex neither confirmed nor denied.

"I'm the trainer and treasurer. I'll get you set up with a new gun and ammo so you don't have to use your own. You pay me when I deliver it. Your escorts this evening have a uniform waiting for you in the car. You pay me for that, too, when I come 'round to collect your weekly dues."

"That's extortion!" Alex looked back and forth from the trainer to Nick, then to Mike, and back again. "I'm leaving. I want nothing to do with you!" Alex turned around to leave and was confronted with a line of black-cloaked figures blocking his way. Two men came from behind him, each taking an arm. He struggled to wrestle free. They tightened the grip on his upper arms. The hooded men approached him with the skill of law enforcement.

"Don't worry. You'll like being a member of the club. You get to go to secret meetings, carry a gun, and everything," the Doberman voice barked from the far side.

"You're one of us now. Once in, there's only one way out," the leader said. "Remember. No names. Total secrecy. One betrayal and we'll find you. If not you, then the ones you hold dear." He leveled the threat. Alex doubted not the man's willingness to execute on his promise.

"One more thing before we go," the voice continued. "You'll know a brother when you meet one because he'll tip his hat three times. When he does that, you respond, 'Under the star of the guard.' You got that?"

Alex withheld a reply.

"I asked you a question. You got that? Now say it. 'Under the star of the guard.'"

"Under the star of the guard." Alex spit into the fire.

The flashlights extinguished. Alex blinked to erase the sight of pairs of red eyes surrounding him. Someone doused the fire. The rocks in the ring sizzled when the cold water hit their hot surfaces. Once again Nick and Mike, now without robes, led him down the path to the car. Mike resumed his spot in the driver's seat. Nick held open the back passenger door for Alex. Nick grabbed Alex by the shoulder, demanding eye contact. Nick's liquid dark eyes pleaded for forgiveness—begged, implored. Alex's shot daggers of cold steel.

Oppressive silence filled the car. Alex rubbed his knees. He hated the cold. Wet snow had penetrated the thin cloth of his trousers. He bolted out of the car the second it stopped, a full block away from his house. He hastened up the street. The Ford coupe pulled alongside him. Nick jumped out and shoved a bag into Alex's arms.

"What's this?"

"Your uniform. I'll be in touch." Nick scurried back to the coupe. Alex watched the Ford turn right at the next street and heard its engine rev as it gained speed. In the backyard, he yanked open the slanted metal doors to the cellar. He proceeded to the incinerator, lifted the lid, and dropped the bag. Good riddance. He exited the cellar doors into the backyard. The windows to the bedrooms were dark. Good. He didn't want to go inside. Hastings Street. He'd go there.

Neon signs glowed through the haze. Up ahead, Sunnie Wilson's club beckoned. Sunnie had built a booming business showcasing the best contemporary jazz musicians. Alex didn't care who was performing tonight. He needed to calm his nerves and figure out what the hell just happened. Who were these Black Legion people in their infantile costumes? When he approached the entrance, Jake, the doorman, was engaged with other people. Alex was glad he could just nod and avoid conversation. He sat at the bar, disinclined to join the crowd in the ballroom. The first martini hadn't calmed his nerves so he ordered a second. The ridiculous trappings of those men disguised something evil, even lethal. At first he thought it a joke, some Boy Scout-type initiation. Nick had said it was a club. Nick. What was his involvement? He didn't seem to be gung ho—more apologetic, reluctant. The hate the men espoused wasn't Nick's style. As soon as possible, he'd confront Nick. Then, when he learned more, he'd choose the extent to which he'd uphold these responsibilities foisted upon him. He relaxed into the bar chair, losing himself in the music wafting from the ballroom.

He stayed until the band finished the set. Reaching in the pocket of his slacks for cash to pay his bill, he felt the two bullets. One for his head, one for his heart, they'd said. His choice may have been made for him. In fact, he may have no choice at all.

On his way out he stopped to talk to Jake.

"Good to see you, man. You're not staying long tonight." Jake shook his hand.

"No. Tomorrow's Sunday. Church in the morning."

"You don't fool me none. If I was a bettin' man—which you know I'm not—" Jake winked, "I'd say you'll be catching some z's, maybe with a sweet patootie all snuggled up."

"If life were that simple. Have a good evening."

"Wait, you don't have a bet you want me to run in for you?" Jake ran the numbers for Paradise Valley's most successful businesswoman, Mama Queenie.

"Not tonight." Alex fingered the bullets in his pocket. "My luck's not running high tonight."

"All right then. Catch you next time." Jake tipped his hat.

Alex headed home, threading his way through Paradise Valley, the entertainment district, then the Black Bottom residential neighborhood. An ambitious woman, Queenie started her own numbers game. Like many other ethnic groups, Blacks flocked to Detroit from the South, answering industry's call for labor. In the 1920s, lack of employees girdled manufacturing output. As did the Germans, Jews, and Poles before them, Blacks were doing their time in Black Bottom when the market crashed. They had landed in the squalid neighborhood not long before the economy shattered, throwing more than half of workers out of their jobs. He respected the economic microcosm built here. Mama Queenie traded on hope by taking bets that certain numbers would appear in the newspaper. For years the numbers games were cottage industries. Anyone could start their own and each had their own way of pulling the winner. Finally, it was decided the number of financial transactions reported daily by the US Treasury in the newspapers would determine the winning number. Queenie also offered hope in a practical way. The pool of cash was used to lend money to people who otherwise wouldn't have access. Maybe they started a business, or bought a home, or just needed to make one end meet the other. Alex won often enough playing the numbers to stay in the game. He hoped his luck would continue.

CHAPTER 9

Wednesday, February 10, 1937 (Ash Wednesday)

The community of Poletown descended upon Dom Polski once again. Temperate weather made for muddy boots, and women stationed at the door scolded those who didn't remove their messy footwear upon entering the community home. Florence saw to that. The ever-burgeoning crowd gathered in the garden basement as usual. She ran downstairs to check on the arrangements. The buffet table, austere in its Lenten offerings, provided adequate sustenance for those arriving directly from work. Good. Romek stood behind the podium, as usual, speaking seriously to Alex, who occupied the adjacent chair once reserved for Henryk. Joan busied herself with setting up her typewriter and selling copies of *New Masses*, the newspaper of the John Reed Club of social realist artists and journalists. Florence ran upstairs to herd the latecomers so they could start. Tonight was important. Everyone needed to hear. Romek signaled to Joan, who advanced to the podium. Romek called for attention and quiet before stepping aside.

Once the crowd settled itself, Joan led them in singing "Internationale" using the pencil she kept behind her ear to conduct. She took the verse.

> The state is false, the law mockery,
> And exploitation bows us down;
> The rich man flaunts without a duty,

And the poor man's rights are none.
Long enough have we in swaddling languished,
Lo, Equality's new law
"Away with rights that know no duties,
Away with duties shorn of rights."

The attendees joined in the refrain.

Tis the last call to battle!
Close the ranks, each in place,
The staunch old International
Shall be the Human race.

As the last notes of the rousing chorus faded, Romek resumed his place behind the podium. Florence and Basia sat in the front row. She envied how Basia beamed at her husband. Earlier, walking home from the cigar factory, Florence confided in Basia about Alex's opinions and her surprise at Alex's newfound involvement. A bit of a lone wolf, Alex wasn't one to engage in community activities. Basia'd said maybe underneath he was beginning to change his mind.

"*Dobry wieczór, przyjaciele!* Good evening, friends! You warm my heart by being here tonight." Romek's eyes twinkled as he panned the crowd, appearing to look into each individual's eyes.

"First things first. *Dziękuję*, many thanks, to our sister Joan for blessing us with your gift of song. Your voice, so beautiful. So strong. Unwavering. You're an inspiration." The crowd joined Romek in a round of applause. Joan stood up from behind her typewriter and offered a quick nod of her head.

"And you can type this into your news story: 'Joan sang prettily as a songbird yet sonorous as the trumpeter in St. Mary's in Krakow.'" Appreciative laughter warmed the room. Basia smiled at her husband.

With a change in tone, Romek continued, "My friends, we have some serious business to discuss tonight. Work slowdowns."

"We've been slowing down, Romek. My chrome bumpers are so polished you could hang them in a fancy parlor," a bumper installer shouted.

"Me too! I take a three-minute snooze across the front seat once I install it and two more in the back." The crowd chortled.

"I know, boys, you've been doing a great job of it. Assembly lines stopped twice as often as usual last week while waiting for stations to catch up. But here's the thing. Individuals are getting in trouble. Tuesday, Joe was fired. They say he purposely caused those electrical shorts. Now what can he do? No one's hiring. He's been blackballed. His name's on the list. At least he's got a place to live with Alex here, who's not going to kick out Florence's brother."

Florence watched Alex's face. Dispassionate.

"But what if he didn't?" Romek continued, "Look at Peter over there." Romek pointed to a man standing in the back, leaning against the wall, with his hat pulled low, looking at his feet. "Sorry to single you out, Peter, but you're a good example of what's happening. Fired, no recourse. No family here in America. But you do have friends, Peter. We've got your back. You won't starve. And neither will your family in Łoniów. My friends, Florence will collect at the door tonight for Peter and his family. Give what you can. It's all right if you can't."

"Peter," shouted Mrs. Koseba, "you come eat dinner with us tomorrow tonight." Peter, ashamed, looked up and nodded, tears breaking the dam of his blonde eyelashes.

"Sunday, you're with us!" Another cried.

"I've got Monday. My pierogis are better." And another.

"Wait till you taste my czarnina." And yet another.

"*Czarnina*? Where'd you find a duck?" Women chimed in, kidding each other, one after another, until laughter permeated the room and Peter had scads of dinner invitations.

"So you see," Romek resumed, "we can't put the burden of our struggle on just one or two people. We can't continue to sacrifice our neighbors, our friends, for us all to benefit."

"If we all agree to slow down at the same rate, then slowdowns should work, right?" Someone from the audience asked.

"The problem is that management has control. They can make an example out of anyone they just don't like. They're not going to fire us all. So it's not fair."

Florence continued watching Alex, who offered not a hint of his thoughts. She knew he didn't support slowdowns. They'd spoken at home, argued, in fact. When her brother lost his job, Alex ranted about the stupidity of the slowdowns. He couldn't lose his job. He had to pay the mortgage. He was close to fully owning his house, paying off the bank loan. He had much to lose. He didn't have anybody in Europe to support, so he was able to get ahead. Now his brother-in-law, Joe, might weigh him down. Florence defended her brother and challenged Alex to get involved if he knew a better way. His temper exploded. His extreme reaction surprised her. Alex was friends with Joe, if only in the guarded way he knew how. Why he'd agreed to come tonight was beyond her. She prayed he wouldn't cause trouble. Maybe something said here tonight would open his mind.

"Basia and I, we talked last night. Sure, it's bad at Dodge Main. But it's worse for our women." Romek gestured to Basia, who joined him at the podium. Once there, she took a moment to gather herself. Her winter-pale fair skin was framed by a dark black updo, hairpins sagging in back after the workday.

"First of all thank you for hearing me out. Romek tells me all the time the troubles at car factory. After working twelve hours a day, sometimes more, in foundry furnace, he comes home so exhausted his head falls into the soup! You all, we all, work hard. I'm not saying women work harder, just different." Basia drank from Romek's water glass. "We all know young Alicja from Denton Street. Alicja couldn't bring herself to be here tonight because she knew I would talk about what happened at cigar factory. She's embarrassed, more than embarrassed. How you say? Mortified! Her father's here, standing in back. Thank you for coming." Basia nodded to the sad-looking man still wearing his overcoat. "Alicja's a child, just a little girl. A good girl. Smart girl. She works every day for ten hours. More. She does fine work. She quit high school when her father was injured, lost his job." Her father looked down.

"No need to feel shame," Romek, standing a few steps behind Basia, interjected, directing his comment toward Alicja's father. "If that factory weren't a death trap you wouldn't've lost your arm. The company should've paid you, then Alicja wouldn't have to work."

"That's right, don't blame yourself," another man chimed in. "They just throw us to the wolves, and if we get eaten? So what?"

Basia continued in a soft, lowered voice, "Alicja wants to be doctor one day to help people like her papa. She spends nights, what little time she has after work, reading books." The audience leaned forward.

"But what happens to our fine little girl?" Basia's booming voice slammed the audience back in their chairs. "That devil at cigar factory. Resnick. He intimidates her! Terrorizes her. That menacing *dupek*! Now Alicja can't go back to work. She's too afraid." Basia let that thought land on the audience for a moment. "Do you think that supervisor, Resnick, cares? No. Tomorrow another young girl will take her job. Another, and another. Happens all the time. Over and over. I've seen it before. And I've heard of worse. I've had enough." Basia drew out the words through gritted teeth, her determination writ large in her expression. "Romek and I have plan. He'll tell you." Basia returned to her seat next to Florence, who grabbed her hand, sweaty from her fervor.

"Here's the plan. After mass on Sunday, come here."

That evening in bed, Florence and Alex rested against the headboard, each with a book in hand.

"Florence, what's Basia cooking up? With these plans for Sunday?"

She'd been surprised Alex hadn't commented on the meeting earlier.

"I don't know. She hasn't told me. She's getting to the end of her rope. With Henryk and everything. You should hear her at work. The other day—"

"Don't tell me. I don't want to know."

Florence shrugged and resumed reading. If he didn't want to know, she wouldn't tell him. Alex had not caused any problems and hadn't even drunk alcohol.

"Whatever she plans, you're not getting involved."

"Truth be told, I'm not sure I want to." She laid her book in her lap. "Basia has the energy. I don't."

"That's right. It's not your strong suit. Good. I'm glad you're being sensible."

"Sensible? I said I wasn't *sure* I wanted to—that means I'm also not *sure* I don't."

"Flo, you have an artist's soul. Mr. Rivera shuns politics. He told me 'his art is his weapon.' You could be like him." Alex had closed his book too.

"You compare me to Rivera! Alex, are you flattering me to get your way?"

"It's just that I—" He rolled toward her and planted his mouth on hers. She dropped her book to the floor and pulled him on top of her. He caressed her face and ran his finger over her lips. What was this? Alex being so gentle, so loving. Lately their lovemaking had been perfunctory. She was usually too tired to care. She massaged his neck, his shoulders. His tentative explorations heightened her anticipation. He tried to extricate them from beneath the thick down comforter.

"Damn *pierzyna!*"

She laughed.

"What's funny?"

"You're funny." She shoved the covers aside and stood, kicked her book out of the way, and drew her flannel nightgown over her head. She pounced on him. They rolled back and forth, searching and exploring each other's mouths and bodies.

Alex, now on top of her, breathed heavily. She removed his glasses and set them on the nightstand.

"Florence, I do love you. I just want what's best—"

"I know. You always have." She covered his mouth with hers. They provided pleasure to each other until they were spent.

Their well-rehearsed marital routine differed tonight. They were both so alive, joy in each other rekindled. Alex had returned to his side of the bed, barely. She nudged him over to make room when she crawled in after retrieving her nightgown. She sighed and prayed. Perhaps this ray of sunshine portended better days ahead.

CHAPTER 10

Sunday morning, February 14, 1937

"I thought that homily would never end!" Basia said to Florence. They stood just inside the door of Dom Polski. So far about fifty women, and a few men, had gathered in the hall. Excitement mixed with anxiety permeated the air. Everyone wore overcoats and gloves. They wouldn't be staying long, so no need to heat the building.

"Florence, we missed you last night. Where were you?" Mrs. Koseba asked.

Basia began to answer when Florence placed a hand on her arm, quieting her.

"Alex didn't want me to come. He doesn't want me to get involved."

"Fine for him to say! Everyone knows he gets special treatment at the plant. He's allowed time in the experiment room. He's treated with respect. The men talk about it all the time," another woman said.

"He doesn't really." Florence bowed her head, yet she knew he did.

"Well, whether he does or he doesn't, we could've used you last night," the woman said, doing nothing to hide her indignation.

"It's not like she let us down!" Basia defended her friend. "You should've seen her sneaking those paint cans out of the garage into alley. Then all I did was swoop them up."

"Really? Won't Alex mind?" queried Mrs. Koseba.

"Maybe . . . when he goes to paint the fence in the spring." Florence grinned.

"Does he know you're here now?" a woman asked.

"Not exactly. I told him I'd be home late from Mass. He didn't ask." Florence shrugged. When she left home she hadn't been sure she would go to the hall. She left the option open. During Mass she'd thought about the Westside women from Ternstedt she and Basia visited. They were taking action, doing something to relieve people's suffering. Remembering the poor souls on the streetcar, she thanked God for her good fortune and decided to put her toe in the water. Joining one cavalcade couldn't be too harmful.

"Come look at these signs." Helen, Wally's wife, led her and Basia through the crowd to the back hallway. Leaning against the wall, myriad signs painted on flattened cardboard boxes and butcher paper attached to scraps of wood and lengths of metal poles awaited their debut. Florence scanned the ragtag bunch of them.

CLEAN BATHROOMS
BREAD, NOT CRUMBS
8 HOUR DAYS
WHEN DO WE WANT IT? NOW, NOW, NOW!

Colors bled into one another. Letters shrank in size toward the right edge of the paper. The signs, perhaps not eloquent in their delivery, told no lies. The brushstrokes oozed the conviction and fervor of their makers—the colors, mostly red and white, the colors of Poland.

"Flo, your painting skills from your convent days would've helped," Helen said, offering a wry smile.

"I won't deny the signs wouldn't pass muster in art school, but I think they're beautiful. Every one of them." Pride surged through her very being. "Is it time?"

The women engaged a few others and passed the signs down the line toward the front door. The group, now too large for Dom Polski, gathered in the street.

The women organized themselves into rows, eight to ten abreast. Basia and Romek were in front, facing the crowd, along with Father Maletski and another priest from a parish on the other side of the neighborhood. An experienced union organizer agreed to help and occupied a position in front. Joan walked up and down the sidelines of the formation handing out song sheets. Women who previously snubbed each other or had a petty quarrel exchanged smiles as they jabbed their makeshift signs high into the air, making them dance. Someone blew a whistle, and they advanced.

The planned route departed Dom Polski on East Forest Avenue, proceeded up Chene past East Grand Boulevard to Joseph Campau, right to Mt. Elliott, and right again down to Warren Avenue, which would land them at Perrien Park. In the heart of Poletown, the park had served the community as a place of protest during the meat strike a few years prior. The park was also near the White Eagle factory. The press descended before they reached East Grand Boulevard. Joan from *Głos Ludowy* provided the tipoff. Today Joan participated rather than chronicled. Reporters shot questions at the women on the ends of the rows, cameras shooting off every few steps. All the while the women chanted, repeating their demands. Now and again Joan led them in song. The women belted out verse after verse of "Internationale," then other songs. The union organizer led the group across the trolley tracks. Trolley riders hung out the open double-hung windows, and the women played to the captive audience. Chants grew louder, signs flew higher. For just a moment time stood still for Florence. Her friends, neighbors, the priest, all together, silent no more. She started to cry. Anushka, her goddaughter, looped her hand through her arm and smiled. Florence laughed, cried, and sang, all at the same time. Uncurling her shoulders, lifting her feet higher, arm in arm, she and Anushka proceeded over the tracks. Fear of reprisal slid down her straightened back, cast astern.

They paraded past most of the cigar factories. They cut through the neighborhood to include White Eagle and Mazur Cressman.

Men, women, and children came out of their houses to watch. Many fell in step. Marching women beckoned them to join. Crowds grew deeper. Word spread like wildfire. Women took turns carrying the heavy wooden signs, giving their arms a rest. Sometimes a pair of women would carry a sign to share the load.

As they marched past her house, Florence waved to her sons, Lucien and Frank, who'd climbed out their bedroom window onto the top of the porch overhang to watch. "You be careful up there!" Florence shouted. Distracted, she tripped on a rogue wooden block. The uneven street was paved with creosote-soaked white pine. Another verse had been sung when Florence felt warm, heavy breath at her shoulder. Singing drowned out the *clip-clops* of the police horse approaching from behind. The uniformed officer, with practiced skill, directed his mount up the middle of the marchers. Chestnut brown withers looming at head height cleaved the crowd. She pushed into the others to avoid the boot nested in the metal stirrup. Looking behind her, she observed about a dozen horses wending their way through the people, along with a lineup of police cars at the cross streets. In front, the leaders raised their knees higher and their voices louder.

Alex allowed the living room drapery to slip back into place. Police horses had arrived. The scene looked too familiar. He donned his fedora and long navy blue coat and descended the front porch steps. With his long strides, he overtook the marchers, soon arriving at the forefront. Alex turned to face the approaching throngs. Humbled for a moment by their sincerity, their fervor, and their devotion, he needed to protect them from their innocence. He saw Police Chief Packett. Sirens and the arrival of fire trucks and paddy wagons drew residents out of their homes. Now police hovered around the journalists taking notes. The scene did not bode well. Alex backed away from the marchers, receding into the crowd, not wanting to be noticed. He backed right into someone.

"Oh, pardon me!" He came face-to-face with Diego Rivera. The artist hugged a sketchpad with his left arm and waved a charcoal pencil with his right.

"Mr. Falkowski, I see. We meet again." A glint of amusement danced in his dark brown eyes.

"Yes. I hope I didn't cause you to mar your drawing."

"No matter. It's just a sketch."

"Ah. You must specialize in marches. You sketched the march on the Rouge plant, didn't you say?"

"I like to capture faces expressing raw emotion. Full of life. Bigger than life, eh?"

Alex followed the artist's gaze, trying to see what he saw. Rows upon rows of women, all ages and sizes, presented a collage of fury and hope. Jutting chins, round open mouths, straight downstrokes of spines.

"What brings you to this event, Mr. Falkowski? As I recall, you don't see value in such demonstrations."

"My wife. She was coerced into being part of this mess." Alex searched the rows for Florence.

"Was she now? She didn't choose?"

"No!" Alex yelled to be heard over the singing.

"Then I hope you find her soon."

Standing next to Rivera now, Alex gazed at the artist's pad. He'd captured the vanguard. Father Maletski, arms out to the side, shoulder height, sleeves of his vestments billowing, a protective shroud for his flock. Alex could see the motion in the draping of the garment. Romek, his brawny bulk dominating the front line, oversized. Basia, fierce with fury and fervor, stood tall and strident. He could almost hear her voice emanating from the page, even in the surrounding din, so real had Rivera replicated her image. Police horses' flanks appeared to breathe. Lyrics to "Internationale" twisted with torque in his head. He froze. The coda. He knew the coda and how this would end. He snapped to.

"I have to go." He walked away.

"I hope you find her soon," Rivera said. "Before it gets ugly," he added, only for himself to hear.

Alex headed back along the march route and found himself face-to-face with Chief Packett. He'd never met the man in person, but he knew the face from the newspaper. Was the whole world at this march? Alex looked quizzically at the chief who, with three small gestures, tipped his cap three times, almost like he had a tic.

"Well?" Packett drew the word into multiple syllables.

"Good morning," Alex replied. He needed to distance himself from the chaos in the street and save Florence. He started to sidestep the policeman. Packett grabbed his upper arm and escorted him a short way down an alley.

"Let's try this again. Look at me." Packett repeated the troika with his hat, then looked down at his extended hand in which a bullet lay. "Until death."

Alex sighed. The secret greeting of the Black Legion. Visions of the night of his coerced initiation hurtled through his mind. Three tips of the hat initiated a call and response. Should he say it? Maybe he'd be arrested if he knew the response and the police thought he was a willing member.

"One last time, Falkowski. I say, 'until death.'"

Alex's head snapped up at the use of his name, then he lowered his eyes in silence. The glossy shine of Packett's rounded police boots reflected the rays of the sun tunneling through the alley. In his mind Alex saw those boots poking out from a long black robe, reflecting lumens of a flashlight. Then he knew.

"Under the star of the Guard," Alex stuttered. He remembered the response. He just didn't expect the chief of police to be one to ask for it.

"I knew you'd remember. Now I'm assigning you the task of disrupting this brazen display." Packett gestured expansively toward the rows of women marching.

"And if I don't care to?"

"You got a wife out there, ain't you? You wouldn't want those youngsters of yours on your porch roof to see something happen to their mama now, would you?"

"What do you want me to do?" He never expected he would actually be given orders by the Black Legion.

"Figure it out! I'm busy. But it better be quick. And don't let me down." Packett pumped his open palm up and down as if assessing the weight of the bullet.

Packett walked away, leaving Alex resigned to devise a plan. After a moment of hawing, he bounded down the alley to the back door of Wally's Bar. He pounded loudly. He knew the bar was closed; it was Sunday. Wally lived in the second-floor flat. Soon Wally leaned out of the window above.

"Alex, how ya doin'? I'm watching the parade from here. Care to join me? Somethin', ain't it?"

"It's something all right. Can you come down for a minute?" Waiting for Wally, Alex paced across the alley and back multiple times. He raised his coat collar and tugged on the end of his sleeves. He laced and unlaced his fingers and punched one fist into the palm of the other hand. Unnerved. Packett had unnerved him by mentioning Florence and the boys. Damn Nick! How could he have roped him into this predicament?

"Alex, you all right? Your face is red. Are you sick? Here, c'mon in." Wally backed away from the doorway so Alex could walk past.

"I need a favor."

The men whispered in the dark hallway.

"I forgot my wallet. I'll pay you at the bar tomorrow," Alex promised.

"I know you're good for it," Wally said.

Minutes later Alex slipped out the alley door, his arms crossed with his long blue coat folded over them. He considered his options. A block away, the old stables occupied the corner. When Germans occupied the neighborhood, horses were kept to draw beer wagons. Now Poles employed horses for milk wagons and fruit and vegetable carts. Alex walked along the side of the street against the flow of the protesters. Close to the stables a delivery wagon full of dried hay was perched where the driveway met the street. He knocked a bundle of hay onto the street, then drizzled *Spirytus*, 95 percent alcohol, from the bottle concealed under his coat onto the pile. He doused the street with a generous amount, then dropped the bottle under the hay wagon. He paused, tucked his coat up under his arm, retrieved a cigarette from his shirt pocket, and pretended to light it, dropping one hot match onto the wagon and a second into the puddle of alcohol on the street.

Whoosh! The street was on fire. Flames, burning hot in the high-proof alcohol, ignited both the hay and the creosote in the wooden blocks paving the street. Immediately, yells of "fire" permeated the crowd. Alex hoped the trifling fire and subsequent cries would incite enough of a disturbance to fulfill his forced commission without anyone getting hurt. At this bit of provocation, the fire truck and police cars rolled into the streets and faced the crowd head-on. The police Packards and fire trucks advanced tentatively at first, then moved without regard to people in their path. Discordant shouts, screams, honking horns, and sirens usurped harmonious singing and chanting. Now turned about, Alex hastened through the melee of people. He found Florence toward the front of the group. He grabbed her by the arm.

"*Chodź tu!*" Come here, Alex commanded Florence.

He yanked her through the crowd. In the slipstream of the public safety entourage he pulled her through the detritus from the march. Signs dropped in the street and run over by the trucks lay mangled and broken. Song sheets matted with dirty footprints lay forgotten, no more enthusiastic voices to bring the words to life. The boys climbed back through their bedroom window as their parents approached their house.

Once inside Alex lambasted her, berating her for her naïveté. "Do you want to lose your job like Joe? Then I'd have two millstones around my neck? Parading around out there with communists!

What were you thinking? Nobody cares about your damn march! You could walk from here to the ends of the earth and no one would care. You work in a lousy, cheap, dying company. They're not going to pay you more."

"You don't know that!" Florence dropped onto the upholstered sofa and lifted her feet onto the coffee table. "Besides, it's not all about the money!"

"What is it then? That loony friend of yours? Did she talk you into it? Thinks she's smart, eh? She's trouble! That's what she is." Then he left. The slam of the front door reverberated through the house.

Before long, Florence sensed movement at the bottom of the staircase. She looked up to see her older son, Lucien, watching her as she wiped tears and her nose in her ever-present handkerchief. She patted the sofa seat next to her.

"I'm sorry, Mama." Lucien hugged his mother from the side from his place adjacent on the couch. "I know you wanted the march to go well."

"Get your brother. You boys must be hungry." When Florence tried to stand, her son pulled her back to a seat.

"I'm sorry about Papa. He's so mean. He shouldn't say those things to you and call you those names."

"I know," Florence whispered. "You have to understand him. He doesn't know any different. He tries to protect us in this mixed-up world. He loves us in his own way. Let's get something to eat." Florence rose and Lucien ran toward the stairs to summon Frank. Florence stopped in the hallway to straighten the painting of the Black Madonna. She made the sign of the cross.

"*Proszę, szczesc Boże!*" Please, sweet Jesus.

CHAPTER 11

Sunday, February 14, 1937

Resnick entered the second-floor office of the cigar factory. His uncle Steve required that he work every Sunday along with him and his other uncle Mort. His uncles reviewed the week's financial performance and he took inventory. Steve preferred details of the business to remain in the family. He finished tallying tobacco leaves in their various forms on a paper marked with numbers in weight of raw leaves, stripped leaves, filler leaves, wrapping leaves, and wasted leaves. These, the wasted leaves, caused him the most grief.

"Here you go, Uncle Mort." Resnick poured himself a cup of coffee from the buffet in the office. He leaned against it while sipping from a solid blue pottery mug. Mort, in his early fifties, hunched over a pad of buff-colored ledger paper with a dizzying array of green lines. He wore brown tweed suit pants, a vest, and a white shirt with the sleeves rolled up to his elbows. The suit probably came with him from the old country.

"Did you include the bin from the workroom?" Mort pulled on his bushy, graying eyebrow.

"I forgot those again. I'll go." Resnick pushed himself away from the console and put his mug down. A bit of coffee spouted over the rim.

Uncle Steve glared from under his equally bushy eyebrows, barely lifting his head. Once through the doorway, Resnick heard Steve make some disparaging comment about him. He couldn't parse the specifics. He didn't have to—he knew the tone.

On his return to the office, he reviewed the weights. Compared to last week, though he couldn't quite remember, the waste number seemed higher. Wasted leaves. He resembled them, disintegrating, going nowhere, his uncle's lackey.

"Here it is." He retrieved his mug and sauntered over to the windows overlooking the main street. His uncles could berate him to his back.

"Hmm. I see," Mort muttered. Resnick flinched at the sound of the adding machine.

"Robert, we need to talk," his uncle Steve commanded.

"Wait! Look! Come here." He beckoned his uncles over. The three men gaped at the spectacle at the end of the street. A crowd of women filled the street. Ten or twelve abreast. They just kept coming from around the corner.

"What do those signs say?" Mort adjusted his thick glasses.

"It's our workers. I recognize some of them."

"Write down their names. Every single one of them," Steve ordered his nephew.

"I think that sign says clean bathrooms." Mort squinted at the advancing throng.

"Well damn it, then they should keep them clean!"

"Fair wages. Eight-hour day." Mort kept the tally of signage. "Representation."

"Robert, lock the doors downstairs. I'll call the police."

"I see them down there, Steve. The police. They're on horseback. A squad car at the intersection. They're putting up barricades. Turn on the radio," Mort reported like an experienced sportscaster giving a play-by-play.

When Resnick returned, Uncle Steve had gone from rabid to full-on foaming, pacing back and forth in front of the windows. Cuss words in English, German, and Yiddish spewed from his mouth. Resnick felt relieved when the phone rang. It probably saved his uncle from a heart attack.

"Yes. They're in full force below our windows right now. Can't you hear them?" Steve held the earpiece away from his ear for a moment. "The police are here but aren't doing anything. I think they're headed your way. Yes. Yes. I'll let you know. Make sure your place is secured."

Back at the window, the three men watched the marchers. Fervor fueled their song. Many locked arms in sisterhood. Resnick found himself smiling as a few of his secret favorites paraded by, glancing up at their place of employment.

"What are you smiling about? Did you know anything about this?" Steve challenged him.

"I don't know why I'm smiling." He truly didn't.

When the crowd thinned and quiet prevailed, the three relatives looked at each other not knowing what to do next. Then Steve sat at his desk and retrieved a bottle and two glasses from his bottom drawer. Resnick drained the now-cold coffee from his mug to make room for what his uncle had to offer.

"You can't say those women lack pluck. That's for sure." He swung a chair around backward and straddled it. He centered himself between his uncles, who faced each other at a partners' desk.

"Before the disruption, Mort and I wanted to have a talk with you." Resnick hoped he'd forgotten. "I see now it might be more important than ever."

Uncle Steve announced he and Mort would leave in the morning for a fact-finding trip to Florida and Cuba. They had an early train. The death knell had sounded for the hand-rolled cigar industry. Automation had already taken over much of the industry. Cigarettes threatened to displace cigars of any kind. Decisions had to be made.

"You see, we need to find our way forward." Uncle Steve refilled the glasses.

Resnick could not have cared less about business, especially this tawdry, mundane enterprise of cigar rolling. Now the rug had been pulled out from under him. What would this mean?

"I don't think you understand your position in the world. Your responsibility."

"What do you mean?" He watched Uncle Mort, who'd returned to working his pencil across the ledger pad, a short cigar, not lit, hanging from the side of his mouth.

His uncle explained how when the Jews emigrated to the United States to find a better life, not being as welcome as expected, many turned to bootlegging during Prohibition and slid into other criminal activities.

"That is not our way. Mort and I bootlegged for a while, just until we saved enough to buy this business from a man we knew in Germany. You see, we pick up the scraps. We live where the Germans moved out. Buy their dying businesses. Now we eke out an existence. Not glamorous. But not criminal."

"Seems to me we're doing more than eking out an existence. Some might say we live a very affluent life."

"Yes. We live a very nice lifestyle. Some of that is for show. To buy respectability. And this is where responsibility comes into play. You see, our people have no home. No country. We moved east across Europe. Then further east. We were all right. But the tsar and his pogroms threatened to exterminate us."

"Yes, I know. I've heard all of this before. Rabbi talks of nothing else." He grimaced at his uncle's obvious signs of exasperation.

"Do you read anything in the papers? Do you pay attention to anything besides fast cars and going out on the town? Do you?" His uncle's questions were punctuated by the ding of the adding machine.

"Yes, sir. Sometimes." How he wished his uncle would pass the bottle again, but it had been stowed away in the drawer.

"Then you might know Nazis are making laws against us in Germany. We're banned from the army, government jobs. We can't graduate from university or practice law. They will legislate us out of existence! We must bring as many Jews here as we can. We need money to do that."

Resnick didn't understand why his uncle always felt he was responsible for the whole world.

"Mort and I will decide the most prosperous route for us going forward after we've evaluated the options. We may invest in the industry, or we may squeeze every penny out of this factory as long as it stays afloat, but then move into real estate. How was the week, Mort?"

"Not good. Production down again. Three percent. Lost inventory, and waste was up again, fourth week in a row. Cost of raw materials rising from this week's purchases. Sales down 5 percent, month to date."

Resnick relocated to the window. He wanted to be clear of any shrapnel from the explosion he knew was imminent.

"I see." The blast never came. Its containment was more ominous.

"Robert! You'll be in charge while we're gone. I've shared our plans with you, though God knows why, and I expect you to prove yourself. I want these figures Mort has given us to be reversed."

"Yes, sir." He knew better than to argue.

"Now leave us. Mort and I have business to discuss."

Relieved to have been dismissed, Resnick strolled down Warren in the wake of the march. Maybe he'd follow and see where it went. Likely they headed toward Mazur Cressman and onward toward General Cigar. Sunday afternoon and the streets were quiet. With shops and diners closed, he had no place to be and nowhere to go. What did his uncle think? He could magically snap his fingers and solve all the factory's problems? The coming week would be the same as the last. Weren't they all the same? He stopped to peer into the window of a small shoe store. He admired the two-toned leather dress shoes with the patterned stitching. Maybe he would come back and buy them when the shop was open. Buy some respectability. Isn't that what his uncle said? They certainly would be snazzy if he went dancing.

Something rubbed against his trousers.

"Oh, hello." He scratched the scrawny dog behind the ears. "What's with you? Are you lost?" Resnick assessed the dog's stature. Skinny, knotted tan fur. Overgrown nails.

"You're not lost, are you, buddy?" He stooped down, eye to eye with the mutt. The pup was one of the many feral dogs wandering the streets. People couldn't afford to feed their pets anymore.

"Come with me. I need a friend who knows how to feed on scraps."

Alex rubbed his cold hands together. He'd forgotten his gloves. Sunday night and no place was open, at least not legally. Maybe a back door off the alley behind Monroe Street would be accepting visitors. He could sit a hand or two. He patted his pocket. No wallet. He'd left the house in such a lather. The Detroit River, which divides the city from Canada, wasn't far, so he headed that way instead. Perhaps a cool breeze would clear his head. What was happening with Florence? She was acting like that friend of hers, Basia. What was happening to them? He'd brought Florence here to Detroit to follow a dream.

When he'd first met her at her parents' grocery store, she was just a schoolgirl. Her comportment and speech were elegant. They talked while stocking the shelves. Sometimes she would mention a book or an idea that he didn't know. The next day he'd go to the library and study the topic. Little did she know, she was educating him in a roundabout way. He'd had no formal education, coming from rural Russia as the son of a serf. His parents christened him Aleksander in honor of the tsar who abolished serfdom.

Once he landed in St. Petersburg, though, he learned to read. Absorbing everything, he listened and observed. He worked his way into a Cossack regiment in service of the royals. He studied their behavior and learned proper Russian, French—often spoken by high society—and some German. He made no mistake about who they were or who supported their lifestyle. Regardless, he envied their access to art, music, ideas . . . all that was smart and beautiful.

Florence was smart and beautiful, a kindred spirit. Like his parents, who encouraged him to migrate to the city, hers sent her to the elite school in Montreal. Her parents were good-hearted and kind yet very provincial. Even by her teens Florence had outgrown them and yearned for more. They'd shared a hunger, an appetite for life. He reached for his cigarettes. No luck.

His life was out of control. He crossed the parking lot toward the terminal building of the Boblo Boat. He dropped on a bench placed for those waiting to board the Columbia, the 2,500-passenger ferry that went to the island. Florence loved going to the amusement park there. In the city she maintained a vestige of her convent decorum suitable for upper-class society. On Boblo, she was free. Her hair swung out behind her on the roundabout rides. She danced with abandon, everything they'd come to Detroit to experience.

"Hey, this is private property. Move along."

Alex looked at the security guard who approached. The tip of a cigarette glowed red in the guard's hand.

"You wouldn't happen to have another one of those, would you?" Alex stood.

"Guess I could spare one." The guard offered his pack. "What are you doing here? Not like any boats going in the middle of winter."

"No, I was out walking. Came to sit. Watch the water." Alex exhaled.

"It's Sunday night. Don't you gotta a home?"

"Yes. I have a home. A nice one at that. I just don't want to be there right now."

"Ah. Trouble with the missus. Did she throw you out?"

"No. Florence would never do that!" He started coughing. He couldn't stop.

"Hey, it's too cold. Wanna go in the waiting room over there? I spend most of my time there."

He was shivering. Maybe he would go in and warm up before heading home. The guard led him across the parking lot and unlocked the building. WAITING ROOM was emblazoned in large capital letters above the door.

"Funny being in a waiting room." The guard put a few scraps of wood in the corner stove. "That's all we do these days. Wait and wait. For something to get better." He drew up an old folding chair for Alex.

"Why do they need a guard here in the winter?"

"It started during Prohibition. Owners didn't want rumrunners using their dock."

"That ended four years ago."

"Yeah, but now we get a lotta drifters here. Setting up all sorts of makeshift shelters. It's private property. So I deal with the riffraff. Scare them off. Boring as hell, but it's a job."

Alex saw a small pile of clothes, a pillow, and a blanket near the stove. "Where do you live?"

"The missus threw me out. Ran home to mama. So I catch as catch can. I'm saving up, waiting till I can blow this town."

"Where would you go?"

"Anywhere."

Alex stretched his hands toward the stove. He opened and closed his palms, begging circulation to return. "Detroit's been hit hard. No doubt about it. But during the 1920s? There was no place like it."

"I wasn't here then. Came in early '29. Bum luck, huh? Tell me, what was it like?" The guard pulled a pint from his jacket pocket and the men took turns while Alex spoke.

"Everything was exciting and new. People were optimistic about the future. New buildings were under construction—taller than ever, with new aesthetics, clean lines. Companies begged you to work. People came in droves. All of us were new, in the same boat, and there was plenty of everything to go around. My wife—"

"Florence, right?"

"Yes, Florence. She's an artist. New paintings, new fashions. The new wealth supported the arts and it was like Vienna or Paris! When we first arrived from Canada, Florence worked at the D. J. Healy Company on Woodward. Their new building was terracotta, in the new Sullivan style. She sold art. She reeled in the tony clientele." Alex looked at the flames dancing behind the small glass window in the stove. The guard opened the door and threw in some more scrap wood.

"And what did you do?"

"I worked at Studebaker. That building was innovative too. Do you know they had a 25,000-gallon water tank on the roof. If there was a fire, water flowed through the pipes to put it out in no time. One of the first in the country."

"You don't say?"

"That's one example. Patents flew around here like barn swallows. New inventions all the time. Even down to the cocktails."

"Studebaker's not still there, are they?" The guard offered another cigarette.

"No, they moved on. Sold the building in '33. But so had I. The Dodge Brothers. Now there were some innovators." Alex took a pull on the pint. "Last one's yours." He handed over the bottle. "I moved to Dodge Main."

"On the line?"

"That's where I started. Guess it's where I still am."

"Least you got a job."

"That's what everyone says. Florence. She believed in me. See, I'm an inventor. I thought I could get somewhere at Dodge. After the brothers died, it took a while, but the company changed. Then the crash."

"Yeah, a few months after I got here."

"D. J. Healy didn't need Florence anymore. I didn't lose much in the market, but our wages were cut. We wanted to start our company. Florence always said I was creative. But—"

"Yeah, 'but—.' Seems all the stories end that way today."

The men looked at each other when they heard noises outside.

"Guess I better check." The guard stood.

"I'll go with you. I should get home anyway." Alex donned his coat. The guard picked up his flashlight and reached for the doorknob.

"Wait." Alex extended his hand. "Thank you. Thank you for listening."

"Anytime, man. Feels good to talk sometimes. Here." The guard offered him a cigarette. "One for your walk home." Alex nodded. Behind him, he heard, "Hey, this is private property. Move along now."

What a good man. Alex didn't even know his name. What was he doing, spilling his guts to a stranger? He never did that. He never joined secret organizations either. It was fun to think about those heady days. He and Florence. They never wanted to sleep with so much going on in Detroit. They'd stay up late. He designed and tinkered, she painted. She didn't mind his tools and prototypes all over the kitchen table. They'd clear away a little area for plates for dinner. After the boys were born, she took care of them. She was capable, never needy.

The dream of Detroit had turned into night terrors. Could he blame her for wanting more than a back-breaking job in a suffocating factory? Maybe she had been right to march. But if she got hurt? Like those people a few years back, the ones who marched on the Rouge plant. What would he do? He was nothing without her. He loved his boys but he didn't know anything about children. He couldn't raise them. He'd only raised farm animals a long time ago. Anyway, even if she were right to march, he couldn't encourage her. Those hoodlums in the Black Legion tied his hands. Even if he'd wanted to, which he didn't think he did, he couldn't hint at supporting a labor action.

The front door was unlocked. He checked the hall table, and yes, his wallet and cigarettes were there. Maybe tomorrow he'd leave a pack and a pint at the waiting room for that guard. He undressed and folded his Sunday clothes. Florence wasn't sleeping, he could tell. Her long brown hair spread out around her head, the ends falling over the edge of the pillow. He slipped his arm across her. She rolled away from him. He pressed his mouth against her ear.

"Flo." Silence. "Flo. I know you're not sleeping."

"What?"

"Look at me. Please." She rolled toward him.

"I'm sorry."

"You're sorry? About what?" Florence sat up and bolstered herself with her pillow. "That you yanked me away from my friends? That you humiliated me?"

"I never meant to, Flo."

"Well, you did!" She rolled away from him again.

"I can't lose you. I was scared. What if they started shooting? Like at the Hunger March? You could get hurt." Should he tell her about the Black Legion? No. That was his burden to carry. Alone.

"Sometimes you have to stand up. Fight back."

"You sound like Basia. She's dragging you into this. You should stand up to her." He rolled onto his back and released a heavy sigh.

"You set a fine example for your sons! Lucien, he was so upset for me. He's trying to be a man. He looks to you. But he thinks you're mean."

"He needs to toughen up. You coddle him too much."

"He's not you."

Did she say "thank goodness" into her pillow? He turned away. His family was all he had. They were slipping away. He slid his hand under his pillow and grasped the small box hidden there. He had intended to give it to Florence tonight. It was Valentine's Day.

CHAPTER 12

Thursday, February 18, 1937

Florence offered Nick a refill of plum brandy. "The weather is so bitter tonight. This will warm you up. Alex should be home soon."

"Thank you." Nick welcomed Florence's generous pour.

"I'm so glad you came. It's been a long time since people took time just to visit one another. It's none of my business, Mr. Starovitch, but are you courting anyone?" Florence looked sideways at Nick.

"No, Mrs. Falkowski, 'fraid not. Working on Hastings Street, I don't meet many eligible women. Besides, being from Russia's not real popular right now. Girls'd be afraid of someone named Starovitch."

"Yes, that's probably true. Well, a nice man like you would make a fine husband no matter what your name. You sit and have your brandy and I'll get you a little *przekaski*." Florence retreated to the kitchen to fetch what might be available to serve an unexpected guest. Alex should be home shortly, but maybe he wouldn't. She didn't know. She returned to the front parlor to find Nick standing by the window holding back the sheer curtains.

"You must hear a lot of the new music played in the clubs. What do you make of it? Big band and jazz?" Florence wanted to speak of topics that might interest Nick.

"I like it real fine. There's nothing like it anywhere in the world."

"I know Alex likes it. And Lucien. He's always listening to the radio. Oh, I forgot the horseradish sauce." While she was retrieving the sauce, Alex entered from the back door.

"You'll never guess who came to visit. Nick Starovitch! He's in the parlor."

Alex continued walking right through the kitchen, galoshes dripping icy slush. Horseradish in hand, Florence trailed behind Alex.

"Nick, let's go," Alex said by way of a greeting.

"You two're going out? I put out appetizers for Nick. No need for you to go. I can prepare dinner, then you can visit while I go upstairs."

"We've some business to attend to." Alex pulled his gloves out from his pocket where they'd just been deposited. Nick reached for his coat.

"So good to see you, Nick. You're welcome here anytime," said Florence.

"Thank you, ma'am, for the delightful food. I enjoyed it thoroughly." He tipped his hat and proffered a slight bow. Florence always appreciated Nick's courtly manners. Alex possessed polished manners too.

"If you'll wait for just a minute, I'll pack up some cake for you to take home." Florence turned to retrieve the cake and came face-to-face with Alex.

"He doesn't want any cake," Alex said, still wrapped in his navy blue wool coat.

"Oh," uttered Florence. "It'll just take a minute." Florence started to bypass Alex.

He grabbed her arm. "I *said* he doesn't want any."

"It's fine, ma'am, don't trouble yourself. I'll have it some other time."

Alex pulled the door shut behind them. Florence shivered in the backdraft of numbing cold.

"That was strange." Florence perched in the wing-backed chair Nick had vacated. She peered through the sheers at the backs of the men halfway down the block. She put her feet up on the footstool, poured herself some plum brandy, and helped herself to some appetizers.

NOT YET LOST

"I'm not too impressed with your black-hooded friends. Why did you bring me into it?" Alex glanced sideways, head tilted down against the chilling wind.

"Don't talk about it here. Don't know who might hear." Nick swiveled his head back and forth. Alex glanced around too. The streets were empty.

"Let's go to the Schvitz. It's safe there." Nick led the way.

The Jewish bathhouse in Northtown was a distance away. The men walked in silence. Alex supposed his friend was right. Not likely any Black Legion members frequented the spa since Jews were among those targeted by the hateful vigilante group.

"They don't mind you going there? With your Russian heritage?" Alex knew Nick had ingratiated himself with the primarily Jewish Purple Gang during Prohibition. Nick had managed a blind pig for them, one of the many outlets for the Canadian whiskey the Purple Gang smuggled across the river into Detroit. They spoke a common language. The Schvitz was located down Oakland Street from one of the Purple Gang's facilities.

"One thing I've learned since coming to America is that survival for immigrants makes for some strange bedfellows."

Nick checked Alex in as his guest at the front desk. They proceeded to the second-floor locker room. Alex surveyed the room, its countenance shabby splendor. When new, the mirrors, stone countertops, and intricately patterned carpet would have embodied the zenith of modern design. Now the fixtures with poorly maintained grout and chipped corners conveyed the club's weariness. They changed into cotton terry robes and slide sandals and descended to the basement pool area. A strong odor of chlorine permeated the damp air. They disrobed and entered the adjacent sauna room—large, tiled in black and white, with tiered wooden benches. Alex climbed to the top tier to rest his back against the wall while Nick attended to throwing water into the large oven doors. Nick joined Alex on the top tier. They had a view of the entrance.

"We're here. Now talk," Alex demanded.

"Here's what happened. I spent time in New York when I first came to America. I was taking English lessons at a Russian club. You know? I wanted to fit in. Make my way. Unfortunately, I got caught up in one of the raids by the Justice Department several years back."

"I was in Montreal then, but I heard about them." Alex remembered the news stories.

"Yeah, well, I was almost deported. Scared me to death. Can you imagine going back to the Bolsheviks?"

"No, I don't imagine they look kindly on Cossacks."

"Exactly. Ever since, I do everything I can to prove I'm not a communist or labor agitator. America's running so scared. A hint of Eastern European accent and they think you're a communist. You know Hoover's gunning for them. He's against the Jews too."

"I understand," Alex said in well-articulated English, even though they'd been speaking in Russian. "So how did you get into this Black Legion, as you call it, and—I'll ask again—why did you involve me? You've put me at risk. Florence and the boys too."

"I made a mistake getting involved with the bootlegging racket. What did I know? With Prohibition it was a good way to make a few bucks. I was living down in the cheap part of town. I knew all those guys and, yeah, I drank with them. We talked about the old country. We all kind of miss it. Sorry place it was—and still is—but it's home."

Steam wafted just below the low ceiling, condensation beginning to form on the wood planks. Alex focused on a drop of water coalescing, lengthening, and eventually liberating itself into free fall.

"It's lonely here for men without families."

"You still haven't answered my question," Alex pressed on, cracking the knuckles of one hand, then the other.

"The Purple Gang was falling apart. Head men shot right in the street. The heat was on. The Feds, the cops. Even some rival gangs,

Sicilians, looking to take them down. I got scared. I started carrying a gun."

"I thought you weren't really in the gang."

"I'm nobody. You know, I could be in the wrong place at the wrong time. Guilty by association. You know over two hundred Jews were deported on that ship, the *Buford*?" Nick referred to the mass deportation of immigrants deemed to have leftist leanings. Alex nodded at his friend. Photos in the paper had shown J. Edgar Hoover, Mitchell Palmer, and a number of congressmen watching the deportees being forcibly boarded onto the old rattletrap vessel bound for Lenin's Russia. Newspapers posited that at least one thousand people were deported: members of socialist and communist parties, trade union leaders, so-called agitators, activists, and anyone else whose face government officials didn't like.

"I started going to the gun club. No use having a gun if you're no good with it, eh?" Nick looked at Alex, who nodded. Nick could be so tedious. Alex summoned the last of his self-control to refrain from pummeling him. He needed Nick to talk, to explain.

"The owner of the gun club's a White Russian. He supported the tsar in the civil war. We get talking one day. I tell him my situation. He says he can help me. We go to an initiation, like you did, but I went willingly. These Black Legion members. It's all very secret, but they're everywhere. You won't believe it! Cops, government officials. Businessmen. Electricians."

"So I've found out. You were right earlier. Strange bedfellows indeed."

"It's my ticket. I know it's no good. But now I've got someone to vouch for me. If they start those raids again, I don't want to be deported."

"That's all well and good for you. Last time I'm going to ask, Nick. Why bring me into it?"

Alex couldn't tell if the rivulets running from Nick's basset hound eyes were tears or sweat.

"I didn't want to," Nick said. Alex leaned in to hear his words.

"They want more members. We were ordered to bring in two new ones. You'll see. They'll make you do it too. See, they have detachments, like battalions. Crews doing different jobs. Arsonists, hit men, factory spies." Nick stopped talking. He breathed with deliberation, holding his head in his hands.

"They're extortionists!" Alex jumped up and began pacing, towel tied around his waist. "You bring in members, they get more money. They gouge you for a gun and cheap black cloth they call a uniform."

"I know. And then they con you out of monthly dues. It's a racket."

"And you thought this was such a great club you didn't want me to miss the opportunity. Is that it?" Alex faced Nick, down a step, forcing Nick to look up with the power of his voice.

"They targeted you. They wanted someone in Dodge Main. Then Fred saw you shoot at the club. I couldn't disobey an order. The oath. You heard them. I'm on thin ice. They'd kill me. I had no choice."

"You had a choice! You chose to drag me, my wife, my children into your wretched circumstances."

Nick didn't reply.

Alex descended the steps. He crossed the slick tile floor to the lone showerhead and pulled the chain. Cold water shocked his skin. Had he spoken the truth? Did Nick truly have a choice? Did *he*? Remnants of warmth in his body, heart, and soul spun down the drain. Alex dried himself off with a towel much thinner than what he would have expected.

"I'll meet you outside by the pool." Wisps of steam escaped the door to the steam room as it swung shut behind Alex. He donned his robe and paced up and down the length of the plunge pool while Nick, presumably, was showering. Small black tiles an inch square and inset in the white tile background commemorated the year the men's club was built, 1930. Only an illicit gang would have the funds to build a facility like the Schvitz in the year after the market crash. Why was Nick dawdling? Likely he preferred hiding in the steam room to facing Alex in the naked light. At last Nick emerged.

"Are you hungry? They still serve up a great steak here. Come as you are." Nick extended both his arms wide, indicating their attire acceptable for the dining room.

The men proceeded to the dining room. A few groups dined at heavy oak tables strategically placed a distance apart. Nick chose a table in the corner, the premium ones near the fireplace already occupied. They spoke of Poland and Russia, Petersburg, and politics. Nick, the more conversational of the two, recounted escapades from their Cossack days. Nick slapped the table and doubled over, remembering the time his favorite mare tossed him off in chase of a stallion.

"Not the first time I've been thrown over by a woman."

Alex realized his friend's conviviality was a form of apology, an attempt to make amends. After dinner, they each savored a small glass of cognac, neat with a twist. Alex relished the burn of the amber-brown liqueur, his insides now as warm as his exterior. Nick grew serious again.

"Back to your question, Alex. Do you see? We're ships without a port. No place to land. No one'll have us."

"There we're white, here we're red. The colors of the Polish flag." Alex twisted the stem of his cognac glass in circles.

"This has been a wonderful evening, Alex. I can talk to you. You understand. Let's stay in touch. We can do this more often. Shall we?" Nick drained his glass and rose from the table. Alex did the same. Outside, the bracing cold felt all that much colder now they'd been in piping hot steam. They walked back up Oxford Street.

"Alex, thank you for listening to me. I've gotten myself in a mess."

"Yes. You have. Now I'm in one too."

"I told you, Alex, I didn't have a choice. I really didn't."

Alex glanced at his companion, who'd seemed a bit tipsy when they dressed in the locker room. Now Nick appeared relaxed, his gait almost jaunty. He walked like a man released. Either the Schvitz worked its magic or Nick's conscience was lightened by the proffered apology. One Alex didn't accept.

"Nick, that's the question, isn't it? Whether you had a choice or not. If it were only me, that's one thing, but you've endangered my wife and boys. My family, Nick, do you get it?"

"I get it. These men are brutal. All this 'secret club in the woods' stuff. Makes them seem like silly kids. But I'll tell you, they murder for sport. They put a price on your head and you're gone."

"That's my point! How could you do that to me?"

"Maybe you and me, we can buddy up, fight these guys. You know, like the old days."

"No, Nick. This is different. I've got something to lose now. I enjoyed the evening. I miss men like you, at least the way you were, but we can't be friends. I never want to see you again." Alex shielded his heart from the pain in Nick's sorrowful eyes.

They'd arrived at the railroad crossing near the Poletown neighborhood. A train whistle shrieked and Alex clutched his companion's arm to prevent him from crossing.

"I know I dragged you down. Forgive me. Please forgive me, Alex."

Alex squinted into the conical light of the train's engine bearing down on them, then looked down at the track, iced over by refrozen slush. He faced Nick, and their eyes met. Nick looked past his shoulder toward the oncoming train.

"I'm just a sorry excuse, Alex. Not worth your friendship. I've failed here in America. I've failed—" Nick started toward the track.

"No, Nick—" Alex reached out.

Nick's body spasmed as if he'd been kicked in the back. He fell on the tracks. The train, loud and heavy with cars filled with iron ore, hurtled past. Alex spun around in shock, realizing his friend had been shot. He could hear only the train, nothing else, and he couldn't see far in the dark. He flung himself flat to the ground in the muddy snow abutting the street, a mere two feet from the hurtling train. Squealing metal-on-metal abraded his eardrums, the vibration rattling his bones. The last train car passed. He waited as wet snow seeped down his neck. Nothing. Finally, he stood, then peered into the dark. Whoever fired the shot must be long gone. At first he thought Nick had jumped, but then he recognized that spasm, the arching back, the flailing limbs. He brushed the snow off the front of his coat. Wait! He and Nick had been close together. What if he was the target and not Nick? The engine's roar waned in the distance. He forced himself to look down, the last time he would see Nick. He crossed the tracks, and rather than heading home, he turned toward Hastings Street in Paradise Valley. Alone.

The aroma of shrimp wafted from the shack on Hastings but didn't appeal tonight. Alex was still full from dinner at the Schvitz. A train whistle blew in the distance. He whistled to block out the sound. Passing Sunnie Wilson's Forest Club, notes of Cab Calloway's scat singing "hi-de-hi-de-hi-de-ho" roared out to the sidewalk. The crowd inside sang in response to the call from the famous headliner performing tonight. Alex stopped whistling now. Sounds of the street offered plenty of distraction. Walking on, he'd find a place with low-key entertainment, but not before tipping his hat to Jake the doorman.

"Evening, sir. How's tricks?"

"Here you go. For Queenie. Got it?" Alex passed some money and a slip of paper into Jake's hand. Maybe he'd be lucky tonight.

"Yes, sir." Jake looked at the ticket before pocketing it. "There's some mitt pounding goin' on tonight."

"So I hear."

"You work late tonight?" Jake eyed him up and down. "You're usually sportin' some fancy togs."

He forgot he walked straight through his house without changing clothes because Nick was there. He'd also rolled in dirty snow.

"Extra hours. You know how it is."

"That I do. I sure do. Set's almost over, man, but he might play some after hours. Can't promise. I'm surprised I didn't see you here earlier. What, with Cab Calloway here."

"I'm looking for something quieter tonight. Besides, I'm not dressed." Alex opened his coat a bit to expose further his tired canvas pants and chambray shirt. Perhaps Jake's comments were intended to dissuade him. He knew Jake prided himself in managing the clientele.

"Do you know Vickie Spivey? She's singing up the street. At the Flame. She sings real sweet," suggested Jake.

Alex nodded.

He traipsed on toward the Flame. The hostess seated him at a corner table next to the window. Shortly after, he had a vodka martini, up, in front of him. Pulling one of the two olives off the toothpick with his front teeth, he rolled it around with his tongue, noticing the salty, bitter taste. His hand trembled as he reached for the stem of the martini glass. What just happened?

Alex was angry enough to kill Nick, a friend of sorts. In a way, it would be self-defense. Nick's group of deluded vigilantes threatened him and his family. He couldn't do it. Nick was a good man. Also, he'd promised himself never again. Did his anger make Nick want to jump on the tracks? He tried to stop him. Where had the shot come from? Could it have been meant for him? He'd been a smart aleck with those Black Legion men. He'd hardly embraced them. With the train, he hadn't heard the shot, but it hit Nick in the center of his back. What recourse? He couldn't go to the police, as it was a cop who threatened him if he didn't disrupt that asinine march. Nick's remains were in no condition for an autopsy, as if they'd do one. Just another Eastern European soul lost. No matter.

Alex thought he escaped such subterfuge when he fled Russia. Ha! It wasn't even Russia! It was Poland unwillingly masquerading as Russia. He signaled the waitress for another drink. From his corner perch he could watch the entertainment both on the stage and, through the glass window, on the street. After the second drink, his hands stopped shaking. He could applaud now for Victoria Spivey and the Chicago Four.

"Apropos!" He chortled when Spivey announced the next number would be "Detroit Moan."

NOT YET LOST

> Detroit's a cold, cold place and I ain't got a dime to my name
> Detroit's a cold, hard place and I ain't got a dime to my name
> I would go the poorhouse, but Lord you know I'm ashamed
>
> I been walking Hastings Street, nobody seems to treat me right
> I been walking Hastings Street, nobody seems to treat me right
> I can make it in the daytime, but Lord these cold, cold nights

The brass sang his soul. Lee Collins breathed life into that trumpet, then made it wail in pain.

> And if I ever get back home,
> I ain't never comin' to Detroit no more

Mournful notes, bolstered by the martinis, soothed the rough edges of his soul. Life had been cheap along the rivers of Eastern Europe. Conscription, wars, and famine gnawed people to their demise, chumps for some political ideal. Did the banks of the Detroit River offer anything different? The price of life here was none too high. Although, some lives were pricier than others. It was irrational. He couldn't have heard anything above the train engine. Had Nick moaned? The band took a set break and he flagged the waitress over again. He was in the mood for a B & B. The honeyed liqueur might help on this cold, cold night.

A ruckus outside the window hijacked his attention. Some ruffians were throwing punches at each other, a circle around them egging them on. The beat cop Alex knew by sight blew his whistle and swung his club, more to threaten than to make contact. The bystanders dispersed, and the cop was addressing the combatants under the glare of the streetlamp.

No nie! Was that Lucien? His son was wiping his face with his sleeve while arguing with the cop. Alex stood, grabbed the edge of the table, and fell into his seat. He felt woozy.

"Are you all right, sir?" the waitress asked, setting down the snifter and clearing the martini glass.

"Yes. I'm fine. I just need a minute." He waved her away. He rubbed his forehead. Too much booze? The steam bath? He made a second attempt. After steadying himself, he laid some bills on the table and bolted out the door.

Florence, attempting her needlework, could no longer struggle against her falling eyelids. She guessed the men had gone to Wally's, so she decided to go to bed. Upstairs in her flannel nightgown, Florence slid under the covers. She luxuriated in the warmth. Alex said they couldn't spend more on heating oil, so the bed and its multiple quilts offered the sole respite from the bitter cold coursing through her bones. Florence especially loved the *pierzyna*. The cotton covering showed wear, but the thick down stuffing bestowed weight and warmth. Alex, for all his faults, took pride in providing. She checked the clock on the bedside table. Too late for Wally's. They probably went to Hastings Street. Alex enjoyed the contemporary jazz music played in clubs in the entertainment district. She preferred classical. She remembered the elegant music of her convent training. Joyous liturgical music resounding through Notre Dame Cathedral in Montreal had elicited tears—the sheer beauty—when she'd been a girl. She drifted off, accompanied in her mind by strains of the "Magnificat."

Boom! The sound of the slamming door yanked Florence from her slumber. She reached over for Alex, but he wasn't there. She hesitated to climb out of bed.

"Don't you ever sneak out of the house like that again!"

Florence cringed at Alex's voice. She threw back the covers and arrived on the landing just as Alex landed a slap across Lucien's face. Lucien's arm cocked back.

"*O, Boże!*" She raced down the steps and inserted herself between the two. "Now what is going on here? Will somebody tell me?"

"Stay out of this, Florence. I found him on Hastings. Outside the Flame. He and some boys fighting. Fancy themselves boxers. Cops had to break up the fight. They were drinking hooch. Here's the bottle." Alex pulled an empty pint bottle out of his coat pocket, held it up, and threw it on the floor. He pinned Lucien to the wall by his shoulders. Florence wanted to tell her son to wipe that defiant look off his face.

"It's all right for you to drink and listen to jazz but not me?"

"You're just a kid. You shouldn't be in that neighborhood."

"I'm not just a kid. I'm fifteen."

"Fifteen! You know nothing. You don't know who's who down there. You think you're so smart? You don't know a thing about the streets."

"I do too! The drummer from the band, he told me—"

Florence restrained Alex's arm as he raised it again. This time his palm wasn't open.

"You deal with him!" Alex commanded his wife.

"You left home at fifteen. You said so yourself!" Lucien yelled toward Alex's back, his father now ascending the stairs.

"Let's go in the kitchen. You can tell me what happened." Florence took her son's arm. She shivered in her nightgown, either from cold or nerves. She hadn't had time to don her robe, so she retrieved her coat from the hooks by the back door. She put milk on the stove to heat, then laid eyes on her son, who sat at the table with his long legs outstretched and his arms crossed over his chest.

CHAPTER 13

Tuesday, February 23, 1937

"Just about ready?" Florence queried Basia while sweeping tobacco leaf litter off her table.

"Almost. Just few more."

Florence retrieved her shoes from under the worktable. She'd kicked them off earlier to relieve the swelling in her feet and ankles. After ten hours with little movement, most of the blood and water in her body pooled in her extremities. Florence massaged each foot before slipping it into a shoe, leaving the laces untied. One of these days her feet might just burst wide open.

"What's the hurry, Mrs. Falkowski? Do you have a meeting tonight?" Resnick questioned. Florence looked up and uncrossed her legs, placing her hands in her lap and smoothing her dress.

"Meeting? What meeting?"

"I've heard your neighbors host political meetings. Party meetings. That's all you Polacks do these days, meet and talk, meet and talk." His bullying was long past wearisome.

"Bah! Who's got time for politics?" Florence waved her hand dismissively. "I just need to shop and cook dinner. I've got kids and a husband at home. You know that." Florence reached for her handbag under the worktable—better if she didn't make eye contact. Even if she were telling the truth, which she was, Resnick had a way of twisting her words. He interpreted "good morning" as a communist threat. Resnick's uncle had made him paranoid, put the fear of something into him. She almost felt sorry for him. One could understand the makings of a bully, but that didn't make working for one any easier.

"There must be some kind a doin's going on. You all worked faster than usual today. I walk through your neighborhood on my way home. I see things."

Florence imagined Resnick walking through her neighborhood and felt violated. She always felt her community sacrosanct. It wasn't that he wasn't Polish. Non-Poles lived in and wandered through the neighborhood all the time. It was him in particular. She noticed Basia watching her over her shoulder. Resnick addressed the women only with "Mrs." or "Miss" when he spoke tongue in cheek. Otherwise, he took the right to employ the familiar. Her interchange with Resnick must have put Basia on high alert. She started rolling the leaves faster, no longer needing her eyes on her work after all these years.

"And what're *you* gawking at? No one's talking to you, our dear *Mrs. Sikorski.*" Resnick turned his attention to Basia. She was arranging her worktable for the next day. "Do you think you're finished here?" He perused her worktable and the stacks of finished product. "I don't think you are. Your output's down. Sandbagging again?"

"*Mr.* Resnick, you know *I* wouldn't do anything like that. My heart, mind, and soul belong to White Eagle. I simply *live* to make money for you."

Florence covered her mouth with her hand. She could tell her friend was about to explode. Basia was already on thin ice with Resnick. Florence shook off the cardigan she had just donned in preparation to leave and rerolled up the sleeves of her cotton work shirt.

"Basia, we can work another half hour. I'll help. We can fill another box." Florence wedged herself between the two and hoped Chaveta knives wouldn't fly. Again.

"See, *Mrs.* Sikorski? You should be more like your friend here. A little more willing. I demand you stay another full hour. Maybe two, just for your cheekiness. I forbid you to leave."

"Is that right, *Mr.* Resnick? You think you can forbid me to leave?" Basia drew out the words, arms across her chest, left eyebrow up, head cocked to the right. Here it comes! Florence cringed.

"I won't leave! And I don't work!" Basia plopped herself down on the dirty, cement floor, steadfast. Her arms were folded, her legs pulled up and crossed under her dress, unbudgeable.

"Get up off that floor! Roll that box of cigars like your friend said."

Basia sat, rooted. Women across the entire factory floor watched. Some froze, others slipped out, afraid.

"Get *up*! You stubborn cow!" Resnick kicked Basia in the hip.

Florence watched tears well in her friend's eyes, yet she knew Basia would not cry. What could she do? She sat down next to Basia, adjacent to the assaulted hip. Basia took Florence's hand in her own and squeezed it in gratitude.

"You two are trouble!" Resnick spun around, both hands on top of his head. "I'll report you. You'll be gone tomorrow. Just like those women over at General Cigar. Twenty-five of them. Here today, gone tomorrow. Just like that." Resnick wiped his hands in quick succession, one, two, three.

"Okay. That's how you want to play it? Fine! You grovel on the floor." Resnick stomped toward the little room with the glass window he called his office. Before he could reach it, another woman spoke from across the room.

"If she stays, we all stay." The woman, Anna, sat down with a flourish. Others joined her. Florence exchanged a smile with Basia.

"Anushka!" Basia barked. Florence turned to see the young girl sidling toward the exit door.

Anushka faced Basia. Her cheeks flushed at being called out.

"I'm sorry, Basia. I have to go. Stephan and I, we meet at the church tonight with Father Maletski. Pre-Cana."

"It's all right. That's good. Here's what you tell Father." Basia spewed forth in rapid Polish. "And stop by my house and tell Romek."

The hours wore on, the women on the floor, Resnick locked in his office. After a while, the women began to move around. Some began to eat the remnants of their lunch. Others rose from the floor and reoccupied their chairs. Florence, who'd taken to her wooden Windsor chair, stretched and put her feet up on her worktable to ease her swollen ankles, though the chair was minimally more comfortable than the floor. Basia mirrored her at the adjacent worktable. They could see Resnick in his office. He was playing solitaire at his desk. Voices from the radio filtered through the glass.

"What now?" Florence asked Basia.

"Not sure. I've got to think about this." Basia began pacing the small aisleway, staying close to Florence.

The phone rang in Resnick's office. Basia stopped pacing. Florence watched through the expansive window.

"Yes, your wife's still here. She won't leave! They're pulling some kind of stunt. Yes, I'll tell her." Resnick put down the receiver, and just as he stood to leave his office, the phone rang again. "I'll tell her to go home right away. And if she doesn't leave? What am I supposed to do about it?" Resnick slammed the receiver down and stood up once again. After several more calls, he departed his office and addressed the group.

"You dames better go home now. Your husbands want you home. Now go on, get out of here!" Resnick walked to the door leading to the hallway and held it open, beckoning the women to walk on through. Several did, throwing backward glances of apology to Basia. Florence looked with anticipation at Basia. Her friend, nonchalant as on a sunny day's walk in the park, continued her pacing. Her hands were clasped behind her back, and she whistled a jaunty little tune. Florence stretched her shoeless feet out on the table, making a show of rotating her ankles. She stretched her arms above her head and yawned. Knowing looks darted among the women faster than a metal ball in a BallyHoo game. Some who started to gather their belongings stopped. Some who were standing sat. Some sitting did so more determinedly. Florence saw resolve in the expressions on her coworkers' faces. Time ceased. She surveyed the tableau, Resnick holding open the steel door, a silly, obsequious grin plastered on his face. No one else was walking through.

Basia stopped pacing. She leaned against the wall with the bottom of one foot up against it and her arms folded across her chest. No light-heartedness danced in her eyes now. A cadre of supporters planted in their chairs exuded the confidence of the virtuous. She nodded. This was it. The moment had arrived. The point of no return.

Scraps, Resnick's dog, frolicked around his legs. An open door portended a walk. Resnick restrained him by his collar.

Buzz, buzz!

The doorbell at the loading dock. Resnick let the steel door slam behind him. Presumably, he was going to answer the call. Scraps trotted along joyfully. Basia launched herself off the wall.

"Quick! Follow me!" Florence recognized the flare in Basia's dark eyes. She had a plan. The urgency in Basia's voice propelled Florence and the rest to jump up. Women crowded through the door Resnick held open just moments ago. It opened into the hallway that led past the lockers to the back receiving bay. Florence, with white cotton socks on her feet, skidded behind her friend, who sprinted toward the loading dock. The women fanned out in the hallway. Florence could see Resnick standing in the alley outside the open dock door. He spoke with a delivery driver. He pointed at his watch and threw his hands up in the air. Basia wasted no time closing the dock doors and maneuvering the lock. Florence and the others who'd caught up braced themselves against the door. Some of the last to arrive understood the situation at once and moved the desk from the receiving office against the door. Others piled on chairs and boxes for good measure. The barricade was superfluous. Doubtful Resnick could break the fortified and locked steel door, yet they continued building the barricade with zeal. Resnick shouted to be let in and pounded on the door.

"Quick! Make sure all other doors—windows!—are locked. See who else is in building. You, check upstairs! You two, go downstairs." Basia barked orders like a Napoleonic general, making eye contact with each soldier. Each sprinted off to her assigned role.

"We need a plan. I must call Romek. Anushka must've talked to him by now," said Basia. Florence followed her friend through the workroom. As they weaved their way through, the women who neither bolted home nor ran to the loading dock applauded and cheered. Florence beamed at her friend. She was proud of—and admittedly a bit envious of—her friend's moxie.

They tiptoed into Resnick's office, though there was no need to, really, other than the aura of tasting forbidden fruit. Workers rarely entered there. Florence listened to Basia's side of her conversation with Romek and watched the women on the other side of the glass. They walked around and put their feet up, tentatively as newborn colts, their actions incongruous with the surroundings. Three of the younger women set off on an excursion upstairs to explore the offices.

"Romek's going to call back. He's going to contact people he knows from Local 3." Basia referred to a division of the nascent UAW union.

"Do you think we should call Mary Zuk? She'll know what to do next," Florence advanced.

"So you think she's not so bad after all?" Basia chided.

"I don't know what to think!"

"Romek thought he might get Stanley Nowak to help. He'll let Mary know." Basia organized and shuffled the playing cards Resnick left on his desk.

"*O, Boże!* What've we done?" Florence wrung her hands, massaging her aching fingers.

"Stood up for ourselves for once! That's what we've done!" Basia slapped the top of Resnick's desk as she rose from his chair.

"They could fire us! Like at General Cigar," Florence explained.

"I don't care!"

"But Romek's not Alex. Let me use the phone. I should call home." Florence traded places with Basia and sat in Resnick's chair.

"I'm going see what everyone's doing." Basia exited the office.

The phone rang and rang. Florence hung up and tried again.

She counted the rings. She replaced the receiver in the two-pronged hook. Where were the boys?

Basia returned. "The girls have so much energy! I told them Romek is delivering some food and blankets. It won't be enough, but it'll do for tonight."

Florence relinquished Resnick's chair to Basia and began straightening up the office.

"What did Alex say?"

"No answer."

"Aah. Well, Romek should be calling soon. Now we wait."

Florence pulled her clean handkerchief from her pocket and began dusting. File cabinets, bookshelves, the guest chair, even the coat rack. Not much here in Resnick's office. No photos or art or framed certificates. Just a bulletin board with ragtag notices and schedules pinned onto the cork surface. She ran the handkerchief over the top and adjusted the papers to hang straight. She started humming, mostly to counter the noise of playing cards being endlessly shuffled and reshuffled.

Brring!

"Romek? Yes . . . uh-huh . . . okay. . . . The back door is best . . . by loading dock. . . . We'll be waiting."

Florence had plopped down into the guest chair when the phone rang. She surveyed her friend's face, trying to guess what Romek was telling her.

"Oh, and Romek? See if you can find Lucien and Frank. . . . Okay . . . and be careful!"

Florence stayed put. She saw the grime on the window facing the factory floor, but she couldn't bring herself to move. The turmoil had sucked every ounce of energy out of her being. She'd attend to it tomorrow, depending on what happened. Tomorrow. She faded in and out of sleep right there in the chair. The ticking of the Westclox Big Ben on the desk and the incessant card shuffling, once annoying, provided a comforting backbeat to these strange new circumstances.

NOT YET LOST

Resnick collected himself in the alley. He rubbed his right shoulder. Stupid of him to use it as a battering ram. That door was designed to be solid to keep alley vagrants from coming in at night to sleep. Now that he was gone, the women might go home. He should've thought of it sooner. If he'd departed on his own, they would've stayed a bit, just for the novelty, and gone home to cook dinner. His uncles, Steve and Mort, and the manager, Miller, were away on a business trip, sourcing new raw material and evaluating machinery to automate the rolling process. He'd been left in charge. Thoughts of dining with his aunt and young cousins left him cold. In fact, he was cold. His jacket was inside. If he did return home, he could go straight to his room, feigning a headache or a cold coming on. His aunt might bring some soup or a light dinner to his room. Like her husband, she wasn't one to suffer the feeble, but she liked to fix what was broken, in a practical way. He was hungry now, though, so he should eat before being relegated to an infirmary supper. He entered a pub. With a draught and a brisket sandwich in front of him and his dog, Scraps, at his feet, Resnick relaxed. Perhaps if he said nothing, tomorrow would start like any other day.

The men at the bar formed a convivial group. The usual chatter about baseball and spring training diverted Resnick's attention from his troubles. After another few steins, the collection of casual strangers became a group of friends. The conversation turned to politics. Franklin Delano Roosevelt, in the first few weeks of his second term, rendered plenty of fat to chew. Outside, church bells rang at the top of an hour.

"Hey, Karl, turn on the radio. Let's listen to the news," said one of the men.

Obligingly, the bartender turned on the Philco receiver next to the cash register. The small box resembled a cathedral with its arched shape. WJR's news announcer reported national events first. Stories of labor unrest throughout heavy manufacturing industries in Boston, Chicago, and New York dominated the airwaves. Then, turning to state and local activities, the announcer's stoic voice bellowed, "Disruption continues at General Motors' Ternstedt factory. Prohibited from striking by the UAW contract signed after the sit-down strike in Flint, workers slowed down production by 50 percent. According to Stanley Nowak, the UAW labor organizer, General Motors intentionally stalled negotiations at Ternstedt by offering no concessions. Without the ability to strike, workers started to reduce production one department at a time. Nowak said this tactic is used all over Europe. He also said the move was necessary to encourage General Motors to negotiate in good faith. It's unusual for a workforce comprised of women to engage in labor actions. Nowak said he found the women quite dependable, vocal, and militant. Their determination is unwavering. Demands advanced by the workers include—"

"Turn it off! Turn it off! I've heard enough," Resnick snarled. Karl switched the radio off and stared at Resnick. The vehemence in his voice surprised even himself.

"What's eatin' you?" one of the men at the other end of the bar asked.

"Nothing. I'm tired of hearing about all of it." He shoved the last couple of bites of his sandwich into his mouth. He drained his stein while digging in his pocket for money.

"Hey, I got it. You run that cigar shop full a dames, don't ya?" Another man down the length of the bar quipped. "They giving you trouble? Like at Ternstedt?"

"C'mon, Scraps, let's go." He set his money down on the counter.

"You and your mutt there running away from some girls, huh?"

"Let him be," Karl said. He nodded his thanks to Resnick as he picked up the money.

"Turn the news back on," someone suggested.

"Yeah, before it's over," others agreed.

Once outside, Resnick gave Scraps a moment to answer nature's call before walking forward.

"What do you think, little buddy? Should we head home or go somewhere we're wanted?" About a block down he turned left into an alley behind a business district and headed toward Gagen's. Canadians liked to frequent the dance club, and there they were always friendly.

CHAPTER 14

Wednesday, February 24, 1937

The night in the factory proved less than comfortable. Romek had delivered a paltry number of blankets, his best effort given short notice. Some of the women gathered large tobacco leaves from the hopper in the intake room and piled them high, creating makeshift mattresses. Others shunned them due to the smell. Some slept in chairs, outstretched legs bridging from one seat to another. Younger ones curled up like kittens on the floor. A few older women appropriated tabletops. Dawn had yet to arrive. Women were awakening if, in fact, they'd been sleeping at all. Few spoke.

"What should we do when Resnick gets here?" Florence stretched her neck from side to side.

"I think we be all right. The way we barricaded the doors last night should hold. That bully's too lazy to break it down."

"We're lucky his uncle's traveling. He'd barrel right through it like a Panzer tank."

"Buys us some time. I hope Stanley Nowak agrees to come."

Brring!

It was still early, before business hours.

"I'll get it." Basia scurried into Resnick's office. "Good morning! White Eagle cigar factory.... Oh, it's you. Thank goodness!... Yes. Yes.... *Boże błogosław!*"

Basia hung up and announced to the ladies, "*Damski!* Listen up! Wally just called. Helen and others were up all night cooking at bar. They're bringing food. Panfuls!"

NOT YET LOST

"Wonderful!"

"I'm so hungry! Bless Helen."

Florence clasped her hands. She found Andrea, who she knew was pregnant but did not yet show. Brushing the young woman's hair off her forehead, she whispered, "*Malutka yeden*, you must eat first, my little one."

For the next hour or so, before Wally and Helen arrived, the newly energized group swept and cleaned and organized the workroom. They arranged tables in anticipation of the upcoming feast. Several women waited by the back door. The furniture barricade was disassembled in anticipation. Florence opened the heavy delivery doors, and Wally, Helen, Anushka, Stephan, and a small crowd of women arrived. All carried bundles of food and supplies. Loaves of bread and sausages peeked out the tops of brimming bags. Florence waved the visitors in and scanned the alley for Resnick.

"Mr. and Mrs. Koseba donated so much of this food. He had to go open the store now, and poor Mrs. Koseba, she was so tired from being up all night, she went home. She said to tell you how proud of you she is," Helen reported.

"Helen, you're our savior." Basia hugged Helen, then she and Florence helped her arrange the large pans on the makeshift buffet table.

"Listen. Mary Zuk came to see us. She's been helping over at the Ternstedt plant with Nowak," Helen said.

"Yes, we know Mary." Florence nodded along with Basia.

"She advised we set up a strike kitchen close to here. We'll use the bar until we have it arranged."

"We have to be quick! Let's go," Wally entreated.

"We're staying here. And there's more coming later today," a woman who'd left the day before said. The small crowd of workers in tow behind her all nodded. Before the women could finish the welcome breakfast, they heard pounding on the front door. A shroud of silence blanketed the room.

"Let me in! Let me in, goddamnit!" It was Resnick.

"Some of you go to back. Keep it secure. Be ready to let us out if we need to escape," Basia commanded. Florence led the way.

The pounding on the front door stopped, but the women hesitated to relax.

"You'll pay for this. You think 'cause my uncle's gone you can run roughshod over me. Well, you can't!" Resnick pounded on the back doors. Florence rechecked the iron bar she had put through the door handles. Others dragged more furniture to block the way. Basia ran from the front.

"That's exactly what we're doing, Mr. Resnick." Basia planted herself as close to the door as possible so she could be heard. Florence shook her head at her friend's pluck.

"I'll call the police. That's what I'll do. That's exactly what I'll do!"

"Are you convincing me or yourself, *Mr.* Resnick?"

Florence pulled her friend away from the door. "Don't taunt him!"

Resnick appeared to have retreated. Two women stayed back to keep watch, while the others returned to the workroom. They finished their interrupted breakfast.

"Should we go upstairs and see if there's an ice box there? We can't let this food spoil," Florence said while taking stock of the leftovers. Basia took the lead, and each woman carried armfuls of food, mostly dairy products, up the stairs to the offices. They pushed open the door, expecting to land in a palace. They didn't. Two humble wooden desks faced each other in the center of the room. Each had an upholstered office chair, matching only in their level of shabbiness. An adding machine peeked out from behind a neat stack of papers on one desk while the other supported shorter stacks and a telephone. The women laid the food next to the coffee pot on the nearby wooden buffet.

"We can take this pot downstairs. There's enough coffee grounds here for everyone. Maybe for day or two," said Basia, assessing the spoils of war. Florence walked around the office.

"No ice box. Maybe if we put this on the windowsill it'll stay cold enough." She now looked out the windows onto the street where they marched just a short time ago. She turned to see her friend had commandeered a chair at the desk with the phone.

"Come sit down," Basia's eyes twinkled as she summoned Florence to the other desk.

"I expected something grander. Plush carpets. Fine leather chairs. Still, to sit here does feel deliciously irreverent." Florence settled herself in the chair. "Look at this." She held up a short wooden pencil stub. "I thought the old man would have a fancy fountain pen."

"Good to know that old man is just as tight with himself as with us!" Basia started opening and closing drawers. "Look at this." Basia pulled out the bottle of Seagram's scotch whiskey and held it up to the light. "Not enough for everybody. We leave it here. Besides, don't want to be accused of stealing."

"Aren't you the funny one. What're we going to do if the police come?" Florence wrung her hands in her lap.

"I don't know yet. Let's go down and see who's got backbone."

"*O, Boże!*"

They returned to the workroom with the same armloads of food, which they arranged on a windowsill.

"*Damski! Damski!* Listen. Resnick said he's calling police. We need to make plan," Basia commanded. The women gathered and sat on the floor, in the chairs, and some on the tables. For hours, the women hypothesized, discussed, argued, cajoled, and fought among themselves like only loving families can. They broke for a late lunch, once again blessing the generosity and support from their friends and neighbors. Most of the women spent the afternoon in idle pastimes. Resnick's decks of cards were put to good use. Hair was brushed and styled on one another. Dances were danced. Turns were taken on the telephone. All the while, Florence and Basia designed work details to ensure functionality and harmony in the new living arrangement. This must be what organizing is all about.

The strikers transformed the workroom into a communal living center. Women hung clotheslines for their laundry and arranged their sleeping quarters. Outside labor organizers might bring cots in the next day or two. Florence sure hoped so. Her back felt like she'd slept on sharp rocks. The novelty of the day spent, the women were subdued. They listened to the news on the radio. No mention of their sit-down on mainstream programs. Only the Polish program hosted by Stanley Nowak reported on their strike.

"Let's tell stories," a young woman—a child really—suggested.

"Basia, how 'bout you start?" Florence always appreciated her friend's ability to spin a yarn.

"Yes, Basia, tell us, how did you become such a mischief maker?" another younger woman asked, her curiosity affirmed by several others.

"Tell us! Yes, tell us!"

"I've been *podżegacz* all my life I guess." Basia shrugged. "At least that's what my mother always said."

"Were you involved in revolutions in the old country?" The young woman, who'd been brought to America as a child, persisted.

"Let me tell you what it was like where I came from," Basia began.

Florence knew her friend's story well but hadn't heard it recounted in a long time.

Basia's family farmed the tired land in Łoniów, a region once part of the Polish-Lithuanian commonwealth but that was ruled by Russia at the time. Generations of her family served in serfdom on an estate. Once emancipated in the middle of the 1800s, the Szczesny family, yoked by debt, continued to farm a small piece of land. Then, the Great War. Threats came from Russian soldiers traveling west to the front, defeated Russian troops returning east from the front, and sometimes terrified army deserters. Hungry and desperate Polish countrymen, exiles anxious to hide from the German army terrorizing Polish lands, sought refuge in Łoniów. Her father fought in the Great War and was absent much of the time. The Szczesny family that remained on the farm was exposed and vulnerable—caught in crossfire.

Then the world became even more unhinged with the Bolsheviks and their soviets. Farmers were expected to feed the cities, the armies, feed everyone but themselves. They no longer drank milk from their own cows. Forced to sell it to the government, they bought it back at the store for *less* money.

"None of it made any sense. Crazy!"

Basia explained how, while her father was gone, she and Krisha became inseparable, a mother–daughter relationship as symbiotic as any. People moved into, out of, and through Łoniów in increasing numbers due to the war, uprisings, and the Russian Revolution. These outsiders brought not just their woes but their diseases with them to the isolated farm village. The Szczesny family managed to avoid the Spanish flu epidemic in 1918, but scarlet fever afflicted Krisha soon after. Her heart, with its new fragility, could no longer withstand long days of farm labor. Basia, the eldest, managed the family and farm side by side with her mother. Basia took over while Krisha raised Basia's two younger sisters and managed somewhat in the kitchen.

"Papa built small shelter near our summer kitchen. It wasn't much. Just canvas thrown over posts and birch ridgepole. He hung crucifix centered in view from the slit canvas entryway. It was small act of resistance against the atheist communists. With couple of long tables and some benches, the farmers had meeting hall."

When they visited, she listened to them jabber as she worked in the summer kitchen, fed the livestock, weeded the vegetable garden, or split and stacked firewood. Over the summer, their musings became pensive, combative at times. Their voices more boisterous as the *Spirytus* egged them on. Everyone had opinions about politics, the church, the village, the crops—all as changeable as the weather and equally unpredictable. Most of the seasoned farmers spoke with wisdom or yearned for days past before the Great War. Those in their middle years tried to make sense of current-day politics and social changes. The newly minted men were just that, inexperienced. Some quiet, observant, watchful. Others strutted like roosters, false bravado masking their youth. One of them, Feliks, the neighbor boy, pushed the limits to beyond obnoxious. Down the road his family owned a farm, a poor one. Resentful of others, Feliks became a

Bolshevik through and through. If he couldn't climb the ladder, he would break it so everyone would grovel on the ground.

One night, as the men dispersed, she pushed her way through the rabble of chickens to the outhouse. No more talk to overhear, she was eager for bed. Summer days are long in the north, and she had labored since before the full orb of the sun cleared the horizon. Her mother, Krisha, already deep in slumber, would have to wait until the morning to hear what she learned listening to the farmers.

"Even now, I can see that night." Basia chewed on her knuckle for a moment. The women, especially the young ones, sat spellbound.

"Dark clouds covering half-moon. I started to walk back to house. It didn't matter that I couldn't see. My feet knew way. I took a few steps from outhouse, and something struck me behind my knees. Hard."

She was felled. Then a body hurled itself upon her back, and her face smashed down into the dirt path.

"I had mouthful of dirt and chicken shit. I couldn't scream." Her mouth twisted in disgust.

"Now you'll have me. Or should I say, *I'll* have you." Feliks, the Bolshevik, stretched on top of her, spewed his foul breath on the side of her face, his head swinging low next to hers like a bull preparing to charge.

"He yanked my head back by my hair. Every time I tried scream, he shoved my face back down into dirt." Her audience was rapt.

Feliks's knees straddled her hips.

"I fumbled for my apron pocket with my right hand." Her hands acted out her words. "Then I reached out with my left for tall grasses next to path. I started slapping around like sea lion and barking." Basia demonstrated, her movements growing more exaggerated as her bewitched audience roared with unfettered glee.

"What did you do that for?" a young woman sitting on the floor asked.

"He said, 'You're crazy! What're you doing?' When he was distracted, I bucked and reared like wounded buffalo."

She threw Feliks's drunken body off her.

"I didn't hesitate one minute. I plunged boning knife from my apron pocket into his neck. And not just once, I'll have you know." Basia surveyed her audience.

Florence grinned as Basia placed her hand on her cocked hip and scanned the silent room, making eye contact methodically, lapping up the reaction. She would have been a splendid entertainer in a different day and time.

"Then I wiped blade on his shirt. Why should I soil my own?" Basia's coquettish question stirred pockets of nervous laughter.

"Did you *kill* him?" a young voice asked.

Basia looked point-blank at the woman who posed the question, her arms across her chest. "Yes."

"What did you do with the body?" another asked.

"I think that's enough of a story for the night," Florence interceded. "Let's get in a circle and pray." Stifling protests from those who wanted more stories, Florence herded the women and they held hands while she led them in prayer. After reciting Our Father and Hail Mary, Florence finished with the Act of Contrition.

"Oh, my God, I am heartily sorry for having offended Thee—" Florence eyed Basia. Her head wasn't bowed. Her shoulders were squared. Florence sighed. Try as she may, she might never succeed in saving Basia's soul.

The women cleaned up and arranged themselves for the night. Streetlamps glowed behind the resin-hazed windows, a nightlight of sorts. Odd rustling noises popped up here and there. The room and its occupants were unsettled. Bodies tossed and turned, seeking comfort. Florence wondered if Basia's story might best have been saved for another time, or perhaps at least toned down. She first heard the story years ago and knew much of it in further gruesome detail. Even she shuddered at its retelling. She also worried about her friend every time she told the story. How would replaying those memories affect her?

JANIS M. FALK

— — —

Basia rolled herself up in one of the blankets Romek had brought from home. She lay on her side, looking out the windows on the east side of the room. She'd padded her space with her wool coat. The blanket wasn't long enough to accommodate her legs, so she pulled her knees up to her chest. If there were light from the moon, the streetlights overtook it. Her cache of memories had been unlocked, her own Pandora's box. She might as well reacquaint with the full cadre of demons.

In the aftermath of the traumatic incident, her mother's heart succumbed. The constant threat of being under siege from every direction had beaten her down. Basia and her father agreed it would be better if she left the village. The priest arranged for passage to America.

On the day she departed, Basia walked to the cemetery in the churchyard. The rusty wrought iron gate, askew on its hinges, wobbled as she pushed it open. Just a few steps in, she found the roots of her family tree, starting with her great-grandfather—whose name, smudged from the elements, stretched across a small rock one could easily trip over. She knelt, crossed herself, prayed, then kissed her fingertips and ran them across the fuzzy, chiseled indentations. No sign of a great-grandmother to honor.

From there she moved toward the edge of the cemetery and found actual headstones, upright, marking her maternal grandparents' resting place. Again, she knelt, centered between the two adjoining plots, and prayed. Her fingertips lingered as they delivered her kisses. On the outer ring, adjacent to the fence, she found her mother's grave. The edges of the chiseled letters still as sharp as her pain. She knelt in prayer, gazing at the photograph of her mother, slightly distorted by the convex glass covering the small picture. Her wedding photograph—her only photograph. Basia had sliced her image away from her father's for use in the headstone. Now she would have no image of her mother to carry on her voyage other than the one in her heart. Basia prayed. And she wept. Sobbing in grief, she collapsed forward, lying across the grave. She dug her fingertips into the dirt on either side. If she could only hug her mother goodbye.

After a few moments, her outburst spent and tears and trembling quelled, she lay with her cheek on the cold ground at the base of the headstone. She heard the rusty wrought iron gate open. Glancing over her shoulder to see who'd witnessed her private moment, she saw the priest standing in his robes with his head bowed.

"We must leave now."

Basia faced her mother's headstone once again. She concentrated on the photograph, taking a picture of the picture in her mind's eye. At the same time, her mind's ear heard her mother speak, "Basia. You have strength I never had. You are powerful. You can do this. You *must* do this."

"I will, Mama, I will!" Basia had kissed the picture, clenched her fists in resolve, and joined the priest at the gate.

CHAPTER 15

Tuesday, March 2, 1937

Packett, the chief of police, straddled the bar stool at Jacoby's and nursed a Guinness. The mayor had called a meeting and should arrive any minute. The place was always busy in the afternoon. Court proceedings were over and lawyers, fighting tooth and nail just hours ago, lifted glasses in friendship. Sitting alone, he draped his overcoat on the adjacent stool for the mayor. Not that the mayor wouldn't be able to commandeer one, but the less disturbance upon his arrival, the better. With his eyes, he traced the patterns of lead in the stained glass, an old habit that calmed his nerves. He saw the mayor in the smoky mirror behind the bar and rose to greet him.

The mayor tipped his white felt fedora to a few constituents as he ambled his way through the room.

"Good afternoon, Packett." The mayor assumed his place at the bar next to the chief of police, and almost immediately, his favorite draught was set in front of him. "Thanks, Eddie. Keep the riffraff away, will you please? The chief and I have some important business to discuss." Eddie, the consummate professional, nodded and engaged a group in loud conversation at the other end of the bar.

"I need your help with some labor problems," the mayor beseeched Packett.

"We've been keeping the protests down to a minimum over at the tool and die. I got patrols there and guys walking the beat all hours, day and night. More than three people together, we break it up."

"Good. That's good, but we've got something else. I met today with owners of three of the five cigar factories in Poletown. White Eagle, General Cigar, and Mazur Cressman. Workers staged a sit-down at White Eagle and then word spread. Mazur Cressman sat just last night. General Cigar is expected to sit tomorrow."

"I see. It's harder when they're inside. It was easier in the old days. With Murphy up there in the guv's office we gotta be a little smoother," bemoaned Packett.

"I know. He's a sympathizer, that's for sure. It's what got him elected."

"We can go light, we can go full bore. You tell me what you want," Packett offered.

The mayor studied his beer. "The thing is, I'm not sure. The fact that they're mostly women complicates matters."

"That was the problem at that damn march a few weeks ago. Could hardly've run them down."

"No, that we couldn't have done. That fire near the stables was indeed serendipitous." The mayor shot a sideways glance at Packett, who nonchalantly sipped his beer. A small dribble of foam escaped from the upturned corner of his mouth. He dabbed at it neatly with a cocktail napkin.

"Maybe the way to go is to start with a scare. Try a few things to get them outside. It can't last forever," Packett proposed.

"The sit-in at the Fisher plant in Flint lasted over forty days," countered the mayor.

"Yeah, but those were a bunch of factory toughs."

"Don't underestimate these women. They've stayed in there a week so far. They're no hothouse flowers by any stretch, these women." The mayor drained his glass.

"How about if I—"

"I don't need—or want—to know the details. Do what you have to do. Just get it done!"

"Yes, sir."

Pervasive labor unrest jangled not only the city of Detroit but also Packett's nerves. At least he harbored a secret weapon in his battle to quell the insurrections. Now that the strike at Kelsey Hayes had settled, he would pay some attention to these cigar factories. He'd let those hot spots languish in favor of addressing the hardcore industries, Zenith Carburetor, Timken-Detroit Axle, Murray Corporation, Ferro Stamping. Men needed to get back to work. Mostly women sat down in the cigar factories; they were not nearly as dangerous. He allowed them their week of fun, playing dress-up in a man's world, but now it was time they went back to work. He would trigger the network of the Black Legion. No one hated communists more than Black Legion members. Packett thought it had to be the Communist Party behind these labor actions.

"Damn immigrants from Eastern Europe. Polocks, Russkies, and Jews. Communists, all of them!" He knew just who he'd call when he got to his office. Fred Lynch's boss, Moore, would get the party rolling.

"Moore? Hey, it's Packett. Listen up." Packett summoned Moore to assemble a team of counterprotesters. Packett could count on Moore.

"Lynch? It's Moore. Listen up." Moore could count on Lynch.

"Falkowski? Fred Lynch. Listen up." Lynch could count on Falkowski. Alex wouldn't like it, but he would do it.

Alex cranked up his black Dodge coupe. He hadn't driven his car in a long time. Gasoline was expensive. He headed up Michigan Avenue. He'd been "invited" to another barbecue in Rouge Park. At least this time he was accompanied by his firearm. Since his initiation, as the Black Legion called bald-faced coercion, he had been providing names to the group. His assignment was to call out men at Dodge Main who might be organizers for the burgeoning United Auto Workers. Once each week, he would drop into the drugstore and slip a piece of paper listing names to the proprietor. On occasion he'd been directed to attend secret meetings in the basement. To gain entry one had to ask the proprietor for the correct bottle of liquor and identify the shelf it was on, according to the code of the week. Alex hadn't engaged in such juvenile games since he was a young farm boy. Back then, the stakes had been low. The games he played might get him a beating with a birch switch if his antics caused food waste or damaged equipment. Now, he knew all too well that any beatings would be less kind.

The weather wasn't as severe as the first time he visited Rouge Park—frozen mud replaced hard ice on the path to the clearing. His galoshes were slick, and he hoped there would be a fire. He detected the flow of the River Rouge and knew he was close. He caught a whiff of burning wood. He reassured himself with a hand on his pocket.

"There he is! The nonbeliever. We weren't sure you'd grace us with your presence," a voice from his Black Legion initiation boomed. Alex had since learned the voice belonged to Keen, one of the most active hitmen. The masterminds of the Legion manipulated this dimwitted brute to execute their dirty work, or "wet" work, as killings were known.

"Where's your uniform?"

Alex observed that each and every man wore the black-hooded uniform punctuated with the white skull and crossbones. He'd thrown his in the incinerator.

"I didn't know it was required." Alex reflexively caught the bundle thrown at him.

"Put it on."

"Is this necessary? You all know who I am. I don't know who all of you are."

"Put it on!"

Alex unfolded the voluminous black robe and pulled it over his head. While doing so, he slipped his gun out of his pocket and held it concealed in the bell-shaped sleeve. He brought the silly hood over his head and adjusted the ragged eyeholes so he could see.

"Do you know whose robe that is?" Keen asked.

"How many guesses do I get?" Alex retorted. He knew it was dangerous to poke the bear, but he couldn't capitulate entirely.

"Don't be smart. It's your friend's. Nick's."

Alex froze.

"When we saw what happened at the tracks—" the leader now spoke. Alex had learned this man was the state commander of the Black Legion.

"So it was you—" interrupted Alex, then he stopped.

"We keep an eye on our new members, especially ones who don't seem to have dedicated their heart and soul."

"Once that train passed, we broke into Nick's room. Retrieved our property."

The folds and sleeves of the flimsy robe drooped as Alex exhaled.

"Don't worry. We don't mind that you offed Nick—"

"Me? Me? I didn't off Nick! I held him back. I thought he was going to jump. Then that bullet hit him in the back." Alex envisioned Nick's body convulsing in the air before it thumped onto the railroad tracks, then after the train had passed. "You killed him!"

"Who's to know you didn't?"

Alex understood the rattrap they'd caught him in.

"Nick was a nervous Nellie anyway. No great loss."

Alex looked at the myriad feet making a wreath around the fire. None stood out as excessively polished, but he couldn't be sure. Maybe Police Chief Packett was there, maybe he wasn't. At least in the old country you saw the enemies you fought. He felt unmoored.

"Let's get down to business. You see, the problem is cigar factories are near and dear to our director of operations' heart." The Black Legion's state commander walked back and forth, his hands clasped behind his back, almost professorial in his long black robe. Alex watched the fabric dragging across the ground, hoping it might catch in the fire.

"He lives in a town, in a state, dominated by cigar factories. Many owned by friends and relatives. They lived through strikes twenty years ago, before some got smart and automated. The others don't want this sit-down strike contagion going their way, so it needs to end."

Another voice spoke. "The police, the mayor, they don't have time to deal with this little gals charade. There's serious strikes goin' on at Zenith, Timken-Detroit, Murray, Ferro Stamping. So we need to make this disturbance go away. Men need to get back to work."

"Maybe you should be talking to the cigar factory owners. If they would concede, the strike would end," Alex said.

"We don't have time for such nonsense. Let's talk about our options. How can we use your—how should we say?—talents? To bring this nonsense to an end?" The robed men bandied about ideas from the mundane to the fantastic, barely noticing that Alex didn't contribute. They seemed absorbed in one-upping each other in wild suggestions of methods to tame the recalcitrant women. One hooded thug demonized them more than the next.

While they were talking, Alex slid his arms in opposite sleeves, assuming the posture of an Orthodox monk. He emptied some shell casings from his gun into his hand. He wouldn't be using his gun tonight after all. He edged toward the fire and dropped his hands to his side. He cleared his throat.

"You've offered many good suggestions. I'll mull them over accordingly. I have my marching orders, so I'll be on my way."

"I'm glad you're starting to see things our way. Make sure your assignment is completed. Promptly," the leader commanded.

Alex took his leave, but not before he doled out, one by one, the bullets at the edge of the fire. As soon as he shut his car door, he heard the *rat tat tat* of shell casings flying. He reveled in the last laugh. What did it matter now?

CHAPTER 16

Saturday, March 6, 1937

Morning sun slipped above the building across the street. Florence darned a blue sock, Frank's or Lucien's, which she pulled from the basket of mending Lucien had brought her. A few women sat on the floor playing cards. Some of the younger girls designed dresses on paper absconded from Resnick's office. Others questioned Anushka about her wedding plans. Basia, ever watchful, served as scout upstairs in the offices on the top floor. One of the younger girls, whose legs could better run the stairs, served as messenger. Some women peddled small talk. Florence pricked her finger with her darning needle, startled by the distant sirens. She made the sign of the cross and sucked her bleeding finger. Silence blanketed the room as the women listened to the fast and furious footsteps descending eight flights of stairs from the top floor.

"They're coming! They're coming! Just a few minutes now." The messenger bent over, hands on her thighs, attempting to catch her breath. "Basia says to come look."

Florence dropped her mending into the basket, Anushka rose from the circle of girls, and a few others joined in behind the messenger for her return trip up the stairs. Basia met them at the landing. Wailing sirens, louder now, announced the arrival of Packett's men. Florence wiped her sweaty palms on her cotton dress. The women huddled in front of the windows in what must be a meeting room.

"See, look out there! They're coming." Basia pointed to the left.

"No, they're coming from that way." Florence pointed right, toward the source of the sirens. "Maybe it's the National Guard."

"Those are just cops. Look this way." Basia pulled on her arm.

Florence swiveled her head. "Oh, my!" Tears ran down her cheeks, rolling over her hand that covered her mouth.

A throng of people marched in the street, filling it side to side. Voices raised in song competed with the police sirens.

"Look, Father Maletski's at head of group. And look, there's Romek. There must be hundreds behind them." Basia placed a knee on the windowsill, pushing her nose to the glass. Florence craned her neck to see around her friend.

"At least! The neighborhood turned out for us. I don't see Alex anywhere, do you?"

"No, not yet." Basia scanned the marching crowd now approaching the front of the building.

"Not surprised. He doesn't much go in for this sort of thing. The boys told me he's hornet mad at me for staying here."

"He'll get over it. Especially when you start bringing home more money. Don't worry. Let's go watch from second floor."

"We can open a window and hear what's happening. Police are lining up too."

The women ran down the six flights of stairs to the second floor. In the owner's office they threw open the sashes and waved to the throngs.

"Like our march but bigger!" Basia exclaimed. Florence leaned her chin on Basia's shoulder, craning to see who was there. Father Maletski's baritone belted out a song of unity. People filled in behind the priest. He stopped the crowd in front of White Eagle and led the group in a call and response, voicing their demands. A multitude of signs punctuated the responses:

FACTORIES ARE NOT JAILS
FIVE DAY WORK WEEKS
8 HOUR WORK DAY

Policemen on horseback muscled their way through the crowd, and policemen on foot impelled their way through, infiltrating the throng.

"Look at that! They break up the people."

"Yes," Florence agreed with Basia, "divide and conquer."

"Hope for no fire this time. They say what needs saying and move on."

"Look, Joan is coming our way. Joan, Joan, up here!" She waved above Basia's head to their journalist friend. After a few minutes dodging marchers, police, and horses (and what they leave behind), Joan stood beneath the window.

"Have you heard the news? It's not just factories anymore! Shop girls are on strike. Women took over Woolworth's drugstore. The downtown location. Even some customers refused to leave in order to support the workers."

"That's wonderful!" Basia clapped her hands.

"Over two hundred saleswomen! They let me in to take a photo. A bunch sitting on the counter reading the paper."

"*O, Boże!*" Florence couldn't imagine. "A drugstore?"

"And shoe stores and hotels. The world's with us, ladies. It's our time now. Look at these." Joan waved a stack of leaflets. "I'll leave some by the door. We're handing these out everywhere. Even at church!"

"Isn't that police chief over there?" Basia pointed across the way.

"I'd better go. I'm sure there's a story to be had there." Joan dived back into the throng to make the return crossing.

By the time Florence and Basia cracked open the front door to retrieve the leaflets, the marchers were progressing forward. Inside, they passed around the leaflets for all to admire.

That night the mood was jubilant. Such an outpouring of support renewed their resolve. Others had tried to organize before in the hand-rolled cigar industry, but the AFL union didn't support them. Not that there had been many men to begin with, but most had transferred to jobs at the newly automated factories where cigars were rolled by machine. Others had joined on at the cigarette factories, also automated. The AFL either thought these workers were on their way out or not worthy of representation. The cigar factory women may not have been the most powerful or plentiful, but they mattered. Florence thought so. Basia told everyone so.

Irena, the head of the entertainment committee—which Mary Zuk insisted they form—not only procured an accordion but knew how to play it. She struck up a mazurka, followed by *Polka Staroswiecka* and *Kasuby* dances. When she completed her repertoire, she started over. With no men available, the women danced by themselves, in groups, and with each other. Gaiety and mirth enlivened the dun-colored factory, at least for a short time. Basia took the center of a dance circle and stomped, twirled, and leaped, imitating the men's peacock moves from *Opoczno* dances. She played for laughs, and soon many of the women were overcome with tears of hilarity. Several collapsed in chairs, clutching their chests as they caught their breath. Florence brought Basia a glass of water.

"*Dziękuję!*" Basia gulped down the beverage.

"You're something else!" Florence took back the empty glass.

"Fun, eh?"

Irena called for attention.

"Before we settle down, let's not forget who we are. Let's pay homage to Poland." Irena played the notes of a *Polonez*. Pairing off, the women lined up at the room's perimeter. They circled the room and ventured through the other workrooms at a moderate tempo. Florence looked around as she hummed the tune. Women of all ages, humble, tired, bedraggled, and disheveled, paraded solemnly. Heads held high, they exchanged respectful nods to each other, as was the custom of the dance. If she could only use one word to describe the ambience, she would choose resolve. That is what she saw in her friends, neighbors, coworkers, and countrymen. Resolve.

CHAPTER 17

Monday, March 8, 1937

Alex had been summoned upstairs. He stopped to wash his hands and tidy his hair. He'd been angling for a new position, but he hadn't expected it would happen now. They needed the money. Reserves were dwindling. Florence hadn't been paid in a few weeks now with the idiotic sit-down at the cigar factory. Labor actions at the tool and die shops disrupted supply chains, and the auto factories stopped production intermittently. No production, no pay. The wage rates had not yet returned to pre-market crash levels, even after seven years. After this promotion, he still wouldn't be making the same.

Alex rapped on the frosted glass window of the door. Fred Lynch swung it open. Fred's boss, Mr. Moore, whipped his legs off his desk.

"Mr. Falkowski, please have a seat here." Moore indicated a chair across from his desk. "Mr. Lynch here speaks highly of you and your work. A cut above the rest."

"Thank you, sir."

"Now it has come to our attention your wife—"

"My wife! What's she got to do with anything?" Alex grabbed the arms of the chair, almost catapulting out of it.

"As I was saying, Mr. Falkowski, your wife seems to be engaged in a sit-down strike at the cigar factory."

"How do you—"

"Her name appeared on a list."

"A list? What type of list?" He knew all too well the type of list.

"A list of undesirables. Deplorables, really."

He fell back in his chair and rubbed his chin. What could he say?

"And then there's this." Moore shoved a photograph across the desk toward him. Without touching it Alex leaned forward and perused the image. Centered in the grainy, blown-up picture, Florence and Basia hung out a window of the White Eagle cigar factory, waving and smiling as if President Roosevelt himself were stumping in the street. He deflated back into the chair.

"Now, to talk about the promotion. We think you could demonstrate your supervisory capabilities by reining in these women. Ending the strike." Moore leaned forward, elbows on his desk.

"How do you expect me to do that?" Alex asked.

"You're the head of your household, are you not?"

"Besides, it's your patriotic duty. You're a patriot, ain't you?" Fred, sitting in the adjacent chair, swatted his arm. If Fred didn't stop cracking that chewing gum, Alex was going to swat him.

"What do you say, Falkowski? Show us what you got, and we'll talk about that promotion." Moore rose, ending the discussion. Not one to be bullied, Alex stood to his full height, cap in hand, and locked eyes with Moore. Snapping gum marked the count. Moore coughed and resumed his seat.

"You're dismissed. I have work to do."

That evening, Alex sat in his reading chair. The evening edition of the paper lay limp across his lap. He scanned the want ads. Nothing. He didn't suppose the situation in Canada was any better. Besides, how could he sell the house? He was stuck.

"Bastards!" He knew he couldn't let them get to him. He'd faced tougher, meaner men than them before, but the rules of engagement differed.

A knock on the back door. He strained to see through the glass as he traversed the kitchen.

"It's me. Romek."

Alex opened the back door for his neighbor. He was not in the mood for company, but he had invited Romek over to discuss the cigar factory. While he and Romek always had been cordial, Florence truly was the neighbors' friend.

"We need to talk about the strike. That's why you called?" Romek wasted no time.

The men retired to the front room. Alex brought two shot glasses and a bottle of vodka with him. After a salutary shot, Alex opened the conversation. "The strike? What are your thoughts?"

"I'm afraid it's dangerous."

"Absolutely it's dangerous! In many different ways," Alex agreed.

"I know Basia. She's a stubborn cat. And I love her for it. Where there's a wrong, she will right it."

"And Florence will follow. Can you go see Basia? Talk her down?"

"I don't know that I want to, but I'm worried just the same."

Alex leaned his forearm against the mantel. Using his toe, he directed unruly bark and wood chips back into the hearth. He looked over his right shoulder at Romek, who stared into his empty shot glass.

"Under the star of the guard," Alex mumbled.

"What?"

Alex repeated.

"What are you talking about?" Romek looked confused.

"Nothing. Talking to myself." So the Black Legion hadn't recruited Romek. Good to know. Then again, why would they? Romek reveled in the thick of the labor movement.

"Do you ever get tired of it all, Romek?"

Smash!

The mirror above the mantel shattered in Alex's face. He whipped around to see his front window broken and shards of glass gathered in the puddled sheer curtains. Tires screeched as a car hightailed it away. Romek picked up the fist-sized rock lying at Alex's feet. Alex snatched it from his hand.

"I blame you for this!" Alex shook the rock in Romek's face.

"Me?" Romek stepped back and his immense hand flew to his chest.

"Yes, you! You riled everyone up after Henryk died. Talked to them from the podium like you're some goddamned preacher." Alex's face reddened beyond the flush of the vodka.

"We must stay together. Keep our community together."

"And that hot-headed wife of yours! Dragging Florence off with her harebrained schemes. Causing trouble."

Romek stepped further back. His nostrils flared.

"No one. *No one* disparages Basia."

"Her loud mouth got everyone into this mess!" Alex accused.

Romek hurled himself at Alex, who found his shoulders pinned up against the wall.

"Now you listen to me," Romek growled. "Basia is worth more than you could ever understand. And she does something you don't do. She understands your wife! If you think Flo's not there by her own choice, you're wrong! Very wrong!" Romek released his hold on Alex's shoulders.

"Get out! Get out now!" He followed Romek as he left by the back door. After Romek cleared the alley, Alex entered the garage to look for wood to board up the window.

He picked up the glass and began to install the plywood over the window opening, a temporary fix to repel the cold. The phone rang. Perhaps it was Florence and he could try to talk sense into her.

"Hello?"

"It's been several days now."

"Who is this? Who's calling?"

"We're watching you. That broken window is to wake you up. Do something to get those dames to give it up. Before anything else happens." *Click.*

CHAPTER 18

Wednesday, March 10, 1937

Alex lay on his belly below the foot-high parapet wall of the building across from the cigar factory. He was glad he brought an old tarp he used to cover the lawn mower in his backyard. Puddles, sporting an oily rainbow sheen, riddled the neglected asphalt roof. The tarp protected his clothes, and he wore his galoshes. He sighted his Winchester Model 69 through the scupper in the parapet, aiming at the windows of the White Eagle. He was familiar with the bolt action and the .22 rimfire cartridges. Fred had let him use this late-model long rifle at the gun club. Alex always knew a price would be exacted for his membership at the club, but he hadn't expected shooting a gun at his wife would be the levy.

Police, arriving from the left, set up operations. Several officers milled in front of the cigar factory, bull horns hanging at their sides. He would take his cue from them.

"This is the Detroit Police Department. You are unlawfully occupying private property. You need to vacate the premises immediately."

Crack!

A window on the far left of the third floor shattered. Alex noticed women huddled by a window on the fourth floor. He didn't intend to kill anyone, just frighten them into leaving the building. Damn Nick for getting him involved in the Black Legion. Alex peeked over the top of the parapet and saw a tall, stout man in a long camel's hair coat, a fat cigar stuck in the side of his mouth, pacing behind the line of police officers. Must be old man Schwarz, the factory owner. He watched as the man verbally assaulted a policeman, all apoplectic, waving his fine-finished cigar around before he returned to pacing.

Alex resumed cover behind the short wall. He set up his sights again, this time focusing on a window on the fourth floor but away from the one in which he'd seen the women. He couldn't be sure, but he thought Florence was one of them. Basia definitely was one, so Florence was no doubt nearby. He saw the policeman in charge lift his megaphone.

"Repeating. You are unlawfully occupying private property and you must exit the building at once."

Crack!

Another window shattered. Packett, the police chief, looked up and around. What a fool. From what Alex could see, the occupants had descended to the first floor. Maybe they would come out and put an end to this fiasco. He aimed at the far corner of a first-floor window. He rotated the lever up and slid the bolt back, loading another cartridge into the barrel. Then, moving ever so slightly to the left, he pulled the trigger. The bullet missed the window by an inch or so, shattering the mortar between the bricks and the window frame. Shrieks ensued. He could not imagine the terror he was inflicting. He locked his eyes on the front door. He hoped, and even prayed, the door would open. Maybe they were leaving by the back door or sneaking out the side employees' entrance. Movement near Packett distracted him. Two officers were huddled with the chief. Each man walked away with something in his hands. Individually, they advanced to the windows on either side of the main entrance.

"*Kurwa!*" He sped to the rooftop entrance and hurtled down the stairs, abandoning his lawnmower tarp.

Florence felt the sharp metal bite the skin of her leg as the tear gas cartridge exploded. She fell onto her hands and knees. Acrid smoke enveloped her head as the cloud of gas swelled to fill the room. Cries of pain echoed through the chemical fog. Her bare forearms burned, and she couldn't catch her breath. Caustic smoke tendrils seeped behind her eyelids. She opened her eyes but couldn't see. Stand up! She needed to stand up! She groped around her and found the leg of a chair. Tracing its form, she found the seat and pulled herself up. Her knees wobbled. Blood dripped down her leg, and she lost her footing in its slippery pool. Her fingers found purchase on the edge of a worktable. She fell into the chair. Coughing. Coughing. She doubled over. Someone pulled her by the arm.

"Go upstairs! Have to get upstairs!" Basia wheezed. They headed toward the stairs. Florence heard labored breathing all around her.

"Hold onto the wall. Follow the wall," Anushka hollered.

Florence heard talk from every direction, disoriented by the smoke.

"It burns!"

"I can't see!"

"Watch out!"

The first ones to reach the top of the stairs barreled into the second-floor offices and threw open the sashes. Bad idea. The open windows drew smoke toward them like a chimney. They hastened back to the landing.

"Go higher! Up! Up!" Before leaving the office, Anushka grabbed the adding machine from the desk, ripped its cord from the wall socket, and placed it as a doorstop.

The women crowded into the third floor. They opened the windows a short way. Smoky gas continued to coil up from the lower floors, mere wisps compared to the dense fog they just escaped. Taking turns in front of coveted window positions, the women crouched or kneeled, still wary of the gunshots, which seemed to have stopped. After clearing their lungs the best they could, they gathered in the center of the room.

"Anushka, get Andrea out of here. She's expecting. Listen up, everyone. Anyone who's with child or might be with child go with Anushka. She'll get you out the side door." Florence wiped her leg with the hem of her dress.

"When you . . . uhh . . . see those bastards . . . 'ell 'em . . . uhh . . . we not leavin' . . ." Basia gasped. Her chest rose and fell with the effort to eke out the words.

"Come over here. Now." Florence compelled her friend to the window and gently pushed her shoulders so she would sit on the floor facing the windows. "Make room, girls. Basia can't breathe." Florence sent one of the young girls for water and knelt, her arm around Basia's shoulder. "Breathe. In. Out. In. Out. Deeply." The women quieted, as the situation was serious.

Anushka returned from releasing the mothers-to-be and nodded at Florence.

"How is it down there?" Florence asked.

"Tolerable. Most of the smoke is gone."

"It'll be better if everyone washes. If they can, change clothes and wash what they're wearing. Get everyone moving," Irena instructed.

"I'll get a group to clean the workroom," the girl who returned with water for Basia offered.

"Good. Wash the dishes and throw out any food that wasn't covered. *O, Boże!*"

Once each woman recovered and caught her breath. One by one they left the room to start the arduous task. Florence helped Basia into a chair. She was out of the direct line of the window, which had a bullet hole in it, but close enough to breathe in air from the outside.

"You scared me!"

"I scared myself." Basia held her hand to her chest. "The burning. Never felt such . . ."

"Shh! Save your breath."

"Out . . . side . . . What's happen . . ."

Florence peeked out the window. "Some people milling about. Police're still there. Wait. It's Schwarz!"

"Must be . . . back . . . traveling," Basia stuttered.

"Don't talk."

"Let's go . . . down. I want to hear . . . radio." Upon rising, Basia suffered a coughing fit before the women descended to the first-floor workroom.

Irena directed the cleaning and washing chores. Still aghast and in shock, the women moved about in near silence.

"How long can this go on?" Florence shook her head.

"As long . . . as it . . . has . . . to. Not give up!" Basia settled herself in a chair and put her feet up.

"I'm going to call your Romek. I'll have him bring fresh clothes and blankets. You rest." Florence proceeded to Resnick's office to use the phone. She exhaled heavily as she sat in his desk chair. She picked up the phone and clicked and dialed. Nothing. She tried again. Nothing. She dialed 0. Nothing. Again. Nothing. She collapsed her head on the desk and cried. The phone lines had been cut.

CHAPTER 19

Friday, March 12, 1937

Late in the morning, the kitchen detail in the factory, of which Florence was a part, assessed their pantry. Food supplies had dwindled. Police presence hindered deliveries from the strike kitchen. Patrolmen on horseback circled the factory almost nonstop and often queued up to block the alley. The routine was becoming tiresome. Dry bread, thin ham slices, and a modest number of sausage disks were laid out. Coffee ran out the day before. They drank hot water. The number of workers remaining had dwindled. After the tear gas incident, several had slipped out the back door and gone home. Was it worth it? Families in need of their wives and mothers had become ill-humored, often begging, even demanding, the women return home. Deteriorating conditions inside made acquiescence easier. Some outside the factory discouraged continuing the strike. Despair trumped hope of a productive resolution. Father Maletski came as often as he could, but other parish business demanded his attention, especially with Easter fast approaching. Stanley Nowak and Mary Zuk came and went sporadically. Workers trying to organize all over the city needed their help.

After laying out meager provisions, Florence's knitting needles clicked and clacked away on a baptismal cap for Andrea's baby. Her completed mending had been sent home with one of the women shuttling between homes and factory. Alex had demanded she quit the strike too. She couldn't. She believed in it, down to the marrow in her bones. They heard a noise like something thrown at the window. Several women, all needleworkers around a table, looked at each other and shrugged. They heard it again. And again. Florence rose to get Basia, who was in Resnick's office tweaking the list of demands.

"Let's go check it out." Basia stood.

The women looked out the tiny window next to the loading dock. They didn't see anyone. The two women standing guard said they thought they'd heard someone, nothing menacing. Carefully, they removed the iron bar from the door handles and twisted the thumb lock. Basia peeked out. From across the alley, Alicja darted toward her. Basia pulled the young girl in, opening the door no more than required.

"Alicja!" Basia exclaimed while Florence relocked the door. "What're you doing here?"

"Here, I brought you my lunch." Alicja proffered a worn cloth sack. "I heard there wasn't much food here now."

Basia held the girl's cheeks between her hands and kissed her on top of the head. "Bless you, child! This is just what I needed."

Florence, too, recognized the gesture was the encouragement Basia needed, what they all needed, and it wasn't the lunch. Florence gave the girl a hug and sent her on her way. They returned to the workroom with nourished spirits. It was almost time for the midday radio news. The radio had been relocated from Resnick's office so they could all listen.

"The women at Webster Eisenlohr cigar factory have joined in the sit-down strikes. This is the fourth in a wave of strikes sweeping Detroit's cigar industry. Only one factory remains working, but there's speculation workers at Essex will sit down by the end of the day."

Cheers resounded off the ceiling. Florence cried. Basia shouted, "It's working!"

The knitting needles picked up tempo. A new energy suffused the room, tepid compared to two weeks prior, but energy all the same. The impetus moved them through the afternoon.

"Bless Alicja! That dear girl. How brave coming here," Basia uttered in a soft voice to Florence as they prepared for bed.

"Yes. What a child." They removed hair pins and brushed their hair.

"Basia?" Florence's voice quivered.

"Speak up! What is it?"

"Alex demanded I come home. Lucien dropped off a letter."

"What're you going to do?" Basia's fingers worked strands of her dark hair into a braid that hung forward on her shoulder.

"He says it's not safe. After what happened, he may be right."

"*Psia krew!* He's just tired of all the work himself."

"He said the boys need me." Her voice caught in her throat.

"What your boys need is world where people not treat them worse than ants. Work, work, then get stepped on!"

Florence settled down on her cot.

"You do what you think best. Not what Alex wants. Not what I want. You're smart. You sleep. Decide tomorrow, eh?"

"Good night." She rolled over to face away from Basia, not an easy task on the narrow cot.

CHAPTER 20

Friday, March 12, 1937

"Packett, that fiasco over at White Eagle has caused us some problems. Martin, the UAW boss, called me. They're threatening a general strike if we keep using these tactics to break up the sit-ins." The mayor wiped his brow with his handkerchief. Despite the winter's chill, sweat exuded from the pores on his forehead.

"I see. What choices do we have? Asking politely's not going to work." Packett sat across from the mayor and held his hat on the knee of his crossed leg.

"Hardly."

"Some cigar factories have settled. Not sure why Schwarz's holding out, why he's so goddamn stubborn. The outcome's inevitable."

"It's a changing world, Packett. Thirty industries. Thirty goddamn industries across this city have labor turmoil."

"You don't think I know? Jails are full. We're going to stop arresting agitators. I got nowhere to put 'em. Brought in at least twenty from that skirmish over at Newton Packaging yesterday. Couldn't do anything with 'em, so they're back at it today. My men are discouraged. They ask, 'Why bother?' and I don't blame them."

"I'm worried, Packett. So worried. I worked construction. I understand hard work. I really do. But what if these work stoppages slow the local economy again? This city can't weather another setback. People have just gotten on their feet. There're still lines at the soup kitchens. There'll be anarchy. Uncontrollable violence."

NOT YET LOST

"Will be? *Will be?*" Packett jumped out of his chair. "My men and I can't keep this town in line now. We don't have time to mollycoddle people." Ropy veins bulged on Packett's neck.

"Don't get all riled up. Sit down. I recognize you have it tough, but—"

"I've seen the petitions going 'round demanding your recall." Packett remained standing. "That's what this is all about!"

A knock on the office door.

"Excuse me, please," the mayor's secretary said. "Chief Packett, your assistant chief wants you to call him immediately. He says it's urgent. And, Mayor, here are your phone messages from the last hour." She handed a considerable stack of notes to the mayor before retrieving papers from his outbox and crossing the Oriental rug with crisp efficiency.

"Thank you." The mayor nodded. "All right, Packett. Go take care of business. But keep in mind what I said."

Packett tucked his captain's hat under his arm, nodded, and left in silence.

The mayor shuffled through the stack of messages and sighed. He'd been talking and arguing with Packett for much too long. Replacing the stack on his desk, he stood and peered out the window. A small group of protesters gathered in Cadillac Square below. He heard the call and response chants. He saw the moving signs, now more ubiquitous throughout the city than umbrellas. In the dimming light the pane glass mirrored his image. Nose to nose with himself, he took stock. The hair, receding and graying, not unusual but perhaps premature for thirty-five years old. The cleft chin, still strong and distinctive but now bookended by fine jowl lines. The laugh lines around his eyes had become furrows of worry. This job, in these times, would tax any man. Yet still, he couldn't bear the shame of recall, not with his father being the former mayor and now a United States senator. It could happen. Mayor Bowles had been recalled in the first year of his term in 1930. He was accused of being soft on crime, in bed with criminals. His own crime was being unable to quell labor unrest. Powerful people blamed him for stalling the economic engine that drove this city.

The mayor's immediate predecessor, the ever-popular Frank Murphy, assumed office after Bowles. Murphy, now governor, courted labor organizations. The mayor hoped to ride Murphy's coattails to governor himself. First, he needed to stay in office, then get reelected. The question of managing crime and labor organization vexed him. He noted the shadow on his cheeks and chin. He rubbed his neck. He would have to shave and get cleaned up before his daughter's school performance this evening.

"Please have the car brought around," the mayor spoke through the intercom.

CHAPTER 21

Friday, March 12, 1937

"I'm hungry," complained Frank. Lucien looked up at his younger brother, who stood holding the cupboard door open. He rose from the table and looked over his brother's shoulder. Not much to see. He moved to the ice box—not much in there either. His mother, absent for a time now, had not brought groceries home.

"Let's go to Koseba's and get potatoes. I think Mrs. Koseba is cooking at the strike kitchen so she won't be home. I'll cook them for us out back." The boys retrieved their jackets from the hooks in the vestibule by the back door. Ordinarily, their outerwear was strewn around the kitchen chairs, the banister, or their bedrooms. With their mother gone the boys tried to keep order, Lucien in particular. Being older, he set the example. Frank was young and self-absorbed, unobservant. Lucien, to the contrary, didn't miss a thing. His father seethed just below the surface at his wife's refusal to leave the cigar factory. Lucien avoided his father's wrath since the incident in Black Bottom. By keeping the peace, he supported his mother. If there were trouble at home, who knows what his father might do? Physically pull her from the factory floor?

Lucien started a fire in the middle of a small circle of stones in the backyard. Frank crossed the alley to take potatoes from the Koseba's larder. The chickens in the coop next to the garage made a racket. His father didn't let them out in the yard during the winter even though their yard was surrounded by a fence. Each of the boys rubbed a potato on each pant leg. Frank had brought four. Once the dirt had been transferred, Lucien stoked the small fire by adding a few still-damp twigs. The twigs generated more smoke than flame. Creating proper embers in which to nestle the potatoes might take a while. Days were edging closer to spring, a few more minutes of daylight extended each afternoon. Even so, the boys were surprised when their father entered the yard from the back door of the house.

"Dad, you're home early." Lucien spoke in a neutral tone, not wanting to poke the bear.

"I came straight from work. All anyone's talking about is the strike at the cigar factory. I don't need to listen to that."

"We're baking some potatoes. Do you want one?"

Lucien wasn't sure what to make of his father's exasperated sigh.

"Put the fire out. I'll take you to get some supper."

Lucien went inside and returned with a pitcher of water to douse the fire.

"I'll get another, just to be safe." Lucien noticed Alex staring at his feet as he walked into and out of the house.

"Do you have any other slacks you could change into?" his father queried.

"I can wash the dirt off." Lucien headed for the door with the empty pitcher in one hand, the other brushing off potato dirt from his thigh.

"No, I mean longer slacks. Those look like they belong to Frank."

Lucien blushed. He'd grown another two inches since the first of the year. He hated how so much of his socks showed, but his mother said they couldn't buy new clothes until summer.

"No, sir."

"We'll get you some proper-fitting slacks and supper."

Behind Alex's back the brothers looked at each other and shrugged.

The boys followed Alex into the house, but not before Frank remembered to feed the chickens. His mother was relying on him.

Once the family reached the main street, Alex hailed a cab, a rare occurrence.

"Take us to 1200 Woodward, please."

"J. L. Hudson's, yes, sir." The cabbie slid back into traffic. Lucien brimmed with anticipation. His mother shopped at neighborhood stores. Father Maletski encouraged Polish people to support each other. He once said in a sermon it was imperative Poles supported Poles for the community to survive. Lucien's mother took heed and patronized stores owned by Polish immigrants. He didn't like the clothes at those stores. They made him look like a DP—Displaced Person, they were called. Once inside the opulent department store, the trio went down the escalator to the boys' department. Finding nothing suitable, they switched to the men's department on the second floor. Nothing there was appropriate either. Lucien had the height of a man and the rail-thin body of a teen. The helpful salesclerk said the waist could be taken in without a problem. It could be done within the hour. Lucien saw his father hesitate.

"Mom could do it?" Lucien suggested. He really wanted the nice slacks.

"Your mother is not at home." Alex acquiesced to the clerk.

On the mezzanine level they proceeded through the cafeteria line at Piccadilly Circus restaurant, boys in front. They secured a table by the railing, and Frank occupied himself observing the early evening activity on the first floor.

Sitting across the table from his father, Lucien asked, "Papa? Why don't you think the strike at White Eagle is a good idea?" He watched Alex's face.

"Labor actions don't end well. People get hurt. Things can happen."

"Is mother in danger?"

"Possibly."

"How so?"

Alex recounted to his sons a seldom-told story of his life in Russian-occupied Poland. He had traveled for a month to reach St. Petersburg, the beautiful and cultured port city on the Baltic Sea.

Along the way he'd survived by hunting and selling game in villages. On the last leg of his journey he followed the Neva River into St. Petersburg. Exhausted and dirty, he wedged himself behind a column on the side of the even-then historic Narva Gate, the entrance to the tsar's Winter Palace. Attempting to dispel muscle kinks earned by sleeping on the ground, he stretched his back against the hard stone wall. He would allow himself a short nap, his rifle tucked up under his arm, then find a public *banya*. After making himself presentable, he would find work. He needed a good deal more to pay for his passage to America.

"I didn't know how I was going to get to America, but I knew that I would."

"How come?" Frank asked.

"I couldn't stay. People were starving. There was no food. An inept tsar bankrupted the country in a foolish war with Japan. We tried to farm on land where even weeds wouldn't grow. In the factories you might as well've been a slave. There was nothing there for me. Or anyone."

Distant singing had roused him from sleep. Church songs were accompanied by the low rumbling of a crowd marching, boots stamping and sloshing through snow. From the other direction inside the palace square he'd heard a staccato clickety-clack of horse hooves on the pavement punctuated by gruff commands spewing forth from those in charge. The Cossacks sat tall in their saddles. Pride in their military heritage dripped from the tips of their black boots and bubbled up through the tops of their cylindrical wool *papakha* hats.

"What's a *papakha*—" Lucien stopped his brother's interruption with a swift kick under the table. When Frank looked up, Lucien shook his head no. He could see their father had sunk deep into memory. The sharp blue eyes had turned opaque. He'd switched to Polish, peppered with Russian. A woman behind him bumped his chair and excused herself. He took no notice.

Louder and louder, the rumble from outside the gate and the roar from inside the gate converged, about to crash like cymbals.

NOT YET LOST

He peered from his burrow behind the columns. A mass of people, thousands strong, approached. Families, including children, followed behind a priest in Eastern Orthodox garb, arms outstretched with sleeves billowing. Crosses held high danced with pictures of Tsar Nicholas II above the heads of the crowd. A dozen Cossacks astride their stallions exited Narva Gate, mimicking the sculpted warrior horses crowning the arch. The priest read from a paper in his hand. He beseeched the officer high above on his steed. The horse's breath steamed in the frigid air.

"I'd never been so cold. I remember how I ached to lean against that horse's warm flanks." Alex rubbed his long white fingers together as if treating frostbite.

"What did the priest want, Papa?" Frank asked, wide-eyed and curious. Lucien glared at his younger brother, but their father was back in the present, for the moment.

"The priest asked for some very basic things for the people. To improve conditions for factory workers."

"You mean like Mama and her friends are now?" Frank asked.

"Yes. Exactly."

"What happened? How did it end up?" Lucien still sought to understand his father's opposition, the connection to the present eluding him.

The Russian officer kicked the priest's hand, raised his own in the air, and shouted a command. Decisively, his arm dropped to his side. Horses exploded through the gate by the hundreds, their riders shooting, clubbing, and slicing with abandon. Men, women, children, crosses, and pictures of the tsar blanketed the street. Blood ran. The marchers, the workers, never reached the Winter Palace.

"It's just like what happened in Dearborn a few years ago when Ford's men shot into the crowd near the bridge. They were marching to get their jobs back." Lucien referenced an event dubbed the "Hunger March" by the press. He'd been young but remembered the uproar in the community. His father met his eyes with a puzzled look as if seeing a stranger. Lucien adjusted his posture, sitting a bit taller, two men discussing worldly matters.

"What did you do then?" Frank slurped his chocolate pudding. Lucien watched his father retreat inside again.

He walked among the carnage of the massacre. No time for sentimentality. Pockets of the dead yielded a meager harvest but worth the effort nonetheless. Hopscotching over the limp and moaning, he spotted an expired Cossack, one of the unlucky few of the Imperial Security Force. Wasting no time, he dragged the fallen soldier by the armpits behind a bosque of birch at the road's edge. The soldier might have fallen from his horse and been trampled by the crowd, judging by the head injuries. He pulled the high boots off the man, taking a moment to appreciate the leather's suppleness, then started to strip him. Naked, thin, and white, he blended with the winter trunks of the birch trees as he slipped into the Cossack's uniform, replete with a black felt overcoat. He relished the warmth. Now, with saber in hand, his lineage had changed.

"So, you see, then I was no longer a mud-slopping slave. In uniform I could be descended from the mighty Caucasian Cossacks. I could join the Imperial Forces." Alex resurfaced.

"Why would you want to? They sound awful."

"I didn't think. It was impulsive. All I saw was an opportunity. A chance at something. A way out."

Lucien had forgotten to eat his chocolate cake.

"Finish up. Your slacks should be ready now."

"How come you never told us any of this?" Lucien took large bites of his dessert.

"It was a long time ago."

"You can't forget something like that. Did they make you do terrible things?" Lucien challenged his father. His father was not affectionate, cold even, but riding with Cossacks?

"No. You can't forget. It was a high price I paid to get to Canada, then America. Even now, people I knew there haunt me. Let's go." Alex rose.

Lucien and Frank would never hear the real ending to the story their father told.

The soldier's head flopped from one side to the other and a moan oozed from his lips. Without a thought Aleksander took his farm-worn knife from his belt and slaughtered the soldier. For as many animals as Aleks had vanquished since he was a young boy, he could never tolerate the moaning.

On the way out of the cafeteria a man caught Alex's arm. He tipped his hat three times. Alex pulled some bills from his pocket and handed them to Lucien.

"Get your slacks and meet me out front."

CHAPTER 22

Thursday, March 18, 1937

Daybreak found tranquility at the cigar factory. Florence basked in its richness. Rough blankets provided by strike supporters compared poorly to her feathered *pierzyna*. The narrow cot, hovering close to the floor, couldn't rival even her worn sofa. Yet she luxuriated in these early hours in a bounty of a different kind, affirming her decision to stay. The community of women had created their own life rhythms. Florence relished the extravagance of not rushing to cook breakfast, pack lunches, shoo the boys off to school, hurry to work. For over three weeks now she had woken to quiet sounds of creaking cots, murmuring, dreamy utterances, and, of course, snoring. As hard as they tried to clear tobacco dust and resin from the air, the nasty irritants clung with dogged resolution. Particles infiltrated their lungs with each breath.

Bang! Bang, bang! Bang, bang, bang!

Pounding on the metal lockers lining the hallway. Florence identified the sound, but who? A thunderous wave of noise rolled through the doorway. Harsh voices amplified by megaphones directed them to move out. Women's screams joined the fracas.

"They must've broken through back!" Basia yelled as she shoved her feet into her shoes. The women, still half asleep, clamored for their clothes and shoes. Garments flew every which way as the women tried to cover themselves. A torrent of police officers in wide-belted, long, blue jackets barged onto the factory floor. Gun barrels and billy clubs swung wildly through the air. The uniformed marauders herded the women toward the front doors.

"Game's up!"

"Get going. This is private property."

"You girls should be at home."

The men trampled the cots with little regard for the belongings surrounding them. Most of the workers bolted for the door and were pushed and shoved from behind to squeeze through the narrow exit. Like herding cattle, a few policemen rounded up the stragglers. Once outside, the stupefied strikers huddled in small groups, trying to understand what just happened. Florence had held onto Basia as they were expelled outside. Now she looked to her for direction.

Basia's line of sight rested on the group of law enforcement and men in suits across the street. Florence observed them too.

"Make a chain! Make a chain!" Following Basia's direction, Florence linked arms with her on the right and another woman on the left.

"What good will this do? They're already inside," she shouted.

"I don't know. We must hold each other dear. Stay together," Basia commanded.

Before long, Stanley Nowak and a group of supporters arrived, as they had for several mornings now, to show solidarity. They inserted themselves as links in the human chain. Nowak tucked himself on the other side of her, with Florence bookended by the two vociferous labor leaders.

"I'm sorry we weren't here earlier. Others are coming too. What happened?" Nowak asked, leaning across Florence to address Basia. Florence peppered in tidbits as her friend recounted the shocking event.

"The others will be here soon, including Mary Zuk," Nowak stated. "We can relieve anyone who needs to leave. You've been through a lot."

"No turning back now," stated Basia. Florence, as always, smiled at her friend's fortitude.

Throughout the morning, the strikers and their opponents across the street exchanged words. Chants and songs were met with orders and directives, summarily ignored. Women from the strike kitchen distributed hot drinks, often simple hot water, but welcomed just the same. Late in the morning, pieces of rye bread spread with lard were passed down the line. Periodically, Nowak walked the line, assessing the welfare of each human link. Some were sent home if they felt weak or ill. They were asked to try and send a replacement. Mary did the same.

Florence silently said the prayers of the rosary, pressing her fingers on the buttons of the adjacent sleeves as beads. She listened as Basia and Nowak yelled, chanted, and made plans. Gray clouds finally revealed the soft-edged sun in its decline. The factories would be letting out soon unless there was enough work to stay late. The school day would end. Florence hoped the boys or Alex would come see the predicament. The changing timbre of the chatter from across the street hooked her attention.

Schwarz strutted toward the policeman in charge. Miller followed. Resnick followed Miller, his hands in his pockets, shuffling, his head down. Florence noted Basia and Nowak had seen them arrive too. After a brief conversation between the factory owner and law enforcement, Schwarz commandeered a megaphone.

"You've been illegally trespassing on my property. Effective immediately, you are all fired. You have no reason to be here. Any further occupation will have consequences. Of that, you can be sure."

"Stay in place, stay strong!" Nowak yelled. The directive was repeated up and down the line.

Not long after the factory whistle heralded the end of the day shift, Romek's bearlike figure ambled up the street. He hugged Basia in greeting.

"You crazy woman, you! You're something else!"

"I agree wholeheartedly." Nowak shook hands with Romek.

"May I?" Romek linked himself into the chain between his wife and Florence.

"How are you holding up, Flo? You, too, crazy, right here with her. And I couldn't be prouder." He squeezed both their hands.

"It's getting late. I think everyone's fading. I'm going to talk to them. See if we can get somewhere." Nowak broke the chain and crossed the street.

Other men and teens joined the chain or replaced women who wanted to leave. Stephan, Anushka's fiancé, waved from down the line.

"Romek, how're things at my house? Have you seen?" Florence asked her neighbor.

"I think the boys've been going to Dom Polski. Several women supervise the children after school. They help with homework. It doesn't hurt that old man Kowalski donates cookies and honey cakes."

"Have you seen Alex?"

"I'm sure he's been busy at work. I think he eats at Wally's while the boys are at Dom Polski."

"Hmm. I hope the boys are eating."

"I think they are. I know Alex took them out to dinner and to get some new clothes the other night. I heard they even went to Hudson's."

"That's good. That's very good." She was relieved. Possibly Alex might be connecting more with the boys. That might be a good outcome from the strike, if nothing else.

"Look! Nowak's coming back," Romek bellowed with hopeful excitement.

As he came nearer, Nowak shook his head. "No go. Nothing. Won't concede an inch."

"What're we going to do?" Florence rubbed her hands together. "We can't stay out here all night."

"I don't know yet. I must leave now for the radio show. I'll be back."

Another hour passed. The chain grew shorter. Streetlights turned on. Across the street Schwarz and the police talked and talked. Packett, the police chief, was now on the scene.

Sirens sounded from both directions of the street. More police cars amassed, pulling off onto the sidewalks. Looming behind them came fire trucks. The red behemoths inched toward the center. The fire chief hopped out of the command vehicle and conferred with Packett. Ladders unfolded from the trucks as if levitated by the chief's command. Schwarz, Miller, and Packett huddled. All three had stogies hanging out of their mouths. Resnick was nowhere to be seen.

A cream-colored Cadillac limousine separated the crowd of spectators that had gathered on the far side of the street. The mayor emerged from the rear door. He was tall, thin, and topped with a pearl gray felt fedora wrapped in a matching Petersham ribbon hat band. He consulted with Packett. In a short while, the mayor, smoking a trendy new cigarette, returned to his car and was whisked away by his chauffeur.

In an unusual spectacle, Chief Packett climbed a ladder extending from a fire engine. Firemen hastened to unreel the hoses from their berths. Packett hung from the ladder like a military band director on a perch. He surveyed the firemen lined up with hoses over their right shoulders, bronze nozzles cradled between their hands.

"One last chance. Clear out of here immediately. We will remove you forcibly if we have to." Packett dropped his megaphone to his side.

The women looked at one another, murmuring, uncertain. Florence searched the perimeter for signs of Nowak. She tightened her grip on Romek. Basia stepped forward.

"I'm not afraid of you," Basia shouted. "Turn your hoses on us, your guns. We will *not* be silenced." Basia waved the others forward to join her.

Packett's arm extended straight up as if in salute to the sky. Decisively, his arm dropped to his side. Freezing water spewed from hose nozzles and pummeled the protesters. People ran for cover, screaming in shock. Both the bruising force and the frigid water temperature thrashed and scourged the women. Basia took another step forward, her balled fist reaching high. "We're *not* afraid of you!"

Florence screamed when the awning over a picture window collapsed. A window down the way shattered.

Basia stood until the punishing force of the water knocked her off her feet. She rose. A fireman targeted her. She fell again. Romek, who'd been tending to the injured, picked his wife up from the slushy sidewalk.

"I'm sorry, my love, it's time to go home."

"I won't leave. Not now." Basia stood again with her fist in the air. Her chest heaved up and down. She held her rib cage. No words came out of her mouth. Others uncurled from their cowed positions and stepped to Basia's side. Most—drenched, hurt, and humiliated—fled.

Florence rattled the double front doors of the factory. Locked. All the open windows were high up and out of reach. She searched among the wreckage on the sidewalk. She picked up one sopping wet blanket after the other, abandoned by women fleeing for their lives. Her wet, bare legs stung. The wound on her calf from the smoke bomb seared with pain. She needed to get a dry blanket for Basia, or she would catch her death of cold. She pounced upon a stray metal pole, a broken appendage of a protest sign, and beat on the door lock. Changing tactics, she tried to insert the rod between the doors. Maybe she could pry them open. The rod didn't fit. With two hands and every ounce of ferocity she possessed, Florence railed on the doors with the rod. It wasn't until Father Maletski clasped her shoulders that she stopped. He wrapped her in both his dry coat and an embrace. She let him. She fell against his chest and sobbed.

"Father, you'll see she gets home?" Romek approached, his shirt-sleeves wet and bloody.

"Of course."

"I'm going to the police station. They arrested Basia."

CHAPTER 23

Thursday, March 18, 1937

Once inside the tiny vestibule of her home, Florence handed the priest's coat back to him.

"You're a brave woman, Mrs. Falkowski. Take care of yourself and let me know if you need any help."

"Thank you." Florence shut the door and leaned her forehead against it for just a moment. She turned and saw Alex sitting in the front room, an open newspaper on his lap.

"Hello, Alex."

"You're a fine sight! What happened to you?" Alex laid the paper on the ottoman.

"It was awful, Alex! They broke into the factory, and then outside they turned the fire hoses on us. People were screaming and sirens—" Florence cupped her hands around her ears. She rushed to hug Alex.

"You'd better get cleaned up." Alex sidestepped the embrace, wasting no time dismissing her. She was stunned.

"Where're the boys?" Florence surveyed the front room, so familiar, yet a memory.

"Frank's at Dom Polski. I don't know where Lucien is. I'm going to Wally's for dinner. If you'll excuse me."

Florence stepped aside so he could access the coat closet. In a moment, he was out the front door and gone. She hadn't expected a hero's welcome, but this? She went upstairs, retrieved her bathrobe, and went into the bathroom. Pushing aside the shower curtain, she saw the dirty ring around the tub. Her knees gave way, and she collapsed on the commode. Wild sobs echoed off the surrounding tile. She doubled over, arms crossed over her stomach. The pain so real. Everything lost. Alex. Her job. The fight. Her torso straightened, and she howled toward the ceiling, unrestrained and unabashed. A deluge of sorrow gushed from her soul. Reverberating wails engulfed her, and she reeled with vertigo.

"Mama? Mama? Are you all right? *Mama!*" The door handle rattled. "*Mama! Answer me!*"

Florence gulped and sobbed. Taking a minute, she took control of her agony. Lucien continued to beseech her. She hadn't heard him come home. She inhaled before answering, though her hands shook with tremors.

"I'm fine, dear. I'm really fine. I just got home. I'm going to bathe now. I'll be down soon, and we can talk." She heard his reluctant feet descend the stairs.

Florence willed herself to stand, then cleaned the tub, sink, and commode with supplies kept under the sink. While hot water filled the tub, she assessed her reflection. A tangled nest of gray-tinged brown hair perched on her head, Medusa-like tendrils reaching out at random. Tobacco dust entrenched in the furrows of her skin made her face appear wooden, carved and burned in relief. She washed her face repeatedly in the sink. When she immersed herself in the tub, her taut body began to unbind. She drained and filled the tub twice more, once to scrub with a washcloth and once to soak. Her muscles eased but her mind and soul remained snarled. She couldn't linger, so she extricated herself from her tiny vestige of comfort—the most she'd experienced in weeks—then dressed and proceeded to the kitchen.

"Mama, I've made us tea." Lucien gestured in grand fashion at the table. The floral oilcloth covering had been laid with cups, saucers, a steaming teapot, some pickles, toast, and farmer's cheese. An odd assortment, as there must be little food in the house.

"Mama?" Frank hesitated in the doorway, just returning from Dom Polski.

"Come here and give me a hug!"

"Are you home for good?" Frank nestled close to her.

"Yes, I'm home now. How I missed you!"

"Mama, I think this might help." Lucien pulled a hip flask from his pocket. "Brandy. It'll warm you up."

She gave her son the requisite stink eye but nonetheless accepted his proffered flask. Cup and saucer rattled against each other in her still jittery hands. "Now put that away!" she scolded her son. The front door opened with a slight groan, a result of the damp weather. She expected Alex, but it was her brother, Joe.

"I'm surprised to see you," Florence said as her brother planted a kiss on her head.

"How *are* you?"

"Maybe a little worse for wear." A small smile crept onto her face. "I won't deny it's good to be home."

Joe greeted his nephews and proceeded to unpack the bag of groceries he'd set on the kitchen table.

"These two have been swell soldiers while you were away. Just swell." Joe assembled sandwiches of Krakow ham on rye dressed with horseradish sauce. The four were quiet. Joe pensive, Lucien's gaze latched onto his mother's face, Frank gobbling down his sandwich, and Florence spent.

"Uncle Joe took us to the show last Saturday. Laurel and Hardy. It was really keen," Frank piped up.

Joe ruffled his nephew's hair. "Now I need to talk to your mother, so why don't you boys go upstairs and do your homework. Lucien, I'm sure Flo won't mind if you listen to the radio in your parents' room." Over the years, Joe had garnered the boys' affection. She was glad. He was like their own mother.

Brother and sister relocated to the front room, carrying their drinks and plates.

"*O, Boże!* What happened here?" Florence observed the wood covering up the picture window and the small shards of glass pinned into the carpet.

"That's part of what I want to talk to you about." After starting a fire in the fireplace, Joe perched in one of the wingback chairs near the boarded-up window. Florence plopped on the sofa. Uncharacteristically, she put her feet up on the coffee table.

"It's about Alex. Something's going on. He may be in some kind of trouble." Florence heard rustling at the top of the stairs.

"*Parles français.*" Florence rolled her eyes upward to direct her brother's attention to the stairs where she guessed at least Lucien would be listening.

"He's been acting very strange while you've been gone. He's often out at night. A few times he's come home with the smell of gunpowder on his clothes. You know I try to make myself scarce. Well, with you gone, I've been home more. For the boys."

"He went to the gun club that time with that boss of his. You know him, Fred? He's probably going there to shoot." She wanted to defend her husband.

"I'm not sure. At work he's been strange too. The guys've been asking me about him. He's often called upstairs to the offices. There's rumor of a promotion, but nothing yet."

"A promotion? Alex would be so pleased." She swung her feet off the table and sat forward on the edge of the couch.

"Romek was here when that happened." Joe gestured at the boarded-up window. "Someone threw a rock."

"Do they know who?"

"No. A car pulled away right after, so probably wasn't kids. I was upstairs. I don't think Alex realized I was home, and I knew to stay out of his way. Whoever it was, the way they squealed the tires made me think a message was being sent." Joe's warm brown eyes held steady.

"But who? What message?"

Joe shared his theories. The union-organizing activity at the factory was becoming intense. Men were jockeying for position. Paranoia ran rampant. Workers didn't know who was for and who was against. Who was a communist and who was a spy.

"You know how Alex is. That chip on his shoulder. Acts like he's better than everybody else."

Florence lowered her eyes. She knew her brother spoke the truth. She was all too familiar with her husband's foibles. "But he *is* so clever. So intelligent. He could run that factory."

"I know that. And I should be an electrical engineer. That's not our world. See, because he's so aloof and the bosses talk to him all the time, people suspect he's spying for the company."

"He'd never!" Indignation was her first reaction. Would he?

"After the window was broken, Alex argued with Romek. He blamed Romek for stirring up trouble." Joe moved over to sit next to his sister on the couch. "And he said some not-so-nice things about Basia."

"I see."

"There's something else. There's talk about town. I don't know for sure how true this is, but there's rumor of a secret society. A vigilante group. Maybe Alex—"

"*O, Boże!* Now you're really talking nonsense. Alex join a society? No, thank you. That's not something he would do." Florence was running on adrenaline. This gibberish was all so confusing. A secret society? She couldn't think it through.

"Maybe so. I'm still worried. There's a strong undercurrent running through Alex. Always has been. It was best you never told Maman and Papa about his real background. Who he truly was in Russia. I guess now we should call it Poland. It's been almost twenty years now. Hard to believe."

"*C'est vrai.* Maman and Papa, they saw a hardworking young man with aspirations of living a cultured life."

"And he saw that cultured life in you. Let me get some more wood to stoke this fire."

While Joe fetched the wood, Florence considered the beginning of her journey with Alex. It was 1915 in Montreal, Quebec. She worked at her parents' grocery store after the school day at the prestigious girls' school, Congrégation de Notre Dame. Handsome and hardworking, Alex was hired on at the store after having been a meat supplier. The courtship had been quick, and though her parents worried about the ten-year age difference, they approved a marriage upon her graduation.

Joe shuttled in and out with armload after armload of chopped wood. On his last trip he picked up the brandy bottle from which Lucien swiped for his flask and topped off Florence's teacup.

"Joe, do you remember when Alex caught me sketching him at the store?"

Her brother chuckled. "*Mais, oui!* You were so embarrassed. You made up an improbable story about an art project for school. You were so lovestruck. And young."

Florence and her brother talked of those days growing up in a bygone world. Maman had hoped Florence would marry into Montreal high society. Their papa emigrated from occupied Poland to Montreal and found kinship, or at least familiarity, in Alex. The door to America was no longer wide open to Eastern Europeans. Restrictions applied. Many took a detour through Canada. On the cusp of the 1920s the magnetic pull of Detroit's promise of prosperity and modernity triumphed. She and Alex crossed into Vermont illegally.

Her brother indulged her recollections, for which she was grateful. So rarely did she speak of herself or reflect on who she was or who she'd become.

"Alex was my white knight in a pauper's visage. Even in his work clothes he looked and behaved like a prince."

"He still does. Which is what causes him trouble at the factory." Florence set her cup and saucer on the table. Joe's harsh comments extracted her from her dreamy remembrances.

"I just want you to talk to him and get to the bottom of it. I'm afraid he's carrying a burden all on his own. And I'm afraid of trouble for you, Florrie." She softened at her brother's use of her childhood nickname.

"Do you still love him?" asked Joe.

"I understand him. What more can we ask for in the here and now?" She met her brother's questioning eyes.

"You're exhausted. You should go to bed." Florence rose and reached for the dishes. Joe put a hand on her arm. "I'll clean up."

She shuffled up the stairs. Once beneath her feather *pierzyna*, she was down for the count.

CHAPTER 24

Friday, March 19, 1937

The alarm yanked Florence from the deep abyss of sleep. Alex rustled around to silence it. She'd not been aware of him. Remaining still, she moderated her breathing to feign sleep, not yet ready to face him. He dressed and left. He'd probably get breakfast from one of the food trucks in the factory parking lot. She counted the footsteps going downstairs and the number of times the outside door opened and closed.

"Frank, come on! We'll be late. I'll pack our lunches." Lucien was trying so hard to be grown up. She smiled underneath the quilt, which was pulled up almost over her head. Once the house was hers, she descended in her bathrobe to the kitchen. She ate bread and ham left over from the night before while the coffee percolated. What to do? What to do? If she wasn't going to go to work, she supposed she would go to the market and clean house. She started to make a list with a pencil stub on the back of a church bulletin, now a month old. If she didn't have a job, she would need to be frugal. Potatoes for latkes, sauerkraut, maybe a small pork shoulder she could shred and stretch, or pig's feet. Another shrill bell startled her. The phone rang. She roused herself from the kitchen table to answer the phone in the hall. "Hello?"

"Good morning, Mrs. Falkowski. This is Margaret Nowak calling on behalf of Stanley."

"Yes, of course! What can I help you with?" It was unusual for the wife of the labor organizer to call.

"I'm calling everyone I can reach from the cigar factory to see if they want to return to work."

"I don't know." Florence paused for a moment. Then she realized she still clutched the old church bulletin with her market list scribbled on it. "Yes. Yes, I do want my job."

"Good. Stanley plans to meet with the owners this afternoon. He's confident he can pave the way for everyone to come back."

"If anyone can do it, he can. You have a wonderful husband. Thank you, Mrs. Nowak."

"Unless you hear otherwise, plan on going to work Monday. Please listen to the radio show tonight. He'll announce if anything changes."

After pouring another cup of coffee, Florence returned to the kitchen table and her list. Now she wrote fast and furiously. For the third time a shrill bell assaulted her ears. Once again she answered the phone.

"Florence, it's Romek. I was hoping you'd be home."

"Tell me everything." She sat down on the petite chair next to the hall table.

Romek recounted the scene at the jail. The arrested women had been crammed into a cell with wooden planks lining the concrete walls. The guards wouldn't let anyone in for the longest time. He knew Basia must be freezing. All the women from the factory who'd been arrested huddled together for warmth. There were others from other factories too. Romek told how, as the evening turned to night, other women from the streets were brought in. Panhandlers, drunks.

"You get the idea," Romek said. "When one new person was booked, one of our women was released. I waited and waited. No Basia. Finally, I demanded to see her. By then it was late. The night guard didn't care, so he let me in. But it took more hours until they let her out. We took a cab home this morning. Just at dawn."

"*Boże!* How is she?"

"Sleeping. Exhausted. She was shivering so bad. I couldn't warm her up, so I put extra blankets on the bed." Romek's voice cracked, just a little.

"Romek, you've been up all night. You should go sleep beside her. Let her know you're there. Be warm for her. You need sleep too. It's been quite an ordeal."

"Unimaginable. We came here for this." She knew he meant moving from Poland.

"I don't know if it will make you feel better or not, but Stanley Nowak's making sure we keep our jobs. We're to go to work Monday unless we hear different on his show tonight."

"Bah! She's not going back. I don't know if I'll ever let her go back."

"She'll want to go back. She'll want to prove she's not beaten."

"Florence, you're a dear friend."

Florence rung off with a promise to stop by after going to the market. Even without work, she had a busy day ahead, so she had better start.

Her next problem to tackle would be Alex.

CHAPTER 25

Monday, March 22, 1937

Florence followed the well-worn steps like a daily breakfast dance across the maroon and putty linoleum floor: ice box, stove, table. This morning her steps plodded like a funeral dirge rather than a mazurka. She scooped up the breakfast sausage on the first beat, shook it on the second and third, and on the fourth placed it on Alex's plate. She almost tripped over the polished work boots at the end of his extended long legs. Today would be the first day back at work. A church calendar hung on the wall. She checked it to confirm it really had been a full month since they'd sat down in the factory refusing to work.

Alex hid behind the open newspaper, enabling her to scan the headlines. Nothing about the factories or the firehoses. After all, cigar companies advertised extensively in the newspapers. Coffee percolated in the tin pot on the stove. Using her apron as a hot pad, Florence poured the fragrant brew into a cup from their wedding set. It was a cup, once broken, which she had painstakingly repaired. She paused to reach for another, then decided to serve this one to Alex. They'd settled into a lukewarm truce.

She hauled herself up the stairs and knocked on the boys' bedroom door before opening it a few inches. Once certain they were awake, she reminded them to get to school on time and not to dawdle. Florence washed the dishes, making circles with the dish rag more times than necessary. She placed her lunch in her canvas tote bag. On her way to the back door, she first kissed her fingers and touched the cheek of the painted Black Madonna hanging in the hallway. This morning she hesitated, looking—really looking—at the replica of the revered icon. Two slashes on the lady's right cheek and one at her throat were inflicted by aspiring conquerors of Poland. The original painting was never able to be repaired. She inhaled sharply and brought her hand to her mouth. She realized the cuts she'd seen on Basia's cheek yesterday resembled those on the Madonna's painted visage. Hopefully, Basia's wounds would heal.

The morning routine resembled hundreds of others. She paused at the end of the path to the alley where she usually waited for Basia. Today she would need to walk alone. She crossed herself again and prayed for Basia's health to be restored. In the melee at the cigar factory, Basia had incurred cuts and bruises. Now, in the aftermath, she suffered from a severe head and chest cold.

With no companion Florence walked several blocks in silence. Then she rounded the corner at the mid-rise apartments and saw her neighbor, Delores, a widow since her husband died in an industrial accident. She had been evicted and now stood alone, curbside, among her furniture and other belongings. Florence stopped and greeted her with a simple "Hello" since there was nothing good about this morning.

"Delores. What're you going to do now?"

"I'll stay at the rectory until my cousin gets here from Pennsylvania. He'll take me east. Maybe I'll go back Poland. Not so good for me here."

"I'm sorry. I wish we could've done more."

"Not your fault. We do what we can." Delores opened and closed each drawer of the furniture pieces on the curb. She reached way in, ensuring nothing of value remained.

"You couldn't sell this?" Florence ran her hand over the top of a chest of drawers.

"Nobody buys now. Everybody sell."

"I'm buying! I need a chest for one of our rooms." She rummaged in her handbag, then pressed a bill into Delores's hand. "I'll send my boys to get it."

"*Na zdrowie.*" Delores blinked back the tears as she blessed Florence.

"*Powodzenia!*" Florence hugged Delores.

"Good luck to you too."

Florence was halfway down the block before she heard Delores yell.

"And give 'em hell!"

Florence turned, smiled, and waved before continuing toward the factory. Poor Delores. Emigrating to America failed her miserably, as it had so many. What would she do if Alex were killed or maimed in an accident at work? Return to Montreal and work at her parents' grocery store? Though that presented its own problems. Fortunately, Alex focused on his work. She'd heard from others he didn't often join in the banter and hijinks pervasive on the factory floor. To alleviate boredom the men created diversions. At least for safety's sake, Alex's aloofness was an asset. He acted and moved deliberately, even at home. He may be right, thinking home ownership bought your freedom. No one could pull the rug out and alter the whole course of your life.

"*O, Boże!*" She stopped. Denuded awning frames jutted out from the factory's brick facade, skeletons that had provided shape to the forest-green canvas. Remnants of fabric, ripped and torn, hung limp, defeated. Plywood panels shrouded window openings. Just three days ago, water blasted from fire hoses had shattered the glass. Had it really all happened? Minute glass shards glinted in the crevices of the sidewalk. Hunched women shuffled toward the alley that led to the employee entrance. Straightening her shoulders, she joined the flow through the vestibule to the hallway lined with lockers.

"Florence!" Women huddled around her, spewing inquiries.

"How are you?"

"How's Basia?"

"Did she really spend the night in jail?"

"Is she coming to work today?"

Florence donned her battered, yet serviceable, oxfords after drying her feet with a rag she kept in her locker. She removed the layers between her cotton dress and the moth-eaten wool overcoat.

"I'm all right. Basia did spend the night in jail and she's sick. So, no, she's not coming to work today. Romek's taking good care of her." She shared the detailed update Romek had provided her the day before, and the women were relieved Basia was home. They proceeded to organize themselves for the workday.

Florence paused in the doorway from the locker hallway to the workroom. The cots were gone. Nowak's people must have removed them to take to another sit-down strike. Worktables were once again organized in stripes across the floor. A heap of clothing, books, hairbrushes, socks, shoes, and blankets occupied the far corner of the room. The items had been tossed with little decorum, abandoned in a forlorn and messy heap. A small ray of the morning sun pierced through the dull resin-coated windows. The light zeroed in on a shiny object in the heap. Florence marched toward it and retrieved her knitting needles. As she strode toward her worktable, her blue and pink yarn trailed behind her, connecting her to the pile as if by an umbilical cord. The baptismal cap she'd been knitting dragged across the floor, forging a trail through dust and dirt. Scraps, Resnick's dog, snatched it between his teeth. Resnick snickered.

"You got a joke you want to tell us, Mr. Resnick?" Florence turned the tables using his oft-repeated phrase as she pinched the dog's jaw to reclaim her needlework. She set up her workstation and surveyed the room. About three-quarters of the workers had returned. Had Margaret been able to reach them all? Her eyes landed on the empty chair in front of her: Basia's. She headed toward the trough of leaves to fill her basket. Resnick blocked the aisle.

"Where's your friend, *Mrs.* Sikorski? Too afraid to come back to work?" He folded his arms and arched an eyebrow.

"Bah! She's not afraid of you or anyone else." Florence squeezed her way past him. At the trough her practiced hands selected the best leaves by second nature as she stacked them in her basket. She pushed past Resnick while returning in the aisle. "She'll be back. If for no other reason than to spite you." She dropped the full basket on her table.

The morning dragged on until the women shuffled into the lunchroom. Florence shared her usual bottle of vodka for handwashing. Lunches were meager. Weeks of no pay had cost the families dearly. Women complained about their maladies and soreness. Some were silent. Florence felt lost without Basia.

"That's it, lunch break's over. You got a lotta work to make up."

Irena, sitting next to Florence, started to rise. Florence put her hand on her arm, signaling to remain seated.

"No, *Mr.* Resnick, lunch break is *not* over. Is it, ladies? We will sit until one o'clock." Was that her voice speaking?

"But you have to—"

"Anushka, dear, tell us about your wedding plans." Florence's voice, loud and overexaggerated, surprised even herself. Pairs and threes of women followed suit. One after the other asked their neighbor a question.

"Have you heard from your brother in Poland?"

"What are you preparing for dinner tonight?"

"I heard you're sewing new vestments for the priest?"

Resnick stood at the door for a few minutes watching, mouth agape. Florence felt him staring at her, but she willed herself not to look. Soon a flicker of movement caught her eye. She stole a glance—he was gone. Voices relaxed. Artifice dribbled away, and conversations normalized. At three minutes to one o'clock, Florence rose and tidied her area.

"It's almost one o'clock. Let's go back to work." Shoulders back, head held high, she walked out of the lunchroom straight to her workstation. Irena and the others followed her as if she had commanded "forward march." What sustenance they lacked from their lunches was compensated for with their well-fed pride. Pockets of chatter sprung up like spring crocuses, lightening the morning's somber mood by a few shades. Resnick sulked in his office. Production picked up speed. Pay was still based on piecework after all, although—fingers crossed—that would change soon.

Florence fumbled a bit with the leaves. After a month, movements that had been second nature felt foreign. She stopped rolling and stretched her fingers. Along the edge of her worktable, as if it were a piano, she silently played a Chopin piece. Her knobby knuckles prevented her from adequately spanning the pretend keys, and she cringed at the imaginary dissonance. She'd forgiven Alex's many trespasses over the years, but selling her piano remained a burr in her waistband. At least she could play at Dom Polski. Four o'clock. She looked at the modest pile in her rack. She'd better hop to it.

"Good afternoon, *Damski*," Father Maletski greeted the group. He removed his hat as he entered the room, followed by Mr. Nowak. Resnick bolted from his office.

Resnick confronted the new arrivals. "What business do you men have here?"

Nowak spoke.

"We're here to escort our friends and neighbors home." Nowak stood, hat in hand.

"They're not going home yet. They have a lot of work to catch up on after their little event."

"Ah, but Mr. Resnick, you don't know what you don't know," Father Maletski said.

"We've been upstairs meeting with your uncle. He understands the hardship these women endure trying to work late, rush to stores, prepare dinner," Nowak said.

"Not to mention worrying about the whereabouts of their children," Father Maletski interjected.

"In the spirit of cooperation, and to avoid further 'events,' as you call them, we agreed to end the workday at five o'clock." Nowak said it as if he were announcing the streetcar schedule. "Time to go home now."

Sounds of chair legs scraping across the floor muffled excited whispers. The women hurried to clean up their workstations. The men walked on, straight past Resnick. The men helped the women gather their things and led them out.

Florence considered going to Kowalski's Delicatessen but wasn't sure she had enough money after buying the chest of drawers. If she didn't bring some meat home, Alex might berate her for the loss of income during the strike. She'd find another way to scrimp. Once at the deli, she perused the meat case. Selecting the smallest pork shoulder, she planned meatballs with breadcrumbs and leftover rice. At least leaving work at a reasonable hour would afford her time to grind the meat. She reveled in the normalcy of preparing a meal in her own kitchen.

The mushroom sauce started to burn. Not again! Where was everybody? The front door opened with the wind of a typhoon. Lucien swung around the door frame into the kitchen.

"They sat down! Mama, they sat down! Papa's there inside. He must be. I can't find him anywhere."

"*Boże!* What're you saying?" She moved out of Lucien's way so he could reach the radio. The farm report blared through the speaker. They would wait for the news.

"At the plant. They started a sit-down strike. Just like you did! They won't leave. The cops are there." Lucien snatched a meatball from the casserole dish that sat on the warming burner. Florence sat on the corner of the banquette, wrapping her hand in her apron. She couldn't imagine Alex enduring a sit-down strike. Lucien reached for another meatball.

"Go wash up and get your brother. It's time to eat." She began to lay out the table. Alex wasn't well-liked at the factory. If he stayed in, would the men bully him? Though he was a hard man to bully. Maybe the men would get to know him if he let them. The camaraderie in the cigar factory had been inspiring, the knit of the community pulled tighter. Would it be the same?

"Mama, Luc said Papa is locked in the factory. Is it true?"

"We don't know for sure. We'll have to wait and see. I just don't know." The boys devoured their food. She didn't bother to correct their manners. The front door opened and shut.

"Florrie, just me." It was her brother, Joe. She stood to greet him as he entered the kitchen.

"Come, eat with us. Tell us what's new."

"Alex isn't coming home for dinner?" Joe asked.

"I don't know. He can eat a sandwich. Sit." Florence filled Joe's plate.

"I was at the factory and—"

"The factory? Why were you there after the way they treated you? Firing you to make an example."

"Romek thought I should go. Still be an example, I suppose, of what shouldn't happen. Besides, I've got to support the men. I'm sure *you* understand that." Joe winked at her.

Florence laughed. "Was Alex there at the factory?"

"I don't know. It was a bit chaotic. Could've been. Doesn't seem quite his style though." Joe thanked his sister for the abundant plate.

"You boys are finished, so why don't you go do your homework and let your uncle and me talk." The boys reluctantly obeyed.

Joe recounted the events at the factory. The strike had been planned but kept under wraps for some time. Even though the police were there, the entire perimeter of the factory was too big to guard. There were places in the fence where people could slip in and out.

"I'm going back in, but I knew you'd worry if I didn't come home and you didn't know my whereabouts." Joe washed down the meatballs with the beer Florence had retrieved from the refrigerator for him.

"Bah! I'm used to that." She stood to clear the plates and to dodge her brother's sympathetic gaze.

"I'll call you or find some way to let you know if Alex is there."

She and her brother discussed the many arrangements now familiar to her. Mary Zuk was organizing a strike kitchen. Yes, Florence would rally her friends to help. She would listen to Nowak's show to stay abreast of developments. Florence lost focus for a moment when she heard the front door open and close quietly. Lucien was sneaking out again.

"And now I should get back. I'm going to run up and get a few things."

Florence cleaned up the kitchen, setting a pie tin of food in the oven to stay warm just in case.

Joe and Frank were talking in the living room.

"All right, Uncle Joe. You can count on me."

She heard Frank seeing his uncle out the door. He was probably instructing him to behave and take care of her. She crossed herself and thanked heaven for her brother.

CHAPTER 26

Tuesday, March 23, 1937

Her broom drew thin lines in the damp dirt, which, over the winter months, had built up on the wooden planks of the front porch. No matter. Florence was glad to be using a broom instead of a shovel. She descended to the narrow concrete walkway lined by tufts of brown grass struggling to turn green. The hopeful fringe visible now where snow receded. She kept a watchful eye on the street for her ride. Men with their jackets flying open popped out of front doors at scattershot intervals. Odd, watching the neighborhood wake up from the front of her house instead of the alley. Odd, too, how life's rhythm had been disrupted. First the cigar factory, now Dodge Main. Alex had slipped in late last night. She'd feigned sleep. With the auto plant stymied by the sit-down strike, apparently Alex decided to sleep late. When he didn't come down for breakfast, she packed his sausage for her lunch. Alex's behavior had become so unpredictable. Even the boys had changed. Lucien sneaking out at night. Frank had become a bit more childlike. They all needed to find their way again.

Stanley Nowak slowed to a stop in his black sedan. Florence snatched up her purse and tote bag, which were perched on a porch step.

"Good morning, Florence," Stanley welcomed her into his car.

"Good morning, Stanley." She arranged herself in the back seat behind Basia. "How are you feeling today, Basia?"

"Oh, all right."

"What did the doctor say?"

"Ha! Nothing I didn't know! My lungs don't sound good. Chest cold. Nothing to be done."

"Should you be home in bed today?"

"Probably. But I must—" Florence winced at her friend's barking cough. "I have to go."

"We thought she should at least make an appearance," Stanley stated as he merged into traffic.

"But your health, Basia, is more important. Is this wise?"

"Florence, you take care of her at work. See if our Basia can make it through just this one day then we'll decide about the rest of the week." Stanley explained the reason he felt it so important for Basia to make an appearance. She had made herself the de facto leader at the factory.

"The women need to see her to know the fight continues. And the factory owners need to know she's not beaten. We're so close. I'm trying to set another meeting with Mr. Schwarz. Continue working on solutions. I'm approaching Governor Murphy too."

The black sedan turned into the alley behind the White Eagle cigar factory. Stanley eased to a stop at the end of the little path to the employees' entrance on the side of the building. He jumped out of the car to open the passenger door for Basia. Florence exited from the back.

"I'm fine." Basia waved away Stanley's proffered hand. "I'm not invalid."

Stanley and Florence exchanged glances. Stanley checked his watch.

"Let's give it another minute. Everyone should be at their stations before you walk in. Then I have to get back to Dodge."

"You're kind to take your time away from the UAW for us. Should I go in now?" Florence asked.

"Yes. Good idea. Make it look just like yesterday."

Florence nodded and headed down the narrow sidewalk to the employees' side entrance. She followed her usual routine, putting her belongings in her locker and changing her shoes. The hallway in which the lockers stood was empty except for the few stragglers who were habitually late. She then slid into her workstation.

"Slipping in under the wire, I see, Mrs. Falkowski." Resnick tapped a rolled-up newspaper on her workstation. Florence ignored his remark and collected an armful of rolling leaves from the supply bins. As she returned to her station she stopped mid-step. Basia stood in the doorway. Resnick followed her gaze.

"Well, well. Look who decided to join us. If it isn't our own Mrs. Sikorski."

The women looked up from their work.

"Basia!"

"It's Basia!"

One of the women jumped to her feet and started clapping. The room exploded. Everyone stood, and applause drowned out Resnick's cries for order. Basia proceeded to her workstation.

"Good morning, ladies."

"How *are* you?"

"I heard you were in jail. Was it awful?"

"What did Romek think?"

Florence hung back, outside the circle of women crowding around her friend. She knew the answers to the questions already, but more so, she allowed her friend to revel in the well-earned adulation. She expected a reaction from Resnick and was surprised when none came. After about twenty minutes, Resnick, in a relatively pleasant voice, announced work should begin. Florence was relieved. Basia's vocal cords sounded rough as a metal rasp.

The women worked in silence. Once seated, Basia didn't speak at all. Sounds came from open-mouthed breathing, throat clearing, and wretched coughing. None of the women rolled at their previously frenetic pace. Working fast in the morning had ensured a reasonable departure time, but they'd agreed on this new plan. Florence stretched her hands more often. The women conversed pleasantly, though of nothing of great import. She scanned the workers in her line of vision. Good. They worked as had been decided. Steadily, efficiently, but not inhumanly fast.

The air hung thick with anxiety or anticipation. Normal sounds of cutting, boxing, and chairs scraping were amplified. Florence couldn't put her finger on it. Basia's presence imbued an expectation of action.

"How're you holding up?"

"I'm all right," Basia murmured.

"Do you want to go home?"

"No! Lunch soon." Basia shook her head.

For the next hour or so, Florence worked with one eye on her product and one eye on Basia. Not a single sigh or shudder escaped her notice. Once in the lunchroom, Basia indicated she didn't want to answer any more questions. With only five days left until Easter Sunday, the women discussed their preparations. A group planned to convene at Dom Polski the next night to fashion lambs from the softened butter they'd been saving up for a few weeks. Others planned to share hams to pepper the breakfast borscht with meat. All would bring baskets of provisions to be blessed at the Saturday vigil. Serendipitously, Passover would begin on Friday and the factory would be closed.

"Basia, you need to eat more. Keep up your strength." Florence noticed the partially eaten sandwich.

"Too much effort."

After a bit more cajoling, Basia acquiesced.

Before lunch, Florence noticed the paltry pile of crooked cigars on Basia's worktable. Her friend was struggling. Florence asked others to join her in contributing to Basia's quota in addition to their own work. Several women offered. The anxiety over how Basia's return would be received had dissipated and a sense of familiar calm enswathed the room.

Desperate wheezing and gasping shattered the calm. Basia sounded like she was trying to breathe through a mask. Florence fetched a tin cup of water. Perhaps it would douse the strangled hacking. Her friend drank greedily.

"Careful with that water on your table." Resnick appeared from nowhere. "Can't get that filler damp."

"No? Watch me!" Basia tilted her cup, now almost empty, over her work. "Not quite fire hose, is it?"

Sharp footsteps heralded Schwarz's arrival. When he whooshed into the room, the air whooshed out.

"What's going on here?"

Florence snatched the cup from her friend's hand and shoved it below the worktable.

"Nothing. We're just getting reacquainted," quipped Resnick.

Schwarz marched straight to Resnick's office. The nephew followed him as if he were a pull toy.

"What you think that's about?" Basia uttered over her shoulder. Silence enveloped the room, enabling Florence to hear Basia's strained murmur.

"I couldn't guess. Doubt it's something good." Florence noticed, like she and Basia, many others glancing sideways into the office.

"*Boże!* Look at that."

The men gesticulated wildly. Their voices were restrained and low.

"That pot's going to boil over," Florence predicted.

Basia laughed. Her laugh turned into a hack, which turned into a choke. Florence jumped up to help. She thumped her friend's back.

"Get some more water!" She handed the tin cup to one of the women surrounding Basia. A few sips of water quelled the attack before Basia started gasping for air. Out of the corner of her eye she saw the men had stopped arguing. They stood frozen behind the glass. Resnick exited the office, the door banging into the wall. Schwarz followed.

"What's wrong with her?" Schwarz demanded. "Does she have TB?"

No one answered. Tuberculosis ran rampant among immigrants due to overcrowded housing. Florence wondered the same.

Basia's hand flew to her chest. She inhaled, exuding the sound of an injured animal. Then the coughing, hacking, choking. In projectile fashion she expelled a wad of bloody phlegm. She fell back into her chair with a thud. Her eyes rolled back, then closed. Florence felt her forehead. Burning hot.

"Get me a cold towel."

"I recognize her. The troublemaker. More of your theatrics, Mrs. Sikorski?"

"Leave her alone. Can't you see she's sick?" Resnick seized his uncle's arm. "You shouldn't be near her."

Basia took quick shallow breaths. Her hand still rested on her chest. Florence didn't take her eyes off her friend's face. A pinpoint spark of glee ignited below Basia's drooping eyelids. Florence's brow creased quizzically. The corners of her friend's faded lips twitched. Florence watched her friend's limp hand drop from her chest to point at the floor. Her eyes scoured the floor to see what Basia saw. Schwarz's new white and black spectator shoes had been defaced by Basia's bloody sputum. The women looked at each other. Laughter peeled out from each, Basia's arrested by a virulent coughing attack.

"These two are crazy!" Schwarz declared. Resnick pulled his uncle away. He nabbed a rag off a table and cleaned his uncle's shoes.

Schwarz's face turned red, apoplectic with ire, and departed in a fury. "I'm ordering you to leave. I can't have this whole crew sick. I'm shorthanded as it is. And it's a short week."

It was true. Only two-thirds of the women returned after the strike. Several didn't return because their husbands forbade it, while others had become sick after enduring the assault by the fire hoses. Ah, maybe the tables had turned. Schwarz needed them at least as much as they needed him. That could bode well. Resnick escorted his uncle out of the workroom and approached her and Basia.

"Go home. Please. You've made your point, Mrs. Sikorski. I'll call you a taxi."

Basia's eyebrows darted up. "A taxi?"

"Even I'm not enough of a cad to make you walk!" Resnick returned to his office while she and Basia looked at each other, mouths agape.

CHAPTER 27

Wednesday, March 24, 1937

"Alex? I'm making this ham for dinner tonight. It's big enough so there'll be some left over for dinner tomorrow." Florence whisked together the ingredients of a glaze.

"Uh hmmm." Alex didn't look up from the drawings and pencils spread out over the kitchen table.

"There'll be some kasha and some cold beet salad."

"Uh hmmm."

"Later this evening, I'll make babka so you'll have it for dessert."

"Florence, can't you see I'm trying to work? Why're you bothering me with talk of tomorrow's meals?"

"I won't be home for dinner tomorrow." She vigorously rubbed dry mustard over the raw meat.

"All right. Something going on at church or the hall, I suppose." He extracted a clean sheet of paper from a tablet.

"I'll be home very late."

"All right." Alex removed his glasses and bent over the paper. He guided the graphite of his mechanical pencil in small, precise moves. Not having joined the sit-down strike at the factory, he stayed home working on his inventions.

"I'm going to Lansing with Stanley Nowak tomorrow." She shoved whole cloves deep into the ham.

"What?" The tip of the lead snapped off the point of Alex's pencil. "*Kurwa!*" He scrunched the paper into a ball and threw it on the floor.

"Basia can't go. She's too sick. And Stanley wants someone from the factory to give witness to the governor."

"The governor."

"We don't know if we'll meet the governor himself but maybe a staff—"

"You're going to parade yourself in front of the governor like some sniveling socialist?"

"I'm not a sniveling socialist. I'm a human being and I deserve to be treated like one." She fought to keep her voice neutral.

"Your name's already on a list. At least with . . . Now you want the government to label you a labor agitator?"

"So what if my name is already on such a list?" She clenched the potato peeler.

"You and your friend Basia." Alex was standing now, pacing, two steps in each direction across the tiny kitchen. "Do you know what that could do to me at the factory? If they think I'm part of all this, this nonsense? I could lose my job." He sat down at the table, head in hands. "Or worse."

She swung around to face Alex, thrusting the potato peeler at him.

"Don't you talk about Basia. She's sick. Very sick. She's been in jail. She could die!"

"Stop waving that thing around."

She looked at the metal device in her hand, shrugged, and resumed flaying potatoes.

Silence settled over the kitchen. Alex resumed drawing.

"Damn!" Alex threw his pencil down and pounded his fist on the table. The pencil rolled to the floor.

Startled, Florence peeled the edge of her index finger instead of the potato. "Damn yourself!" she cried. She sucked on her finger and picked up the pencil and the wad of paper still on the floor, chucking them both on the table.

"You can't go. I won't allow it."

"I don't need your permission."

"Lower your voice! It's dangerous."

"Dangerous? What's dangerous? Going to Lansing? Stanley's a good driver."

Alex continued to rail about all the incidents that had occurred targeting labor organizers. He spoke of spies in factories. Retaliation. Threats. He reiterated the tragic events when Henry Ford's security forces shot and killed marchers on their way to protest.

"Didn't that fire hose teach you anything? You said yourself—Basia is sick and might die."

"And does her life mean nothing? She was willing to take a beating and go to jail so we could all have a better life. And I can't even ride in a car to Lansing? It'll be a pleasure outing compared to what she's been through."

"What she does and what you do are two different things."

"I want them to be the same things. I believe in the cause."

"It's going to *cause* you to end up like her. Halfway in the grave. If not wholly underground."

"You're so suspicious. No one cares about a *staruszka* like me begging for a couple of nickels an hour? Huh? Do you think some thug will pull me out of Stanley's car and beat me up? You're nuts!" She wadded up a tangle of potato peels, stared at them, faltered, not sure where to aim. *Splat!* Wet potato peels landed in the trash can.

"Then I'm nuts! Because it can happen, and it *has* happened."

"Not to anyone I know."

"No. But to people who associate with Nowak."

"I'm proud to associate with Stanley. And Margaret. They're good people. They care."

"I care."

"About yourself!" She slapped the dishrag down in the sink, untied her apron, and jammed it on a hook. Her slippers thudded against the wall. She crammed her feet into her shoes.

"I care about you," Alex's voice trailed from the kitchen.

Florence walked out the back door. Cool night air sliced through her heated temper, and by the time she crossed the alley and reached Basia and Romek's back door, her hands no longer shook. The steps to the porch, on which they'd found Henryk dead two months ago, hadn't been shoveled. She wiped her hands on her house dress; she'd failed to pick up a jacket in her hasty retreat. Better to knock—though usually she let herself in—to afford Romek some privacy. She'd check in, be helpful but not a bother.

"How is she?" she asked Romek, who invited her into the kitchen.

"Hard to say. One minute she rallies, then the cough seizes her." He shook his head. "It's like a devil spirit squeezes and squeezes her insides."

"Do you want me to heat some broth for her? Or I can warm up some towels to lay on her chest."

"Florence, you're a dear, but no. I will do it. Makes me useful. There's so little I can do."

She watched as his mammoth hands moved pans around the stovetop. He was so kind, so empathetic.

"I can't help my wife. I can't help at the factory while I'm here. I can't do anything but wait. We always wait for something to get better, eh?"

Florence didn't respond. Maybe she'd been waiting too long for the situation at her own home to improve. The recent spat might make Alex realize the extent of her commitment to labor affairs. Alex probably was shocked. She'd never argued so vociferously with him, much less walked out the door. She fanned her face. Her blood pressure must be through the roof.

"I'll let you do your work here. I won't be able to come by tomorrow because I'll be with Stanley in Lansing. Tell Basia I'll come over Friday and tell her all about it."

"Yes. Please do. We're eager to hear. It will lift her spirits."

On the way out, she borrowed Basia's spring jacket—a bit small, so she didn't fasten the buttons. They'd shared so much, clothes being the least of it. She stepped into the bracing air, crossed the yard, and pulled up short at the alley. Her wooden gate swung on its stave because she'd failed to secure it in her fury. The open gate to her home offered no appeal. She stood on the alley side of the gate, secured the latch, and proceeded down the alley away from home. A short way, and she paused in front of Dodge Main. The behemoth appeared eerie in the dark. When second and third shifts operated, the plant loomed large at night, alive and productive. Now the building was limp. No smoke exuded from the stacks. No longer did cars swing in and out on outdoor tracks like barn swallows. Police guards hovered at gates in the chain link fence. She looked up at the water tower, half expecting to see a sentry aiming a rifle at her. A veritable prison. Like the city itself. Her brother Joe was in there. Romek would be in there if he weren't tending to Basia. Most of the neighborhood men were in there. But not Alex.

Her brother's words came back to her. Last week Joe had said Alex might be in some type of trouble, that he carried a burden. She couldn't imagine what it might be. When he worried about money, he'd nag them to turn off lights, close the refrigerator door. If distressed about his job, he'd grumble about his supervisor, Fred. When the boys disquieted him, he'd discipline them "to make them better men," he would say. When she annoyed him, he found fault. Lately, he'd been subdued, preoccupied, or simply absent, excepting his vehement opposition to her union involvement. How weighty a freight crushed a man into silence? Especially a man like Alex. Perhaps Joe was right. Alex could be suffering internal strife. From what? She should go home.

Could she talk to Alex and draw out what was bothering him? Married for so many years, he should trust her. After all, didn't she always try to help? She remembered her father would retract into himself when facing challenges, become distant. Her mother had offered a steady hand, maintained life's routines, waited. The last two months had been anything but routine. Some things couldn't wait.

She closed the front door, trying not to make noise. Frank bounded down the stairs and wrapped her in a hug.

"Mama! I didn't know where you went. I'm all alone."

"Your father's not home?"

"He left not long after you did."

He probably went to Wally's to get a drink and cool off. Just as well, as she wasn't sure she was ready to face him.

"What were you fighting about?"

"He doesn't want me to go to Lansing with Mr. Nowak tomorrow."

"I don't like it when you fight." Frank's voice was still that of a child.

"I know, dear. Are you hungry?"

Florence checked on the ham, basted it with the glaze she'd made earlier, and closed the oven door. The potatoes must have boiled over, judging by the blotch of starchy residue covering the stovetop. That must have taken Alex by surprise. She poked a fork in the potatoes, then drained the pot. She'd mash them, though they were cold, and make potato patties. Together they ate dinner, and her son relaxed. She let Frank lead the conversation, so they spoke of things of interest to a ten-year-old boy. He updated her on the latest radio shows. He particularly liked the intrigue of the mysteries. They had fun, and they both relaxed. After dinner, she told him he could go to his friend's house. Alone, she put the food away and decided to leave the dishes for later, or even tomorrow. She poured a small plum brandy and retired to the living room. Soon she had a fire roaring in the fireplace.

How could she explain to Alex what this trip meant to her? The impact her engagement in the strike had on her? She'd been only seventeen when she met Alex. She'd yearned for something beyond the routine of her own life. Her life was so small. School at Notre Dame was pleasant but confined, her interests channeled. Then at home, the grocery store. Always the grocery store. Predictions of the weather, the winter, how would prices be affected? Her mother discussed recipes with the neighborhood women, a guise to interest them in purchasing a specific vegetable they'd ordered in quantity. After school, she would unload cartons, stock the shelves, sweep the floor. She was grateful for the privilege a successful business bestowed on the family, no doubt.

But Alex brought her the world. Then to come to Detroit? She won the jackpot. It was exciting and new, energetic. She couldn't wait to jump into the center of the modern world, the avant-garde. Then she realized they'd only be tolerated, not welcomed, as the newest wave of immigrants. It was the Poles' turn to serve as the bottom rung of the ladder. Their Slavic language made them an oddity, taking the rung down a peg. The crash of business broke the ladder entirely. Now the ladder was being rebuilt and she wanted to climb it. She wanted all of them to climb it, to do what they came here to do. Basia and Romek. Anushka and Stephan. Wally and Helen. Delores. And Henryk. It was too late for Henryk. But if she could make a difference in their lives?

A car backfired on the street. The noise startled her. The plywood behind the sheer curtains caused unease, intruding on her thoughts. Alex had yet to repair the window broken by a projectile rock while she was in the factory. They hadn't found out who threw it, or why. Maybe that still bothered Alex. She averted her eyes from the plywood and instead looked at the small writing desk she'd brought from home when they'd married. In the grocery store office she'd do her homework or draw on the kidney-shaped walnut desk. Now she wrote letters to her parents. That's it! She settled herself in the petite chair, opened the single drawer, and withdrew a few sheets of stationery. She loaded her fountain pen with ink and, in the beautiful italic style she'd learned at Notre Dame, began to write.

Dear Alex . . .

CHAPTER 28

Thursday, March 25, 1937

Florence readjusted her hat in the hall mirror again and checked the wall clock. Stanley Nowak would be there soon to pick her up. She strolled about the living room and checked out the front window, the part without plywood, though she knew she was early and Stanley wouldn't be there. On top of her writing desk lay some stationery she'd left out after writing the letter to Alex the previous evening. She slid the small stack into the drawer, the pen as well. She had perched the letter against the salt and pepper shakers on the kitchen table. When she'd made coffee this morning the letter was gone. In it, she'd articulated her thoughts, tried to explain why her participation in these labor events was of such consequence to her. Also, she'd beseeched him to open up to her if, in fact, he faced turmoil of some variety. Alex hadn't been home when she returned from Basia's the night before, but she'd heard him return in the early morning hours. He must have made a fire because she remembered the homey smell of woodsmoke wafting into their bedroom before she fell back asleep. As she brushed dust off the mantel with her hand, she spied a small white triangle resting in the ash, a corner of an envelope. Had he even read it?

Two beeps of a horn: the headlights on Stanley's car came to rest in front of the house and Florence bounded out, not wanting to keep him waiting. He drove, his assistant sat up front, and Stanley's wife, Margaret, joined Florence in the back seat. Pleasantries consumed the early part of the journey. Florence had met Margaret a few times but didn't know her well, though she knew her to be supportive behind the scenes during the sit-down. They ambled northwest on the highway, and it wasn't long before they passed by Dearborn's River Rouge plant, then in Ann Arbor, the University of Michigan. Would it ever be possible for her boys to attend? Soon farm fields lined either side of the two-lane highway. Florence rolled the window down just a bit, enough to smell the fresh air but not enough to muss her hair. She needed to stay presentable. Spring was her favorite season. It brought the promise of new beginnings, and today certainly felt like one.

Florence had never been to Lansing, the state capital. The governor's office had contacted Nowak just a few days ago to say a time slot had opened. She wasn't prepared. Basia should have been the one going, but her fever spiked, and she felt weak. Romek had called. He delivered the message that Basia was "excited for Florence to go in her place and thought she'd represent their fellow workers better anyway. She wanted to make sure Florence enjoyed the trip, and her day off work, and wanted to hear all about it when she returned." Florence agreed to go and contacted Nowak to make plans.

Stanley said they could go into the gallery and watch the legislators if they had time after meeting with the governor. Of course she was familiar with Frank Murphy, in the public sense, from when he was the mayor of Detroit. She listened to him on the radio, and newscasters seemed to skewer him lightly, not a bad endorsement.

"Look at that farm." Florence pointed at a particularly tidy spread. Tilled rows lined low rolling mounds, making patterns for the eye to follow. White and black Holsteins dotted the adjacent pasture. The clean red lines of the pentagram structure cut the light blue sky. The cylindrical silage silo seemed to pin the barn to the earth. "That's beautiful! So perfect."

"Yes, isn't it? The Kaminskis own that. They've been a big help to labor. During all the milk strikes a few years back, they were so kind. They brought the milk they couldn't sell to schools and hospitals."

"Sometimes I think it would be nice to live on a farm. Get away from the dirty city and all the upheaval. Having some space would have been so good for the boys while they were growing up."

Margaret smiled. Florence considered all that might have been, as people do when they have time. With her ankles crossed and her pocketbook perched on her lap, she enjoyed the pastoral scenery. Soon the farms became smaller and closer together. Lansing rose in the offing.

Florence marveled at the luster of the conference room table, mahogany with inlaid accents of exotic wood. She allowed her fingertips to fondle only the edge. She didn't want to leave a fingerprint. The four of them—she, Stanley Nowak, his wife, Margaret, and his organizer colleague—had been led into the conference room by a starched secretary. Efficient, perhaps even haughty, in her demeanor and dress, the peplum of her silk suit jacket defied motion. Government jobs must pay well.

"The governor won't be able to see you himself. He has many important meetings. He designated a staff member to meet with you. He'll be in shortly."

"Fine, that's fine." Stanley accommodated the woman's need for importance with an obsequious smile. Florence bristled but Stanley flashed her a mischievous smile.

Artwork on the walls of this small room intrigued her more than the portraits of former governors that lined the hallways. The oil paintings, in series, depicted the settling of Detroit. Kinship with her French heritage compelled her to ruminate about Montreal.

Examining her gnarled hands caressing the table, she wondered if she would be able to paint again. At one time she envisioned herself an artist, or maybe a gallery owner. At Congrégation de Notre Dame her skill had been encouraged and lauded. She'd garnered a plethora of prizes and was recognized at juried exhibits. She was educated in arts, literature, religion, culture, and decorum. On the path to becoming a society lady of Montreal she dreamed of an urbane match. Perhaps one who'd finance her own gallery on Rue de Saint Sulpice facing the Place d'Armes square. Then she met Alex. If she'd remained in Quebec, what course would her life have taken?

"Good afternoon! Sorry to have kept you waiting." The quartet rose to greet Governor Frank Murphy himself.

"Governor, I didn't expect you were going—"

"Yes, my deputy will be in soon, but I had a minute between meetings and thought I'd duck in to say hello. After what we've been through with all the other strikes, Nowak, I feel we're at least old friends, if not brothers." Murphy referred to the many protracted negotiations to settle the strikes in other industries.

"I'm glad you did. We know you're a busy man." Stanley took the lead, first shaking hands with Murphy and then introducing the members of his entourage.

"Please, let's sit. Mr. Nowak, every time we meet there is some crisis in the world of labor."

"Yes. It is true."

"I've been briefed on the situation that brought you here today. However, I'd like to hear a summary of the facts straight from the horse's mouth, as they say."

"Of course. And I am ready to provide them." Stanley slid a folder of papers toward Murphy. "I've prepared these documents for you to review later since our time together is short." The deputy arrived, and after introductions, Stanley continued. Murphy leafed through the folder of papers and photographs.

"Our request today on behalf of the workers of White Eagle cigar factory, of which Mrs. Falkowski here is one, is that you mediate with factory owners to obtain recognition of our union. Our right to bargain collectively."

"I see."

Florence searched his face for clues to his answer, but it proved as difficult as reading tea leaves.

"Other factories have settled with owners and workers received wage increases. There have been promises of improved working conditions. A local union with the AFL already exists. Why not join with them?" Governor Murphy queried.

"Allow me to explain. Two reasons. First, the wage increase was paltry. A small scrap to the dogs, eh? To stop the barking?"

"Perhaps that's true, Mr. Nowak." Murphy proceeded to explain the dynamics of pulling an economy out of depression while staving off monetary inflation, which would bring a recovery to a screeching halt. "We have to take it slow."

"Economic dynamics are complicated. But I ask you, should Mrs. Falkowski here, and her fellow workers, pay the price for the whole country?" Stanley argued.

Florence tilted her chin up, striking a pose of indignation.

"Well, no, of course not!" Murphy adjusted himself in his chair and straightened his tie.

"Which brings me to my second point. Hand rolling of cigars is a dying industry. Do you smoke, Mr. Murphy?"

Florence knew the answer since the governor's well-tailored three-piece suit emitted the undeniable odor. She was sure Stanley knew too.

"Well, yes, but I prefer cigarettes."

"Exactly! You and many others. You see my point. Cigarettes on one hand and machine-rolled cigars on the other. Together, they squash the industry Mrs. Falkowski and many others like her work in. The AFL union you referred to—they don't want to represent us."

"Why not?"

Murphy's deputy leaned into him and whispered in his ear, then Murphy waved him off.

"If you need to attend to other matters, we understand—"

"No, keep going, Nowak, you've intrigued me."

"Mostly men work in the automated plants. Mostly English-speaking men. The majority German. They've forgotten they, too, were once the new immigrants."

"Perhaps the industry is dying a natural death in the name of automation. The future. Progress."

"You're Irish, is that correct, Mr. Murphy?" What a puzzling question for Stanley to pose to the governor. Florence thought it almost rude.

Stanley continued, "I'm not against progress, Mr. Murphy, for it will come, whether we approve or not. You see, this low-level industry serves a great purpose for America. For immigrants who need jobs, like your Irish forefathers did."

Florence couldn't anticipate what he would say next.

"The industry is a portal. Like an extension of Ellis Island. Eastern European immigrants come. They can work in these factories while they learn English, learn to assimilate. Wages earned contribute immensely to the well-being of families. Imagine. In these last several years, with half the men out of work in the automobile industry, if these women hadn't worked, how many more would've we had in the bread lines? How many more children would be malnourished or dead? These workers have taken it on the chin to contribute to this great country. Do you not think they deserve some basic recognition?"

"Hmmm. Mr. Nowak, you offer an interesting perspective. I see what you're saying. These factories do serve society as a whole."

Florence straightened her posture and smoothed some rogue wisps of hair from her face. She glanced at Margaret, who beamed at her husband.

"Mrs.—Falkowski—is it?" The governor switched his focus to her.

She offered a single nod, well accustomed to people having difficulty with the simplest of Polish surnames.

"Obviously, Mr. Nowak brought you to represent the workers. Please tell me about your situation. At work, and your family."

Stanley had warned her she may be questioned. She was ready. Florence recounted the hours, the stultifying air, the pitiful pay, leaving nothing out.

"We decided to take matters into our own hands. We took possession of the factory. You see, Mr. Murphy, we wanted to be heard. Everyone has their own struggles, their own way to cope in these hard times."

During her entire chronicle, she had locked eyes with the governor. When she spoke of Basia, firehoses, and pneumonia, her eyes welled. Murphy's did too. He was truly hearing her.

"We are not so different, you and I, Mr. Murphy. Irish people came to America to escape hunger and imperial rule. Poles are doing the same, sixty, seventy years later. Eastern Europeans suffer from bad timing. The war, the Russian Revolution, the stock market crash."

"Therein lies the dilemma, Mrs. Falkowski. Our government has to stimulate the economy. President Roosevelt is doing what he can. It's a delicate balance. We're on the brink of getting back on track. And when we do, and the marvelous Detroit engine of prosperity is chugging along again, we all will be better off. That's why I need to focus on the automobile industry."

The car industry. Always the car industry. Were they destined to live in that shadow forever?

"I'm no economist, Mr. Murphy. What I do know is my best friend is near death. A wonderful, hardworking woman. Loving and kind. And she is no communist. She killed a Bolshevik and was forced to abandon her family and her country." A jolt of surprise registered on Murphy's face.

"We need to weigh business interests against workers' rights. We can't jump too far too fast or it will all come crashing down again," Murphy admonished.

Florence thought about how Basia would tell the tale. She let loose.

"Men sacrifice their limbs to that great engine of prosperity, then drink themselves to death because they can't provide for their families. Our cigar industry may be dying, Mr. Murphy, but I'll tell you what," Florence thrust her index finger at the governor, "it kept us alive. Our work prevented more people from dying in the streets. On the streets of your state. We spend our hard-earned money. We feed your economy, even if we can't feed ourselves." Florence stood. She glanced at Stanley, who nodded. "Is that the kind of state you want to run? We don't ask for handouts. We work. What good is your economic theory if it doesn't serve people? What else is there? People, Mr. Murphy, people!" Florence slammed her hand on the mahogany table. Her sweaty palm left its mark. "We want our fair share and we want our union to be recognized."

For a moment no one spoke.

"I've said enough." Florence sat. She clasped her hands in her lap. Maybe she'd overdone it, embarrassed Stanley. She hoped not.

"Stanley," the governor addressed Nowak, "I see why you brought Mrs. Falkowski with you today. She makes a compelling argument." He turned to Florence. "I sympathize with you. My lieutenant governor, Mr. Nowicki, was born in Poland. I do know a little of that world. Again, I sympathize with the conditions that forced you to leave Eastern Europe. But, as you say, what is the economy if it doesn't serve people?"

Florence nodded.

"Mrs. Falkowski, you are very convincing, very articulate. I'll give you that. I can't condone the tactics used by the police. Never should violence be a tool against those seeking to organize. The mayor is well aware of my position and I will chastise him accordingly." Everyone nodded in endorsement. "As far as intervening with the factory owners? I'm not going to say I won't, but I can't right now." Her group remained silent. "I have an untold number of labor actions I'm dealing with at the moment. But I assure you, when my plate is cleared, I will give your plight some attention. Your friend, Nowak here, will see to it that I don't forget." The governor stood, ending the meeting. They all rose.

"Nowak, as long as you're here, may I have a quick word about Dodge Main?"

"I'll meet you in the car." Nowak motioned for the others to leave. They regrouped near the car and waited for Stanley to join them. Florence had been riled up, infusing her narrative with emotion, and now, with inaction as a response, she was spent. Stanley returned in short order. They planned to have lunch in the downtown area, then Stanley promised some sightseeing. After lunch, though, Stanley suggested the women see the sights on their own. He needed to meet with some of the governor's staffers regarding other labor actions. The afternoon spent with Margaret was pleasant and engaging. "You were really something in there," Margaret had said. Florence wasn't so sure. She wanted to believe the governor would get involved, but . . . They had a light dinner before meeting again with Stanley on the capitol steps. Florence was ready to go home.

A shroud of silence enveloped the car's interior. Florence rested her head on the cold window and used her lightweight coat as a blanket. The day had been exhilarating and exhausting both. The nights were still cool in the spring and the sun had long ago set. Instrumental music slid from the radio. Stanley kept the volume low. Florence loosened the straps on her shoes and her feet wiggled in their freedom.

Stanley broke the silence. "Look at that. See that? I wonder what that is. It's a strange glow."

She raised her head for a moment to see what Stanley saw, but she wasn't that interested and let her head drop.

"Fire. It looks like fire," Margaret said, alerted by her husband's concern. "Could it be a field on fire?"

"I don't think so. It's still too wet." Stanley sped up.

"I think it could be the Kaminski farm! I hope not, but there's nothing else around here." Stanley pushed the accelerator even further to the floor. Florence couldn't help but sit up.

"That beautiful farm? *O, Boże!*" Her feet pressed against the floor. She willed the car to go faster. She gripped the handle of her handbag as tightly as Stanley gripped the steering wheel. Soon they turned into the long gravel road leading toward the flames. After taking a hard turn, blinding lights in sets of two assaulted them head-on. Stanley swerved off the narrow road and stopped. Florence's head hit the seat in front of her before being flung back against her seat. The four passengers watched a cadre of cars race past, flinging dirt and gravel in their wake. Florence rubbed her forehead, then her neck. Her scrambled brain bobbled in her skull.

"What?! Did you see that? Was that Alex?" She perched straight up, gripping the front seat. For just a moment, in the wild swinging of light beams, she thought she saw a glint of Alex's fine blonde hair.

"Alex? You saw Alex?" Stanley swiveled his head around from the driver's seat.

"No, yes, I don't know. My head's scrambled. *O, Boże.* Just for a moment. Light hair."

"Could've been anyone. If everyone's all right, let's go up to the farm. See what's happening."

Stanley was right. It could have been anyone. But a spouse knows.

They proceeded as close as they dared. Vicious flames engulfed the house and barn.

"Wait here." Ambient heat rushed in when Stanley swung open his car door. He returned in a few minutes. "No one here. Thank goodness they weren't home."

"The animals?" his wife queried.

"I couldn't get close enough to the barn. I'm sorry."

Clanging bells announced the arrival of three fire trucks. Once again, Stanley exited. This time the heat ratcheted up. They watched as he spoke to the firemen and returned.

"I told them what we saw. About the cars."

"What did they say?" Margaret asked.

"To go home." So they did.

Florence waved to the others from her front porch. She knew Stanley would wait to see her in safely. She made a show of putting the key in the lock and feigned opening the door. As soon as the headlights turned the corner, she tiptoed to the backyard and slipped through the side door to the garage. Heat emanated through the stamped metal hood of the car into her palm.

"*O, Boże.*"

Florence slid into bed next to Alex. He lay on his side facing her. Could he have been at that farm tonight? He wasn't a destructive man—angry, intensely angry, at times, but not destructive. She wanted to shake him awake but had not an iota of energy after the wearying day. She examined his face. The crow's feet around his eyes no longer disappeared in sleep. His once strong jaw slacked, the bottom a bit receded. He was still handsome in a cavalier way. She had no trouble envisioning him on horseback in his Cossack days, regal, like the tsar himself. Wisps of blonde hair created a lace veil over his eyes. She could peek through and see his eyes bobbing beneath the lids. His porcelain skin belied his virile whiskers. At night, did he dream of the past, or, as in the day, did he look to the future? She'd let him sleep. She'd sleep. After rolling over to face the wall, Alex's arm slid over her, a habit of their long-married lives.

CHAPTER 29

Friday, March 26, 1937 (Good Friday and start of Passover)

Steve Schwarz's frayed suspenders hugged the cotton of his chambray shirt, worn yet pressed. Resnick had never seen his uncle dressed down. He'd been taken aback when, upstairs in the office, Uncle Steve had shed his tie, starched white shirt, and gray wool suit, donning instead these humble clothes of a working man.

"Where did you find those?" Resnick asked in disbelief when his uncle pulled the clothes from a small valise. Resnick could be more casual with his uncle since they weren't in front of the workers.

"Don't look so shocked. I've always kept sets of working clothes. You never know when your basement might flood or some other disaster may occur. Like now. Let's go."

Resnick followed his uncles, Steve and Mort, down two sets of stairs to the basement of the White Eagle cigar factory. Empty boxes stood next to an enclosed hopper filled with tobacco leaves. When the older man shifted the heavy metal lid off the hopper, his chambray shirt pulled taut across his muscular back, a back not unaccustomed to manual labor. Uncle Steve required that he work today. The women were off for the Christian holiday, Good Friday, when most every establishment was closed. With the strike and slowdowns, the factory had slipped behind on fulfilling orders. Uncle Steve declared it unacceptable and demanded they take matters into their own hands.

"Go on, get a box." Resnick swiped the top box off the stack and held it out for his uncle to fill with leaves. This process continued for a while, with Uncle Steve filling the boxes, Resnick running them upstairs, and Uncle Mort sorting the leaves depending on their suitability. The three men convened in the workroom normally occupied by the Polish women. Resnick was directed to find gum, filler, and the extra Chaveta knives he kept hidden in the back of his desk drawer.

"All right, I'm quite rusty of course, but I'm sure it'll come back to me," Uncle Steve said. "Let's get started."

"Come back to you? You know how to roll these?" Resnick couldn't believe his ears.

"Of course. I supported myself." Uncle Steve settled into a workstation and began arranging materials. "What are you smirking at?"

"You're sitting at Basia's table. The woman you sent home the other day for being sick."

"Yes. The woman who stood up against the fire hose." His uncle made no effort to relocate. "Good."

"I thought you hated her."

"I don't hate anyone who works hard and stands up for what they believe. Don't just stand there! Close your mouth and get some stripped leaves over here."

Resnick picked up a stack of leaves from one of the piles next to Mort. He laid them out on a worktable and began stripping the flat surfaces away from the center stem. The trick was to maximize the amount of the leaf without any stem pieces. He fumbled, unacquainted with this type of work.

"Once in a while, it's all right to have some small stem pieces in the filler. Adds flavor." His uncle must have been watching him. "Let me show you." Uncle Steve demonstrated.

"I never knew you worked in a factory. Is that why you bought this place?"

"It was a long time ago in a different world. We, my family, moved away from the East to Germany. It was never our plan to stay there. We ran out of money. We did odd jobs along the way, working our way northwest. Closer to Hamburg and Bremen. Port cities where we could get passage to America. In the Bunde area, cigar factories needed labor. Germany lost so many working-aged men in the war. So, we worked. I was ten years old."

"Was it your plan then to own your own cigar factory?"

"Own this sorry place? *Nein.* I'd burn it down if I could." Uncle Steve transferred a pile of leaves back to Basia's workstation and resettled himself to begin rolling.

His uncle was such an enigma. Resnick returned to stripping leaves, trying, with marginal success, to copy his uncle's technique. The scrap pile grew.

"The world is a complicated and confusing place, Robert. Things—and people—aren't always what or who they seem." That truism Resnick knew all too well.

His uncle continued to explain that he couldn't seem too eager to capitulate to union recognition. Maintaining relationships in the business community was paramount. Yes, the Cigar Makers International Union of the AFL had been recognized decades ago, but members had been skilled artisans who'd been sucked out of their at-home workrooms into factories. Machines made upfront capital necessary, and the cottage shops were all but wiped out.

"The world changed for those workers. And it'll change again. Recognizing this new union of unskilled workers will quicken the demise of an industry already in its death throes. Especially with Detroit becoming such a union town." Uncle Steve held up a specimen he rolled and admired it before placing it in the wooden mold. "Did you see how I did that? Wrapped the outer leaf around to cover up the tear in the leaf below it?" Resnick hadn't been watching but nodded his agreement anyway.

After a bit, Resnick heard his uncle muttering, almost chanting, under his breath as he filled the wooden molds and stacked them on the adjacent table. Then Mort joined in and the brothers spoke louder in unison, and in Yiddish. They laughed.

"What's this?" Resnick's day was becoming even more unusual.

"That's a poem written by Morris Rosenfeld. Twenty, thirty

years ago now, it was popular to write Yiddish poems about working in the sweatshops in New York. These poems were very good and translated into German and Polish."

"Some even became songs." The usually quiet Mort piped up. "Do you remember the one that went like this?" Mort whistled a bit of a tune.

"Yes, of course!" The older men tried to piece together the lyrics from their collective memory.

Rarely did Resnick see his uncles so relaxed. He'd never heard about these poems or songs. They were fun and serious. He asked his uncles why they'd never spoken of them.

"You see, Robbie, if you're Jewish, whether German or Eastern European, they see us all the same. We must make an effort, make a huge show, to be different from the Yiddish-speaking unions. Those are tied up with socialists and communists. At least that's what some people think. We want no part of that. We must manage our position in the world." Uncle Steve explained the thin line he walked. He extolled the need to fit in with business leaders and politicians, to be part of the fabric of society, not the outcasts they were being made out to be in Germany.

"It's like walking on broken glass."

"Did you agree with what the police did here? Attacking our workers?" Resnick focused on his leaf stripping. He had finally gathered the courage to pose the question. Since that day, the day of the fire hoses, his estimation of his uncle, which had not been high to begin with, sunk. He dared not look at him when the room remained silent. He was moving toward Mort to fetch another stack when his uncle eventually spoke.

"No."

Resnick stopped in his tracks and looked at his uncle. Gone was his uncle's lighthearted tone.

"No. I did not. I'm ashamed."

"You didn't tell the mayor—"

"No, I told the mayor no such thing. I only asked to assert our rights to possess our property. It's the law." Resnick's uncle began pacing around the room. "I didn't tell him how to do that."

"But you must've known it—"

"We can't afford to be closed down for long. You may think we're well off, that this factory churns out cash, but we're not. This industry is dead." Uncle Steve's voice, now hard, rose in volume. "How do you think we can make much money when half the people who buy our cheap cigars have been unemployed for the last seven years?" He snatched a cigar off the top of his pile and held it up. "Do you think we make any money selling this for a nickel?" He shoved it in his mouth and continued pacing, exerting his frustration on the unlit cigar. "It's a lot of responsibility to manage all of this exactly right. Sometimes things happen that shouldn't." Steve spit onto the floor. "I'm not proud of what happened. Made me feel like a goddamned Nazi."

"You see, Robert, Mort and I are no strangers to work. And you shouldn't be either." Uncle Steve returned to Basia's seat and rolled with a vengeance. Resnick watched his uncle's manicured hands, now tobacco-stained, twist the leaves and cut with surgical precision. He sat next to his uncle to watch him roll and shape. Maybe he should learn. Besides, he was tired of stripping.

"You'll recognize the union then?" He had nothing to lose, as he'd already poked the bear.

"In due time. All in due time."

Steve turned on the radio. Resnick kept his head down and worked into the afternoon. Mort announced the number of completed mold trays stacked under weights and the number needed to be completed to fulfill the backlog.

"We'll need to come back on Sunday. We've not made much of a dent and we'll need to leave soon for seder."

Resnick knew better than to let his groan be audible. Nothing existed that he hated more than this stinking cigar factory.

CHAPTER 30

Friday, March 26, 1937 (Good Friday and start of Passover)

Florence closed the door to the Sikorski's master bedroom, the mirror image of her own. She left Romek sitting next to the bed where Basia lay wheezing and coughing. The doctor suspected pneumonia, possibly tuberculosis, which ran rampant in the jail. Florence cleared the dishes from the tray she carried down to the kitchen. She would give them some time alone before returning with more peppermint tea and honey. In the meantime, she would wash the kitchen floor.

Florence knew Basia's house as well as her own, so she easily found the buckets and rags. She moved the kitchen chairs into the hallway and began under the table, first sweeping away crumbs. Warm water felt good on her aching hands, and she dangled them in the bucket for a moment before using the scrub brush and rags. On her knees Florence moved from under the table to the area in front of the stove. She saw close up the mess she had made yesterday when hastily preparing chicken soup. Monday, Romek would need to return to work, so she would take the day off to stay with Basia. Father Maletski arrived just as she was drying the floor. Romek had summoned him as a precaution. He'd told her that Basia might take some comfort in praying with him.

Florence set aside cleaning and prepared the tea. On the tray for Basia she included a small ramekin of honeyed onion syrup with minced garlic. She set a small teaspoon next to the plates. At the

NOT YET LOST

top of the stairs she paused to listen. The priest's quiet words were punctuated with mumbled "amens." She balanced the tray on one arm and with the other made the sign of the cross in unison with the priest, signifying the end of the prayers. She elbowed the door open.

Darkness shrouded the crowded room. Romek lay beside Basia on top of the covers, making her gaunt body appear all the smaller. Father Maletski, who was wedged between the wall and the side of the double bed, retreated to a corner adjacent to the wardrobe.

"What is this? All this darkness?" Florence settled the tray on the nightstand on Basia's side of the bed. She parted the dark maroon velvet drapes she and Basia together had sewn. The late winter dullness offered little in the way of cheery light.

"Now that's better." Romek offered a wan smile at her efforts.

"I've laid out tea and some cakes in the kitchen. There's some sandwiches and coffee too. Father, you and Romek should go down and eat. Romek, you haven't eaten in some time." The priest took the hint to get Romek fed. His head cowed like a wounded bear, Romek lifted his heft and shuffled out the door.

"Now let's get you up here a bit." Florence adjusted the pillows behind Basia's head, then placed the back of her hand on her forehead. Still a fever, and quite a high one at that. The patient opened her eyes.

"Flo."

"Don't you talk. Save your strength. I've brought some honeyed onion syrup with garlic. It'll help." She offered her friend little tastes of the compound from the tip of the teaspoon.

"Flo—always—optimist," Basia spoke, breathing shallow breaths. For a few minutes the women continued as such. Florence fed Basia and brought the teacup to her lips intermittently. After a bit, Basia raised her fingertips indicating she'd had enough. "Lansing. Tell me."

Florence recounted her day with Stanley Nowak and the trip to the state capital. She belabored every aspect in the hope Basia would experience it vicariously. She described the furniture, the paintings, the clothing of the government officials, any minute detail she could remember.

"Won—derful. Will they—help?"

"The governor promised. Not for a while. Not until some of the auto industry conflicts are resolved."

"Typical."

"I truly believe he will keep his word." Florence busied herself around the bed, straightening sheets and tucking in corners. "Tomorrow, we'll get you up and I'll put some fresh sheets on." Florence stopped chattering when she saw Basia had drifted off. She gathered the tray and headed downstairs.

In the kitchen, she found Romek sitting in silence at the table. Father Maletski had departed. Florence rinsed the dishes and put the food, mostly untouched, away. She poured herself a cup of coffee and perched on the end of the corner banquette.

"She's resting."

"You're a good friend, Flo, the best!" Romek's eyes crinkled at the corners.

"I know you're worried, Romek. I am too. If anyone's strong, it's Basia. She'll pull through. She'll find a way. She has to." Florence's voice faded at the end of her sentence.

"She is strong, but her lungs are not. At night they rattle. She wakes herself up trying to catch her breath."

"Yes, I've heard it too."

"At that rat hole of a jail they wouldn't even let her have dry clothes. And it was cold there, so cold. The women huddled together. They tried to keep warm. Walking in circles."

Florence thought of the hot bath and hot tea with brandy she'd enjoyed at home while her friend shivered in the stone-cold dampness of the old jail.

"They didn't need to keep her there. They just wanted to prove a point. They threatened to send her and the others to DeHoCo."

She shuddered at the reference to Detroit House of Corrections out west. It was well known the prison staff there was harsh.

NOT YET LOST

"How frightening it must have been for Basia. And you." Florence put her hand on Romek's arm. He turned away, his hands rubbing his temples.

"You should get some rest, Romek, while you can. I'll go now but I'll be back with some dinner."

Florence gathered her things and shut the back door behind her. She made her way across the muddy alley and through her yard. She noticed the chickens had been fed. Must have been Frank. Inside her own kitchen she assessed her cupboards and ice box and started to think about dinner. Feeling quite tired, she sat down. Before long she laid her head on her crossed arms on the table and dozed off. Then Alex came home.

"What's with you?" Alex retrieved a bottle of beer from the ice box.

"Oh. Hello. I must have dozed off."

"I'd say so. All this running back and forth. Trying to manage two households. It's not necessary. Romek can manage."

Florence's fist tightened around the saltshaker.

"His wife is dying."

"Of her own doing."

"How dare you!" Florence rose, slamming the saltshaker down hard on the kitchen table, surprised when Alex flinched.

"She didn't have to be a martyr. She likes the limelight. And she dragged you with her like the Pied Piper."

"The limelight? Well, there's not much limelight over there lying in bed gasping for breath! You think that's glamorous?"

"Like I've said before, you'd made your point. You didn't have to turn it into a marathon. You could've come home."

"Come home? Then what? Go back to work with nothing changed?"

"Where did it all get you? A nickel? A dime? You don't have a union."

"Not yet. But we will!"

"Are you sure about that? Even if you do, at what cost? You don't even know!"

"I'm going to continue fighting. I'm not going to let all our hard work and Basia's go up in smoke!"

"What's for dinner?"

"Get your own."

On her way across the yard to the alley, Florence tucked an unsuspecting chicken under her arm. Once in the Sikorskis' yard, she entered their shed and retrieved a bucket and a hatchet. She placed the chicken on the overturned bucket and severed its neck. She released the body to the ground and watched it take a few steps blindly. She recognized herself in that chicken, walking without sight. No more. No more would she walk aimlessly. After gutting the bird she sat on the tree stump and plucked the feathers, one by one, with more force than necessary. Using matches she found in the shed, she singed the close hairs of the chicken's skin. Each match hissed as she dropped it in the watery snow, extinguished. When the burning was completed, she placed the chicken in the bucket and entered the Sikorski's kitchen. She called out her arrival. Adrenaline fueled her movements as she prepared the chicken for roasting. She'd just closed the oven door when Romek entered.

He sat down with the weight of the world on his shoulders. He planted his elbows on the table and buried his face in his hands. She noticed his shoulders heaving. How could such a bear of a man cry so quietly?

"She's gone."

Florence sat down next to him and they cried.

CHAPTER 31

Wednesday, March 31, 1937

Florence retrieved her black wool dress from the bathroom, where she had put it to steam. She'd worn it each of the last two days of Basia's wake. Tonight would be the third and final evening. Visitors turned out in astonishing numbers. So many people who didn't even know her paid their respects. So many women from other cigar factories honored her, their hearts brimming with gratitude that someone had spoken for them. Before going to the funeral home, she would swing by the Sikorski's to organize the vast amount of food delivered by the community. She didn't want any to go to waste.

"Do you need a shirt pressed?" Florence asked Alex as she pulled on her black wool tights. He was lying on the bed with a crooked arm behind his head. His eyes were closed.

"Why would I?" he answered without opening his eyes.

"It's the last night. You haven't gone to pay your respects."

"No. I haven't. I'm sure there're plenty of people. I won't be missed."

She hovered over Alex. "I don't know what's happened to you. You're not the man I married." Her fists clenched and unclenched at her side, her voice low and controlled. "You've become a mean, cold bastard. You won't get off your bed to offer comfort to Romek?"

"I can't."

"What does that mean, you can't?"

"I can't forgive her for pulling you into this mess. You've put everything I have worked for in jeopardy. You can't fathom what could happen."

"And what about me? Do you not care that my heart is broken? Basia was my best friend." She turned away, her tears threatening to spill over. While looking in her drawer for her best earrings, a gift from her mother, she heard Alex leave the room, then leave the house.

Alex headed out on foot toward the downtown business district. His hands were jammed deep into his work jacket pockets and he'd traded his fedora for a brown tweed cap.

"*Kurwa!*" He kicked an empty beer bottle but didn't bother to watch it break against the concrete wall of the liquor store. He paused at an alleyway and saw lumps of blankets served up on trays of cardboard. He took in the snorts of passed-out men, smelled the urine. The homeless. He averted his eyes and marched forward lest the tentacles of despair envelop him in their grip. How could this city, this engine of innovation and prosperity offering hope and salvation to the downtrodden of the world, fall flat on its face and fail to rise?

Poles lost their country when it was violently ripped apart, not once, but three different times, divided among Russia, Prussia, and the Austrian–Hungarian empire. Poland had been erased from the earth for over one hundred years. Poles came to America to find a new home, only to lose their houses to rapacious lenders and landlords. Something had to give, and soon. Seven, almost eight, years had passed since the stock market crashed. Companies were thriving again. Workers were not. What to do? Politics here were as Byzantine as in Eastern Europe. He had understood those. Here, he tiptoed through minefields. Incensed that Nick embroiled him in the doings of the Black Legion, he understood Nick's misstep. Alex didn't forgive him, but he understood how it could happen.

NOT YET LOST

Now he was on his way to another imbecilic secret meeting with codes and drama. At least the black robes weren't required tonight. He'd had to wear the ridiculous garb at the previous meeting when they'd planned to burn down the Kaminski place. He passed beneath the neon Rx sign and entered the drugstore, hoping tonight's assigned task wouldn't be too egregious.

"I want that bottle of Bacardi. Over there on that fourth shelf. At the end."

The druggist nodded and came around the front of the counter. Alex followed him through the black curtains into the back room. Without exchanging a word the druggist unlocked the painted wood door to the basement. Men's muted voices wafted up the stairwell. Alex braced himself and descended.

"There he is! The man of the hour." Fred walked over and escorted him to a group of chairs forming a circle. "We're laying out the plan now."

A few days ago, a man in J. L. Hudson's passed him a note commanding him to attend a meeting at the drugstore. Ever since Nick corralled him into the Legion, these vermin had come out of the woodwork in unlikely places. He didn't spook easily, but when this stranger approached him while he was with his boys, he was rankled. How dare they invade his family life? He was glad he'd been speaking Polish with his boys. The incident reminded him of how few qualms these men had. Until now, he'd managed to keep his involvement separate from his family.

The men discussed a wave of evictions that was going to take place. A Legion member who owned apartment buildings coordinated with other members in the police force.

"We expect the Unemployed Council will show up to protest in the streets as soon as they catch wind," the leader from the Black Legion initiation explained.

"Damn commies!" The voice of the man who'd assaulted him from behind at his initiation was now known to Alex by sight. His name was Keen. Alex found him vile.

The Communist Party had formed Unemployed Councils. Over the years, their tactics resisting evictions became more violent as they faced firmer resistance. The senior officer of the Legion passed two photographs across the table toward him.

"These men need to be eliminated before Friday. Without those two the Unemployed Council won't rally."

"Eliminated?"

"Don't act stupid, Falkowski!" the senior officer sneered. "The cops need to be able to remove the furniture and belongings of that scum that don't pay their rent. It needs to happen before Friday when the evictions will take place. You see, the landlord's a good friend of the Legion's."

Alex walked around the room, now silent. He stretched his entwined hands over his head and cracked his knuckles. He faced off with the leader of the Legion.

"I've gone along with everything you've wanted. I gave you names of agitators in the factory. I disrupted labor actions. Set fires. Shot out windows. I'm finished." Alex approached the stairs, but a beefy hand on his shoulder pulled him back.

"That is where you're wrong, Mr. Falkowski. It's because you've done all those things that you are *not* finished with us," the senior officer retorted while Keen pushed him down in the chair. "We have witnesses to all of it. Whether you know it or not, Legion members never work alone."

Mentally, Alex scrolled through the various tasks he'd done for the Legion, trying to recall who may have been a witness. His fingertips dug into his knees. If he'd brought a firearm, he would've done them all in then and there, and maybe the druggist on his way out the door. He knew he'd be patted down, so he hadn't bothered bringing his gun.

"Look, Falkowski, I know you're hesitant. But there's more to it." The Legion member changed his tone, taking the empathetic approach. "It's not just these crumbs we're kickin' to the curb. The commies take advantage of the unemployed. They do 'em a favor, rally behind 'em. Fight their eviction. Then comes election time and they're beholden. The commies expect votes in return. They're grooming candidates now. Highland Park. The mayor's race."

Alex nodded, rubbing his now less than perfectly smooth chin. This Black Legion goon wasn't wrong. He knew survivors took refuge in any port in a storm. Hadn't he done so, too, when he fell in with the Cossacks? The Red Party leaders were snakes with fangs. They bit in hard and swallowed people whole. Their rhetoric intoxicated people with hope of a better world, just like the Bolsheviks. Unemployed masses, reeling with disappointment from their expectations of the New World, were happy to be drunk. He remained silent.

"You're an intelligent man, Falkowski. I knew you'd see it our way." He shook hands with Alex and clapped him on the back. "We'll be in the know. Let's stay clear of each other for a while."

Alex nodded and took the stairs two at a time. He peered between the curtains to make sure the drugstore was empty before making a beeline for the front door. He ignored the druggist who bid him good night from behind his cash register.

The night air still had a bite even though spring was around the corner. The sky was clear. He walked. And walked. He stopped across the street from the White Eagle cigar factory. Streetlights shone on the icy slabs at the curb, the result of fire hoses having flooded the street. He envisioned Florence, Basia, and the others standing in defiance. A subdued, chaotic energy lingered. Broken awnings and windows; glass strewn on the street. A hunched man picked through the orphaned articles of clothing, stuffing a few under his coat. He examined a cup that must have been from the strike kitchen before shaking it out and plunging it into his pocket. Alex coughed so as not to startle the man, then handed him a few pennies from his pocket, less than the price of a movie ticket.

"Thank you, sir!" The man wouldn't look at Alex. Even in the dark, he sensed the anemic man reddening.

He continued walking. Tonight he didn't feel like going to Hastings and he didn't feel like going home. The wind picked up and the frigid barbs of the weather sought his bones. A neon sign ahead shouted the availability of warm coffee and homemade food. He picked up his pace. The café's warm vestibule couldn't rid him of the chilling cold coursing through him.

Warmth from the white ceramic mug tried to thaw his hands. Swirling steam rose to caress his cheeks. Simple pleasures provided immense comfort, especially living in such a complicated world. These penny cafes provided a good service: nutritious food, cheap, available all hours. He didn't want to splurge again like he did with the boys at Hudson's. He observed the clientele and assessed their clothes. Apparently, moths ate better than they did. Exposed faces and hands were burnished by the grime of the streets. The patrons shared a gray pallor. He watched the other men at the counter devour hunks of bread with dirt-encrusted fingers. The waitress placed the three dishes of his meal in front of him, a welcome diversion. Pea soup, a bowl of beans, and a large piece of brown bread. He laid a scrap of paper napkin across his right leg and dined.

Between bites he watched the baker. He could see into the passthrough to the back reaches of the kitchen. The baker had several bowls across a stainless steel counter under warming lights. He tended to them one by one, lifting the cotton dish towel and punching down the dough, then replacing the towel. He didn't know how many times the dough needed to be punched down—though he'd watched Florence many times—before the yeast rose in victory.

"Ready for your dessert? We have a dish of prunes tonight or spiced tomato cake." He didn't warm to either of the waitress's offerings, but it was included in his meal.

"I'd like the prunes, please."

With the small dish of prunes and a refilled cup of coffee in front of him, Alex knew he needed to get down to business. What to do? What to do?

NOT YET LOST

He'd just agreed, tacitly, to commit murder. He'd done it before in vastly different circumstances. He'd vowed never to do it again. That ignoramus in the Legion was right about the communists. They were a bunch of jackals who preyed on desperate people. The downtrodden found solace in a willing ear. The Communist Party found votes. He wondered if that goon at the drugstore realized how similar they were. He caught himself half smiling in the mirrored backsplash below the passthrough.

Could he muster the audacity to kill again? The world might be better off, but was it worth the risk? Like the goon said, no Legion member ever worked alone. He looked around. He'd probably been tailed tonight. If he followed through, the Legion would hold more power over him. At first, the assigned tasks weren't too egregious. Or at least he could tamp them down. He only started a small fire, shot out windows. The names he gave them from the factory were names they already knew. He didn't turn in anyone new. But torching the Kaminski farm? Who had he become?

If he flouted the directive, what would these halfwits do? They weren't afraid to inflict damage. He could take it, but what of his family? And what *of* his family? He left Florence looking like she'd gone a full fifteen in the ring. Simply walked out on her to meet with thugs. His predicament defied the logic he was trying to impose.

"You look like a man with troubles. Here, I'm not supposed to give you second refills but it's the bottom of the pot anyway."

"Thank you."

She was right. The coffee definitely came from the bottom of the pot. He pulled coins from his pocket, almost twice the cost of the meal, and headed toward the exit. In the booth next to the door, the man he'd seen scavenging the debris near the cigar factory slept, head slumped on the table.

By the time Alex returned home, Florence was lost to the world, deep in slumber under the feather blanket. When he pulled a beer from the ice box, he saw that her brother must have brought groceries again. A good man, Joe.

JANIS M. FALK

— — —

For all three days Florence visited the funeral home, remaining there for most of the day and the evening. Repeating the prayers of the rosary comforted her. The hand-carved facets of the wooden beads provided her nervous fingertips a place to rest. The funeral home attendant placed a hand on her shoulder.

"Someone is here to see you."

"Me?"

"Yes. He's out front. He said he wasn't sure if he should come in."

Puzzled, Florence pocketed the rosary beads and, without retrieving her coat, stepped out front. Her hand flew to cover her mouth when she saw Resnick standing under the portico.

"Mr. Resnick!"

"Mrs. Falkowski." Resnick removed his cap and wrung it between his hands. He shifted his weight from one foot to the other. "I'm sorry about Mrs. Sikorski. I truly am."

Stunned, Florence did not respond. She just looked at Resnick.

"I wanted to pay my respects but didn't know if I should go in. I don't want to upset anybody. Stir up any trouble. It wouldn't be right."

Still, Florence remained silent.

"Well, you should go back in. Don't need you getting sick too." Resnick replaced his cap and turned to leave.

"Wait!" Florence implored. "Come in. Please."

Resnick held the door open for Florence. She took him by the arm and led him into the room. Perhaps she imagined it, but quiet blanketed the room. She led him to the kneeler in front of the open casket and knelt. Resnick knelt beside her. Together they prayed. After a few moments, the two stood and receded to a quiet corner.

"Thank you, Mrs. Falkowski. You're so kind. You see, I admired Mrs. Sikorski. I wish I had her moxie. I know I made her life, and your life, harder than it needed to be. And I'm sorry for that." She nodded both her agreement and acceptance of the apology.

After Resnick left, Florence stood at the back of the room to make way for the multitude of mourners gathering around the casket. Her heart ached as Romek encircled each person, one after the other, in his generous embrace. His unbridled tears stained wet rivulets on his tie. The pace of the receiving line stopped. She noticed Stanley Nowak and his wife conversing with the widower. Undoubtedly, they had more to say than simple condolences. After Romek released Stanley from a second embrace, the couple assumed positions at the side-by-side white kneelers adjacent to the coffin. Somewhat brief in their prayers, they crossed themselves and rose. Margaret gazed for a moment at Basia's face, then blew a kiss to bid her adieu. Stanley urged her along by taking her hand. He wended his way through the crowd, nodding to and acknowledging many people who recognized him.

"Dear Florence." Stanley took both of her hands in his. "I'm so sorry. Basia was your closest friend. Like sisters. It's so hard to lose someone like her."

Florence nodded. She pulled her damp handkerchief from her sleeve and dabbed at her eyes. Margaret hugged her.

"I've been in touch with Lansing." Stanley referred to the governor's office by the name of the capital city. "Murphy's under pressure from business leaders and the mayor to address the sit-down strike at Dodge Main. At least we've got their attention now." His eyes shone bright. "I'm afraid the issues in the cigar industry will have to wait a little longer."

Florence nodded. She feared to open her mouth. Tears might pour unfettered, but words may as well. Involuntarily, she looked to the front.

Stanley's voice softened. "I know. She fought with all her heart. We won't forsake her. I promise."

Finally, the long receiving line tapered off and Romek joined them. His brown eyes, rimmed with red, displayed the colors of fall and the stark desolation it portended. His slight smile was grim as he met her eyes, and the abyss of grief lay between them.

"It's been a long day, eh?" ventured Stanley.

"Yes. You know. It's to be expected."

"All these people here." He gestured to the crowd. "Quite a testament to Basia, I'd say."

"Yes. We're just ordinary people. If it hadn't been for the last two months, would all these people have known her?"

"I don't know, but she lived large the last two months, and all these people *do* know her. She was remarkable," Stanley declared.

"*O, Boże*, there's nothing ordinary about Basia. She's so special. A gift from heaven!"

"I'll agree with you there, Florence." A warm spark of fire ignited in Romek's autumn eyes. "Stanley, how's it going at the plant? Some of the guys filled me in a bit."

"Good. So many men stayed in. Some you wouldn't have expected. We're holding our own. Getting quite good at these sit-ins."

"I'll be there. After. The funeral is tomorrow."

"No, take some time for yourself. No one expects you—"

"Basia would expect me to be there. She'd want me to stay as long as it takes. And I can't disappoint her, can I?" He looked at the casket centered at the front of the room. Flower arrangements, ranging from twine-tied posies to elegant cascading blooms, flanked the simple coffin.

"Yes, I will be there," Romek vowed.

CHAPTER 32

Monday, April 5, 1937

Stale air in the cigar factory rested like a shroud. Florence coughed. Basia's worktable remained empty even though new workers joined the group. By silent agreement, her place became a shrine. Occasionally, a flower or trinket adorned the work surface. Even Resnick didn't disturb the area. He didn't dare. Florence didn't mind the subdued ambiance. She was digesting the whirlwind of the past several weeks. The latest puzzlement occurred that morning in their bedroom after breakfast. She had been gathering her things when Alex announced he was joining the sit-in. Stunned, she'd sat on the bed and watched as he collected his razor, shaving cream, a comb, soap, washcloths.

"I think that's good. I'm surprised." She kept her tone neutral. "What changed your mind, if I may ask?"

"Romek. If a man can go soon after burying his wife, then so should I."

"Good. It's very good." She stood. "Let me help you. Now you'll need this tooth powder. I can get another. Here's some underwear and undershirts. Socks. How many pairs? You'll need at least three pairs. And how about these?" She held up a pair of his pajamas. He shook his head no. She kneeled with her head almost touching the floor and lifted the bed skirt. "Here's the small satchel you can take. Everything should fit." Standing, she faced him, an arm's length away.

"Florence, it's not a vacation."

"Don't I know it! But still, you'll be more comfortable if—"

"I'll be fine." The look in his eye told her to stop.

"*O, Boże*, I'm sorry. I'm just—oh, Alex!" She hugged him tight and kissed him goodbye before she left for work. "Call me if you can. I'll send food. And look after Romek." He had nodded but said nothing. What was this change all about? Did he feel guilty for not attending the wake?

At the factory Florence stopped rolling to refill her small dispenser with glue. She was taken aback by the number of cigars she finished in no time while she was replaying the morning's events in her mind. It was spring and change was in the air. Some changes had been better than others. The room was so empty without Basia's laugh. Oftentimes, Florence noticed when she was staring at Basia's seat, her hands would freeze mid-task. Each time, she renewed her vow to continue their work, knowing full well she could never replace Basia.

During one such moment, two men, very starched and buttoned-up, appeared in the doorway. They blinked unnaturally, acclimating to the low light levels. Florence glanced at Resnick, who was leaning back in his chair with his eyes closed. He'd arrived late that morning, disheveled, wearing a rumpled suit jacket. She knocked on the door and poked her head in without being invited. Resnick swung his legs off the desk and lifted a sheaf of papers.

"There's some men here to see you." She pointed through the window. Resnick followed her gesture.

"Hmmm. I don't know them. Thank you, Mrs. Falkowski." He slipped on his suit jacket, which was hanging on the back of his chair. He started to walk past her.

"Wait!" She put a hand on his shoulder. "Let me remove this before you go out there." She removed a wilted green carnation from his lapel. She looked Resnick in the eyes. She studied their depths, seeing myriad emotions.

"They look like government types. We can't have them thinking you're a man about town now, can we?"

"You're a gem." She thought he was going to kiss her cheek.

Resnick left to greet the men, and she returned to her table but remained attentive to the doorway. They exited, presumably to the upstairs office.

Ah, Resnick. He was, in so many ways, an innocent. All he'd known in his young life was fear. First in Germany, then here, without a loving family. They'd had a pleasant conversation when he'd attended Basia's wake. Ever since, they'd been friends, of sorts. He was well-read. They discussed books now and again. He was quite timid underneath the false bravado.

Schwarz's knuckles grazed the top of his desk as he stood to address the two men whom Resnick ushered into his office.

"You do realize I'm Jewish. Hardly would we tolerate Nazi activity or propaganda in my factory. And, frankly, I am insulted you would insinuate as much!"

"No need to get upset, Mr. Schwarz. We're just doing our jobs," the tall, slender man with a pince-nez said.

Resnick hovered by the credenza, fiddling with the cups and coffee, intimating he would offer some to these intruders. He had no intention of it. He watched the other man check his notebook and point something out to the tall one, who nodded. He must think himself a regular Phylo Vance, the popular fictional detective.

"As I'm sure you're aware, being commissioned by the McCormack–Dickstein Committee, our job is to root out *any* un-American activities. Yes, that includes Nazi propaganda, but also communist activity. That includes labor activists. We know the American Communist Party infiltrates labor unions in an attempt to garner votes. We are to identify anyone with such proclivities."

"I don't think we know anyone with such pro-cli-vi-ties, do we Uncle?" Resnick couldn't help himself, though he suffered his uncle's reprimanding eye.

"Look." Schwarz, now seated, folded his hands in front of him on the desk. He leaned forward. "We came here from Germany. We want to live just as you. Free. Independent. We work. We raise our children. We look after our own."

"Even though recent activities at your factory didn't warrant much coverage in the newspapers, we've stayed informed. You have some employees, women, who we think are backed by the Communist Party. What are their names?" The tall one turned to his sidekick, who replied, "Sikorski and Falkowski."

"Is that so?"

"Yes, we think some party members are egging on these women. Maybe their husbands. The UAW is backing their activities. We all know the Communist Party has them in their pocket."

"Do we now?" Schwarz sat back in his worn leather chair, his elbows on the arms, fingertips together forming a triangle. Resnick always thought his uncle exuded a professorial air.

"You have mostly Polish women here, right?" The slender man checked his notebook.

"We do. And you think you can judge them summarily by their ethnicity? Is that right?" Schwarz stood.

"Well, many people, immigrants from Eastern Europe, have different ideas from those of us who settled—"

"You need to go now. I don't harbor any political groups in my factory. Neither Nazi nor communist sympathizers." Whenever his uncle spoke in that eloquent tone, Resnick held him in awe. "You can look for yourselves. I only abide those who work hard and endeavor to better themselves. I dare say, your employer might consider doing the same. Good day, gentlemen." Resnick took his uncle's cue to lead the government employees out of the office.

Florence looked up when Resnick and the two buttoned-up men returned in the doorway. She looked down again at her work but kept the men in her peripheral vision. Resnick cleared his throat and began speaking in an overly articulated and loud voice.

"You can see, gentlemen, there is an empty seat there."

She popped her head up and met Resnick's gaze. His eyes bored into hers as if trying to send a message. "Mrs. Falkowski is not here today." Across the room heads swiveled toward Florence, though they just as easily could have been looking at Basia's empty chair.

"And how about Sikorski? Which one is she?" The one with the notepad scanned the room.

"She's dead."

The starched ones nodded and left. Resnick strode past Florence and motioned with his head for her to follow him. She was barely seated across from him before she blurted out her question.

"What was that about? Who were those men?"

"They're from a government agency. At first we thought they were here looking for Nazi propaganda, but they're actually here looking for communists."

"Communists! What's that got to do with me?"

"They think labor activists and union organizers might be communists."

"*O, Boże!*" She slumped back in her chair. "Am I in trouble?"

"I wouldn't worry about it. Uncle Steve dispensed with them quite matter-of-factly."

"Why did you stick your neck out?"

"One good turn—" He patted the left lapel of his suit jacket.

"I see. Since you brought it up, I have a bone to pick with you." It was time.

"Brought what up?"

"Good turns." She was comfortable in their newfound kinship.

He leaned forward with his elbows on the desk, hands folded in front of him.

"Why do you torment the young girls like you do?"

"I don't know. I really don't. I'm supposed to be in charge. Uncle Steve put me in this job. I don't know how to do it. All he does is berate me. Tells me what he was doing at my age. I'm not him."

"I understand. You're afraid. But so are those girls! They're young.

They *don't* understand." She sat on the edge of her chair, back straight. "They're afraid too! Look at Alicja. She couldn't face you again."

"She's too young to be working in a place like this. She should be in school."

"Is that so? Well, she has to work. Her father was injured on the job and the company didn't pay him much. He can't work. She helps support the family."

"I didn't know," he mumbled.

"She'd love nothing better than to be in school. She wants to study medicine and help people like her papa."

Resnick buried his face in his hands. Were his exhaustion and his hangover as much to blame as his shame? Through the window to the work area, she could see several women stealing glances her way, undoubtedly wondering what was transpiring. They'd heard the charade, Resnick's misdirection. She waited. Resnick lifted his head.

"I'm sorry. I truly am. I'm as lost as poor Scraps here." He rubbed the dog behind his ears. "I didn't really want to come to America. I have friends in Germany. My parents gave me no alternative."

"From what I read, you should be glad you came here, with everything happening there."

"I know. I don't belong in Germany now. I don't belong in America either. I don't belong in my family. And I certainly don't belong in this job!"

"That all may be true. But do you think you're the only one? What gives you the right to take out your problems on these women?" Florence pointed to the window overlooking the factory floor. "We're just trying to feed our families." She stood now, towering over Resnick, who remained seated at his desk. "I don't belong here either! Did you know I was educated in Montreal? At an elite girls' school? I wanted to be an artist. Do you think I'll ever paint again with these fingers?" She held her hands in front of her as if they were foreign objects to be reviled. "They hurt. From morning till night, they hurt. The pain even wakes me up at night." Her voice, now loud, commanded the attention of the workers. She glanced through the window at the sea of gawking faces. "You see, Mr. Resnick, I don't know you well enough to know what kind of man you really are. But I do know one type of man you could be. A kind man. Everyone likes a kind man. A kind person. Maybe then, you wouldn't be so lonely!" She opened the door with a flourish. It slammed into the grimy plaster wall, leaving a divot. Over her shoulder she said, "*How far that little candle throws its beams! So shines a good deed in a naughty world.*"

"Shakespeare."

She gave him a quick nod and left. At her worktable she rolled leaves with savage ferocity. A hush settled over the room.

Later that evening after dinner Florence settled herself into the living room. She was tired. The kitchen was clean, and she didn't feel like washing clothes. She retrieved her knitting needles, made two mistakes, and threw the needles into the basket on the floor. The hearth was cold and covered in soot. Lacking ambition to light a fire, she closed her eyes and leaned the crook of her neck on the walnut trim of the sofa. She searched for a feeling, any feeling, but she had none to spare. She had none at all.

CHAPTER 33

Wednesday, April 7, 1937

Alex swept metal shavings off the workbench using a hand brush and staccato strokes. He liked a tidy work surface. He fingered the metal object he'd created, using a file now and again to smooth a burr.

"Alex," Romek whispered, standing in the doorway of the inventor's room. Alex turned.

"I thought I'd find you in here. What's that you got there?"

"Just an idea." Alex held his device in the palm of his hand.

"The strike runners brought some food in. I brought you a plate."

"*Dziękuję.*" He washed his hands at the small sink and transformed his workspace into a place setting, draping a clean rag across his right leg. Romek perched on a metal stool nearby.

"You surprise me, Alex. Several days now, you've stayed inside with us."

"It's almost like a holiday. I can work in here uninterrupted. Use the equipment without those *dupeks* looking over my shoulder."

"But Alex, they're countin' on you. You're going to come up with the next big idea for them to steal." Romek chuckled.

Alex raised his eyebrows, nodding his head in knowing agreement. "We may not have jobs after this." He jerked his thumb over his shoulder toward the main factory. "We'll have to do something. I want to work for myself anyway."

NOT YET LOST

"If anyone can start their own company, you can, Alex. But I think we'll be able to work. If we want to."

"That is the question, isn't it?"

"The women are back rolling cigars."

"Uh-huh." Alex ate.

"You and me, Alex, we got us some good women."

"Uh-huh." Alex noted Romek didn't acknowledge his good woman, Basia, was gone.

"Come on. Talk to me, Alex. Why're you really here? The guys think you're a spy."

"They're right." He cleared his place setting and returned to his metal object.

"What! What're you saying?" Romek yanked on Alex's shoulder, swinging him around on his stool to face him.

"That's right. I've been a spy. But a poor one."

Romek's eyes widened almost beyond their physical limits.

"Fred hoodwinked me into reporting names of people who were organizers. Activists. Communist sympathizers."

"Who'd you turn in?"

"No one they didn't already know about." Alex picked up his metal file again and applied it to a rough spot.

"What about me?"

"I didn't need to tell them." Alex smiled at Romek.

"I'll be damned." Romek plopped down on his stool and ran his massive hand through his overgrown, thick hair. "So that's why you're here?"

"No. It's not." Alex inspected a round metal piece, holding it close to his eye. "Can I trust you?"

"Me? Of course!" Romek scoffed.

"Trust in the most serious life and death way."

"Really, *braciszek*, my brother, after all these years?"

Alex rose and paced the room, idly picking up and organizing tools on the benches. Slowly, haltingly, he revealed his predicament with the Black Legion.

"It's beyond belief, Romek. You don't know who belongs, who doesn't. When you're being watched. What they'll ask you to do. What'll happen if you don't."

Romek did not interrupt but nodded encouragement.

Alex struggled to meet his eyes. "Now you know why I'm here." He stopped pacing.

"What does all this have to do with this strike?"

"I'm hiding, Romek! Hiding! Like a scared little *dziecko* behind his mother's skirts. I'm not noble. I'm not here for a cause. I'm not here to support you. I'm just hiding." Alex began pacing again. Neither spoke for a moment.

"Why now?" Romek asked. "Why tell me now?"

"They ordered me to murder."

"What!" Romek joined Alex in pacing the room. He swung his arms and drove one fist into the palm of the other hand.

"Who, Alex? Who do they want you to murder?"

Alex leaned against the workbench, holding on to the edge to brace himself.

"The two primary leaders of the Unemployed Council. Alleged communists."

"Yes. I know them."

Romek stopped across the room, his large brown eyes boring into Alex's. Romek stood to his full height and rushed him. Alex raised his hands defensively, expecting a punch, and was surprised when Romek wrapped him in a bear hug.

"My friend, my friend, you are so strong. You've carried this burden all alone."

After a moment Alex pulled back, hurriedly wiping away small tears.

"Go ahead, *braciszek*. Sob. Let it out. Grieve for your predicament. Our predicament." Romek released him, and he regained his composure. Alex pulled a comb from his back pocket and ran it through his long blonde hair, sweeping it off his forehead. His hair was now dirty from several days of being locked in the factory. He promptly wiped the comb on a rag.

"Does Florence know?"

"No. How could I tell her?"

"Let me help you, Alex. I know it's not in your nature. Please. I beg you. We need to protect each other," Romek beseeched him.

Alex didn't say yes, but he didn't say no. He leveled his icy blue eyes at his friend.

"Give me some time to think. We need to think of a way out."

"There may not be one."

Romek put his brawny hand over Alex's. "There's always a way. Have hope."

"And always a cost." Alex crossed his arms.

"Come. Friends are out there." Romek jerked his head toward the door. "There's some good poker games going. Just try not to fleece 'em too bad."

The corner of Alex's lips turned up ever so slightly.

Frank leaped over the chain connecting two train cars with the agility of boyhood. The train had been stalled on the siding since the strike started. Workers refused to unload the raw materials. Streetlights from the far side cast shadows of the hopper cars heaped with taconite. His black hat pulled low and his matching scarf pulled high, he snaked along close to the train. Now and again, he ducked between cars to stop and listen. He didn't hurry. He relished the game, though he knew it was more than that. At eleven at night, factory security and police were scarce. Throngs of badges had surrounded the factory on the first few days of the strike, expecting violence. None occurred. Unrest permeated the city and the police had been reassigned to quell other labor uprisings. Those remaining had grown bored. The situation was at a stalemate.

As planned, his uncle Joe was waiting for him inside the factory when he scampered beneath the slightly rolled-up dock door. After a brief greeting and hug, Joe handed him a bag.

"Wow! A lot of messages tonight."

"Distribute them as quickly as you can tomorrow. Get your brother to help if need be." Joe lowered his voice and motioned with his hand for Frank to do the same.

"I can do it, Uncle Joe. I'm fast as a jackrabbit."

"That you are, my boy." Joe smiled. "Now what do you have for me?"

Frank emptied both pockets of his dark trousers and pressed wads of folded paper into Joe's hand. He had devised this system of communicating with the families in case authorities tapped the phone lines.

"Now keep this one separate. Deliver it immediately to your mother."

"Is Papa all right?"

"Yes, he is, Frank. He's holding up just fine."

"I'll let Mama know." Frank hugged his uncle and rolled his small frame back under the door into the black of night. Once his eyes readjusted, he crouched and crept along in the lee of the train. At the point where the train walled off the end of his street, he stepped on the chain between cars and jumped down, reaching his arms above his head, exalting in the adventure. His front porch was in view. He scanned the street. A few people walking in the distance, but nothing out of the ordinary. He started down the narrow sidewalk toward home.

A deep voice came from a man who lurked in the shadows. "Hey, kid! Whatcha got in that bag there?"

"Nothing." Frank clutched the bag close to his chest.

"You got a bag full of nothing?"

"It's a rabbit. I emptied my snares. Over there." The man looked up, and in that split second, Frank made a run for his porch.

"Tell your dad he better come through!" The man laughed and receded into the darkness, cracking his chewing gum.

CHAPTER 34

Wednesday, April 15, 1937

Florence tapped her fingers on the steering wheel in time with the windshield wipers. She'd parked their black Dodge coupe near the corner of Chene and Michigan Avenue as the note from Alex instructed. She'd been confused by the cryptic message Frank had delivered but now understood Alex was in a serious predicament. She peered through the gray drizzle, trying to identify people in front of the mid-rise apartment building. Protesters locked arms across the front of the building. Two men shouted through bullhorns. Cars jammed the side streets. Police cars blocked the area in front of the building. Fire truck sirens reverberated off the brick apartment building. She shuddered.

Romek, immediately recognizable, was stationed near the breezeway. She had passed through the arch into the courtyard many times over the years when visiting friends or canvassing for church activities. She noticed Father Maletski joined the human chain just a few links down from the men with megaphones. Often, when he'd caught wind of upcoming evictions, and with other church members, he preemptively moved the families' household items for safekeeping. Some furniture was stored at the church, some at Dom Polski. She wasn't acquainted well with the specific families, but she knew they couldn't afford to have their few belongings destroyed. Those executing the evictions seemed to take pleasure in damaging the victims' property. She continued to scan the crowd. Ah, there he was.

Alex paced back and forth on the sidewalk. He must've stopped at home to get his black raincoat. She knew he didn't have it at the factory. His hat was pulled low over his brow, not unusual given the drizzle, but oddly, he seemed to tip it ever so slightly now and again as if in greeting. His right hand remained shoved deep into his coat pocket. Why on earth was he strutting like a sage grouse if unsavory characters had him in their sights? Finally, he veered from the sidewalk and engaged with the two men with the megaphones. She thought they might be with the Unemployed Council. Newspapers covered the Council extensively, both for its activism on behalf of the unemployed and for its alleged ties to the Communist Party. Joan had written of them in great detail for *Głos Ludowy*. Now she was truly intrigued. What could Alex have to say to them?

Soon Alex led the men toward the breezeway, though not before they handed off their bullhorns. Chants resumed. Alex seemed to be introducing the men to Romek, who, after a moment, waved them beyond his sentry point. The three men vanished into the breezeway. Police charged the protesters, swinging billy clubs. Romek joined the fray. The sound of gunshots rose above the ruckus. One. Then two. Those in the brawl didn't seem to notice. She panned the area for the source, or the result, but found neither. Alex exited the breezeway alone. She gasped. Could he? His gait was brisk yet unhurried. There it was again! A small gesture with his hat directed toward a small group of onlookers. He patted his right pocket. He crossed the street and continued toward her. She started the car.

Alex slid into the front passenger seat and slammed the door. "Drive around the block to the back of the apartments." She did as she was told. This was no time to ask questions. "Pull over here."

The two men who'd accompanied Alex exited the breezeway on the other side of the courtyard. She sighed in relief to see them alive. They crawled into the back seat. She looked at Alex for direction. He peered out his window expectantly, and moments later, Romek lumbered around the corner. He squeezed into the back seat.

"Go!" Alex commanded.

Florence popped the clutch. In the rearview mirror, she saw the wide-eyed men slammed against their seats. She almost smiled.

"Where to?"

"Drive to the back of St. Florian's."

Florence headed toward their church. She felt alive. She wasn't sure what was happening, but she was part of it. Bonnie Parker came to mind. The men in back swayed in unison as she rounded the corner of the church, perhaps a bit too fast. The brakes squealed and the car stopped. They all lurched forward, then back. Alex shot her a disapproving look. She grinned. The two men, strangers to her, pried themselves out of the back and scurried to the stairwell leading to the basement. Still in the back seat, Romek let out a sigh of relief.

"Take us to the back side of the plant. Safely, please." Alex smiled at her.

Was Florence mistaken, or did she detect a hint of admiration? She eased the coupe to a stop at the back gate. Romek got out with a quick nod to her in the mirror. She and Alex looked each other in the eye for a moment before he cradled her face in his hands and kissed her. Romek rapped on the window. They giggled and blushed.

Alex searched her eyes again before he whispered with a raspy timbre, "I love you!"

"I love you too!"

CHAPTER 35

Friday, April 30, 1937

Florence's aching fingers worked with practiced precision as she crimped the edges of the pierogi dough. She finished up the stack of sauerkraut-filled crescents and spun around from the kitchen table to check on the large pot of potatoes, which were taking a long time to boil. She stirred them with a large wooden spoon. Over a month had passed since the strike at Dodge Main started. In the first few weeks the women gathered in the evenings, often cooking together at Dom Polski. They took turns hosting weekend get-togethers at each other's homes. This week, collectively, they were tired. They worked all week, took care of children, did housework, and paid bills, or at least organized them to be paid when their husbands received paychecks again. Here it was, Friday night, late, and she occupied herself making pierogies. Maybe tomorrow she would get to work on the vegetable garden.

Florence drained the water from the large stock pot, added sour cream, and worked the masher vigorously. Once the creamy potatoes were smooth, she decided to put them in the ice box and finish filling the dough in the morning. She put the kettle on to boil and plunked down on the bench seat. She'd enjoy a cup of hot tea before bed. Other than the gurgling of the water, the house was quiet. Her hand twitched. She almost reached for the phone on the wall to call Basia, then remembered.

NOT YET LOST

The cathedral-shaped radio perched on the shelf behind the table. She reached for the knob. Coverage of the upcoming coronation in England and of the Hindenburg dirigible's travels enthralled her. She relished the diversion. After the kettle whistled, she prepared her cup with a slosh of brandy while the tea steeped.

"Just in, the strike at Dodge Main automobile plant has been settled. According to the governor's office, an agreement was reached today between the striking workers and factory owners. Governor Murphy intervened to facilitate a contract to get the city's largest factory back into production. Workers sat down in the plant forty days ago in protest of low pay, accelerated production speeds—"

"*O, Boże!* Alex will come home! I wonder if he'll still have a job," Florence exclaimed out loud. She tipped her teacup all the way up, then began cleaning the kitchen with her second wind. Or was it the third? No matter. She transferred the pierogies from the platter to a baking dish and covered it before placing it in the ice box. Tomorrow she'd call Stanley Nowak. Maybe now the governor would work on the cigar industry union. She brushed crumbs from the counters and table onto the floor and retrieved the broom and dustpan from the vestibule near the back door. After sweeping, she filled a pail with hot soapy water. She grabbed for the table's edge to steady herself as she kneeled to wash the floor.

"*O, Boże*, I'm getting old!" Her arms alternated between arching swaths and short scouring strokes with the sponge. She couldn't believe it. Governor Murphy promised he would attend to the cigar industry once the auto workers were settled, and his comments irked her at the time. Why should the women workers play second fiddle to the men? Then, of course, she realized the pure economics of it. Many more people worked at Dodge Main. The automobile industry was the engine that drove the city, the state. Automobile barons donated to campaign funds, and more workers meant more votes. She *was* getting old. When had the cynicism crept in?

"He promised! He seemed a man of his word." She tried to

rekindle belief. She sat back on her heels and wrung out the sponge over the pail. What would Basia think? Basia! If only—

Navigating around the legs of the kitchen table, Florence put muscle into scrubbing the space where Alex's feet rested.

"Alex!" She reared back, slamming her head against the underside of the table. He had been safe locked away in the factory during the strike. But now what? Would those men in that Legion track him down and hurt him? She backed out from underneath the table. Moving with purpose, she dumped the water from the bucket outside the back door and snatched a coat off the hook in the back vestibule. She better go see what was happening outside the plant.

Inside the factory, the men celebrated. Stanley Nowak had just left after announcing the results of the negotiations. Alex gathered his tools and materials to return to the workshop. He was eager to go home. Romek called a huddle near the drill presses. What's he up to now? It's over. Settled. Alex welcomed the improved working conditions and pay. He doubted if much else would change. The same people, with the same prejudices, would be in charge. Would they retaliate? He looked up at the men slapping each other on the back and passing bottles around, celebrating the right to breathe air. Closing the lid on the toolbox, he saw the huddle disperse and Romek approach.

"*Braciszcek!*" Romek draped a strapping arm around Alex's shoulders and fell in step. "Good news, eh? We get to go home."

"Yes. It's been a long time." The men broke apart to pass through the door to the workshop. Alex arranged the tools and other items into their proper places, then Romek closed the door behind them.

"Alex! Listen." Romek's jovial demeanor vanished like a wisp of smoke. His weighty brown eyes penetrated Alex's. "You've been safe in here. Out there," Romek extended a muscled arm, his index finger pointing through the window, "those Legion men are waiting. From what you've told me, they won't quickly forget our little caper with the men from the Unemployed Council. You're in danger."

Alex smirked, remembering the day they'd whisked away into safety the two men he'd been charged with killing. "You're probably right. But what am I to do? I want to go home. See Florence."

"I understand. She's a good woman, Alex. *Aniołeczek*, for sure. Don't forget that. You never know—"

Romek turned away. An angel. Yes, Florence was an angel. Romek flinched, then steeled his body against what Alex presumed was pain coursing through it, remembering his own *aniołeczek*, Basia. A true angel in heaven, for those who believed in such things, as he knew Romek did.

"Romek, I'm sorry." Now it was Alex's turn to embrace his neighbor. He braced himself as Romek released his bone-crushing weariness onto Alex's tall but thin frame. Alex held him fiercely. After a moment, Romek extricated himself.

"My friend. Let's go. We have a plan, but it'll only work if we leave now."

A few moments later, a small mob of men walked out of the factory in lockstep. The group of them resembled a mountain, with Alex its peak in the middle. They were rambunctious. They shouted raucously and raised their arms in the air. The group moved as an amoeba, out the front door, across the train tracks, past the crowds gathered outside the gate, and down Denton Street. For once, Alex was glad he lived close to the factory. Once in front of his house, the group veered toward the porch and parted like the Red Sea to deliver Alex to his front door.

"Stay inside now. Call me if anything seems suspicious," admonished Romek.

"Take your own advice. They know who you are too."

Romek nodded, a million words unsaid.

The men from the pod dispersed into the melee of the street.

Alex expected Florence would've greeted him. She wasn't in the kitchen. It was late. Maybe she was already asleep. He couldn't imagine, though, with all the noise from the street. He bounded up the stairs. The boys' room was empty. He hadn't seen Florence since the day she'd driven the car like a seasoned bank robber. She was something else. He opened the door to their bedroom. Empty. He turned at the sound of the front door opening.

"Flo?" He ran back down the stairs, stopping face-to-face with Joe, his brother-in-law and boarder.

"A bunch of us are meeting at Wally's. Want to come? I just stopped in to pick up some cash and a clean shirt."

"No. Have you seen Florence?"

"No. She's probably at some women's doing down at the hall."

Joe went upstairs to wash off the stench of alcohol, sweat, and grime from the last forty days of living in the factory. When he was finished, Alex went upstairs to do the same. He stood in the tub, relishing the hot water flowing over his body and the steamy tendrils orbiting his head. The front door opened and closed. He hoped Joe locked the door behind him. Or maybe it was Florence coming home. Just a few more minutes. He deserved it, didn't he? He lathered his face and shoulders, scrubbed his collarbone. He hoped Romek had gone to Wally's to avoid returning to his empty home. Alex towel-dried his hair before flipping it back off his face with a comb. He needed to visit the barber. Now that he was clean, he would attend to the rumble in his belly.

Odd. Half of the kitchen floor was clean. Foodstuffs on the table suggested Florence had been making pierogies. He checked the ice box. A plate of dumplings and a bowl of mashed potatoes sat on the top shelf. He pulled out the plate and lifted the covering. Sauerkraut. The phone rang.

"Hello?"

"Is this Mr. Falkowski?"

Alex tightened his grip. "Yes." He suppressed his fear.

"I'm from the police department. We're holding your son Lucien here."

"Luc? What's he done? Are you at the Beaubien station?"

"No. We're holding him here in the car on Hastings. He's underage. Been carousing down here. Causing trouble at the clubs. Got complaints."

"Can you bring him home?"

"No. You'll have to come get him if you don't want him booked at the station."

"I'll be there." Alex returned upstairs to change out of his robe. He donned nice slacks and a shirt. He sat on the worn chair to shoehorn his feet into his dress shoes. Maybe the police would be lenient with his exuberant son if he, the father, looked respectable. Winter had dissipated while he'd been sequestered in the plant. He could wear nice shoes without galoshes. "Damn him!" Alex cursed his son. Going out was not appealing; he was so damned tired. Where was Florence? Maybe she was looking for the boys. She must know the strike was settled if she was out somewhere. Descending the front porch steps, he noted the lawn had been cut and the garden area tilled, though not yet planted. He nodded in approval.

Florence squeezed her shoulders tight as she edged through the crowd. "*Proszę, Proszę,*" she pleaded for people to let her through. Stretching up on her toes, she still couldn't see well enough to find Alex. He had to be there somewhere. Hundreds of men marched through the gate from Dodge Main, the spring in their step far different from the gait with which they'd entered to work over a month ago. In the dark, distinguishing the men proved difficult, but still she thought she would recognize Alex. People stepped on her feet and jostled her around. Many women had come to greet their men, and she wound her way around many couples embracing.

A loud group caught her attention as they crossed the train tracks inside the gate. She couldn't imagine Alex was among them. He wasn't one to behave so boisterously. But maybe. Living in a factory for over a month may have eroded his sense of decorum. Perhaps it would be best if she returned home. Even if those Legion men were here, what could she do to spare him harm? She'd been foolish in her impulse to protect him. She elbowed her way out of the crowd. It was much easier going with the flow away from the factory rather than against. She decided to stop at Wally's before going home. He might be there, or maybe someone had seen him.

Approaching the door, Florence noted the small round glass window, now whole, which Alex's head had broken just a few months earlier. She hesitated before pulling the knob. Spirited conversation, though thunderous, sounded convivial. Inside, the space was almost as crowded as the street at the gate.

"*Proszę! Proszę!* Let me through."

She clenched the molded edge of the bar and pulled herself up close, then held tight. Men around her clamored for drinks. Wally was at the other end of the bar, but his wife, Helen, met her eyes and rushed over, wiping her hands on her chef's apron.

"Florence! Isn't this wonderful? The strike's over. Look at them. Such joy!" Her eyes followed Helen's gesture, panning the crowd. Florence sought Alex's tall, thin frame.

"*Tak!* It *is* wonderful. Have you seen Alex? I don't see him here." She strained up on her toes.

"You seem worried. I haven't seen him. Let me ask Wally."

Florence craned her neck again and perused the crowd. Still close to the front door, she turned every time it opened. "Mrs. Falkowski," a man to her left greeted her. She didn't know him.

"Yes?"

"Overheard you talkin' to Helen. That Alex of yours is quite a card sharp. We played poker to pass the time in the plant. Alex cleaned our clocks. That stone face of his doesn't give a hint to what he's got."

Florence smiled. She knew that stone face but couldn't imagine him being so social as to play cards. She could see Helen was having difficulty getting Wally's attention. Clutching the bar again, she ran her hand around the neckline of her house dress. It felt tight. Heat and the odor of spilled beer, unwashed men, and smoke overwhelmed her. The room spun. She needed to get out. Then Helen came into focus.

"Sorry, Flo, Wally hasn't seen him. Some of the guys went to Hastings. I've got to go. Haven't been this busy since before the strike!" Helen was off pulling draughts before Florence could even thank her. She expelled herself out the door. Taking a moment, she leaned against the dirty brick wall, her hand to her chest. Her heart raced. Where was Alex? Hastings Street. Maybe.

Florence hastened down Denton as fast as her swollen feet could move. Maybe she was being silly. Alex knew how to take care of himself. Still, an unsettled feeling clutched her chest. In the past, whenever she failed to act on her feelings, she regretted it. She was turning into her superstitious mother.

She crossed into the Black Bottom neighborhood, and the district lay before her. The warmer weather seemed to charm the music right out of the propped-open doors of the nightclubs. People moved about, club to club, sampling the offerings like bees among wildflowers. For a moment she drank it all in. Jazz and blues music. After all, she figured she could understand why Alex and Lucien liked to come here. The street was alive. She didn't like Lucien sneaking around, but what could she do? At least the music provided some common ground for father and son.

"Good evening, ma'am," Jake, the doorman at Sunnie Wilson's club, greeted her. She nodded.

"Not often I see a dignified lady such as yourself walking alone on Hastings. Might I be of some help?" She looked anything but dignified at the moment. What a kind man.

"I'm looking for my husband. Alex Falkowski. Do you know him?"

"Dunno 'bout that last name, but I see a few Alexes now and again. What's he look like?"

"Tall, white-blonde hair."

"Snazzy dresser?"

She nodded.

"I might know him. Haven't seen him tonight though. Why don't you sit over there on that bench, and I'll help you keep an eye out. If it's who I think it is, he'll show up. We got Fats Waller on the eighty-eights."

Florence couldn't help but return his smile. She settled herself on the bench. Relief, if only for a moment. Ladies dressed in all sorts of finery and adornments walked with their hands on the arms of their men. She could see them intermittently across the street between passing cars. Every few moments, she shifted on her hip to watch the crowd on the sidewalk behind the bench. If she stayed half turned, she could see both sides of the street. She felt a bit self-conscious in her work dress. At least she had a coat, but no stockings. She tucked her legs back beneath the bench. That nice doorman had probably wanted to redirect her away from his well-dressed clientele. Anyway, he'd been polite about it.

"Hello. Do you mind if I share your bench?" Florence looked up to see a thin young woman, spindly as a fawn, her hair darker brown.

"Not at all." Florence scooted over to make room. She kept scanning the sidewalks in all directions. Waves of laughter ebbed and flowed from the open doors, each crest knocking back her anxiety, at least for a moment. Maybe Alex was in one of the establishments enjoying himself.

"You must be waiting for someone too." The pleasant young woman smoothed the pleats of her dress.

"Yes. I'm looking for my husband. How about you? A special someone?" Florence offered her a knowing smile.

"Here you go, Jake. Mama Queenie said to give you this right away." At the sound of the familiar voice behind them, both women turned to see Lucien handing a note to Jake. Jake jerked his head toward the bench while pressing a coin into Lucien's hand. "Your girl's over there." Lucien's jaw dropped. Florence couldn't imagine the surprise it must be to see his mother on Hastings Street. Lucien approached the bench.

"Mom! What're you doing here? Hello, Cecilia." Florence stood, swiveling her gaze between her son and her bench companion. She shook her head, trying to clear the muddle. Did this girl know Lucien?

"Cecilia, you've met my mother?" Lucien shifted his gaze between the two.

Florence had no time for pleasantries. "I'm looking for your father. He might be in trouble. The strike settled. All the men are out of the plant. I can't—"

"Why would he be in trouble? Hundreds of men sat down in the strike."

A flash of recognition slammed her in the face. "There he is!" She pointed across the street and down the block. She bobbed her head, trying to see between the passing cars. Alex walked precipitously, his exuding anger clearing the walk ahead of him. Florence started into the street, but Lucien held her back. Just as there was a break in the line of cars, she saw Alex, his arms raised above his head.

"He's waving—" Her voice trailed off as she saw him double over. His upraised arms clenched his torso. He fell to his knees. Mother and son ran into the street. "*Boże Kochanie!*"

Cecilia followed.

"He must be sick."

"Papa—" Lucien pulled on his father's shoulders, straightening him up. Florence, a few steps behind her fleet-footed son, froze.

"*O, Boże!*" She focused on Alex's shirt in clear view with the brown herringbone sport coat open. A blotchy stain permeated the cotton shirt. Red and white.

"Call an ambulance! Tell Jake to call an ambulance," Lucien directed Cecilia.

Florence snapped out of her stupor. They settled Alex on the sidewalk, then she knelt and cupped his head in her hands. Lucien pushed on the wound to staunch the bleeding. When had he grown up? Jake and Cecilia returned. Jake carried a pile of cloth napkins in his arms.

"Ambulance coming, ma'am. Ambulance coming." Jake joined Lucien, staunching the blood flow with a couple of napkins. "He'll be all right. Just you watch now. He'll be all right." Florence saw Lucien's eyes tear up at Jake's kindness, his Southern syrupy voice coating the horror. Alex mumbled. She couldn't understand the words in any language.

"Shh. You rest. Help is coming." While rubbing his temples with her thumbs she prayed. First the Our Father, then, on his behalf, the Act of Contrition. Just in case. Honking horns and sirens provided hope that help was coming. Soon the long white car with wide running boards and a red cross painted on the side arrived. Medics jostled her to the sidelines. She hovered over their shoulders. How could she help? Cecilia wrapped her arm around Florence's shoulder.

"I've ordered a cab to take you and Luc to the hospital. Come this way." Jake pointed at the cab. Lucien's palm was on his mother's back, also directing her toward the cab.

"I've no purse! No—"

"Don't worry. This'll take care of it." Jake pressed some bills into her hand. "You have a fine son here, ma'am. A mighty fine son."

CHAPTER 36

Sunday, May 2, 1937

Police officers stood sentry outside the door of Alex's hospital room. Florence wasn't sure which side they were protecting. On Friday night, she and Lucien had followed the ambulance to the hospital in a taxi. At first, it had been touch and go, then the medical team staunched the bleeding and assessed the damage. The bullet fractured Alex's hip. He would survive. They kept him stable overnight, and a surgical team was assembled the next morning. Still in her housework dress, she slept on the chair in his room, her coat her only blanket. Lucien insisted on staying too. He was relegated to a lounge because no other seating was available in the room. On Saturday morning, when her son entered his father's room, she was bathing her husband with a washcloth.

"How is he?"

Florence noted the worry in her son's face as he scrutinized his father's sedated body. "He'll be fine. But we'll need to be strong, Luc. He may have a long recovery." Lucien had found another washcloth and was about to start washing his father's other side when orderlies arrived. They rolled him away for surgery.

"Maybe you should bring Frank here. I don't want him to be alone," said Florence.

Lucien went home to get his younger brother. As a family, they sipped coffee, nibbled doughnuts, and catnapped in the waiting room. With no knitting or darning at hand, Florence passed the time counting squares on the black and white tiled floor. Occasionally, she'd flip pages of the dog-eared magazines. Cups of coffee marked the passing hours.

"You may go in now, Mrs. Falkowski. This way please." Florence followed the nurse, and the boys followed her. She avoided eye contact with the officers. Alex was laid out on the bed with his chest and shoulders elevated. She recoiled at the sight of the canvas hood with a clear plastic front, from behind which Alex's head looked preserved like museum statuary. Canvas draped down from the hood covered the length of his body and was firmly tucked in below the mattress at the foot of the bed. No part of his body was available to touch.

"It's an oxygen tent. Your father can breathe better with it until he wakes up from anesthesia," a nurse explained to the boys.

"Wow! That looks like a rocket." Frank approached the tall oxygen tank. "Just like in the Flash Gordon comics."

Perhaps she shouldn't have brought the boys. She looked at Lucien. He understood the peril. He'd been around on the streets. She couldn't even guess at the things he'd seen. His face was impassive, so like his father's.

"Maybe you should take Frank home now that you've seen your father is fine. He's sleeping. He's going to sleep for a while," she addressed Lucien. He nodded. She'd pulled a bill from Alex's wallet and handed it to Lucien. "Go get an ice cream soda at Woolworth's."

Lucien raised his hand in protest. "I've got it, Mama."

Throughout the second night, Saturday, Alex had lain on the bed breathing rhythmically in an induced slumber. Florence had wedged herself into the worn chair. Her head rested on the wooden arm. She'd slept on and off, checking on her husband's breathing.

This morning, Sunday, she used the pay phone to call her brother Joe. She didn't talk long but provided an update and asked him to look after the boys. She returned to the room and was staring absently out the window when she heard panicked sounds and sharp movements.

"*O, Boże!*" Behind the window inside the oxygen tent, the wide-eyed look of horror and fear on her husband's face paralyzed her. She'd never seen that expression. His legs and arms kicked at the heavy canvas, a wild animal thrashing for his life. She cringed. His steel blue eyes, distorted through the wavy plastic, pierced hers. She summoned help.

The staff freed him from the hood and the connected heavy canvas, and Alex relaxed. They administered a mild sedative. The doctor visited during his rounds. Throughout the morning, Alex became increasingly cooperative with the medical staff. Perhaps he realized he needed these people. His life was in their hands.

"Florence? We're in Henry Ford's hospital, correct?"

"Yes. The ambulance brought you to the closest one. They said here was the best for gunshot wounds."

"Uh-huh. We'll have to pay for this, you know. Hospital bill."

"Don't worry about that now." She stood and took his hand. "Not long ago I read in the paper that during these hard times, many people can't pay their medical bills. The hospital lets it go. I guess Henry Ford himself mandated the policy."

"Guilty."

"We wouldn't need to feel guilty. This isn't your fault."

"Not my guilt. Ford's guilt!" He struggled as if he wanted to get out of bed. Monitors and tubes restrained him.

"Shh. Let's not get worked up." She pushed a swath of hair off his forehead.

"We're going to pay every last penny of what we owe. I'm not going to be beholden to Ford."

"If that's what you want, dear, we can do that."

Later in the afternoon, just after lunch, a knock on the door disturbed them. A tall man in gray wool gabardine slacks and a navy blue sport coat entered. He introduced himself as Steve Valleau, an investigator with the Detroit Police Department. The investigator pulled a straight-backed chair close to Alex's bedside. Florence tried to blend into the background, though her ears stayed alert as an antenna.

"Mr. Falkowski, we need your help to find the person or people who shot you," opened the officer.

Alex turned his bleary eyes toward the officer. She hoped he wouldn't say anything untoward. Would he speak at all? He appeared groggy, likely from the pills they gave him after lunch. He asked for water, and she obliged. The investigator waited. Alex recounted the events that had brought him face down onto the pavement on Hastings Street, bleeding out like a gutted fish.

Valleau listened intently to Alex's answers to his litany of questions. So did she. A short time ago, she'd learned of this group, the Black Legion—and Alex's involvement in it—from a note Alex dispatched from the factory. Frank had delivered it. The only occasion on which she'd seen her husband since was the day they'd diverted the Unemployed Council leaders protesting the ruthless evictions at the neighboring apartments. Amid the chaos, there'd not been time for a conversation. Reading that note, she'd been surprised, frightened, and relieved. The group must have caused Alex's strange behavior, his mysterious absences, his irritability. What had he done at Kaminski's farm? Had they really tried to kill him? She shifted in her chair. Her hands trembled. She tucked them under her legs. What else could he have done?

"*O, Boże!*" she muttered.

Alex and the inspector turned toward her. "Nothing. It's nothing." She didn't realize she'd spoken out loud.

"Then you were an unwilling participant in this so-called Bullet Club?" The inspector leaned back in the chair, raising the two front legs off the floor. He could have been discussing the latest baseball scores, so casual was his demeanor. Was he weaving a web? Inviting Alex in? She needed to protect him.

"They threatened me, my family." Alex glanced at her. "They threw a rock through my living room window as a warning when I didn't act fast enough for their liking. They held a gun to my skull."

Florence gasped—the broken living room window. How much trouble had Alex been in?

"I feared for my life. My wife and my sons. When the factory went on strike, I saw an opportunity to hide," Alex divulged.

"They couldn't reach you in there," Valleau encouraged.

"No. And they asked more of me than I was willing to give. At the beginning they only wanted me to snitch on labor agitators. I fed them information they already knew. Or could easily get."

Florence was appalled. Had he turned on their friends and neighbors?

"They demanded more and more," Alex continued. "They demanded I disrupt labor actions." A rosy-hued flush spread across his face. He glanced sideways at her. She was horrified.

"I didn't cause any harm." He asked Florence for more water, offering her a wan smile. Was this a confession? She didn't know whether to hand him the glass of water or pour it on him.

"Then what happened?" The inspector leaned forward again. She did, too, standing behind the inspector.

"There were some people. A couple of men in the Unemployed Council they wanted me to kill."

Florence couldn't believe this was real. Flabbergasted, she spun toward the window, unable to face her husband.

"Go on," coaxed Valleau.

"With some friends, we helped them escape. They're in hiding."

Had she been party to that? She'd only done what he had asked. From the note she knew he was in distress, but hiding people he'd been told to murder? Her knees quivered. Through the window, the trees blurred. She tried to hold on to the windowsill . . . smooth, no edge . . . and heat coursed through the veins in her face. She collapsed.

"Mrs. Falkowski, can you hear me?" Black and white floor tiles came into focus. Shoes. White shoes. Four of them. Rubber soles. Her head was level with her knees, a hand on her back. She started to straighten her torso. "Slowly now. You fainted, Mrs. Falkowski. Your kind visitor put you in this chair." Kind visitor? Who? "Please take a small sip of water." A nurse handed her a small cup. "There you go. Now can you hold this ice pack up to your head?"

She looked at the blue rubber bag in her hand. It was cold. What was this for?

"Mrs. Falkowski, you hit your head on the night table." Florence's hand reached for her temple. It hurt. She pressed the blue bag against it. The nurse continued, "Lay back and rest. We'll bring you some food. You've been here a long time. We'll check your vitals, but my guess is your blood sugar is low." She complied.

"How did you come to be involved in this Black Legion?" The inspector's voice! He must've been the one who picked her up. She focused on Alex. He took several slow sips of water and adjusted himself in the bed.

"A friend." Alex stared at the small tent his feet made under the blanket.

"Doesn't sound like much of a friend," Valleau challenged.

"He was a good friend. A good man with limited choices." Alex clenched the hem of the hospital blanket.

"Where is this friend now, Mr. Falkowski?"

"Dead."

"I see." The inspector, now standing, spread his feet wide. "And this wonderful man's name?"

Florence did not care for this man's attitude.

"Nicholas Starovitch. Died a few months ago. He was found on a railroad track." Alex looked at the ceiling and exhaled.

"He was a wonderful man. Kind, courteous," Florence added, leaning forward. She refused to allow Nick's memory to be sullied. His death had been such a tragedy.

"On the tracks, you say? As so many others have been these last six or seven years." Valleau shook his head. "Pity."

Alex sighed and turned his head away. The inspector assured them the department, working with federal agents, had suspicions about a group that might be tied to several recent murders. He thanked Alex for his candor.

"Wait!" Alex blurted just as Valleau placed his hand on the doorknob. The inspector turned, hat in hand, and approached the bedside.

NOT YET LOST

"There's cops. Some high up. That may be sympathetic."

"You're a brave man, Mr. Falkowski. We're aware. I'll take it from here. You concentrate on recovering. You, too, Mrs. Falkowski." He tipped his hat and walked out the door.

Florence studied Alex, who'd turned away and closed his eyes.

"You realize you just accused the police of corruption."

Alex snapped his head around, eyes wide open. "I didn't say this Valleau was corrupt! I said there might be others who are. And I know there are! I can name one of them right now."

A knock on the door interrupted them. A nurse entered. "How are you feeling, Mr. Falkowski? Time to take your vital signs again." The nurse went about her business. Florence looked out the window, counting as the nurse pumped the ball of the blood pressure cuff. *Whoosh!* The cuff deflated. She wished her frustration could dissipate as easily. What deranged type of organization was this Black Legion?

"Your blood pressure is quite high. I saw your visitor just left. Maybe we should prohibit visitors for now." She listened to his lungs before swinging her stethoscope around her neck. "Try and sit up more. We have to keep those lungs clear. I'll be back to check on you again in a bit." She adjusted his pillows, checked on Florence's swelling head, and left the room.

"Florence?" Alex reached beyond the bedrail to garner her attention. He looked small, childlike. "I didn't mean for you to find out like this. I couldn't tell you everything in the note."

Her hands were folded in her lap. The veins reminded her of the roots of the time-chiseled sugar maple in their backyard.

"It must be disturbing for you to hear all of this."

How do they get the corners of the sheets on the bed so tight?

"Florence! Are you even listening to me?" Alex hoisted himself forward using the bed rails.

"Are we in danger?" She faced her husband, realization dawning. "The boys? Me?"

Alex slumped back onto his stacked pillows. "I don't know." He pulled the blanket up just below his chin. The nubby cotton muffled his soft-spoken words.

"Hello-o-o," an artificially cheery voice preceded a stout woman into the room. "Now then, let's not look so down and out in here. Cook's made a nice dinner. Hot turkey sandwich, mashed potatoes, and some stuffin' there. Eat hearty now. I'll be back for your tray." She bustled out.

"What should we do?" Florence helped situate the monochromatic dinner within Alex's reach.

"I'm in no condition to travel right now. Maybe you and the boys could get away. Go to Canada? There is a train from Windsor. You could take it to Montreal."

She hadn't seen her parents in a long time. No one had traveled much for the last several years, the cost prohibitive. Her parents fared well, according to her mother's letters, but they weren't young. They hadn't seen her boys since they were toddlers.

"You will need care when you come home. The doctor said you'd need a chair and then crutches until you work in this new hip." She shook her head side to side, yet still, she was tempted. "No. We stay together." She rose. She walked across the room and back, rearranging her pinned-up hair. "We can pray this inspector catches these people. Now that you talked to him, if anything else happens—"

"I'm tired now. I want to sleep." Alex pushed the table away from him, much of his meal remaining on the plate. He slid down in his bed. "You should go home." That, too, sounded tempting.

"I think I shall." Florence was spent. Immediately after she exited the room, another starched uniform entered. On her way to the stairs, she heard Alex's voice say, "Can't a man get any rest?"

CHAPTER 37

Sunday, May 9, 1937 (Mother's Day)

Alex's wheelchair bucked as Florence wrangled it up the steps to the main entrance of the Detroit Institute of Arts. Her boys navigated the front wheels, with Lucien on the left, bearing more of the weight. Lucien had suggested going to the Art Institute to celebrate Mother's Day. Not only was it a treat she would enjoy *immensely*, but the outing might be good for Alex's spirits. Released from the hospital, he'd been home recovering from his hip surgery. He hobbled around the house but needed the chair for any distance. They'd converted the living room into a bedroom so he could avoid the stairs.

Before entering, she paused to admire the Beaux-Arts facade and pointed out a few details in the plasterwork to the boys, a ruse to catch her breath. Her hips helped her brace the door while she maneuvered the chair, and Alex, through the doorway. Alex had remained quiet during the ascent, whether from newfound patience or defeat, she wasn't certain. Nonetheless, she appreciated he wasn't barking at her as he would have in the past. Once stilled, they continued through the hallway, dodging paint cans, lumber piles, and heaps of canvas. Admission was free of charge on Mother's Day.

"Look! That's the hall to the courtyard where Diego Rivera's painting murals," Alex exclaimed. "Maybe he's working today." She followed his pointing finger toward heavy velvet curtains at the end of a side hall. A spark! A reawakening perhaps. A few months ago,

Alex modeled for the artist at the factory. His pride had seeped out from under his false modesty. She remembered he was equally pleased with the conversation with Rivera. He'd felt connected to him through whatever they talked about.

"Lucien, take your brother to the Egyptian exhibit. Through that door. Go see the mummies."

"Is that because it's 'Mummies' Day?" Frank piped up.

She tousled his hair. "Go on. When you're finished there, you can go through to the armor exhibit. It's in the next gallery. Knights and such." Her sons accepted her direction. They'd been so helpful over the past weeks, but Alex was unaccustomed to the children's exuberance for any length of time.

She rolled the wheelchair through the red velvet curtains into the courtyard, parked it at the short end of a concrete bench, then settled herself next to her husband. Though they'd encountered none in the hallway, helpers of many varieties buzzed around. They collected palette knives in buckets, mixed pigment, assembled scaffolding. No one noticed them. She scanned the walls, top to bottom, side to side. For the second time that morning, her breath was taken away.

High up on the scaffolding, the artist applied color to his pencil drawing on the wall. Plaster on the end of his putty knife was infused with pigment. Florence, mesmerized by his technique, rose from the bench. Her hands began to pantomime the actions, cutting broad strokes and then rotating the wrist to detail with the sharp edge.

"Sit down! You're embarrassing me!"

She froze. The old Alex had broken through. Resuming her seat, she interlaced her fingers in her lap. Still, her shoulders jerked and danced, mirroring Rivera's movements with a split-second delay.

Almost wordlessly, the team of drones elevated the artist to royal status. He raised a hand, and a tool was placed in it. The scaffolding, three stories tall, served as the dais from which he governed. At Alex's request, Florence rolled his chair across the courtyard so they could observe from a panoramic perspective. The mural's color bloomed from left to right. Rivera sculpted tinted plaster onto pencil drawings of the intricate machinations of the River Rouge plant. An assistant announced it was time for a lunch break. It was almost three o'clock, but Florence gathered when Rivera ate, everyone ate. The deity of murals descended the scaffolding rung by rung. The loose dark smock caught occasionally on a bolt. The artist's boots had just landed on the floor when an assistant rushed forward with a tray of food.

"Where shall I set it, *patrón*?"

"Over there." Rivera pointed across the room. As he did, his eyebrows arched up. Florence blushed when he looked directly at her, standing behind Alex's chair. They were caught. Rivera approached.

"Ah, Mr. Falkowski. What has happened here?" The artist's arm swept over Alex's legs in the wheelchair. Alex started to rise but couldn't. Florence stood nodding while her husband rendered a brief, and rather sanitized, account of the events that had put him in the chair.

"It's very kind of you to remember me, Mr. Rivera. May I introduce my wife, Florence Falkowski?" She came around the chair and offered her hand to Rivera. He cleaned his hand on his smock before shaking hers.

"I do not forget a visage such as yours, Mr. Falkowski. I'm going to take my lunch now. Won't you sit and provide company?" Rivera arranged his chair to face the north wall of the court. "Of course it's still in progress. What do you think?"

Florence bit her tongue. How she wanted to answer! She would have exuded praise and asked questions, inquired about the symbolism. Alex remained quiet. His eyes panned the wall. Rivera didn't press him for an answer and instead focused on eating his lunch. She held her breath and hoped Alex would, indeed, answer. These days she never knew what to expect.

"It is absolutely brilliant." Alex's eyes roamed over the wall. Florence sighed in relief. Alex expressed his appreciation with a tone of awe seldom heard in his voice.

"And you, Mrs. Falkowski?" Rivera sliced a generously sized apple.

"It's the most amazing work I've ever seen. So many industries and themes portrayed. And styles! Would you explain the panels? How they relate?"

"Florence! Let Mr. Rivera finish his meal!"

"It would be my pleasure." Rivera set aside the unfinished portion of his lunch and wiped his lips with a napkin. He explained the layout of the panels surrounding the room, three courses of panels totaling twenty-seven separate friezes. Florence twisted and turned Alex's wheelchair as the artist described his reasoning behind depictions of agriculture, raw materials, and people of all races working together. The huge blast furnace on the south wall symbolized creation.

"You've captured the force, the energy." Florence could see her husband was captivated. She was too. She almost felt the heat from the orange, umber, and bronze licks of flame leaping like a tiger from the wall.

The pharmaceutical industry was represented, and vaccines, with an infant surrounded by family, a clear nod to a Christian creche.

"The Holy Family!" Florence uttered. "A semblance, anyway."

"Yes, I'm afraid it has caused quite a controversy. Religious right groups are calling for the whole courtyard to be whitewashed."

"That would be a travesty! You're not really—cover all this up?" How could people think that a good idea?

"Fecundity represented by female nudes is apparently pornographic." He glanced at the images of nude women embracing the agricultural goods of Mother Earth. "As I recall from our conversation, Mr. Falkowski, you are not a religious man. You see, though, I painted many religious themes into this work. I summoned the ancient gods, the Aztec pantheon. Look here." Rivera led them to the north wall. "The stamping press alludes to Coatlicue, goddess of creation and of war."

"I see! Good and evil. Like over there." Alex pointed to the panels that depicted menacing gas masks. He also singled out the passenger plane and the warplane.

"Yes, like Coatlicue, technology can be productive and destructive. It's for the world to choose."

"Your art, your weapon, as you said," Alex stated, bowing to the artist and recalling their conversation from when he modeled.

"Coatlicue provides much bounty, as I've displayed there." Rivera gestured to painted apples and peaches indigenous to Michigan. "She also requires sacrifice. A symbiotic relationship. It is said warriors were sacrificed to Coatlicue. They then spend years in the sun, after which they become hummingbirds. Statues of her show a clutch of hummingbird feathers, representing the warrior who impregnated her."

The trio continued around the courtyard, with Rivera pointing out details and connections. From her school days in Montreal training to become an artist, Florence recognized the melding of several different artistic styles, from Renaissance to cubism. They chuckled at Rivera's mischief. He'd included his own likeness in a bowler hat amid, yet observing, the factory workers. Henry Ford's image was also woven into the mural.

"You must be wondering where your face is in my work, Mr. Falkowski."

"I didn't want to be presumptuous, but I am curious."

Rivera directed them to the north wall and pointed to a man who resembled Alex: muscular, determined, just left of center, chambray shirtsleeves rolled up, working on an engine block. Florence's gaze swiveled between her husband on the wall and her husband in the chair. The one on the wall, intense, focused, surrounded by men and machinery, laboring in raw geniture. The one in the chair, intrigued, discerning, solitary, erudite. Rivera had captured them both. She watched her husband examine the wall. His minuscule facial twitches indicated his satisfaction with his likeness.

"Thank you. I am proud to be included in this monumental achievement." Alex extended his hand to Rivera, who accepted it. The artist smiled with all the warmth of an Aztec sun god.

"I must return to work now. It's been a pleasure, and I thank you for your interest. Please return after the opening."

Florence nodded and was about to shower the artist with gratitude and praise when Alex spoke.

"One question, Mr. Rivera. What does old man Ford think of all this?"

"I don't know if he realizes the socialist paradigm he's fostered on the assembly line. Humans of every flavor collaborating."

"No, I'm sure that's not what he sees. I don't see any finished automobiles anywhere on these walls."

"You didn't see it? Come here." Rivera led them back to the south wall. Florence didn't want to impose, but Alex motioned for her to push his chair.

"Right there." Rivera pointed to a tiny red car in the far distance of the perspective, maybe four inches long.

Alex threw his head back and laughed and laughed, chortling with vigor Florence hadn't heard in years. Alex saluted Rivera, who returned to his scaffolding.

"Let's go find the boys."

CHAPTER 38

Friday, June 25, 1937

Chatter filled the streetcar. Florence listened attentively to a story Irena was telling about her children. The women laughed. The story was cute but lacked the highs, lows, twists, and turns of those Basia would've told. Nonetheless, laughter was comforting. At the stop at the next street, a swarm of women with bags and bundles squeezed into the streetcar, ratcheting up the ambient sounds. After the next stop, she couldn't even hear what her friend next to her was saying. Wiggling her toes, she looked down at her new monk strap oxfords. She'd almost chosen the white, but—always the practical one—opted for the dark navy, though she'd splurged on a removable white kiltie tongue. Her feet luxuriated in the roomy toe box and relaxed into the sturdiness of the low-stacked wooden heel. A perfect shoe for today's range of activities.

She also appreciated the clean window glass. Had the city washed the windows or had the weather's providence cleansed the grime? People on the street walked with purpose and energy. Shop doors opened and closed. Higher wages achieved through labor actions seemed to take the edge off. People smiled. Most of any increase in income would go to pay off accounts, buy food, clothe children. Still, signs of small indulgences popped up everywhere. A line formed at a barber shop.

"Edgewater Park, next stop. Seven Mile and Grand River. Edgewater Park." A buzz rippled through the crowd and people gathered their belongings. Most carried small bags containing alternate clothing, as did hers. Today was the day. The streetcar emptied out except for a few people not with the women from the cigar factories. All queued up, the women filed through the arched entrance gate. Florence and Irena held out their union cards, "Cigar Workers Local 24," which provided free admission. The Committee of Industrial Organization, or CIO, had arranged for today's outing to welcome the women into the fold. A man named Wagner owned the park, and group outings were commonplace. She hadn't been to the park in years. It had even closed temporarily in the early years after the market crash. A quick glance around and it appeared the famous wooden roller coaster, the Wild Beast, was still there. Alex had taken her on that. Another roller coaster, the Wild Mouse, with its zigzag tracks, still hovered in the air not far from the gigantic neon-lit Ferris wheel. Several other electric thrill rides were surrounded by game arcades, fun houses, and the always-popular House of Mirrors. Everyone scattered helter-skelter toward the various amusements.

"I'm going to the Wild Mouse! C'mon!"

"I'm going to the fortune teller."

"This way to Himalayan. It goes *so* fast!"

"It's nice to see the young ones enjoying themselves," Florence remarked, watching their abandon. They all deserved this day. Especially the blossoming ones who'd grown up in grueling times.

"What a perfect day, eh?" Irena said.

"Perfect. It couldn't be more perfect. Unless Basia were here." She bowed her head and made the sign of the cross. "We wouldn't be celebrating today if Basia hadn't charged ahead."

"I remember her clear as day when she sat down in front of Resnick and wouldn't move. I never had that kind of courage."

"Me neither," agreed Florence.

"What do you mean? You were right there with her. You two." Irena took the lead toward the community room, where they'd find lockers to store their bags.

Basia had dragged her into some madcap situations, so impulsive and outspoken. How many times had Florence pulled her back from a precipice? She was always for the underdog. One time she'd even given Father Maletski a piece of her mind when she didn't like his sermon.

Florence closed the locker door and turned to Irena. "I miss Basia. She should be here."

"Yes. I miss her too. Can you imagine her, hair flying out behind her, on the Wild Beast?"

"Oh, can I!" Florence chuckled.

"We can't bring her back, but we can honor her memory. Let's enjoy the park like Basia would've."

"*Tak*, yes, let's!"

"Should we go to the House of Mirrors first?"

"Alex brought me here once when it first opened. *O, Boże*, when was that? Ten years now?"

"Yes, I think so. How is Alex doing?"

"He's making progress. He can walk on his own now, if not for a long time. His bull-headedness serves him well. He's meeting me here later."

"Did they ever find out who shot him?"

"He was just there at the wrong time. They think maybe it was one of those thugs from the Legion they broke up. Targeting someone else and Alex happened to be in the way." She made the sign of the cross, repenting for the lie she just told.

"Yes, it's a blessing he lived."

Florence had been so proud of Alex in the hospital. Knowing he was taking a chance, he'd summoned the courage to talk to the police. He trusted. He lay in a hospital bed unable to move and vulnerable as a newborn babe. Yet he trusted. Desperation may have driven him, with no alternative for a way out of his circumstances. Still, he trusted. There were good people in the world willing to help a lone wolf, willing to do what was right. Alex provided solid information that helped the federal agents bring down the repugnant vigilantes. His coerced participation remained a subterranean secret among her, Alex, and Romek, never to be spoken of again.

"Here we are."

In the House of Mirrors the women made themselves taller, shorter, fatter, and thinner and made faces in the wavy mirrors.

"We have to laugh at ourselves, Irena."

"Yes, the rest of the world has been. Time we did it ourselves!" After they could laugh no more, they proceeded to the arcade.

"Maybe I could win a stuffed animal for Frank. Let's go over there. They're throwing balls at those milk jugs."

"Look. There's Resnick." Irena pointed to their supervisor.

"Good afternoon, Florence, Irena. Enjoying the day? I'm afraid I'm not having much luck here. Why don't you try?" Florence reached into her bag for a coin, but Resnick put down a nickel, and the barker single-handedly placed three rubber balls up on the counter. The women looked at each other with surprise.

"Thank you. You're in quite a good mood today."

"That I am! I have news. Uncle Steve and I have decided I'm going to New York. To the university."

"Really! That will be good for you. You need a change. You're young." Florence was pleased.

Resnick explained about the new university established three years prior. So many professors were being banished from their posts in Germany because they were Jewish. The University in Exile housed the scorned professors who valued freedom of thought, and the university needed students. His uncle had been one of the earliest supporters. He would be leaving before the end of August.

"I wish you the best of luck." Florence meant it.

She tossed the rubber balls, first one and then the second. Neither came vaguely near the milk jugs. What would Basia think of Resnick's news? She remembered they were going to enjoy the park, like Basia, and on the last throw, she switched her grip to overhand and walloped the pyramid of jugs.

"A winner! We have a winner here. Step right up and win a teddy bear." The barker handed her a small stuffed bear with a red ribbon tied around its neck. Red. Frank would like it—small enough to hide under his pillow so Lucien wouldn't tease him. She accepted congratulations from Irena, Resnick, and his companion.

"Been on any rides yet?" Resnick's eyes sparkled with new life. He must be anticipating a more amenable life.

"We want to go on the Ferris wheel, but there was a big group of children there, so we'll circle back in a bit," Florence responded.

"Probably my uncle. The synagogue sponsored a group today too. Children from Europe. So many are being sent here from Germany without parents."

The women and the men parted ways among a flurry of good wishes.

"*Boże*. Children. What a world for them, eh?"

"Let's just forget about the world today. Remember? We're here to have fun."

Over the course of the afternoon, groups of women combined and recombined as they consumed the available fare. Circus acts dazzled and rides thrilled. The women lost themselves in the long light of the day, the summer solstice having just passed.

"*Boże*, it's late. Let's go get ready for tonight," Florence suggested.

"Yes, we'd better go now, or we'll have to elbow the young ones to get to a mirror."

All the women rushed to prepare for the evening's events. In the community building, locker doors slammed as shoes and clothes were extricated with haste. Water ran constantly in the four sinks in the ladies' room. Raised arms twirling and pinning hair resembled tall prairie grass in a turbulent wind. Skirts and dresses flew about. Giddy merriment permeated the darkest corners of the room. This was their moment. In a short time, small clusters of women left the changing room. Free-flowing tresses were tamed and pretty summer dresses replaced loose, comfortable shifts. The new-style canvas sport shoes favored by the young were replaced with T-strap heels or perforated sandals. Sun-tinged cheeks and noses punctuated their newly donned elegance. Neon lights picked up where the sun left off. Florence and Irena headed toward the dance hall. Sounds of the band tuning their instruments guided their way.

"This looks like a whole new park at night."

"Yes, doesn't it? Looks like many of our other halves have arrived." Groups of men stood around smoking and joshing with each other. A sign at the entrance announced,

Private Event
CIO
Cigar Workers Local 24

In no time the hall brimmed with people. Florence remembered from when the ballroom was built that the then-new dome design could accommodate 2,000 people. Probably more than that would cram in there tonight.

"I'm going to talk to Joan. She's over there." Florence headed toward her journalist friend, who stood a head shorter than some of the men in her group. Camera equipment swung from their shoulders and pencils adorned their ears.

"Florence, so good to see you. Quite a gathering, this." Joan gave her a quick hug.

"I have to ask. It's been a secret who's speaking tonight."

"I think they did that because they weren't sure who would be available. You know these organizers are running city to city these days. The word is Leo Krzycki landed at Detroit City an hour ago. Straight in from Milwaukee. I can't wait to meet him!"

"Leo Krzycki? Really!"

The women discussed their mutual admiration for the assistant head of the CIO. Krzycki had spent his career as a hands-on organizer, often joining workers pounding the pavement. He also held a leadership position in the Socialist Party of America.

"Florence." She felt Alex's hand on her shoulder. "Good evening, Joan."

Alex directed her toward the side of the ballroom. The band, Bob Chester's, struck up a tune, and applause dashed the possibility of conversation. Using the microphone, Bob commandeered the attention of the crowd.

"We have a terrific song list lined up for this evening's dancing, but before we enjoy ourselves, let's take care of business. I can't provide an introduction that would do him justice, so without further ado, let me hand the microphone over to Stanley Nowak."

Applause and cheers sent up into the wooden domed ceiling reverberated back down, and Florence covered her ears.

"Good evening, newly minted members of the Cigar Workers Union, Local 24!" Again, cheers thundered off the ceiling.

"It has been a long road for you, for us all." Nowak continued to itemize the milestones of the past several months. Groans, cheers, and laughter punctuated his speech. When he described Basia standing strong while being pummeled with freezing water, Nowak conjured images of Joan of Arc. Silence and sobs perfused the crowded ballroom.

"Your trials may have seemed lonely at times. Let me assure you what you ladies accomplished here in Detroit has been noticed. The world paid attention. Don't ever think your efforts have been in vain. The UAW supports you! The governor, Frank Murphy, supports you! And the Committee of Industrial Organization supports you!" After the ballyhoos subsided, Nowak introduced Leo Krzycki.

"*Dzień Wieczor, Towarzysze!*" The crowd couldn't be contained. Florence glanced sideways at Alex. He must be roiling inside. Couldn't Krzycki have greeted them as friends rather than comrades?

Alex motioned for her to follow him, and he took her hand.

"I want to hear Krzycki." She pulled her hand back. "You go. I'll find you outside." She deserved to stand here with her friends, her colleagues. They earned this recognition.

Krzycki's speech inspired. He tapped into their souls, providing a reprise of the emotions, good and bad, they had experienced during their ordeal. He resurrected their resolve to own their place in the world. She appreciated Krzycki's skill as an orator—his cadence, volume, how he worked the crowd.

"And now, we must work together, all laborers, work together for peace." The crowd roared.

When he finished speaking, Florence worked her way through the ecstatic crowd to the exit door. She located Alex near a bench across the walkway. They perched themselves facing the dance hall. Thunderous sounds threatened to lift the roof off the edifice.

"How was your day?" Alex queried.

"Rather dizzying, in many ways. In fact, I still feel my head spinning."

"You did look a bit peaked in there. May I get you a sno-cone?" Alex gestured toward one of several concession stands. Hot dogs, nuts, soft drinks, cotton candy.

"Yes. That sounds good. All the sun today. Thank you." Alex favored his right leg as he strode toward the stand with the blinking blue lights mimicking icicles. His hip had been shattered, but at least he was out of the wheelchair. His pride prevented the use of a crutch in public, even though it had only been a few weeks. Maybe he'd use a snazzy cane. So typical, Alex had been fascinated with the corrosion-resistant Vitallium metal used in artificial hips and had pondered different applications for this alloy.

"Here you go. Cherry or lemon." Florence accepted the cherry sno-cone just as she heard—

"Leo, Leo, Leo . . ." The crowd chanted, but she saw the commotion behind the hall. They were momentarily blinded by all the flashbulbs going off as men hustled Krzycki into a waiting dark sedan, moving him to the next organizing event.

"I hope Joan gets her story," Alex mused, nibbling his own icy treat.

"Yes, so do I."

"You know, Florence, I never thought what you and Basia wanted was wrong. I was afraid for you. Scared to death. I've seen this before. The tsar—"

"I know. You've told me before." She put her free hand on Alex's knee.

"But you didn't *see* it. Soldiers on horseback. Guns and sabers wielded at earnest workers. Asking, just for asking, for a little help. Horses' hooves ground their tattered clothes and limbs into the muck."

"Let's not talk of that now." She feared Alex would spiral into melancholy. Memories of what was called Bloody Sunday in Russia haunted him, even now, after thirty years.

"I know what barbarism men in power are capable of when their world order is threatened." His eyes were unfocused. What horrors was he seeing? He licked at his sno-cone absently.

"The men in the Legion. They were the same as the tsar. Their pitiful power. Laying blame." He turned and looked at her. His intensity might have unnerved others, but she was undaunted.

"You were right to stand up for yourselves, for us. You accomplished so much."

Sticky syrup and water dripped down her hand from the sno-cone. She'd forgotten it.

"You had your own burden. With Moore and that—that group, that Legion, Nick pulled you into. Still, I can't believe it."

Once the band started playing its signature song, a light stream of people trickled from the hall, mostly younger couples who preferred thrill rides to dancing. Most of the throng stayed to dance. She disposed of their sno-cone wrappers in a nearby trash can and nodded at Anushka and Stefan as they walked by arm in arm.

"This event was good," Florence declared. "Before, it was anticlimactic after everything we did. Agreements taken care of in meetings and documents. This is a victory party."

"It's like the moon." Alex had flung his arms across the bench back, head tilted up.

"How do you mean?" She cleaned her sticky hands with a handkerchief.

"It goes through different phases, one to the next, in small increments. Then finally it goes dark and there's a whole new moon. Like us, and our community, we're starting a whole new phase."

Florence shivered. Was it Alex's words or the cold ice on her sun-heated body? Alex removed his jacket and wrapped it around her shoulders.

"If you're not tired of rides yet, would you like to go on the Ferris wheel?"

"Yes, the line was too long earlier, so we never rode it today."

The neon-trimmed circle was stopped to load the next car. Their car swayed at the very top.

"I was going to wait to surprise you, but I think I will tell you now." Alex put his arm around her. "I have an appointment on Monday. With Smith Engineering. They need a draftsman. I'll show them some of my designs."

"That's wonderful!"

They admired the lighted streets laid out in a wagon wheel shape, the spokes leading to several compass points from the base of the city.

"It's a remarkable town."

CHAPTER 39

Two years later—Thursday, August 31, 1939

Florence crossed herself and glanced upward. "*Djękiuę, Boże!* Thank you, Jesus!" Not for the first time, she felt lucky Alex was so persnickety about his clothing. She always had the newest clothing iron on the market. She laid out the right sleeve of Alex's evening shirt to press in a crease. Over the last two years, their life had become comfortable, almost luxurious by some standards. She was earning a higher wage now and had been since the strike. Alex worked at an engineering firm that he liked, and they appreciated him. Joe was working again, his wage at a level not seen since before the market crash. They all worked fewer hours. The fabric of the community had a tight stitch now, no longer frayed at the edges.

St. Florian's was crowded this morning for the wedding mass. Even the music sounded more festive than usual. Alicja beamed in front of the altar—she and Tomasz besotted with each other. Florence had enjoyed helping Alicja ready herself for the wedding. With her two sons, she'd never have the opportunity to dress a bride. With her friends, they'd braided Alicja's flaxen hair into a crown and woven in flowers. The bride looked every bit a princess. After Resnick had scared her away from the cigar factory, Alicja found a position as a domestic worker for a family in the Boston Edison neighborhood. There, she'd met an electrician, Tomasz, who routinely worked at her employer's house. Older and ambitious, he helped and encouraged Alicja to attend night school. He was kind and stable and a godsend to Andrew, Alicja's father. They would live with him after the wedding. Florence hung Alex's shirt on a wooden hanger and started on Lucien's, spraying starch from a glass bottle onto the collar. She would finish ironing the boys' shirts and run over to Dom Polski.

While the church service was crowded, the reception necessarily would be more limited, at least for the dinner. Alicja's family was of modest means since her father's accident, so the community came together to throw the wedding reception. Some of the women planned to prepare food in the afternoon between the morning church service and the evening reception. Most other people went home to rest in between.

When she arrived at Dom Polski, activities were in full swing. The coordinated efforts of the women were as efficient as the most modern assembly line. Tables were covered with new white linen cloths and adorned with small vases of freshly cut flowers. Younger children ran underfoot. Teenagers, who could have assisted, didn't. The women, in full-bore production mode, kept matters in their own hands. Florence, her Sunday dress concealed with an oversized white chef's apron, managed the stovetop.

"It was a lovely ceremony, wasn't it?" Mrs. Koseba said.

"Yes. Father Maletski always does such a good job speaking to the young couples," Helen replied.

Florence nodded her agreement as she drained the large pot at the sink. She set the potatoes aside to cool enough to be diced for salad. Hopefully, there'd be time enough for them to chill.

"Speaking of young couples, you and Alex seemed all lovey-dovey this morning," Mrs. Koseba said. Florence saw her elbow Helen, both of whom were peeling and slicing cucumbers.

"*Boże!* It's been a long time since Alex and I were a young couple," Florence protested, though she knew they were right. Father Maletski's homily regarding new beginnings for the couple reminded her of the night at Edgewater Park. Alex had spoken of the phases of the moon and how their lives were starting again, like a new moon. Even now, she held those words dear. This morning he had sat beside her

NOT YET LOST

in the wooden pew, a miracle in and of itself. Throughout the service, he managed to follow her lead: stand, sit, kneel. He even moved his lips when he didn't know the words to the prayers, all because he knew it was important to her. He'd been a font of surprises over the last two years. She'd reached over and taken his hand. This evening's wedding reception would be the first really, truly, traditional wedding celebration in a long time. Much more than a marriage would be celebrated tonight.

Crash!

Florence wiped her hands on her apron. The sound originated in the basement where men were moving a piano. "I'll go see what—"

"Let them be. They'll come crying to us if someone's injured." Helen continued shredding the carrots for the cold vegetable salad.

Ted, the bandleader, had insisted on a piano for the evening. The men were rolling the old upright on a makeshift plywood ramp to the yard where the tent and dance floor were already assembled. Ed, the organist from church, stood at the ready to wrangle the piano as near into tune as possible.

"*Boże*, I told them to be careful." Florence returned to peeling potatoes for another batch.

The plan was to suffer the late August heat through dinner inside, then progress outdoors for drinks, dessert, and dancing. She glanced at the clock, blew a few stray strands of hair out of her eyes, and went to the refrigerator to retrieve beets. Cold air escaped like a genie from a bottle. For a moment, she luxuriated in it before digging through the teeming shelves. She turned to see that her boys had arrived. Mrs. Koseba wasted no time directing Frank to fill bowls with chipped ice to hold the salads and sending Lucien to help the men out back.

"How can I help?" Cecilia, Lucien's special friend, had arrived with him. Florence wiped her hands on her apron, brought the girl into the kitchen, and introduced her.

"Have you ever been to a Polish wedding?" Helen asked Cecilia.

"Well no, but I can—"

"Then you're in for a treat. Here, take this red ribbon—there are scissors in the drawer over there—and go tie pieces around the white vases in the center of the tables."

"Red and white. Beautiful colors." Cecilia took the decoration and scampered downstairs.

"I like her already!" Helen enthused. Florence nodded. She did too.

"I heard White Eagle is shutting down." Mrs. Koseba took Florence's arm, and the moment, to question her.

"Yes. The factory building's been sold. Closing for good. Only a few more weeks of work."

"What will you do?"

"No worries for me. Alex's new job pays well, and Lucien is working part time too. We've made up for the time Alex didn't work."

"You're not going to work at all then?"

"I'm thinking about a job at the Art Institute. Maybe even in the café there. We've been spending a lot of time there as of late. It's so inspiring."

"That's right. I remember now—you like to paint!"

"Yes, my first love, before Alex." They both chuckled. "Now Joe's saved up money and is seeing a lovely woman, so he's moving out. We haven't had any other boarders in quite some time. Alex offered to turn a bedroom into a studio for me. It's beyond my dreams." She'd already stocked the chest she'd purchased from Delores with paints and brushes.

"That's so exciting! To be able to pursue your art. Oh, look—"

Mr. Koseba and a helper bustled through the doorway with a box from his grocery store with five fully cooked hams, which he and his wife began slicing. They stacked the slabs on varied platters women had brought from home and covered them with clean towels. After some time, they looked around the kitchen and everyone was satisfied they were as ready as they could be. Salads, relish trays, bread, eggs, beets, meat heaped on platters. Towers of *kolaczki* rose high. And after a last shake of powdered sugar on the *kruschiki*, aprons were flung on the backs of chairs or tucked away in tote bags. They took turns getting cleaned up in the bathroom. Some tried their best to tidy their hair and apply lipstick using shiny pans as mirrors.

"Oh well, no one's going to be looking at us. This is Alicja's day," Florence muttered to anyone who could hear.

The phone rang. "They're on their way. They're coming! Quick! *Szybki! Chodź tu!*"

Mrs. Koseba enlisted teenage girls to deliver dishes to the tables, first the bread baskets lined with embroidered linen cloths, then small plates of cold savories and hard-boiled eggs. Florence also ran a tray downstairs, relieved to see Alex setting up the drinks with Romek. She exhaled. She thought he'd come on time, but better to double-check. The women lined either side of the front steps, several holding baskets of flowers. The black sedan polished to resemble an elegant black mirror, driven by Tomasz's best man, glided to a stop. Tomasz popped out of the rear street-side door, came around curbside, opened the door, and, with a courtly bow, offered his hand to his bride.

"He's such a gentleman!"

"Look at her smile."

"I'm so glad for her."

Words of elation showered the group, which broke into applause. The couple, holding hands, climbed the stairs under a deluge of flower blooms thrown by the women holding the baskets. The party was underway. Father Maletski led them in blessing the couple and the food. Andrew, Alicja's father, stood preparing to make a toast. He held a microphone with one hand and gesticulated with the stub of the other arm he'd lost in the factory accident. At first, he addressed the crowd with extreme solemnity. He recounted how, with each milestone of his life—Alicja's birth, loss of his arm, loss of his job, death of his wife—the community had supported him, provided for him. He was humbled. He was grateful. Tears sliced rivulets down his cheeks. Florence pulled her handkerchief from her sleeve. Then Andrew spoke of his daughter and her mettle enduring these difficult life events. He fell silent. He seemed lost in the past. The crowd fidgeted. Alicja stood and put her arm around him.

"Now, for my daughter's wedding, you, our community, has come to my aid yet again."

Sounds of dismissal eddied through the crowd, claiming their efforts had been nothing at all.

"So, while I bless Alicja and my new son Tomasz, know that I bless all of you. *Sto lat!*"

Everyone burst into the traditional song of good cheer.

> Sto lat, sto lat niech zyje, zyje nam,
> Sto lat, sto lat niech zyje, zyje nam,
> Jeszcze raz, jeszcze raz,
> niech zyje, zyje nam, niech zyje nam.

> Good health, good cheer,
> may you live a hundred years, a hundred years.

Alicja's father cracked open the hearts of even those who protected them most deeply. Everyone mingled, laughed, ate, drank, and floated between the indoor tables and the outdoor dance floor. Romek's cousin, Ted, led the band. They'd donned the costumes of the Polish highlands with decorated black felt hats, vests, and flaxen shirts. Ted resembled Romek with his burly stature and quick laugh. The band fanned the flames of an already ignited crowd. Polka after polka, skirts twirled, hair broke free from pins. Jackets covered chair backs and once-starched sleeves were scrunched at elbows. Florence watched Lucien teach Cecilia how to polka. Soon they, too, danced buoyantly around the floor.

People abandoned the floor for the bar, and the band slowed down the ambience with a lively yet decidedly calmer waltz. Alex slid his arm around her waist and they danced. His patrician visage had aged, yet his demeanor remained princely. Over his shoulder, she observed the twirling couples in finery she'd not seen in years.

Now soused with sweat, white shirts offered a canvas for silk ties, now loosened, in cobalt blue, orange-red, gold, and in all manner of patterns. Paisley, plaids, stripes, large dots, and geometric patterns all screamed "look at me." So different from the worn, drab palette of recent years. Men stood straighter, taller, no longer cowed by the shame of their circumstances. Verve infused their dance steps. She sighed. Alex pulled back and looked at her. His cool blue eyes searched her face, his white-blonde brows peaked with inquiry.

"Nothing's wrong. I'm fine, more than fine really. It's all so beautiful." She leaned in closer, drizzling her dewdrop tears onto Alex's shoulder. His hand pulsated gently on her waist, signaling his understanding. The dance finished smoothly. Dancers and observers alike applauded. The band leader announced over the microphone a change of tempo. An accordion player assumed center stage, flanked by a fiddle player. Excitement percolated as everyone anticipated the up-tempo mazurka.

"Shall we?" Alex extended his hand. The fiddle and accordion tossed out the first few chords and the dance floor was beyond full. After a few measures, Florence felt Alex's leg falter, his muscles tense. She was about to suggest a rest when Romek approached, bowed, and asked Alex if he may have the honor. It was an act of kindness. Romek must have been watching.

There was something desperate in the way Romek held her. His strong right arm enveloped her. His left hand crushed her right. His eyes bore into hers and he searched her face as if committing every pore to memory. Did he see Basia? Romek had become a zealot since he began working for Stanley Nowak as an organizer. She was on the verge of asking if he was all right when he dipped to his left and then spun her around. Over the years, she'd danced the mazurka with Romek many times at community events, once or twice in an evening. Now, since they'd both lost dance partners, Basia to death and Alex to a bum hip, she and Romek stayed on the floor for several dances. The band announced a break and promised contemporary music. American music, much to the young people's liking, would be played next.

"You've worn me out!" Florence started toward the bench at the tent's perimeter and sat next to Alex, relieved to be away from Romek. His intensity overwhelmed her tonight.

"*Boże*, what an evening!" Florence slid her feet out of her shoes beneath the bench. Romek had gone to fetch drinks. He would take a while as the queue parted to allow the band members first opportunity. The band members hovered near the bar, gulping large mugs of beer following their shots of liquor and wiping sweat from their brows.

"It's awfully late. What time is it?" Florence swiveled her head pointlessly since there'd be no clock in sight.

"I think it's about half past eleven. But let's not leave yet. I want to hear the music they're going to play."

Joan flung open the back gate and elbowed her way through to the dance floor. Always late, Joan ranked her duties as a journalist high in her life's priorities. It must be so demanding. She looked crazed, turning about as if she didn't know where to go or what to do.

"That's odd." Florence nudged Alex. "Look."

Joan stepped onto the small wooden stage and snatched the microphone off the top of the piano. "Quiet everyone! Quiet!" she shouted. People started to shush each other. Conversation ebbed under the tent until even those at the edge of the yard took notice. Joan held her stomach with one hand as if in great pain. Florence expected she might double over.

"Just in. Over the wire." She struggled to breathe. She steadied herself with a hand on the edge of the piano.

"Germany invaded Poland."

BOOK CLUB DISCUSSION QUESTIONS

1. In what ways are Florence and Basia the same? Different? Who is the stronger person?

2. How would you describe the relationship between Florence and Alex?

3. Is Alex a likeable character? Why or why not? Is he good or evil? A coward or a hero?

4. How did Basia's background in Poland influence her activities at the cigar factory?

5. What forces are exerted on the factory owners and Resnick? Is Resnick a likeable character?

6. Was the price the women paid for union recognition worth it?

7. How is organized labor viewed today? Is it still necessary?

8. Is it possible that groups like the Black Legion exist today?

9. Discuss how Nick handled the choices in his life. Did he feel remorse?

10. What is the most surprising thing you learned from this book? About Poles? About Detroit?

11. Were you sympathetic toward the mayor? The governor? The police chief?

12. What was Lucien's relationship like with his family?

13. Why do you think the author included Diego Rivera? Would you consider this book an example of ekphrasis?

14. Why did Diego Rivera and Alex laugh so hard looking at the car in the mural?

15. What was the author trying to say with the contrast between the wedding scene and the abrupt ending of the book?

16. Have you had experience with other immigrant communities that are tight like the Polish one depicted in this story?

17. Has reading this book made you want to learn more about Poland and other Eastern European countries? Has it affected your opinions of events in Eastern Europe?

AUTHOR'S NOTE

I happened upon coverage of women cigar factory workers being pummeled with fire hoses while researching the Polish neighborhood of my father's childhood on the east side of Detroit. The topic compelled me to research further, particularly since many people primarily think of the UAW, automobiles, and other heavy industries when associating labor organizing and Detroit. My goal was to shed light on the experience and contributions made by the Polish community in 1930s Detroit.

As a secondary goal, I tried to convey the troublesome dynamics within which the characters were forced to make decisions. It was not an easy time for anyone. The entire world was in political upheaval, exacerbated by the Depression, and lacking in societal safety nets. Survival was the imperative of the time. Good options were not always available.

I "met" some wonderful real people through research, including Mary Zuk, Stanley and Margaret Nowak, and the women of Ternstedt factory. I imagined their actions and conversations. Similarly, Governor Murphy and other public officials are fictionalized.

The Black Legion did exist with all the outlandish attire and behavior described here. It is unlikely they would have recruited a Polish immigrant like Alex. I created that storyline to intensify the conflict between Alex and Florence.

Finally, I have loved Diego Rivera's *Detroit Industry* murals since I first saw them as a child on a school field trip to the Detroit

NOT YET LOST

Institute of Arts. The murals embody everything I love about Detroit: innovation, hard work, and the working class. Rivera completed the murals in 1933, four years before this story. I slid the timeframe forward because of the relevance of the art as well as the bond I created between Rivera and Alex. Rivera did use sketches and photos of factory workers as models, but again, any conversations and opinions are fictional.

Please visit my website janisfalk.com for links to further information about the people and events in the book. Thank you.

ACKNOWLEDGMENTS

Thank you for reading *Not Yet Lost*. I hope you enjoyed the journey.

I used many resources, books, internet searches, public PhD theses, movies, recorded interviews, and family knowledge. Books that contributed most significantly to my knowledge include: *Those Who Were There* by Margaret Collingwood Nowak, *City of Champions* by Tom Stanton, *Diego Rivera* by Linda Bank Downs, and *The World According to Fannie Davis* by Bridgett M. Davis. I encourage reading all these great books.

A litany of mentors has contributed to the writing of this book.

Jerod Santek, Artistic Director of Write On, Door County brings high-quality teaching artists to the writing center. I have learned much from Lan Samantha Chang, Christine Clancy, Andrew Graff, Jane Hamilton, Dipika Mukherjee, Sheila O'Connor, Cynthia Swanson, and many others.

Kim Suhr, director of Red Oak Writing, offers wonderful programs, in particular the Round Table Critique Groups. The Wednesday Evening group critiqued most of *Not Yet Lost*. The group includes Kim Suhr, Darlene Junker, Barb Lucius, Mark Lucius, John Schneider, Jim Nitz, and Bob Zanotti. For a few years now, this group has provided honest, thoughtful critique and encouragement, for which I am very grateful.

Many thanks to Elizabeth Evans of Elizabeth Evans Editorial for her well-honed insight, particularly on character development.

NOT YET LOST

Rebecca Makkai of Story Studio, Chicago for teaching and offering classes with Abby Geni, Michael Zapata, and others, including retreats at Ragdale and the Pub Crawl.

The story sprung from family history, so I owe much to my parents and grandparents. Alex and Florence were modeled after my grandparents (whom I barely knew), and Lucien echoes my father, though much was fictionalized since he died young.

I thank my husband, Jim Bator, and his extended family. I appreciate Jim for his tireless patience listening to drafts, writing, and rewriting, repetitively and frequently. Without Jim, I never would have traveled to Poland or felt connected to Polish heritage. Jim's grandmother worked in a cigar factory in Detroit. His grandfather was assaulted with fire hoses outside of a Ford factory while waiting to apply for a job. My father-in-law, Steve, worked at Ternstedt factory for most of his accounting career.

I am grateful for the support my children provided. My daughter, Camille, for her storyline suggestions, sensitivity reads, cover critique, and promotional support. My son, Christian, for his formatting, proofreading, and challenging questions regarding content.

AUTHOR BIO

Janis M. Falk, in her first act, raised her family, pursued a business career, and lived large and wide—and now she has something to write about. She is a graduate of both University of Michigan and Northwestern University. Now in her second act, she can often be found kayaking the Great Lakes or pruning lavender plants on her organic farm. Janis was born in Detroit, then took a multiyear tour through Chicago. She and her husband, Jim, currently live in a home they built by combining two 157-year-old log cabins in Door County, Wisconsin.

Looking for your next great read?

We can help!

Visit www.shewritespress.com/next-read
or scan the QR code below for a list
of our recommended titles.

She Writes Press is an award-winning
independent publishing company founded to
serve women writers everywhere.